I0561828

DEAD MAN HAND

ALSO BY T. M. SIMMONS

A Dead Man Mystery Series

Dead Man Talking

Dead Man Haunt

Dead Man Hand

Dead Man Ohio

Dead Man Series Collection 1: Dead Man Mysteries Books 1, 2 and 3

DEAD MAN HAND

A DEAD MAN MYSTERY
BOOK THREE

T. M. SIMMONS

Without limiting the rights under copyright(s) reserved below, no part of this publication may be reproduced, stored in or introduced into a retrieval system, or transmitted, in any form, or by any means (electronic, mechanical, photocopying, recording, or otherwise) without the prior permission of the publisher and the copyright owner.

This is a work of fiction. Names, characters, places, and incidents either are the product of the author's imagination or are used fictitiously, and any resemblance to actual persons, living or dead, business establishments, events or locales is entirely coincidental.

The scanning, uploading, and distributing of this book via the internet or via any other means without the permission of the publisher and copyright owner is illegal and punishable by law. Please purchase only authorized copies, and do not participate in or encourage piracy of copyrighted materials. Your support of the author's rights is appreciated.

T. M. Simmons, 2012, 2022. All rights reserved.

Book and cover design by eBook Prep
www.ebookprep.com

August 2022
ISBN: 978-1-64457-344-0

ePublishing Works!
644 Shrewsbury Commons Ave
Ste 249
Shrewsbury PA 17361
United States of America
www.epublishingworks.com
Phone: 866-846-5123

ACKNOWLEDGMENTS

It takes a village to write a book—believe me, I know. I now have twenty e-books up on line, seven of which are new releases, which I have written in the past year and a half. Without the wonderful assistance of numerous other folks, none of these books would have made it to birth.

I always need to thank the Terrell Writers League, a group of fellow creative artists who critique and read my work and always make it better. For this book, *Dead Man Hand,* A. D. Guzman and C. L. Smothers were my final readers. A. D's story, "Ghosts,", part of the *Footprints* Anthology published by Hadley Rille Books, is available now, and she has a fantastic Young Adult nearly ready for publication, complete with a dragon that steals into your heart and the lovable nerd who saves her. C. L. Smothers' *Wormhole* will fascinate you with the story of possible future events I found myself wishing I could live long enough to be part of. Floyd Brigdon doesn't bother to say anything critical, unless it's exactly on point and needs to be addressed by me. He and his wife have a band, Triskelion, and play great Celtic music. They perform at several Faires and are always asked for return visits.

Angela Rogers is a fantastic cover artist. She's re-doing many of my covers now, making them as cool as my books! Her services are available to others, and her contact information is in the copyright section of this book, as well as quite a few of my others.

Whenever I have a question about winter, I go to my brother, K. P. Cantner. He's the best sportsman I know, and can tell me everything from how a snowmobile operates to whether or not the ice is thick enough to drive out on. My sister, Annie Riddle, helps me proof and keep typos at bay, as does my husband. It's a "family affair," also, to write a book. They handle a lot of household matters so I can write.

There have been many others over the years who have given of their time and experience to me. Thank you all very much.

To Dianna Miller, my free-spirited friend who has seen her share of ghosts! I hope this is the first book you get to read on your new e-reader! I still recall meeting you at The Myrtles in St. Francisville and the start of our long friendship. Remember tapping on the mirror in the Blue Room? You're the one who called Cloe forth for Aunt Belle and me to get our first picture of a ghost! Aunt Belle and I loved you from the minute we met and continue to count you as one of our beautiful friends.

I wish you a wonderful life filled with caring friends who are as loving as you.

CHAPTER I

A h, those fateful words after months spent writing this book. But this one didn't want to depart easily.

My gaze wandered to the fireplace, where log ashes now smoldered in a faint red glow. Earlier, the cheery leaping flames had helped chase off the dreary December evening lingering outside the patio door. The stack of firewood lay out there, also, the empty log carrier tilted precariously amidst scattered bark debris. After tossing the last piece of wood on the fire hours ago, I'd started to fetch more, but gotten sidetracked by a new word to use on a problematic phrase. I'd raced back to the computer instead, and now the wood was damp from the rain I hadn't noticed falling.

"Good grief, how long ago was that?" I asked the Casper clock my eighty-year-old neighbor Granny Chisholm had given me, which sat on the mantle above the fire. The digital numbers on the friendly ghost's wide belly blinked just then, and four boo-bongs chimed an answer into the stillness.

The reason for my vexing attitude had to be the time: four in the morning, not afternoon. Exhaustion dragged at me after another marathon stint at the keyboard.

Everything had finally clicked into place on the just completed book...hadn't it? All loose ends tied up, an extremely satisfying ending after an ever-threatening suspense world in which my characters continued to be outsmarted by a devious villain. Yet something niggled me, and a reluctant Muse refused to cooperate. Maybe he needed a nap, too.

After one more of the numerous backups on the manuscript, I rose and stretched, hands massaging a spot on my lower back. Ergonomic safety never seemed to soothe the sore spot, since at times I lost myself in the story and didn't heed the rule to take periodic breaks. Still, the words had flowed from flying fingertips, and I'd taken advantage of the last rush to the ending. I was even a couple weeks pre-deadline.

So why didn't I feel the customary satisfaction? Have a smile on my face and the need to stumble off to the bedroom and crash on the stupendous new mattress I'd bought with my last royalty check? Could there be some glitch in the manuscript I hadn't noticed, one I'd be embarrassed about when my editor caught it instead of me?

After checking to make sure the fire screen was secure, I wandered out of my study and down the hallway to the front door. None of my paranormal residents were around, surprising, since ten ghosts reside in my haunted cabin with my pets and me. Come to think of it, none of the six cats roamed under my feet. Cats sleep a lot, though. More unusual was I didn't see Trucker, my hundred-and-fifty-pound Rottweiler, anywhere. Maybe he'd taken a doggy potty break through the rear doggy/kitty door.

I slipped into a pair of loose sandals and walked onto the front sun deck, grimacing when a mist of rain hit me. Despite the protective over-hang, a pre-dawn breeze off the lake across the road carried rain droplets and snakes of fog onto the deck. And there were at least two of my pets: Trucker and Miss Molly, my Siamese and head honcho of the cat menagerie. Miss Molly abhorred wetness, but she stood between two railing posts, intent gaze toward the lake. Trucker stared in the same direction and didn't acknowledge my presence.

"Hey, guys, what's up?" I asked.

They didn't answer. Animals don't talk. If they ever did, I'd be much more shocked than when a ghost visualized unexpectedly.

I see ghosts. I talk to ghosts. And I enjoy the heck out of my paranormal adventures...most of the time. I even allow the ghosts who "live" in my cabin with me to linger, as long as they follow the rules of The Howard and Alice Ghost Agreement. With the help of my Aunt Twila, by far the more experienced senior ghost hunter in our partnership, I drew up The Agreement after we found this awesome haunted cabin. I bought it within a month of my divorce from Jack. Twila believes in disciplining ghosts, and we named The Agreement for Howard, the Head Ghost in charge of his paranormal cohorts.

"What are you two looking at?" I asked as I joined my pets at the railing. The rain wasn't too bad yet, rather refreshing after the long stint in my study, although I realized I should have grabbed a sweater or poncho. December nights get chilly in East Texas, and we even have a sprinkling of snow now and then. Dawn was a while away; days are also shorter in Texas winters, as they are elsewhere. The Winter Solstice was still two weeks off, and right after that, Christmas, for which I hadn't done a bit of shopping yet.

Since their eyes are much sharper than mine, I assumed my pets could see something over on the lake that I couldn't. Along with the rain, a heavy mist rose from the water, further inhibiting my line of sight. It layered the grounds around my cabin, my white Jeep—which I'd once again forgotten to move into the garage—nearly invisible in the driveway. Yet the mist over the water seemed....

"Good grief. All the ghosts are out there on the lake!"

Most people would beat feet the other way when confronted with one ghost, let alone an entire crew of paranormal entities. However, since my ghosts were residents for whom I felt a certain amount of responsibility, it behooved me to pay attention to their activities. I couldn't recall ever seeing each and every one of them together in a crowd.

I ducked back inside the door and grabbed a rain poncho from a hook on the wall. Shrugging into it, I hurried down the deck steps and along the driveway. Trucker and Miss Molly followed. Trucker's paws thudded on the steps and crunched the oyster shells in the driveway. Miss Molly grumbled about the dampness under her cat's breath, but kept up. I strode on across the road and down a path I'd cleared to the lakeshore. I'd even placed a small wooden bench on the bank under a tree, and two of my residents sat there. Wilma ignored me; still pouting, I assumed, from the scolding I gave her when I caught her needlessly flushing the toilet to watch the water swirl down the drain. Wilma can be petulant.

Beside her sat Phil, one of those lonesome cowboys who returned from the War Between the States to ride herd on the cattle ranging free all over Texas. For some reason, Phil never had the gumption to start a ranch of his own. In fact, Phil hadn't even dredged up the horse sense to cross on through The Light for some reason. I suspected he had a secret crush on Wilma, whom he might have met on one of the cattle drives up Kansas way back in those days.

I bypassed them and strode onto the wooden pier. The rowboat I bought with the cabin was missing from its mooring, but Howard loved to fish, so that didn't surprise me. The Head Ghost even wet a line at night sometimes. And there was the rowboat, a hundred feet or so out in the lake. In it were Howard, along with Rick and Shannon, the two kids who stubbornly rejected my efforts to persuade them to cross over and join their parents. Five other ghosts hovered on the water surface around the rowboat, heads bent and intent on whatever Howard was doing.

And he wasn't liberating one of the fish he periodically caught, Howard being a catch-and-release ghost. Howard leaned over the side, and the rowboat tilted dangerously—not that I had to worry about any of the ghosts drowning, since they were already dead. Still, I didn't want the boat to sink and have to explain to whomever I called to salvage it what had happened. Weightless, ghosts shouldn't tip that boat, anyway, but maybe they were playing around.

"Howard!" I called. "Don't sink the boat! What are you doing?"

Won't, he mentally said, since our relationship has evolved over the last two and a half years to where telepathy works. He didn't answer my question. Howard's also a ghost of few words. Sometimes getting him to talk is like teasing one of the mimes who work the Bourbon Street crowds in New Orleans, where I met Jack a few years ago.

Howard manipulated something into the rowboat, which caused the boat to rock back and forth. Now, I'd normally say a live person heaved something into the boat, but Howard and other ghosts I've known have a way of directing objects they wish to move. I'd never asked them how they do it, just accepted it as part of their other dimension, which interests me so highly. I couldn't make out what he'd evidently pulled from the lake at this distance.

"What are you doing?" I repeated, since sometimes Howard will answer a recurrent question. This time, he didn't. He did, however, maneuver the oars and head the boat back toward the pier where I waited.

Shannon sat in the bow, Rick in the stern, Howard on the middle, rowing seat. The other ghosts vanished rather than follow along in the boat's wake. When the rowboat grew close enough, I could see a heap of red at Howard's feet. It looked like...

...a woman lying there!

The rowboat bumped the pier and I grabbed the bow rope to tie it off. Howard, Rick and Shannon floated up to stand beside me as I examined the heap of red. She sat up, tossed her blond hair back out of her eyes, and stared directly at me. "Well, you wouldn't talk to me any other way!"

Howard spoke aloud this time. "Didn't you know you couldn't swim?"

"Of course," she said as she scooted onto the seat Howard had vacated. "I can't drown, though. You know that as well as I do."

I peered closer. Yep, she was a ghost, even though she appeared as solid as me. Well, not quite, since I still hadn't lost that extra ten pounds and she was slender and well-toned. She was dressed in a low-cut red gown, which reminded me of something a saloon girl would have worn back in the mid-1800's. Black fishnet stocking encased those attractive legs, a pair of button-up shoes with stacked heels on her feet.

And she was dry as a bone, not a drop of water on her. The dress skirt flared out across the boat seat, and her hair was whorled and curled intricately. A pair of sparkly earrings dangled from shell-perfect ears, and a teardrop diamond hung from a bright silver chain around her neck. The jewelry had to be fake, I assumed, since where would an 1800's saloon girl get money for those expensive baubles?

"The house is full," I told her. "I'm sorry, but once in a while I do have to turn away a gho...uh...prospective boarder."

"I know I'm a ghost!" she shot back. "So you don't have to sidestep that issue. And I know who you are. I've been trying to talk to you for over a week now, but he—" She nodded at Howard. "— wouldn't let me."

"She's writing," Howard said sternly. "We don't bother her when she's writing. That's the number one rule of The Agreement. Never—EVER—bother Alice when she's writing!"

Wow. Howard could spout it out when he felt like it.

"Pooh," the woman said. "Some things are more important than some stodgy old book!"

"And you," I warned, "are not going to win any points with me with that attitude. I don't know how long you've been a ghost, or what you want from me, but Howard's my first line of defense. If he says you don't hang around, or see me, then you don't! Otherwise, I'd have slews of your ilk barging into my life and wreaking havoc."

"And I didn't appreciate being tricked like that," Howard added. "I thought someone real was in the lake."

"I'm as real as you are," she spat at him.

Someone tugged on my hand, and I glanced down at Shannon. "She looks sorta like my mama, Miss Alice," the little girl said. "Can't you at least talk to her?"

"Shannon," I said in exasperation, "you need to *be* with your mama. But I can't force you or Rick to go, not when you two play hide and seek with me whenever I try. However, you aren't in charge here, either. I am, with Howard second-in-command. Right now, I'm going back into the house, take a shower, and go to bed. I've had a long night already."

I suited action to words, gently pulled my hand free from Shannon's tiny one, and strode down the pier toward the shoreline. Problem was, the pier wasn't that wide, and Trucker turned sideways on it to block my path. Miss Molly plopped herself on her rump at Trucker's side, stared up at me and cat-growled the irritating meow-ser that sets my teeth on edge. Beyond them, several of the other ghosts lined the shoreline, and I noticed Wilma and Phil had vacated the bench.

A mutiny! I had a mutiny on my hands. Well, we'd just see about that!

"Move," I gritted at Trucker and Miss Molly. The ghosts didn't bother me. I could stride straight through them with no problem.

"Woof!" Trucker responded. He didn't move a muscle to obey.

"That Lady in Red's been slipping him dog biscuits and Miss Molly her Kitty Kisses treats when she could sneak past me into the pantry," Howard said. "Got them to liking her."

"Then let her talk to them." I started to step over Trucker. "I'm going to bed."

Miss Molly zipped beneath Trucker and I barely missed putting a heavy foot down on her back. I ended up spread-legged across Trucker, one foot toward the shore, one still behind me. And that blasted dog finally decided to move...toward that obstinate red-dress ghost!

Trucker shoved my leg out of the way as though it were a slim sapling. My sandaled foot slipped on the wet pier. Waving my arms for balance didn't help. With a screech, I splashed into that winter-cold water. Fortunately for my body, it was deeper out here near the end of the pier. Not lucky for the mutineers. I sank to the sandy bottom, surged to my feet and straightened. The water was waist-high, and plenty of me was available to take care of the defiance, most importantly, my mouth.

"Get the hell up to the cabin!" I yelled at Trucker and Miss Molly—as soon as I spat the water out. "Or you're gonna spend the night in the garage!"

They had sense enough to realize they had overstepped. Both of them deserted Lady in Red and hightailed it along the pier, down the path to the road. I splashed alongside until the water was shallow enough for me to lunge onto the pier. Water streaming from me and cold chills racing over me, I scrambled to my feet and shouted at the ghosts lining the shore, "Out of here! Every one of you! Get the hell back to your own dimension for a while, or I'll sprinkle sea salt all over the cabin and put out protection packets so none of you can stay!"

Whoosh, they disappeared. And I whirled to face Lady in Red...who wasn't there, either. Nor were Rick and Shannon. Howard was, though. He shrugged and said, "Uh...I think I'll go fish."

He dissolved, also, although I could tell where he was. The rowboat rope disengaged itself and flew into the bow. The boat slowly drifted off.

"Get that boat back here before daylight!" I shouted at Howard. "There are a couple other owners in residence this week!"

Will, he agreed, thank goodness. It was starting to be a nuisance to try to explain to Mr. Jones down on the point why my rowboat kept escaping, since I didn't dare admit a ghost utilized it. Mr. Jones was like Jack; he didn't believe in ghosts. Although Jack had changed his tune somewhat the past year....

I stood there and fumed for another few moments, until both the breeze and rain picked up. Not that the rain could get me any wetter, but the chill got to me. The slicker hadn't done a bit of good during a dunking. My hair hung in wet hanks and my sodden caftan—my preferred attire when I sat down to write—clung to me and dripped.

Finally I stormed down the pier and onto the path. I still might pull out the sea salt.

The wispy white figure standing where the path intersected the narrow county road between my cabin and the lake fired my ire again. I wiped rain and lake water out of my eyes as I stomped over to it and yelled, "I told you to get back to the other dimension!" Then bit my lip as a flush of embarrassment heated my cheeks.

"Ain't quite ready for that," the figure said with a chortle. "Hung around here in the livin' world nearly eighty-one years already."

"I'm so sorry," I said to Granny Chisholm. "What are you doing out here this time of night?"

She was dressed in a long, white granny gown, her gray hair hanging down her back, loose from the gold hairpins she usually secured it with. She wore a white plastic rain poncho similar to my gray one, hood up over her head. Security lights burned on my front deck and at the base of my pier, although with the cloud cover and fog, not much light penetrated to where we stood. She had a flashlight in one hand, though, her walnut walking stick in the other.

"Heard someone yelling for help out on the lake," she admitted. "Tho' even with my hearin' aid on high, it didn't sound right. Figgered what with all them ghosts at your place, mebbe they was having a party or foolin' 'round. Figgered I better go take a gander a'fore I called the Coast Guard."

I didn't bother to correct her and say the Coast Guard patrolled the Gulf, not inland lakes. Here we would call the Lake Patrol...although come to think of it, our lake wasn't big enough for a Lake Patrol. We'd have to call Fish and Wildlife. And with her own psychic abilities, I assumed she'd *heard* Lady in Red mentally, given the distance between her house and where I'd first seen the rowboat.

"Good thing you didn't cause a ruckus, Granny," I said. "It was just the ghosts fooling around. Well, one ghost. A new one, a woman, who's trying to find a berth at my cabin. Howard calls her Lady in Red, and she's evidently been trying to force her way past him to talk to me."

"Uh oh," Granny replied. "Sounds like 'nother one of them who might have a story to tell that gets your interest."

"Not on your life," I denied. "Something's wrong with this book, and I don't have time to mess with a ghost who has problems."

"Even if it's one of them life mysteries that always pulls you in?"

"No," I reiterated. "I've got a full schedule coming up. And I've got to find some temporary help for a while. Have you seen the filing mess in my study?"

"Looks more like a piling mess to me," she said. "But whatever. Thought you was gonna take a while off after this book."

I sighed. "I'd planned to, but you know how it is. Best laid plans of mice and men...."

"Well, I's better get back inside a'fore I catch pneumonia. You, too."

"Would you like to come in and have some hot cocoa?" I asked.

"Naw, not even iffen you offer to put some booze in it. Not this time, anyway. I's'll see you later on today. We gots to start them fruitcakes, iffen they's gonna be done a'fore Christmas." She started to turn away, then chuckled and nodded at me. "But you better get that there one in her place. Don't look like she's mindin' you and stayin' where you told her to."

I whirled to see Lady in Red standing a few feet away. Granny's chuckles faded as she made her way down the road toward her small, clapboard house next door to my cabin.

My aunt, Twila Brown, taught me right from the beginning, when she dragged me on my very first ghost hunt, that we had to discipline the ghosts we ran across. Otherwise, they could overstep into our own physical lives. Lives we still had to lead and with responsibilities.

"I just wanted to make an appointment with you," Lady in Red hastily said as I glared at her. "And apologize for taking the wrong tactic to get your attention. If you'll tell me when we can talk, I'll wait patiently."

"Well, since you have all the time you need, patience is what you'll have to have. Maybe after the first of the year—"

"That's too late!" she insisted.

"Too bad," I replied. "I'm going in and having some hot cocoa, then a shower, then bed."

I left her standing there and walked across the road, down the driveway and up the steps to the deck. I found Trucker and Miss Molly in the kitchen—they must have detoured around back and through the doggy/kitty door. I took time to grab towels from the laundry room and dry myself and both of them before I started my cocoa. I didn't bother chastising them, since they would both turn those hurt eyes on me and fill me with guilt.

What did she mean, the first of the year will be too late?

Huh uh. Nope, I wasn't going to let Lady in Red draw me into her problem. She had tried to break the number one rule of The Ghost Agreement, as well as attempted to thwart Howard's authority. That type of behavior could *not* be rewarded; it called for a reprimand.

I nuked my hot chocolate—half a mug of milk and cocoa, the rest luscious marshmallows melted to a decadent gooey delight—and carried the mug to the table. As I passed the wall phone, I absentmindedly pushed the plug back into the funny little socket. People who know me are used to the fact I unplug every phone in the cabin when I settle down to write. I also wouldn't bother checking for messages until I got darn good and ready.

I'd set my small kitchen table in front of a window where I could see into my acre-wide backyard. One lone security light burned over by the rear patio, and it didn't cast enough light to illuminate more than a quarter of the area. Beyond lay darkness, since dawn arrived late in this season we Texans call our winter. I'd sleep through dawn today, but since I was self-employed, my hours varied drastically. Many mornings I managed to enjoy the sunrise.

Lady in Red stood out there on the edge of the light, just past the patio—where I noticed I'd forgotten once again to bring in some of the more fragile plants and made a mental note to do so as soon as I got some sleep. The ghost's dress looked more black than red in that light, but it was her. Her slumped shoulders were a contradiction to her demanding attitude a few minutes ago, and she wandered through the misty ground-fog snakes in a forlorn manner. I steeled my emotions against a stab of sympathy and licked a yummy gob of marshmallows from my spoon.

Trucker padded across the floor and jumped up to place his front paws on the windowsill. He glanced back over his shoulder and whined at me.

"No," I said. "Who do you think pays for those doggy bones you love so well? The ones she's been sneaking you? I have to have some regimen in my life to be able to pay our bills."

Miss Molly drew my attention when she leaped onto the table and sniffed my cocoa mug. "Hey," I warned. "Off the table."

She obeyed, then stalked over and sat down beneath the phone. She stared up at it, and I shook my head. "You're wasting your time. No one has the gall to call me this time of night."

I proved right...for a while. I finished my cocoa, rinsed out the mug and set it in the dishwasher, then headed for the bedroom. I was halfway there before the phone shrilled. Miss Molly meowed loudly, as much of a hint of told-you-so in her voice as a cat could manage.

"Tough," I called back to her. "I'll get the messages later. After I get some sleep."

No, now, that little voice demanded. I knew who it was, too. Only one person could send me a communication. Someone with higher developed psychic senses than mine.

I sighed and headed back toward the kitchen, the only phone plugged in. By the time I got there, the answering service had already taken the call. I waited patiently, though. Well, somewhat patiently. If I tried to call back, the other line would be busy, calling me again. I picked up the second call mid-first ring.

"Hello, Twila. What are you doing up this early?"

"I'm an hour ahead of you in my part of Yankee-land," she reminded me. "And I didn't bother you as long as you were writing."

"Is anything wrong?" I asked worriedly.

"Quite the opposite," she replied. "You're still planning on taking a break after this book, aren't you?"

"Well..." I hedged.

"You are," she ordered. "And I have exactly the break you need. Remember that old hotel out in Red Dollar, New Mexico? The one we've been trying to get to for years?"

"Oh!" My attitude underwent a drastic change. "Of course I remember. But it's closed for the season right now, isn't it?"

"To the general public," she said. "However, seems it's also up for sale, and—"

"Oh, no!" I interjected. "What if they sell it and the new owners—?"

"Hush, Alice," she interrupted back. "We have no control over other people's property. But remember Danny, the balloon pilot we met at the festival up here when you visited last fall? I know you do. We had such a great time with him, and he was fascinated with our ghost hunting. We even took him out to that old haunted inn on the canal. Anyway, he's kept in touch with me. He lives near Roswell, but he also knows the people who currently own the Red Dollar Hotel. The ghosts there at the hotel are evidently upset about it being up for sale. They're causing all sorts of problems."

"What sort of problems?" I asked, my interest definitely pricked.

"Oh, destroying the *For Sale* signs. Scaring off prospective buyers. Every time they put the hotel ad up on their web site, it crashes it. There are a few other things, but you get the picture."

"Wow," I mused. "Sounds like these ghosts need some discipline."

"Exactly. So we've been invited out there next week. We'll have the run of the place to see what we can do about administering that discipline. Danny says it's gorgeous right now. Snow on the mountains, deer and elk in the valley. We should have plenty of time to do some Christmas shopping, too. Get some unusual presents this year instead of the usual shirts and socks. Maybe we can even hop down to Taos."

"I thought we were supposed to be working on the ghosts, not vacationing."

"Oh, they shouldn't take more than a day or so to handle," she said in a self-assured tone. "And they've promised we can stay the entire week. We also get another free week later in the season, if we want. Which you know we do. You can bring Granny, if you want, and if you can find another cat-sitter. And Trucker and Miss Molly, of course, although I had to promise they were well-behaved."

A chill climbed my back, and I whirled just in time to see Lady in Red vanish back into her own dimension. Still, I thought I'd caught a smirk of satisfaction on her face.

"I've got a stranger hanging around here," I told Twila. "Let me check with Howard and make sure he feels he can handle her if I leave. If so, you're on."

"She won't stay long enough to give Howard trouble," Twila assured me. "I'll make the plane reservations and call you this afternoon, after you've had a nap. I'll get us all into Albuquerque as close together as possible, and we can rent a vehicle there. Hey, don't worry about that ending in your book. It's fine. You're just dragged out from staring at the computer screen and living in that creative world so long."

She hung up before I could ask what made her so certain about her last statement. Not that I had to ask. She would never violate my privacy, but once in a while we would tune into each other, even a thousand miles apart. Sometimes intentionally, as she had just now. Other times, when one or the other of us encountered a rocky spot in life's road and needed some emotional support.

A smile spread across my face as I hung up the phone and headed toward the bedroom. It was still there when I woke up six hours later, feeling as though I'd slept a good week, primed and ready for bear...or ghosts, whichever.

CHAPTER 2

Twila waited until Granny and I were actually in the Albuquerque terminal before she called. I anticipated my cell phone ringing, but not due to my psychic powers. On the departure/arrival screen where Granny and I stood, *Cancelled* blinked after the flight number Twila was supposed to be on out of Yankee-land.

"What happened?" I asked instead of hello. It had to be her, with a Yankee-land area code in front of a strange phone number on caller ID.

"Don't you watch the weather?" she answered. "We were only supposed to get a couple inches of snow, but some sort of weather pattern turned it into an ice storm just before I arrived at the airport. We're grounded until they can re-open the runways and get the planes de-iced faster."

"When will that be?"

"My psychic abilities don't extend to weather forecasts, so your guess is as good as mine. They sent some of us to a hotel. That's where I'm calling from."

"Then you might not get out until tomorrow!"

"Go on to Red Dollar, Alice," she said. "You can come back for me when I finally get a flight, or I'll get my own rental if necessary. The drive's not that far, and we'll still have the bulk of our vacation time."

"I'm not sure I want to confront this pack of ghosts without you."

Someone gasped, and I glanced at the man beside me. *Ghost hunter?* he mouthed, and I grinned and nodded at his pale face. He quickly moved on down the line of arrival/departure screens, to the very last one.

"You'll be fine," Twila was saying. "You packed all the protective things I told you to bring, didn't you?"

"Yeah. And I guess I should get going," I agreed. "You'll stay in touch?"

"Will do. And say hi to Jack for me." She hung up before even half of the shocked huff left my mouth.

My gaze traveled around the terminal, but for once she must have been wrong. Even psychics with strong powers like my aunt's get it wrong now and then. Jack was back in Longview, Texas, a good two-hour drive from where I lived in Six Gun, nine hundred miles or more from Albuquerque. By the time I gave up searching for those broad shoulders and dark Cajun eyes, Granny had collared a motorized cart and the elderly, white-haired driver was already helping her into the seat.

"C'mon, Alice." She waved at me. "This nice man's gonna take us down to get the animals and our bags."

And that's where we found Jack. He knelt beside the carrier inside which both Trucker and Miss Molly waited. Miss Molly would only agree to fly if she could ride in the same carrier as her big buddy. She had recognized Jack and vocally made no bones about the fact it was time to let her out. One paw reached through the cage bars, and the people nearby grimaced at the loud meow-sers that echoed in the air.

"Can't do it, Molly," Jack said as the cart driver stopped beside the carrier. "Your mama has the key."

"What are you doing here?" I asked as I scooted off the cart.

He stood, face nearly expressionless—except for the depths in those chocolate eyes. He nodded at the wall behind the carrier, where a pair of skis leaned, a duffel bag beside them.

"Angel Fire," he said. "Got a few days off and decided to go visit a friend."

Male or female? I had sense enough to silence that thought, since we gave up the right to ask questions about each other's personal lives when we signed the divorce papers thirty months earlier. Not that I was keeping track or anything.

Jack continued, "What about you? And Granny? I can't quite imagine Granny on skis, but I'd be willin' to bet, if she put her mind to it, she could even slalom."

"You betcha," Granny said as the cart driver helped her down. "'Specially if I had me a tall, dark, handsome teacher like you hep'in' me learn, Jack. But me'n Alice is on our way to talk some sense into some ghosts."

I mentally groaned, but Jack just shook his head. The cart driver actually looked interested rather than fearful, like the man at the arrival/departure screens a few minutes earlier had.

"Where are you two stayin'?" Jack asked.

Before I could shut her up, Granny said, "Only hotel in some town called Red Dollar."

Jack frowned. "I've heard of it, but thought it closed down in the winter. It's not far from Angel Fire."

"We really need to get going," I said. "We still have to get our car, and I'd like to drive across New Mexico before dark. Twila got held up in an ice storm back home, so we may have to come back tomorrow and get her."

He nodded. "Have a good time. I need to get goin', too. My ride's probably waitin' outside." He shouldered his skis and picked up his duffle bag. "Y'all need a ride anywhere?"

"Nah," Granny said. "Got's us one right here."

"Take care of them," Jack ordered the cart driver before he strode away without a backward glance.

"How the heck did Twila know Jack was going to be here?" I wondered aloud to Granny as soon as he got out of hearing.

"Prob'ly Jack told Jess, Twila's husband," she said logically. "They still talks off and on."

17

"I suppose."

"So you're ghost hunters," the cart driver said. "And you're heading to Red Dollar, where all the ruckus has been."

"Sure are," Granny said, a twinkle in her blue eyes. "Wanna come along?"

"I'd like to," he said eagerly. "But I don't have any vacation time left, and I need this job. Social Security doesn't stretch far enough."

Granny adamantly agreed with him about that. She sometimes supplemented her small monthly check by cat-sitting for me when I was away.

Things went smoothly after that...as smoothly as they can when we travel with the animals. With our help, the cart driver got all of our baggage and the pet carrier loaded, then zipped us to the rental car desk while he and Granny chatted about the perils of fixed-income living and even exchanged telephone numbers. His name was Joshua...Something. I already knew Granny's name. Joshua motored off with a jaunty wave, and at first the harried clerk tried to stick us with a subcompact car. But Granny marched around the counter and took her arm. Led her back to show her our pile of luggage and the huge animal carrier.

"And we want that there four-wheel drive on our vehicle," she also demanded. "I ain't seen much snow in my life, but I seen some. And at my age, I don't want to see it up close and personal, stuck in a ditch beside the road."

We ended up with a copper-tone GMC Tahoe, and it suited Granny perfectly...after she made sure there was a set of *them there tire chains* she'd heard they used *up North* stowed with the spare tire. Outside the terminal, she beamed at the rent-a-car driver when he handed me the keys, her face nearly disappearing in the wrinkles that deepened with her delight at our transportation. We had to listen to Miss Molly's gripes for another few minutes, until we got out of the terminal area and found a service station. Then I stopped and set up her portable litter box in the back of the Tahoe and took Trucker for a walk. Finally, we hit the highway out of town with what I felt was plenty of daylight left to drive to Red Dollar.

Granny gazed out the passenger side window. In the city, the snow was slushy and gray, but outside of town it lay pristine and gleaming in the winter sun on the arid landscape. I thought Granny was enjoying looking at the snow, until she said, "We got's to try out one or two of them before we leave. Joshua, he said he goes once in a while, usually first of the month."

"What?" I questioned as I negotiated an intersection to get on the correct route.

"Why, them casinos," she said. "Ain't you been seein' all them signs? Got's to see if them machines are any loosy-goosier than them ones over in Shreveport."

I grinned. "You're on, since I got a nice royalty check last month. And Twila's started to like playing the video slots. We'll talk her into the penny ones and she'll be fine."

"Ha! Them penny ones'll eat up your dollars just as fast as the quarter ones."

"Yeah, but she has fun when she hits the bonus. You know how she loves a good movie. And maybe we can find her one of those black cat hex slots."

"That'll work," Granny agreed. "She'll forget how much she's stuck in the machine once that cat starts up and down the ladder chasin' that there crow."

Once we left Albuquerque, the two-lane state highway ran through extremely desolate mountainous country, beautiful in its own way. Granny kept watch and pointed out the herds of deer and antelope, elk and even buffalo, so we weren't bored. The only problem occurred when Trucker adamantly insisted on another potty break, and we had to find a pull-off without any animals close by. He's mostly an obedient Rottweiler, but the animals we passed kept him as rapt as Granny. He even woofed and lunged back and forth across the backseat once in a while. He'd seen deer before, but never elk, buffalo or antelope, and I wasn't sure I could hold onto his hundred-and-fifty pounds if he decided to forget hiking his leg and confront one of those larger animals to see who was boss.

We managed the break reasonably well, even though Trucker sniffed the air the entire time he watered a large boulder. I got him back into the Tahoe a split second before a herd of elk walked out from a stand of pine.

Since I can't drive and talk on a cell phone any better than some people can walk and chew gum at the same time, I took advantage of the stop and watched the majestic elk while I called ahead before I got back on the road. Danny answered after three rings.

"Hi," I said in response to his hello. "This is Alice Carpenter. We're supposed to meet you in Red Dollar."

"And not a minute too soon," Danny replied. "Do you know what happened this morning?"

"Well, no," I said, foregoing elk watching when I caught the tense tone in his voice. "How could I?"

"Oh, right," Danny replied. "Maddie had to go to the ER in Santa Fe. She thought she was having a heart attack, but the paramedics said it was just nerves...stress, you know. She swore they were wrong, so they took her down there to be safe."

"And Maddie is...?"

"The real estate lady," he said with a twinge of exasperation. "I told you about her."

"No, you probably told Twila," I refuted. "So what caused her problem?"

"The hotel, of course." His annoyance persisted. "The reason you're coming here."

Patiently—somewhat, anyway—I said, "What happened?"

"Same old shit, only worse this time," he explained. "Maddie had a hot prospect out of California fly in to look at the property. But when they went inside, everything was a mess. Lamps broken, furniture tossed around. Looked like someone'd had a party in the saloon. Drank a dozen cases of beer, even got into the liquor. Left everything all over the place, empty glasses, bottles. Even the rec room was a mess, beer spilled all over the pool table. Maddie asked the buyer to wait outside, and she and I went upstairs to see if they'd done any damage to the guest rooms."

"They?" I broke in.

"The ghosts," he insisted.

"Probably some kids in town," I told him.

"Well, tell me this, then," Danny said. "Why was everything all put back into place and spotless when we came back downstairs after checking the guest rooms?"

"I see."

"So'd Maddie. She grabbed her chest and fell down right at my feet. That lost us the sale."

I frowned for a second—not at the disturbance/non-disturbance. Ghosts definitely could have done that. Frankly, I wondered what Danny had been doing helping Maddie show the hotel. With a mental shrug, I decided to leave that question for now.

"Are the current owners aware of this most recent happening?" I asked.

"Karen—Mrs. Jamison—isn't staying here right now. She got a room over in Angel Fire. I called her. She'll meet us for dinner this evening and talk to you...if you still want to stay at the hotel."

"Most definitely," I assured him. "That's what we're here for."

Trucker let loose with a blast of barks and growls right beside my left ear, and I shrieked in response. The cell phone landed in Granny's lap, and I swiveled to grab Trucker's collar and jerk him away from the window. Ever try to drag a full-grown Rottweiler somewhere he doesn't want to go? He immediately lunged and broke my hold. I scrambled over the console into the backseat as Granny's cackles joined the cacophony. Miss Molly leaped out of my way, into the Tahoe's hatchback.

"Trucker!" I began...and the dog shoved me aside as he roared his fury and dove into the driver's seat. I started to open the rear passenger door to take charge of him, but thankfully looked out the window to see what was causing his ferociousness first. Looked straight at a huge elk head, antlers so massive they extended halfway down his back. He stood sideways along the vehicle, his rear end against the front bumper. He lifted his head and bugled—for some reason, that's what they call it when an elk hollers. Then he smeared his nose against the driver's window as he gazed in at Trucker, as much of a snarl as an elk could manage on his face.

"Hardy-har-har!" Granny chortled. "He must be in heat."

"Rut," I corrected. "This time of year is when they mate."

"Whichever," she said with a shrug. Then she said into the cell phone, "Nothin' to worry 'bout. We'll call you back in a minute."

Snarling and growling, Trucker banged against the car door. The elk never budged. I grabbed Trucker's collar and hauled...again...and managed to drag him into the rear seat with me.

"Behave!" I ordered. "Or I'll muzzle you!"

That word worked. I'd only used the muzzle twice before—the first time when I took him in to get fixed and he'd turned snarly on the vet when the poor man tried to put him under. To this day, Granny believes poor Trucker knew what was going to happen. Now he whimpered and cringed against the far rear door.

"Get out of here!" I shouted at the elk.

"He's got a herd of cows with him." Granny nodded at the windshield. "Guess he's protectin' 'em."

"We aren't gonna hurt his cows." I splatted my palm on the window in front of the elk's nose. "Get!"

Only his eyes moved as he turned his gaze from Trucker to me.

"Get!" I ordered again. "Take your cows and go!"

"I think we's sittin' in front of his food," Granny said. She pointed her thumb over her shoulder to the side of the car. "Bunch of hay over here. Prob'ly ranchers feedin' their cows, but the elk thinks it's his and his family's food."

"Shit," I muttered. Then I scrambled back into the driver's seat and started the vehicle. "Get out of here!" I yelled at the elk again.

"Jist drive off," Granny said in a logical voice.

"The way he's standing, if I move, his antlers might scratch the car," I said. "He has to step back first."

"Had to leave my shotgun at home," Granny said. "They'da never let me through that high security they have now, after nine-eleven. But I guess I coulda put it in one of them locked cases and sent it with the luggage. That's how my nephew shipped his gun when he went over to Africa on that there safari."

"What does your shotgun have to do...oh, I see. We could shoot in the air and run the elk off." I glanced at Granny and caught her eyeing the elk speculatively.

"He'd look real nice over my fireplace."

"Oh, for...I guess it's a good thing you don't have your shotgun."

"Shotgun wouldn't work, anyway," she said. Take a rifle...a big 'un...to bring that old boy down. My nephew, he took a humongous rifle with him to Africa, case he run across a teed-off tiger."

"Get!" I shouted again at the elk.

He blinked at me and didn't obey.

Granny reached over and pulled the keys from the ignition switch. A second later, the car alarm's blare split the air. Trucker set up a howl that broke off when he laid down on the seat and slapped his paws over his ears. But Miss Molly took up where Trucker left off, her screeches more earsplitting than the dog's howls. I covered my ears, too, and watched the elk hightail it back to his coven of cows. They raced away, heads high, majestic...at least in retreat.

"You can turn the alarm off now, Granny!" I shouted.

"Glad I 'membered that from when we lost your car at that there shoppin' center and had to turn on the alarm to find it," she said as she pushed the keychain button again. Blessed silence descended...until someone knocked on the driver's window. I jerked around again, wondering for a split-second how the heck that elk had gotten back here so fast. Furthermore, how it lifted a hoof to the window. But instead of elk's eyes, I gazed into the stern face of a man dressed unmistakably in a game warden's uniform. His broad shoulders and toned body left no doubt he kept in shape, probably to chase elk poachers.

"Oh, crap," I breathed, then pushed the button to roll the window down. Of course, it didn't roll. Granny had the keys. I took them from her as I murmured in a warning voice, "Let me handle this."

Key in the ignition, I rolled down the window. "Sir," I said before he could speak, "we—"

"Can I see your identification?" he interrupted.

"Of course, Officer," I said respectfully, hoping my politeness would make a difference in whether or not I had to pay a fine. "But we weren't trying to scare the elk. Well, we were, but it was only because—"

"Identification," he repeated. "For both of you. And your papers on the animals."

I sighed and stared around the vehicle for my purse. I had a bad habit of tossing it wherever and forgetting where wherever was. Granny picked up her purse from between her feet and had her driver's license out before I spied mine on the rear floorboard. I wiggled around to reach between the bucket seats. Trucker and Miss Molly had sense enough not to antagonize the game warden. Instead, they stared out the rear window, apparently fascinated by the lights whirling on the official pickup truck. Which I hadn't even noticed stop behind us.

The game warden examined our identification and handed it back. "Tourists, huh? I suspected that from your vehicle's rent-a-car plates. The animals?"

"I had to have their health records to fly them out here," I assured him as I dug out the envelope with Trucker and Miss Molly's records in it and handed it to him.

He leafed through the records and handed them back. "And you're heading where?" he asked. "After you get done scaring the hell out of our elk?"

"We didn't mean to," I repeated. "That male elk wouldn't get away from the car. I was afraid his antlers would scratch the paint if I moved!"

"I's the one who set off the alarm." Granny held out her hands, wrists touching. "If you's gonna take someone in, it'd be me."

A half-grin tilted his lips, and he shook his head. "I guess your explanation holds up. Where'd you say you were headed?"

"Red Dollar," I told him. "We're ghost hunters. We've been called in to—"

But I was speaking to his back. At *Red Dollar*, he'd frowned. When I got to *ghost* and even before *hunters* left my mouth, his face was as white as...well, a ghost. He jumped into his truck and barely missed the Tahoe's rear bumper as he squealed out of the pull-off, U-turned and headed away from us.

"Huh," Granny said after a second. "Wonder what that there was all about?"

I shrugged. "I guess he's afraid of ghosts. Anyway, at least he didn't fine us." I started the Tahoe and said, "Can you call Danny back while I drive? Find out where we're supposed to meet him."

"'K-dokey."

* * *

We hit Red Dollar well before dark, and although I was anxious to get to the hotel, we did as Danny asked and first stopped at the steakhouse on the edge of town. In deference to the freezing temperature, I left the engine running and car unlocked, since they'd only given us one set of keys. I didn't expect anyone would try to steal our car or luggage with Trucker on guard. I retrieved our warm coats out of the rear compartment and snugged both Granny and myself into them.

"Do you need your walking stick?" I asked Granny, risking her irritation at my reminder of one of her infirmities.

She replied pleasantly, though. "I took me a couple arthur-itis pills at that there last filling station. I'm good to go."

The restaurant smelled wonderfully of steaks broiling over some sort of wood flames in an open pit in the center of the room. Hickory or mesquite, I thought. Granny and I paused at the *Seat Yourself* sign and I scanned the room until I noticed Danny in a booth near the back of the dining area. He looked the same as when we'd met Up North: five-ten, a bit portly and partly bald, brown hair lighter due to graying. He had been dressed in jeans and a sweater during our initial acquaintance, but now he wore a casual sports jacket and dark-blue shirt, no tie. He obviously didn't care about manners, since he was cutting into a huge steak on a platter in front of him.

"Danny?" I said as Granny and I approached. He had the courtesy to swallow what was in his mouth before he stood to greet us.

"Long time, Alice," he said as we shook hands. "And this lovely lady must be Granny Chisholm. Twila said you were coming with them."

"You keep flatterin' me like that, youngster," Granny said, "and I might jist let you buy my steak."

"I plan on paying for all our dinners," Danny assured us. "But where's Twila?"

As we seated ourselves, Granny explained about Twila's delay. A waitress came over then and took our drink orders, and when she left, I asked Danny, "Karen's not coming either?"

He shrugged and pushed the basket of yeast rolls over to us. "Help yourselves," he insisted. "They'll bring plenty more. And I'm not sure where Karen is. I called and got her voice mail twice. She was due here a half-hour ago. We were going to discuss the...ah...something else while we waited for you."

"I hope she shows, since we need our room keys," I reminded him. "There's nowhere else to stay in Red Dollar. We'd have to go to Angel Fire or Red River."

"I've already got keys for you," Danny said, then forked a huge bite of steak into his mouth. My own mouth watered, since Granny and I had subsisted on snacks we'd picked up at a convenience store on our drive here. We were sitting right where the fans in the open cooking area blew all those delicious aromas straight at us.

CHAPTER 3

K aren never did show. We finished off our steaks and even dessert while we discussed innocuous details such as the elk at the pull off and our flight. We finally gave up and asked the waitress for a Styrofoam doggie box for the scraps for Trucker and Miss Molly, then Granny and I strolled outside while Danny, as promised, took care of the check.

Darkness had fallen, but the snow gleamed under a gorgeous full moon. Here in this tiny town, no factories or vehicle exhaust polluted the crisp whiteness or deep inkiness sprinkled with diamond pinpoints overhead. Granny and I pulled our coats tighter as we enjoyed the beauty until Danny emerged.

"I'll take you on over to the hotel," he said. "You two can go ahead and get settled while I try to find out what's happened to Karen. Hope she didn't have an accident. The roads are supposed to be clear, but you never know about Cimarron Canyon. Deer and elk wander out all the time, and it's a curvy, dangerous drive."

"Wouldn't wanna hit one of them elk, even drivin' slow," Granny agreed.

"If you would happen to hit one," Danny warned, "stay in the car and call for help. Those bulls can be dangerous when they're wounded."

Trucker scarfed up the scraps as we drove behind Danny to the hotel, and he even allowed Miss Molly to gnaw on a tidbit. That cat would turn her nose up if I offered her a bite of anything except chicken, but I glanced in the rear view mirror and saw her happily sharing steak with her buddy. We pulled in beside Danny's monstrous one-ton white pickup when he stopped in front of a two-story gray building. Rectangular, it covered somewhere around half a block and I recognized it from the pictures on the internet. Our haunted hotel. At last I'd made it here, but it didn't feel right not having Twila with me. I started to check my cell phone and see if she'd left a voice mail with her hotel information on it, since the display had shown *no service* several times during the trip from Albuquerque. But Danny opened the passenger door to assist Granny out.

"I'll help you in with the animals, then come back for your luggage after you decide which room you want to stay in," he said. "There isn't an elevator, but there are nice downstairs rooms, so Mrs. Chisholm won't have to climb the stairs."

"But it's the upstairs that's the most haunted, isn't it?" I asked without thinking.

"Then that's where we's gonna stay." Granny smacked her lips and I noticed she'd slipped her false teeth out at some point. "We want's to be up close and personal with them troublemakers."

I leashed Trucker, and Granny decided she could carry Miss Molly and her walking stick both, although I grabbed the cat's leash, also.

Inside the hotel, Granny and I stood for a few seconds taking in the ambience. Even the color ads on the internet didn't do it justice. As much as possible, each owner down through the years had retained the historical accuracy of the hotel. The wood floor creaked beneath our feet, faded fake-Persian rugs scattered about. Dead animal heads stared into space along the walls: elk, antelope, deer and even a buffalo. The lighting was dim, with mostly Tiffany-style lamps on various end tables, and the furniture consisted of several overstuffed couches and armchairs, very comfy looking.

On our left, a staid old antique desk served for check-in, complete with pigeonholes in the rear to store mail and room keys. Even in the dim light, it gleamed with high-polished care. Across the lobby a huge armoire set against the wall, the doors gaped open slightly to show it had been converted into an entertainment center with a TV and DVD player on the shelves.

To our right was the door into the formal dining room. The tables were set with snowy napkins even during this off-season. Next to it, numerous full and not-so-full liquor bottles lined the shelves behind a simple wooden bar in a saloon area. Dozens of hats covered the saloon ceiling, ranging from battered Stetsons to more modern gimmie caps. I caught a glimpse of a huge safe set in one wall.

And ghosts. That's where we got our first glimpse. A cowboy turned around on one of the bar stools and tipped his Stetson at me. The bottle of beer in front of him was shadowy, as he was, but he took a swallow. The cowboy beside him stood, battered boot toe propped on the railing that ran across the bottom of the bar about a foot from the floor. He nursed a shot glass and beer bottle both: boilermakers, I'd heard them called. He nodded briefly, then turned back to his drink.

"Nice butt on that one," Granny murmured.

Then a tall, dark, handsome man dressed in an old-time gambler's suit complete with string tie materialized in front of the check-in desk. He expertly and noiselessly shuffled a deck of cards.

Care for a game? Five card stud.

"Not right now, but mebbe later," Granny said. She'd heard his silent words also.

Danny called, "Are you ready to choose your rooms? You don't have to bother checking in." He stood across the lobby, a few feet outside a door that led to a long hallway. Wall-mounted light sconces shone along the hallway, illuminating it all the way to the end. We walked towards him as he continued, "If you're sure you want to stay on the upper floor, we'll have to go up these stairs."

We joined him, and Trucker erupted into another one of those barrages of ear-splitting barks. Even Granny and I cringed and clapped u hand over our hearts when that monstrous puma glared down at us from its perch beside the first stairwell landing. I swear the tail switched.

Then I noticed the moth-eaten fur, so the twitch must have been my imagination. That animal had been stuffed for a long while. Those brown fake eyes still gleamed, though, as did its fangs beneath the drawn-back upper lip.

"Shush," I ordered Trucker. "It's dead."

"Well, it even skeered Miss Molly," Granny said. She still held the cat in her arms, but I couldn't see Miss Molly's head, since she'd buried it beneath Granny's upper arm. "Guess even dead, it's a tad too big of a tom for her to take on."

Danny chuckled. "I should have warned you, but I'm used to Ol' Tom here. Guess I forgot he might startle you."

His sly tone indicated the lie, but I let it pass. Some men enjoyed showing off their masculinity with shock value.

Then I noticed Lady in Red on the landing where the stairs curved at a right angle before continuing on up. She wrung her hands and shook her head at me.

"What on earth are you doing here?" I demanded.

"Who?" Danny asked.

"Uh-oh," Granny added.

"Do you see ghosts?" I finally thought to ask Danny.

"Nope," he said. "I believe in them, of course. Heard too many tales not to. I'm not sure what I'd do, though, if one of them actually appeared to me."

Lady faded, but not completely. Her shadowy figure hurried on up the stairwell.

"How'd she get here?" Granny asked as, in deference to Granny's age, we slowly ascended the stairs beneath Ol' Tom's vigilant gaze. I placed a warning hand on Trucker's head and kept him on the right, my body separating him and Ol' Tom's, although the narrow stairwell didn't allow much distance between the two. At least he'd decided the crouched monster wasn't dangerous to his mommy or his friend,

Granny, so he haughtily ignored the beast. But Miss Molly peeped over Granny's shoulder and hissed at the puma.

"Despite what some paranormal investigators believe, ghosts can travel, you know that," I answered Granny. "Perhaps she originally came from this area. I really didn't have time to chat with her back in Six Gun. Come to think of it, she disappeared as soon as she overheard Twila and me talking about this trip to Red Dollar."

A gorgeous oil painting at the top of the stairwell distracted Granny. She stared at it as we climbed the final steps. The painting—conquistadors in full regalia—filled nearly the entire wall.

"Purty, ain't it?" Granny asked. "Few years a'fore even my time, though."

I chuckled. "Quite a few years," I agreed as I searched for Danny. The hallway went both right and left here, and he'd gone one way or the other, since he wasn't in sight. To our left the hall ran straight back to the end of the building; to the right, it L-ed at a corner. A faded carpet stretched down the middle of the wooden floor, too thin to muffle his footsteps. Just as I decided to call out, he emerged around the L corner.

"The larger rooms are down this way." He pointed behind him. "You'd probably be more comfortable in one of those."

But something drew me the other way. I stared to our left. All the doors were closed, but over each one was an old-fashioned transom window. Someone had painted western scenes on the transoms nearest us; cowboys and horses, steers and chuck wagons

I blinked and rubbed my eyes. The transom over the door next to last room on the right at the end of the hall had opened as I watched!

Then the lights flickered briefly and died, leaving us in total darkness.

"Damn," Danny muttered. "You'll have to wait here until I go out to my truck and get a flashlight to check the breakers."

"Does this happen often?" I asked.

He sighed. "Mostly when True's on the prowl, at least, so they say."

"Is True's room the next to the last one down the hall?"

"On the right," he agreed. "And don't even think of choosing that one to stay in. Karen closed it off to guests years ago."

"True one of them ghosts?" Granny asked.

"I'll let Karen tell you about him." Danny brushed past me towards the stairwell. "I'll be right back."

He clumped down the stairs, and my eyes adjusted somewhat to the darkness. A tiny beam of light startled me for an instant until I realized Granny had pulled a penlight from her coat pocket. She shone it down the hallway...and there stood Lady outside the open-transom doorway. Ignoring Danny's order to wait for him, we wandered down the hallway towards Lady.

As we drew close, Lady backed away. *I haven't decided if this is bad or good,* she thrust into my mind. *But you'll see.*

"What are you talking about?" I demanded. But she continued to be an independent type ghost, unresponsive to discipline. She smirked at me and disappeared.

"Good thing she didn't stay behind with Howard," Granny said. "That would've been a tale."

"If she's going to hang around us," I said loudly and firmly, so Lady could hear my warning even if she'd transcended to the other dimension, "she's going to learn to behave. Otherwise, Twila and I will banish her."

"You shoulda brought that there satchel of protective stuff outta the car," Granny said.

"You're right. Let's go back and get it before we—"

As I started to turn, my shoulder brushed the room door. It creaked open with an eerie sound, as though the door hinges hadn't moved in a long while. I hesitated, but curiosity got the better of me. Evidently, Granny, also. She shone the penlight in there.

Trucker didn't have an iota of curiosity, though. He nearly jerked free as he tried to retrace our steps.

"Just a minute, boy," I ordered. "Sit. This room has a story behind it, and the owner might not let us in here later."

Trucker refused the *sit*. He whined and maintained a strong pull on the leash. I was too interested in the room to chastise him for his disobedience.

The little light didn't illuminate much at a time. In front of us was an old iron bedstead, pillows fluffed and the hand-sewn comforter pristine. Granny moved the beam across the bed to a dresser against the wall. The penlight reflected in the mirror, giving us twice as much light. A half-full bottle of what looked like Jack Daniels set on the dresser surface beside a shot glass, a slim measure of dark liquid in the bottom. Even in this light I noticed the expected layer of dust in a long-closed room was missing. Glorious, velvety dark-red wallpaper covered the walls. A person would have thought it faded over the years, but it, too, looked as though it had recently been hung.

Still, the room did smell musty...or something. The odor tugged at my senses. It didn't seem to fit with the room's immaculate condition, but I couldn't identify it.

Granny moved the light. The carpet didn't cover the entire floor; at least two feet of polished hardwood gleamed around the edges. But there....

I took the penlight from Granny and focused the beam on the floor. Some of the wallpaper must have peeled off. A red pool of it lay on the carpet over in the far corner of the room. I frowned. It even appeared wet, as though someone had recently spilled water on it. Then it darkened, as though a shadow moved across it.

I climbed the tiny beam of light up the wall. It hit the bare red feet first. Not wallpaper on the floor. Blood caked the naked human toes circling slowly in the glow.

Trucker's nose had told him what we'd find.

CHAPTER 4

Granny gasped. Trucker whined and pulled against the leash harder—not toward the body, away from it. I quickly lowered the light and, heart hammering and nausea roiling—I even had trouble writing about blood—ushered Granny and my pets out of the room. Now my nose, also, identified the coppery scent: blood.

"We got's to call the cops," Granny whispered.

"I know, I know," I replied in a shaky voice. "What the hell's taking Danny so long? I left my cell phone in the car."

The lights came back on. I tried—brutally hard—but irrefutably, my gaze inched back into that room. Beside me, Granny stepped closer, until we stood nearly as intimate as conjoined twins. Trucker continued to strain on his leash, and I slipped my free arm around Granny. She snuggled close, her arm encircling my waist, her hand fisting in my coat material. A low cat-growl emanated from Miss Molly, clutched in Granny's other arm.

We didn't need the penlight. For some reason, even the lights in the room had come on. The poor woman's body hung from a rafter, the rope knotted in a hangman's noose around her neck, head cocked to the side, tongue protruding. The blood congealed on her wrists, down the lower

34

part of her completely naked body. Her arms had been tied at the elbows, her hands severed.

"Jesus, Mary and Joseph," Granny murmured, even though I knew for a fact she wasn't Catholic.

I couldn't possibly speak aloud, but I pled with all the powers of the Universe to please soothe the poor woman's soul. I didn't recognize her. Not that I could have, even if I'd known her, given her contorted face. Black hair, eyes open and terror-stricken. When I could break my revolted fascination, I eased Granny backward and started to close the door.

"Fingerprints," Granny warned. "We's at a crime scene."

I jerked my hand back...and saw the pentagram drawn in blood just above the doorknob.

Footsteps echoed down the hallway. Expecting Danny, I turned away from the gruesome sight. But he didn't appear. Instead, a gunshot nearly deafened us, then the footsteps raced away.

"Ghost happenin'." Granny immediately confirmed my understanding of what had just taken place. A happening across time; someone had been killed here at one time. But since twenty-six men had died here over time—and now one woman—it could be an echo of numerous possibilities. Perhaps even a residual haunting. And right now, I wasn't in any frame of mind to investigate!

Granny's voice seemed to come from down a tunnel at first, but the deafness quickly receded and her next words were clear. "Got's us more'n one crime to look into this trip, huh?"

"No!" I grabbed Granny's arm and dragged her with me...and Trucker, who lunged down the hallway, away from the blood smell. Had I not been forced to hold tight to Trucker's leash, I swear I would have picked up Granny and carried her slight body.

Body. Wrong word to think of now. Frankly, I would have been grateful to find a door marked *Women* before my stomach erupted. Hell, I would've settled for *Men*. I immediately realized we had passed a restroom door a split-second ago...next door to the murder room. No way. I'd puke on the floor first.

We careened into Danny at the head of the stairs. "Whoa!" he said. "What's wrong? One of your ghosts get the better of you?"

Granny and I stared at each other wordlessly. She probably thought the same thing as me at Danny's words. There were already ghosts in this place; we'd seen a few. And though Twila and I made a point not to read too much of the promo literature on a haunted place before we went into an investigation, I had noticed the poster on the internet listing the names of the twenty-six men killed here.

Twenty-six men and now a woman. Equal opportunity hauntings.

"Call the cops!" Granny snapped. "They's a body."

"Oh, I see," Danny said with a chuckle. "Well, as I told you, I don't see the ghosts like you do. I—"

"This one's not a ghost!" I brushed past him and headed down the stairwell, not waiting for Granny. "I'm getting my cell phone. I hope the hell y'all have 9-1-1- service out here in the boondocks."

When Trucker and I hit the lobby, I could hear Granny's raised voice on the stairwell. "Best not go down there and mess with the crime scene!"

"I need to know—" was all I made out of Danny's words as I pushed open the lobby door and Trucker and I raced toward the rental. I jerked open the passenger door, since Granny had been the last one in possession of my phone. There it was, on the dash. A nearly full battery charge indicator filled me with relief...until I noticed *no service*.

Trucker wanted in the car, but I firmly pulled him with me back toward the hotel. Briefly I realized I was walking through a deluge of snowflakes, large, lacy ones falling in a near curtain of denseness to join the layer of snow on the ground. I mis-stepped on the sidewalk and would have fallen had I not caught myself with a hand on Trucker's broad back. But I made it into the lobby with nothing more than a weak ankle sprain. There, I frantically scanned the check-in desk for a phone. Don't ask me why I didn't think of that phone first! Dead bodies tend to confuse my thinking.

There. On the other side of the desk. Still belligerent, Trucker strained on his leash, and I gave up trying to yank him with me as I rounded the desk, looking for a way inside the enclosure. Trucker high-tailed it...somewhere...as I lunged over the lowest part of the wall. My feet hit the floor and I grabbed the phone.

No dial tone! Damn it, what did these people out here do for phone service?

Oh. I pushed the button marked *Outside Line* and a welcome buzz sounded.

"9-1-1. What's your emergency?" the operator answered.

I froze, voice caught somewhere down there with my gag reflex.

"What's your emergency?" the woman repeated, much too patiently for my state of mind.

I whooshed out a breath and managed to answer, "We're at the hotel in Red Dollar. There's a woman dead in one of the rooms!"

Keyboard keys clacked, and the woman asked, "Are you sure she's deceased?"

My gaze flew to the ceiling, then back to Granny's tottering figure as she entered the lobby from the stairwell. "She wants to know if the woman's deceased!" I said to her.

"It's a reasonable question," the woman said on her end of the line. "I need to know whether to send an ambulance squad or the medical examiner's hearse."

"I don't know if she's deceased or not," I admitted. "I didn't check her pulse."

"Why not?" the woman asked in that logical voice.

"Because she's hanging from a rope and there's blood all over her from where someone cut off her hands!" I shouted.

"Oh," the woman said. "I've dispatched the sheriff's department and ambulance. But some of them—the medical personnel, anyway—have to come from Santa Fe, and there's a blizzard starting up. If you're sure the woman's dead, I guess it's all right to let her hang. But sometimes...."

"Sometimes what?" I demanded.

"Well, it takes a while for someone to strangle...."

I gripped the phone so tightly it's a wonder it didn't crumble in my hand. "She might still be alive? You didn't see her!"

"No, I didn't," she responded in a soothing voice.

The phone clattered from my nerveless hand. I stared at Granny. "Do you think that woman upstairs might possibly still be alive?"

"I seen stranger things in my life," she admitted.

I found the stupid gate on the enclosure around the check-in desk this time, flipped open the retaining latch and raced out of there. "You can stay on the line with that operator," I called over my shoulder. "I need to find Danny."

I did...at the top of the stairwell. We barreled into each other as I rounded the steps into the hall. He grabbed my arm and we flew down the hallway toward that bedroom as he shouted, "I need some help! We can't let her hang there like that!"

The room door blocked our way, and Danny grabbed the doorknob and twisted, then shook it.

"I left it open," he said in a frantic voice. "Who shut it? We have to get back in there!"

I glanced overhead. The transom was closed. The thud of Danny's shoulder drew my attention, and the door shattered off its hinges. He dragged me after him—straight over under the poor woman's hanging body—and ordered, "Wrap your arms around her and try to hold her up some."

Stifling my distaste, I did as Danny said. He climbed onto a chair he'd already pulled over beside the woman. Thank the Universe I still had on my coat, so it absorbed any still wet blood...except where my hands touched her bare legs. I also tried to ignore something else I'd only read about in research, never experienced. The poor woman's bowels had evacuated.

Somehow Danny managed to get the rope loose from her neck. Her weight staggered me, but Danny quickly took the burden off me when he climbed off the chair. For an instant, he stared down at the body lolling in his arms, then appeared to control himself and carried her over to the bed, where he laid her down.

I followed, absentmindedly brushing my hands up and down my coat. Danny pressed his fingers to the woman's swollen throat, seeking a pulse, I guess. He shook his head, but the 9-1-1 operator's words kept ringing in my head. I detoured to the window curtains and pulled one of the tie-backs free. Back at the bed, I handed one end to Danny and said, "Just in case, we need to stop any bleeding."

He nodded and we tightened the two ends of the tie-back around her arms, just above where her hands had been cut off. As soon as we had the tie-backs knotted, Danny pulled out a pocketknife from his jeans and sawed at the ropes binding the woman's elbows.

"Should we try CPR?" I asked quietly.

Danny's gaze flew to mine, then back to the woman's face. I clearly heard him swallow.

"Yes," he admitted. "We should."

"I've never had any training...."

"Me, neither. Not lately, anyway, just years ago. Am supposed to take an updated course next year to renew my insurance on balloon trips."

He hesitated briefly. "But what I know is probably better than doing nothing."

He slipped a hand under the woman's neck, tilted her had back and forced a finger past her tongue, into her mouth. Clearing the airway, I knew from research, not actual experience. He lowered his head and breathed into her once. Satisfied, he then fisted one hand on her chest, placed his other hand on top of it and began the count.

"One, two, three, four, five."

He placed his mouth over the woman's and breathed into her again. I frantically watched her chest for any sign of movement. Nothing, after Danny returned to his count.

I helplessly stood there by the bed until some inner sense whispered to me. No, I wasn't completely helpless. Now that the initial panic had diminished—somewhat, anyway—I drew deep into myself in search of the abilities I'd honed under Twila's guidance for years. I should be able to at least tell if the woman were still alive. I cleared my mind and grounded myself. Searched the room around me, mentally seeking any sign of...anyone.

Nothing. But a faint creak sounded and I swung around to see the transom open again.

Danny continued his CPR efforts, and I closed my eyes in order to concentrate better. Still nothing tugged at my psychic senses. I knew what I had to do, yet reluctance surfaced. With a breath for courage, I opened my eyes, then tentatively reached out to touch the woman's leg, hesitating only briefly before my hand closed on her flesh and over the sticky blood. I encountered the same stiffness I recalled when I gripped her to help Danny a few moments ago. But I wasn't probing for body warmth or non-warmth.

Nothing there, either. Both relief and sorrow filled me. She was gone, and since I didn't sense her soul in the room, I assumed she had crossed through The Light despite her violent manner of death.

Block that thought, my senses informed me. How many times have you encountered a soul who lingers just on this side of The Light, yet takes a lot of effort to contact?

I totally agreed with my senses, still....

"She's gone, Danny," I murmured.

He threw me glance after another three-count, which had produced a slight chest movement that died as soon as he lifted his head. "No! We have to be sure Karen's not revivable!"

Four. Breathe into mouth.

"Karen?" I asked in as quiet a voice as I could summon. "The woman who owns...owned the hotel?"

"Owns," Danny said flatly. "One, two, three, four, five." Breathe.

"Danny, the 9-1-1 operator said she wasn't sure how soon the authorities and medical help could get here. A blizzard's started outside."

"Two, three. Where the hell else would a blizzard start? Not in here! Four, five." Breathe.

I started to reach out and impede Danny's efforts, but he outweighed me by quite a bit. And despite the slight belly paunch, he appeared in darn good shape physically. He might react by throwing me out of his way. As I pulled my hand back, the dried residue of blood flakes caught my attention. And that wasn't all. Fecal matter smeared my coat sleeves.

It shouldn't have bothered me that much, I suppose. It wasn't the poor woman's fault her death had happened in such a gruesome, smelly manner. But I was dealing with living senses, unprotected by the distance of a different dimension.

Thank goodness. I wasn't ready to see what the other side was like. Twila and I had a long to-do list of things we wanted to see and experience in this world.

Leaving Danny to his useless ministrations, I wandered out into the hallway and shed my distasteful coat. It, and I, needed washed. First I'd go find Granny and my pets.

No. This time I paid attention to the door marked *Ladies* next to the one I'd just left. First, I'd clean myself and the coat. I couldn't handle leaving that reside on me if the medical personnel took hours to arrive.

Ten minutes later, with still no sign of Danny, I continued back downstairs. Granny waited in the lobby, on the couch in front of the armoire. Trucker lay beside her, Miss Molly curled in her lap. Three pair of eyes met my gaze as I walked over to them. Granny didn't need to voice her question.

"She's gone," I said as I tossed my damp coat on a nearby chair. "But Danny just won't give up. He's performing CPR. Have any of the authorities or medical people called?"

She rose from the couch and dumped Miss Molly beside Trucker. "Was jist gonna call 'em again. But sounds like I won't have to."

She must have had her hearing aid turned on, because now I also heard the faint sound of a siren. The vehicle pulled up outside the hotel and the noise died, although we could see the bubble lights flashing through the window. Trucker lifted his head, but Granny said, "It's the cops, dog. We got's to let 'em in."

Trucker laid back down, but kept a vigilant gaze on the door. Before I could get over there, a man dressed in a sheriff's uniform threw it open and rushed inside.

"We hud a 9-1-1 call from here," he said, right hand propped on his gun butt.

"She's upstairs." I pointed across the lobby. "Next to last door on the right. Danny's up there with her."

"Anyone else in the hotel?" he asked as he hurried across the lobby.

No one living. "Just the three of us, and my dog and cat."

"Watch out for that there mountain lion!" Granny warned.

"I've been here plenty of times," he called back, steps pounding up the stairs.

At a loss as to what to do next, I stared longingly at the saloon room.

"Me, too," Granny said. She was looking in the same direction. "But I s'pose they's gonna want to dust 'em fer fingerprints a'fore we touch anything else."

The tall, dark, handsome gambler ghost appeared over behind the bar. He jerked his head in an indication for us to join him, and Granny and I looked at each other and shrugged.

"Crown and Seven," I called to the gambler.

"Make mine a double," Granny added as we walked into the saloon.

The gambler levitated a bottle of Crown Royal from the shelf behind the bar and floated it over in front of us as we each took a barstool. He added two glasses and cans of 7-UP.

"I's'll mix," Granny offered.

I grabbed my drink as soon as she had it mixed. I didn't even wait until the soothing relaxation spread before I poured a second one.

There didn't seem to be anything to discuss, and Gambler had disappeared, so Granny and I sat silently...waiting...waiting. I'd have thought the sheriff would return by now, but nothing stirred overhead...or anywhere else. I wanted desperately to talk to Twila, but until I got cell phone service and could check my messages, I had no idea how to contact her. My aunt had yet to believe in owning her own cell phone.

Suddenly Granny stiffened. "This here place is awful big. How long do you think that poor woman's been dead?"

I caught her meaning immediately and stared around the saloon. The murderer—I had no doubt the woman hadn't performed that type of death on herself—could still be in the building!

Granny and I eased off the barstools. I grabbed the bottle of Crown and a can of 7-Up to carry with me as we warily crept back to join Trucker, eyeing the shadows and checking behind the furniture. My mind eased somewhat. Trucker would let us know if anyone was still around.

"Still wish I had me my shotgun," Granny said as she sat down on the couch.

"So do I," I admitted.

CHAPTER 5

Now that she was home, Joleen would have to tell Alice that she preferred her given name, rather than the "Lady In Red" Alice has dubbed her with. Clad in her favorite red dress, she sat cross-legged on the hood of the car that Alice rented in Albuquerque and watched the goings on. Good thing the cold didn't bother her in her state. Snow curtained her, not mounding on her non-body. She maintained the state of invisibility she'd learned over the decades from others of her ilk. Wind piled the snow into drifts around the front of the hotel and covered the sidewalk, turning the vehicles into huge white humps, which resembled sand dunes she remembered from some TV show she'd watched one boring day.

Sheriff Carson had left his red and blue emergency lights swirling. They cast dancing colors in the pristine snow, a preliminary warning of the drama playing out inside. Perhaps the sheriff had left his lights on to spotlight the destination for others in the pack of officialdom no doubt trying to make its way to the hotel even now.

Too late, Joleen mused with tight lips. Nothing could help Karen, the woman hanging up there. Joleen hadn't sensed a spark of life in the physical body, nor the lingering presence of a new resident. She wasn't about to go back and check. She couldn't abide being inside the hotel right now, not after the re-enactment of her brother's death.

Why did the echoes of True's murder intrude just at that moment? After all, twenty-six—seven, now—other deaths hung in the ether of the hotel. She'd kept count, even after own death in the yellow fever epidemic.

What about this place drew death in such numbers? Granted, the clientele hadn't been socially acceptable in the early days: gamblers, bandits, rustlers, thieves. Owners over the years had tried to upgrade the surroundings and attract more refined guests, but the bloody atmosphere of the building's history couldn't be quelled. She didn't care that much about a lot of those deaths. Life expectancy in her time had been short, both due to the lawlessness of the land and the lack of medical knowledge. Yet she'd made a promise on her deathbed, and by damn, she meant to keep it!

Well, this most recent death...she supposed she should be concerned, but she couldn't decide if it were beneficial or complicating to her plan. Would it clear the way or hold her in her semi-state? She couldn't cross over until she honored her vow. She recalled the tunnel, the promise at the end of The Light. She nearly reached it...until she made the mistake of looking down. Saw True still there as a ghost and remembered her promise to her mama to take care of her little brother. That's all it took, one split-instant in time. How could she leave him, even if she did have to learn to cope with a new type of existence?

Had she known so many years would pass without her being able to convince True to accompany her and try to cross over again, would she still have chosen to come back? She sighed. Hindsight and all that. And what about foresight? Who could have foretold the path of her remaining family. Dysfunctional, they called it today. She'd learned a few new words over the years, too.

And by gosh darn, here was one of her annoying problems right now!

"Get out of here, LeRoy," Joleen ordered when he materialized in front of the car.

"Nyaa, nyaa, nyaa, make me," her cousin shot back.

Lord, that boy had never grown up. He even stuck his tongue out at her. Generations dead, he hadn't matured a bit. Even his death was due to the boy's—she'd never bowed to giving LeRoy the title of man—stupidity, mixed with a touch of his meanness and laziness. He'd heard some folks paid big bucks for cats, which were scarce in the new settlements. He hadn't counted on mama cat protecting the babies he dug out of the straw in the barn loft and tossed into a tote sack. They didn't have antibiotics to combat infection back then. Cat-scratch fever, they called LeRoy's malady today.

At least the kittens had escaped while poor LeRoy basked in delirium two days out on the trail. She'd manipulated the string to untie the tote sack herself and led them to the river. She could have told LeRoy that he might have saved himself if he'd taken a bath, or at the very least, washed out the cat-scratch wounds with soap and water. But he couldn't see her back then, and his side of the family believed one bath a year sufficient—in the spring. He'd stolen the kittens in late fall. Besides that, the enmity between the two family branches lingered even over here. LeRoy wouldn't have listened to her, even if she could have materialized to him. Before he entered her dimension, he didn't believe in ghosts.

"Have you seen the cat one of the new guests at the hotel brought with her?" Joleen asked with a wicked grin.

"Cat?" LeRoy backed away. "I ain't seen no cat. You's lyin' to me."

"Her name's Miss Molly. Wasn't that cat whose kittens you stole named Golly-Molly? Something like that, as I recall. Could be this cat is a direct descendant of that one."

"I don't know what the heck a de-desen—what your high-falutin' word means. But that there cat better not mess with me!"

"You've got it backwards, Cuz. Plus this cat's owner has powers you wouldn't believe. She doesn't take kindly to ghosts who get out of line."

"I keep tellin' you, I ain't no ghost!"

Joleen chuckled wryly. They'd had this argument before...same song, dozenth verse. "Then what do you think you are? You aren't alive. You aren't in heaven...or hell, if you believe in those places."

"I'm just...me!" LeRoy spat. "Still look like me. Still think like me."

"Then maybe that's why you're still stupid," Joleen said. "And being the you that you are, and being that Alice's cat can also see ghosts, you might want to think hard about hanging around here right now."

LeRoy glanced at the sheriff's vehicle. "You can't tell me what to do. Ain't nothin' happened around here for years and years, and it gets borin'. I got just as much right as you to get a kick out of watching the goin's on."

"Suit yourself." Joleen shrugged. "I happen to know that Alice brought several things with her that work to haul *ghosts* who don't obey her over the coals."

"I ain't scared of her or her cat."

"Neither am I...scared, that is. But I'm not the one Alice's cat won't like. I made friends with Miss Molly a while back. Trucker, the dog, too."

"Can't no animal bother me."

"It's the other way around, you bothering the animals," Joleen explained again. "And then their mistress—Alice—will make sure you don't disturb them. I've been thinking, Cuz. I've got my own reason for staying here...at least, for now. But ever since the first time I ran across you over here, I wondered why you hadn't gone on. You probably had the same chance I did to go through The Light. But I'll bet you got to thinking what you'd face over there. Retribution for your actions, if you know what retribution means. It's payback, Cuz. The kittens weren't the only mistake you made. Remember my momma's egg money, that she was saving to pay for True to study with that doctor in Albuquerque after we moved out there?"

LeRoy sputtered for a bit, then disappeared.

Joleen sighed. Not having been through The Light herself, she wasn't sure if retribution was a part of the existence over there or not. If so, she might have another mark against herself, for meanness. Yet LeRoy would distract Alice if he hung around and caused trouble like he did in life.

So now what? Should she try to talk to Alice, since she was providently here where Joleen had intended her to be from the moment she'd found her? Alice had been quite adamant she wouldn't even talk to

Joleen until after the first of the year, yet here she was. What Fate had led Alice here? Perhaps even more important, what Fate had led Joleen to that tiny town of Six Gun? Did universal manipulations take place even over here?

Chance. Happenstance. Coincidence. Was that how it worked, or were all those just unknown foregones? She'd first overheard Danny and Maddie talking about Twila, the woman Danny knew who could possibly discipline the ghosts here at the hotel—teach them to keep their fingers and maneuvers off the potential sale.

Joleen had found Alice easily enough after she saw her on TV. True hadn't been the only smart one in the family. Between the two of them, they'd figured out this internet stuff years ago, partly out of boredom at first, but eventually out of fascination. Oh, if only they'd been allowed to live out full lives! So many things they could have accomplished.

And where the heck was True now? She and her brother had fought bitterly over the idea of bringing Twila and Alice here. On reflection, Joleen considered maybe it wasn't even her doing. Maybe those interconnecting chains of Fate had made the decision. Maybe it was time for things to come full circle and be resolved.

Maybe. If she could keep things on track here.

Karen's death. Providence or complication?

Where the heck was True?

CHAPTER 6

D anny didn't bother with a glass. He plopped down on the couch beside me and grabbed the bottle of Crown, upended it and slugged down several swallows. Then he shoved the bottle between his legs and leaned his head back, eyes closed.

Granny and I sat quietly, sipping our own drinks, and I surreptitiously studied Danny. He'd somehow come out of his ministrations to Karen nearly spotless. I thought back to the frantic resuscitation attempt and recalled he'd rolled up his shirtsleeves and discarded his sport jacket somewhere. A stain or two did show on his dark-blue shirt. He'd probably cleaned up the same place I had, in one of the upstairs bathrooms.

Granny and I glanced overhead once in a while when we heard footsteps on the upper level. The ambulance squad had arrived, along with one other deputy from Sheriff Carson's force. I stared out the window in the side lobby wall, where a curtain of blowing snow cut off any visibility. I supposed these residents were used to hazardous roads, but I wasn't looking forward to trying to get out of here tomorrow to pick up Twila—if she didn't decide to completely abort her trip, given the murder.

Besides, the authorities would probably nix our staying here now.

Maybe we couldn't even stay here tonight. Then what would we do? Perish the thought of Granny and I out in that blizzard trying to find a bed. Surely the sheriff would understand Granny, at least, needed somewhere to sleep besides a car seat, and that two Texas tourists had no business out on those deadly roads.

And where the heck had all the ghosts gone? No one stood over in the saloon now. No precursory chill indicated anyone lingered near, keeping their energy under control except for those of us tuned into their presence. The handsome gambler would be particularly welcome right now, a different focus for my thoughts.

The phone on the lobby desk rang, and Granny and I both swiveled to stare at it. Danny didn't appear to notice; he kept his head back even while he raised the bottle again. At the second ring, Trucker nudged me insistently.

"I'm sure they have an answering machine or service," I assured the dog when he butted me harder and Miss Molly meowed for me to stir myself and answer the blasted phone. Neither of them could abide a ringing telephone.

"Might be Twila," Granny said.

I stirred, and got to the phone just as the message on the out-of-date answering machine began. I picked up the receiver and pushed buttons, trying to cut off the message, but it continued until the beep. Then....

"Alice? Are you there, Alice?"

What the...? Jack's voice, not Twila's.

"Jack? Jack, can you hear me?"

Despite the fact I was a whiz with computer technology—well, somewhat of a whiz, depending on the program—other machines sometimes baffled me. Jack continued, obviously not hearing me. Damn it, weren't answering machines supposed to click off when a person picked up?

"...Angel Fire," Jack said. Then he added something about spotty cell service and recited a phone number while I frantically scanned the desk for pen and paper. "I heard what's going on there. Call me, Alice. ASAP."

During my frantic gaze around the desk—and at the obstinate phone

—I noticed one of the lights blinking. I pushed it just as Jack said, "...and I mean ASAP," and cut in on him.

"Jack? Jack, are you there?"

"Alice!" Good, he could hear me. "*Chère*, are you involved in another murder? This entire hotel is talking about what happened over there in Red Dollar."

I pulled the phone away from my ear and stared at it. Darn his prissy attitude! Maybe I'd just hang up on him and let him stew. But no, then I'd be the one stewing, thinking of all the comebacks I should have voiced.

"You've got no busi—"

"Shut up, Jack!" I interrupted. "What on earth makes you think I'm involved here? It's not my fault some perp committed murder just before I arrived! I'm here on legitimate business, and I don't appreciate your attitude one bit!" *Well, if you consider ghost hunting legitimate business, and Twila and I do.*

Before Jack could butt in with his usual denigration of what he considered foolishness over hightailing it on the trail of ghosts, I went right on, "Here Granny and I are all upset over that poor woman's death —plus the manner of it, I might add, along with the fact that now we're probably without a place to stay after the long trip wore us out to begin with—"

"Alice—"

"— and do we get any sympathy from you? Oh, no, all we get is a reaming out for being in the wrong place at the wrong time!"

"*Chère*—"

"Why don't you just go up on the slopes and do some night skiing? Forget we're even in your area? Hell, forget we're even here in New Mexico! Go enjoy your *vacation*."

This time he didn't react to my tirade. He didn't utter another word, just let the silence hang. Shoot, it's no fun arguing with someone who won't take up their end of the squabble. He probably expected me to apologize, or at least make an attempt at amends.

I should hang up....

He probably wouldn't call back, though. And given the desperate need I felt right then to hang onto a familiar voice, I couldn't bring myself to slam down the phone. Here we were in an isolated area with no friends, our only acquaintance....

I glanced over at Danny as he took another slug from the bottle.

...our only acquaintance, the man who should feel responsible for mine and Granny's wellbeing, on his way to getting stink-ass drunk. Danny obviously had taken a slug or two since I'd left the couch; the floor light beside where he sat illuminated the nearly empty bottle.

And where had Granny gone? Oh.

Granny took the phone from my ear and held it to hers.

"Jack? Y'all still there?"

She nodded, then continued, "Settle down, Jack. I's know you's worried 'bout us. You alwise lets your mouth get way from you when you's bothered and bewildered. But there ain't a derned thing you can do right now. You can't get over here, given that dad-blasted snow out there. And me'n Alice and Trucker and Miss Molly are in the warm, not out in that weather."

She paused, then said, "Uh huh. Yep. 'K-dokey," then opened the desk drawer and found a pencil. She wrote a phone number on a notepad I hadn't noticed—right there beside the phone—then said, "We'll do that. 'Spect we'll talk to you early in the mornin'. Bye."

She hung up, but before I could ask the gist of the conversation, the phone rang again. She answered, "Hello?" then grinned and handed the phone to me.

Twila. Please let it be Twila.

"It is," her voice said. "What's going on there? I'm getting all sorts of impressions, but something's blocking the details."

I hurriedly explained everything and, similar to Jack's reaction, she grew silent and unresponsive. Well, maybe I *had* babbled on a little. Or maybe she was trying to make connection here through her connection to me—pierce the block she'd experienced.

No, she said, "The reports are that we'll be able to get out of here in the morning. Maybe pretty early. The storm rushed on through, and a warm front actually followed it. Weird thing, this Santa Ana weather. What's the forecast down there?"

"Forecast?" I repeated. "When the hell have I had time to listen to the geedamn weather report?"

She giggled. "I thought you'd cleaned up your language some after your go-round with Granny and the Quit Cussing Trip Kitty. Didn't it cost you a chunk of your royalty check in October to pay off all the IOU's in the kitty?"

I huffed and searched for a comeback, but a stupid film of tears blurred my vision. First Jack's tirade, now Twila's lack of sensitivity to what had happened. No, *first* the discovery of that poor woman's body....

"Shhh, shhh, shhh," Twila said, obviously picking up on how close I was to shattering. "Hang in there, Alice."

I bit my lip. I so wanted someone here to share the burden of both the emotions and responsibilities right now. I couldn't get the sight of that poor woman out of my mind. The blood. The suffering she must have undergone. The responsibility of taking care of Granny and my pets resting on my shoulders. Sometimes being an adult sucked rotten tomatoes.

I held onto the phone with a death grip, not wanting to lose the thin thousand-mile connection to my mentor and source of support.

"I'll hang," I promised Twila as I took advantage of the longish cord on the receiver and walked to the window behind the check-in desk. *Ah, shit. Wrong word.*

Twila muffled a laugh, evidently picking up on my thoughts. "I know how upset you must be," she soothed. "But reality does indeed suck rotten tomatoes sometimes. Even if I were there, it would just mean there was another person needing a bed tonight."

I gasped. "I was hoping we could stay here. There's no way I want to try to find another room for the night. That storm out there is horrible. Remember the blizzard we were out in up there one winter? When we spent hours helping push stuck cars out of the parking lots after the movie was over?"

"That was more fun than fear," she said. "We were a lot younger and...well, in better physical shape."

I inattentively rubbed a bit of frost off the hotel window. "Physical shape be damned. It doesn't matter right now. The mental stress is—holy hell! What's she doing here?"

"Who?" Twila said, a frown in her voice. "I told you, Alice. I'm having trouble connecting down there."

"Lady in Red!" I spat. "She's sitting out there on the hood of my car!"

The ghost—now I knew where at least one of them was—turned to face me. If I hadn't been so upset, her agonized look might have tugged at my heart. Shoot, it even looked like she might be crying. She had to at least be cold, out there in that mess with that flimsy dress on.

Oh, ghosts didn't get cold.

"Is this the first time you've seen here there?" Twila asked.

"No. I saw her...upstairs a while ago. Just before...just before all hell broke loose."

"You need to talk to her. See what her purpose is in all this."

"I suppose," I acknowledged. "She sure seemed intent on butting into my life back in Six Gun. Now here she is in Red Dollar. Oh, crap, she's leaving."

Lady in Red did just that. She nodded at me, then merged with the falling snow and disappeared. Although I didn't actually hear her, I got the distinct impression she meant me to understand we would meet again soon.

"I heard it, too," Twila said. "She has a purpose there, and we're part of it."

"Here comes the law again," Granny whispered beside me, and I turned to see the sheriff entering the lobby.

I dropped my own voice to a whisper as I told Twila, "Well, this time we'll just do our job as soon as you get here. Take on the ghosts and keep the hell out of this murder investigation."

"I agree," she replied. "It's too much hassle otherwise. Look, let me give you my hotel phone and room number. Got a pen?"

Although Sheriff Carson stared at me with a stern look that

demanded I hang up and pay attention to him, I ignored him and grabbed the pencil Granny had used. As Twila recited her contact information, I wrote it under Jack's. Then, reluctantly, I said goodbye and hung up.

"We've got to decide what to do with you ladies," Sheriff Carson said without preamble. "It'll take us quite a while to wind up our investigation here, and we can't have you in the way."

Danny finally stirred on the couch. "They can stay over in the newer part of the hotel. The other building over there."

"Nope, can't do that," the sheriff disagreed. "That's part of this crime scene, until we can tell different."

Danny sighed and said, "Then call someone here in town and find them another place to spend the night."

"Do you have any idea how dead this town is in winter?" Carson said. Then he shrugged apologetically at Granny and me. "Sorry. Not a good way to put it, but it's true. Most of the residents here close up their businesses and take off for warmer climes this time of year. The few folks I know of left around here either aren't suitable company or don't have a spare bed."

"We aren't picky, Sheriff," I assured him. "Just find us somewhere for tonight, and we'll worry about somewhere else tomorrow, after I pick up my aunt in Albuquerque."

He glanced behind me at the window. "You have any experience driving in snow?"

"No," I admitted. "Well, not recent experience. We rarely get snow in Six Gun. Ice storms, though, we get those. But my vehicle stays in the garage whenever that happens."

He shrugged. "We won't abandon you ladies, but we do have a murder to investigate. And..." He sneered at Danny and the Crown bottle on his lap. "...doesn't look like there's anyone else capable of taking care of you."

"Just find us a place for tonight," I pleaded again. "Anywhere."

Trucker slid off the couch and trotted towards me, followed by Miss Molly. I recognized that look on my dog's face; he needed a doggie potty break. Indeed, he plopped down in front of the check-in desk and gazed beseechingly between me and the hotel front door.

"I've got it," Sheriff Carson said with a snap of his fingers. "I'll have one of my men go turn on the heat first, of course. We can take some linens and blankets from here."

Trucker ambled on over to the door, where he cast an insistent look at me.

"Wherever," I told the sheriff as I exited the check-in desk gate. "I need to take my dog out. And ...." I perused Miss Molly as I passed her, then bent down and picked her up to hand to Granny, who hobbled behind me. "Hopefully, Miss Molly can hold it for a minute or so. Her portable litter box is still in the car."

Footsteps overhead made their way towards the stairwell, and the sheriff confirmed my thoughts. "They're bringing the body out. You ladies go on outside, if you want."

Danny set the now empty Crown bottle on the coffee table in front of him, surged to his feet and hurried toward us. He stumbled a bit, but on his way he grabbed my coat from where I'd tossed it on a chair. He walked on past us to the saloon.

"There's a side door," he said, beckoning. "We'll use that one for now."

I didn't argue, even though Danny's condition bothered me. Maybe the icy air would sober him up some. Granny and I followed him, and I called Trucker with us. The footsteps were descending the stairwell, and we managed to get to the side door before the paramedics arrived in the lobby. Danny ushered Granny on out as he handed me my coat. I shrugged into it as I exited.

Trucker bounded on through the drifts, enjoying his freedom and the unfamiliar snow on the ground. It was less windy here, sheltered by the hotel wall and large pine trees. I started to pull the door closed, but Danny jammed a hand against it.

"Let me make sure I remember the combination first," he said. He engaged the lock, then pushed some numbered buttons on the panel above the doorknob. The lock snapped open, and he nodded. "That's the one Karen gave me."

He pulled the door shut, and I briefly gave a thought to demanding he give me the combination also. However, I was fairly certain I'd followed his finger path. I'd been looking for any other point of concentration for my mind to counteract the murmured voices inside the hotel: Sheriff Carson directing the body-carriers....

Crap. Had it been a two first or four? Didn't matter right now. I drew in a calming breath of crystal-clear air. It was beautiful out here; pure, clean drifts on the ground, inches more layered on the dark green pines. Across a courtyard sat another building, probably the newer portion of the hotel Danny had mentioned. Although similar in design to the older, main hotel, it was smaller and looked more like one of the modern motels along the highway.

"Where you think they's gonna put us up for the night?" Granny asked. Miss Molly wiggled in her arms, and I went ahead and set her on the ground. Mistake. She yowled when she sank into the snow and picked up one foot after the other to shake off the nasty stuff. Yet when her buddy Trucker yipped at her, she headed down the path he'd plowed.

Granny and I both chuckled. Miss Molly was determined to reach Trucker, yet she walked stiltedly, shaking off each paw before she replaced it in that icky stuff.

"He said it had heat," I belatedly answered Granny. "So there's that."

Danny had wandered away from us and stood at the corner of the building, probably watching the activity out front. Probably the loading of the ambulance....

"He don't got no coat," Granny observed. "Got's to be freezing."

"He's more used to the weather than we are," I assured her. "Still, you're right. He has to be cold. He doesn't seem to notice it, though."

She cackled. "Prob'ly gots enough Crown in him to make him think he's warm."

I sighed. "I wonder if Twila's aware we've got a contact here who has a drinking problem. I only spent a little time with Danny up north, but I didn't notice he drank that much. Shoot, we'd never have gone up in that balloon with him if we'd had any hint he wasn't stone-cold sober."

"Looka there," she said.

I moved my gaze in the direction she indicated and laughed out loud this time. Trucker lay in the snow, and as we watched, Miss Molly climbed onto his broad back. The dog rose, and Miss Molly clung to him as he slowly strolled back to us, my Head Cat perched well above that disgusting snow, feet and belly protected. Trucker halted in front of Granny and me, and Miss Molly stared up at us with one of those cat-smirks of total aloofness on her tan and black face.

Or maybe it was just the way her mouth naturally curved. She did bat her blue eyes once, and her purr sounded in the still air.

A set of those backing-up warning beeps sounded, drawing my attention to where Danny still stood. Despite the falling snow, or perhaps due to it, the reflections of the emergency lights swirled in the air along the street. The beeps ended, yet no siren split the air as the reflections vanished and the sound of the ambulance's engine faded. No reason for a siren to clear the way. No cars to warn, no hurry to get the body to medical attention.

The side door behind us opened, and Sheriff Carson said, "You ladies want to wait in here for a bit? I sent a deputy on over to turn on the heat in the jail."

"The jail?" I echoed. "You're putting us in jail?"

CHAPTER 7

"Now, now, now," Sheriff Carson said in a patronizing tone. "It's not what you think. There's a building here in town that was once used for the jail way back when. It's been restored as one of the historical stops for tourists. Like I said, it has heat. They had to put that in to keep the pipes from breaking. At times, the temperature gets below freezing even after the town opens up for tourists. There's a bathroom, too, if we can get the water turned on. And my deputy said he knows how to do that. His cousin's a meter reader."

"The beds?" I asked.

"Bunks, of course," he confirmed. "There's four there, if I remember right."

"Ain't never slept in no jail," Granny mused as Danny joined us. "'Nother life experience to 'member to put in my memoirs for my great-grandkids."

"You're writing your memoirs?" I asked Granny in astonishment. "How neat! Why haven't you asked me to help?"

"Will," Granny assured me. "Soon's I get them ready to send to your publisher."

I groaned inwardly. What Granny knew about the publishing

59

industry consisted of being there with a hand out as soon as my author copies arrived from each book. I supposed I could always help her indie-publish her book.

"Forgot about the jail," Danny said, interrupting my thoughts. He sounded more sober, but I couldn't imagine how. "That will work. If I recall, there are even a few supplies there. Refrigerator, coffeepot, some snacks."

"We'll make sure the ladies are comfortable," Sheriff Carson told Danny. "We'll take anything else we think will add to their comfort from the hotel here. You'll be going with me. I want your statement while things are fresh in your mind. Given the ladies' ages, we'll let them rest before we get theirs."

I shot Sheriff Carson a look that would have added to the body count at the hotel, if it had held half the power of my irritation. Of course I wasn't at my best, given the long trip and stress on arrival. Let alone the responsibility heaped on my shoulders and Twila a zillion miles away. Jack might have offered a sympathetic shoulder, but all he had been interested in was heaping additional guilt on me for once again stepping into a murder. The Crown Royal hadn't eased my tension, since the effects of it were only a tantalizing memory right now. Probably all the booze had done was aggravate my wrinkles! Hell, no wonder I looked tired and aged. But no way should the sheriff lump me in with Granny's generation.

I started to lambaste the sheriff, but some inner voice cautioned me not to antagonize the local law enforcement. Last time I'd done that, I'd ended up locked in an interrogation room until I wished I'd worn an adult diaper. Oh what we learn during life's journey.

Danny shrugged agreeably and jammed his hands into his trouser pockets, evidently finally feeling the cold. "Can I go get my coat?"

The sheriff stepped back so we could re-enter the hotel. I hadn't paid much attention when I was hurrying to escape the sight of the body being carried out, but we'd exited through a café area just inside the side door. Much smaller than the formal dining room, it contained four small tables and a mural of a saloon scene painted on the back wall.

"All of you wait in here so you don't further disturb our crime scene," Sheriff Carson ordered. "I'll get Danny's coat."

Trucker plodded in before Sheriff Carson shut the door, and as we headed for the closest table, the dog decided to shake off the snow clinging to his silky coat. Along with the snow, Miss Molly shook off, too. She landed cat-like, feet on the floor, and blasted her buddy's disregard for her queenly stature with a hiss that exposed her sharp teeth. Trucker ignored her and whirled to stare at the mural as the sheriff strode out of the café.

And by gosh darn, Miss Molly wasn't indicating her irritation at her ride. A short, shabbily dressed male ghost appeared in front of the mural—blond, straggly hair; a patchy beard on his face; clothing that could have stood up on its own from the dirt encased in it. I couldn't decide whether the smell came from his clothes or him. The odor permeated the room.

"Huh," the ghost said, then his face contorted in fear. "She was right for once."

As Trucker lunged, Miss Molly snarling right behind him, the ghost dissolved.

"Huh," Granny echoed. "That one's trouble."

"What are you talking about?" Danny asked as he op0ened the cabinet doors along another wall. "What's wrong with the cat and dog? Phew. I think something in here's spoiled."

"Liquor's all out in the saloon," Granny observed. "And doubt the sheriff's gonna figger that a bottle of booze is somethin' me'n Alice need to help us be comfortable. 'Sides, you oughtta be sober to give a legal-like statement."

"I wasn't looking for...ah, hell," Danny said. "I've got a bottle in my car."

* * *

Sheriff Carson insisted he and his men were too busy to drive my car over to the jail. He gave me a door key and directions, assuring me his deputy had the building ready for us. The sheriff did follow me around and make a list of the few supplies he allowed me to gather. I found a liquor box in a storeroom to carry them.

He didn't notice there was one bottle of Crown left in the box. I made a mental note to pay for it, along with the other things I loaded, which thankfully included a six-pack of 7-Up. If there wasn't any ice available, Granny and I could pluck off an icicle from an eave.

"You knows which one of them thingabobbies is that there four-wheel drive?" Granny asked after we pilled into the rental, Trucker and Miss Molly safely encased in the backseat.

I turned the dash light indicator up higher and examined the various knobs, switches and protrusions. "This one, I guess," I said as I maneuvered a small gear shift on the console.

Dread curdled in my belly. I'd rather have taken a beating than drive in this mess. Yet there was no choice. Taking a deep breath, I blew out my mouth, seeking to get rid of as much tension as possible. Another breath. One more. It didn't help much.

I backed out cautiously, the tires reassuringly crunching snow beneath their tread. Shifting into drive, I barely feathered the gas, and the SUV crawled down the street. Heavy flakes still swirled down, dabs hitting the windshield with muffled clicks. I turned on the wipers and defrosters, hoping against hope it wasn't actually sleet. In the distance, only one light glowed—off the street we were on and presumably our destination. Granny's eyes were still sharp, despite her age, and she read the street signs and navigated while I kept intense concentration on the road straight ahead.

"That's the one we turn on," Granny said, pointing out the windshield...

...a second too late, since I was already on top of the side street. Foolishly, I tried to make the turn anyway, and despite the four-wheel drive, the rear end of the car slid sideways. Heart in throat and the spasm of nausea I get in my belly when I'm terrified, I heard the slight *thunk* as the fender hit something. Damn, another reason to castigate Mother Nature for Twila's delay. Twila had plenty of experience driving in these conditions.

"What did we hit?" I asked Granny, who had rolled down her window and stuck her head out.

"Can't see nothin'," she replied. "Brrrr." She pushed the button and rolled her window back up. "Let's worry 'bout that tomorrow."

I sat for a moment, then nodded and eased down on the gas. A wrenching screech split the air.

"Shit!" I shouted as I pounded one fist on the steering wheel. "We're stuck on something!"

"Jist floor it," Granny ordered. "We's got insurance on this thing."

"Yeah, and what if it's something that will disable the car?" I demanded. "Who the heck knows when the sheriff will remember we're over here and send someone to check on us. And I can't depend on my cell phone here."

Granny sighed. "Want me to drive?"

I flashed her a look that contained both annoyance at her inane comment and irritation for her calm attitude. Sure, she could sit there and matter-of-factly offer services she had to know I'd reject. She drove her own red and white 1950 Oldsmobile at a stately thirty-five miles per hour, and absolutely no one in Six Gun had the audacity to honk at her. A newcomer might try that once, but only once. The news would spread on the wildfire grapevine, and every citizen in town would make it a point to let the newbie know that wouldn't be tolerated.

But the last time I'd ridden with Granny in a vehicle, she'd decided to become a race car driver! Until a flooded back road sucked the tires deep into some gluey Texas mud.

Well, all right, I recalled. I hadn't done much better than Granny. My Jeep ended up in the car hospital on that adventure, and I'd been the one driving it. My only excuse was trying to outrun a madman on an ATV, who was shooting at us.

Shifting into park, I said, "I'll get out and see what we hit. You wait here where it's warm."

"'K-dokey," Granny said. "Iffen you need my help, just holler."

"Do you still have that little penlight?"

"Give it to you back at the hotel," she reminded me.

I nodded and dug in my coat pocket. I found the penlight and opened the door to step out into the snow. Immediately, I reminded myself to sit down and take stock the next time I yearned to spend Christmas with Twila in Yankee-land. Snow was pretty to look at—through a window in a nice, warm house. Pretty didn't cut it when you had to wade through several inches and battle wind whipping crystals against your face.

Crap. I'd hit one of those cheap metal fence posts. It was lodged under the fender-well on the rear passenger side. The edge of the fender-well had barely caught it, but hard enough to lift a corner of the metal behind the tire.

It was the only fence post around! Who had been stupid enough to leave a lone post out here in nowhere land? Still, all I had to do was back up a little, then we could be on our way to spend a glorious night in jail.

I got back in the car and told Granny what I'd found. She bobbed her head as I shifted into reverse and edged backward a few feet. Then I moved forward at an angle and, thankfully, heard no screech of metal. Sighing in relief, I slowly drove on.

"They got's any deductible on that there insurance you got on this here rent-me?" Granny asked.

"I don't remember," I answered. "Why do you ask?"

"I's can pay half, if they do," she offered. "Was partly my fault, me bein' supposed to help you drive."

I chuckled and shook my head. "Don't worry about it. It was just an accident."

"Well, I feels responsible," she argued in a huffy voice. "Least you can do is accept my offer."

The irritation of a minute ago dissolved. Granny made no secret of her slim income, yet she was always the first one on the scene when anyone in Six Gun needed help. It might be only a luscious pecan pie baked by her own hands, the pecans gathered one by one from the ground despite her regular bouts with arthritis, but it would be something. Many times when I found myself in deadline hell—which I created myself when I procrastinated—I'd find a pan of muffins or even a tinfoil-wrapped plate of BBQ and fixings on my front deck. She knew I hated to cook, since it seemed I even burned water, and she wouldn't think of disrupting me while I wrote. It always gave me warm fuzzies when I found a gift from my caring neighbor; knew someone was thinking about me.

She had her pride, though, Granny did, and she gave with no thought of payback. *Do as you'd have others do*, she'd said many times.

"Tell you what," I informed Granny as I finally pulled up in front of the lone building with a light on. "If there is a deductible, you can pay me half of it in pecan pies and that wonderful muscadine jelly you make."

"That'll do," she agreed serenely.

Not wanting to hurt Granny's pride again, I didn't object when she helped me carry things inside. I let my pets out and trusted them to stay near, doubting they would wander off in this isolated darkness. Then I slogged through the snow, which was now at least six inches deep. The deputy hadn't bothered to shovel the sidewalk, so I followed his footprints. The key fit, and I opened the door and shoved it back.

As promised, welcome heat drifted out, but I steeled myself to forego its warmth and returned to the car, passing Trucker and Miss Molly on the path. Granny had found the hatchback release and already had her suitcase in one hand. She'd again decided not to use her walking stick, but I knew better than to offer to carry the luggage for her. Granny had been known to employ her walking stick to back up her pride.

It took me three more trips to tote in my bag and the supplies we'd gathered, along with cat and dog food and Miss Molly's portable litter box. I did manage to sidetrack Granny from helping with that, pointing out it had been a while since dinner and wouldn't it be nice to have a snack of the cheese and crackers we'd found at the hotel.

I set the last load inside the jail and pushed the door closed firmly. Shrugging out of my coat, I hung it one of the row of hooks lined up along a crossbeam. Opting to keep my boots on, since the floor was cobblestone and undoubtedly cold, I kicked my feet against the door-jamb to got rid of the clinging snow, then wiped them on a welcome mat.

A couple of faded Indian rugs were laid on the floor, and Miss Molly and Trucker had claimed one. Still, there were bare spaces and the rugs weren't thick enough to protect even feet encased in socks.

The restoration of the jail had included an ancient, scarred desk against the back wall, a slatted oak chair behind it. There was a small, river-stone fireplace in the corner beside the desk, a stack of commercial fire logs in a wood carrier beside it. I preferred real wood in my fireplace at home, although those fire logs were convenient. No one had bothered with the fire, though. The jail obviously had central heat, since the warm air gushed from ceiling vents.

Corners on the brown-paper Wanted posters plastered on the wall to my right curled up. Either they were original or faultlessly-aged copies. I set up Miss Molly's litter box under the poster for a Dalton gang member. She didn't care who watched her when she got ready for business.

On the left was a fairly new refrigerator, and cupboards lined the wall, a coffeepot on the countertop. Good. I didn't do mornings without caffeine. A tiny table with two chairs sat in front of the counter.

"The sheriff promised we'd have a bathroom," I said to Granny, who was setting a plate of crackers and cheese on the table.

"Prob'ly back there." She nodded at a door in the rear of the room.

"Where the cells are," I said with a shiver.

We didn't bother to explore the rest of the building before I fed and watered my pets and Granny and I sat down at the tiny table where she'd laid out our snack. She'd found the Crown, also, and beside the paper plate sat two plastic glasses of Crown and Seven.

"Where'd you get the ice?" I asked as I grabbed a piece of cheese in one hand, my drink in the other.

She shrugged. "Was already here. In that there little plastic bucket on the counter."

"The deputy must have—"

"That deputy didn't think of ice," the handsome gambler who'd served us at the hotel bar said as he visualized over by the door and winked. "But I know from my brief acquaintance that you ladies are the type who enjoy a taste or two of good whiskey."

Trucker's head jerked up and he stared at Gambler. Miss Molly continued to snooze. I trusted Trucker's instincts, and since he didn't attack, this ghost was friendly. He'd seemed so back at the hotel, also.

Granny cocked her head as she munched on a cracker and cheese and studied him. "Y'knows," she mused. "I played a mean hand of poker in my younger days."

"Why, Madame, that must not have been so long ago," Gambler replied.

Granny chuckled and her eyes sparkled. "I's been 'round enough years to knows when I's bein' buttered up," she said. "And iffen that's how you butter up women, you go right ahead and slather it on."

Gambler laughed, a pleasant, totally masculine rumble. "You ladies enjoy your drinks."

He nodded, an indication I took as a prelude to leaving, but I hurriedly said, "You haven't introduced yourself."

A flirty smile lifted his lips. "What you have been calling me in your mind—Gambler—is fine."

"Is there some reason you don't want to tell us your name?" I prodded.

"Haven't you heard?" he asked. "It's part of the Code of the West. You don't question a man about where he came from."

"The Code of the West I've read about also indicates men are polite to women. While we appreciate the ice—and the drinks back at the hotel—it's good manners for people to introduce themselves. Do you have some reason to keep your real name secret?"

"I just might have," he acknowledged with a sly wink, and disappeared.

"How rude!" I said.

"Good lookin' men thinks they can be rude like that there," Granny said as she laid another piece of cheese on a cracker. "They's used to women bein' more interested in their charm and looks than what they's like inside. And some folks think it ain't polite to be nosy."

"I wasn't being nosy," I denied. I grabbed the last piece of cheese before Granny could commandeer it. "He might be able to tell us what happened to Karen."

Granny cackled, then had to take a sip of Crown to wash down the cracker in her mouth. I tensed, afraid I might have to Heimlich her, but she swallowed and fixed me with her twinkling blue eyes. "You ain't plannin' on getting' involved in this here murder investigation, are you? Whenever you play detective, we ends up with more than ghosts on our hands."

"I. Am. Not. Getting. Involved. In. This. Murder. Investigation," I said in my no-nonsense voice. "In fact, we may have to suspend our ghost investigation. We can't do anything with law enforcement in the way."

"Never stopped you before," Granny mused. "'Though I'd be willin' to bet Jack shows up here a'fore long, jist to make sure you keep your nose out of that there sheriff's business."

I bristled. "Jack has absolutely no say over what I do or do not do! We're divorced!"

"Sad, sad thing, too." Granny swirled the ice in her drink. "Some folks *should* call it quits, but others...." She sipped her drink as she watched me, and I avoided her gaze by staring around the room.

"We should be fairly comfortable here," I mentioned. "It's small, but we'll only be here one night." I peered over Granny's shoulder at the door I assumed opened into the cell block. "We can lay an extra blanket down for Trucker and Miss Molly, so they won't have to sleep on that thin rug on the cold floor. Oh, I forgot to bring in the stack of blankets we got at the hotel. I'll get them in a minute."

Granny shrugged and stifled a grin. "Jist make sure we prop them cell doors open. Don't want's to get locked in."

"There's a ring of keys on the wall beside the door. We'll take that with us when we go to bed."

Granny yawned. "Which I's 'bout ready for. Been a long day."

Concern for her filled me. Despite her age, Granny at times had more energy in one hand than I did in my entire body. When we trod the Piney Woods picking muscadine grapes for her jelly, she perkily wielded her walking stick to chase off snakes while I wiped away sweat and huffed to keep up. Well, I knew I needed to exercise more. I would, I promised myself for the umpteenth time, now that this book was finished.

"I'll get the blankets right away," I said as I rose. "Leave the plate and things. I'll clean up."

"I's'll check out our bedroom," Granny said agreeably.

I didn't bother to grab my coat as I went out the door, just the car keys. The car was parked close, the path beaten down now from trips back and forth. I flicked the key switch to turn on the car lights and a second later, opened the rear passenger door to get the blankets. Tried to, anyway. The door was locked. I must have instinctively locked the car, even though I doubted there was anyone around who might want to steal anything.

Sighing, I clicked the key button to unlock the vehicle. No go. The door handle only slid in my fingers. *Click-click.* Nope, it still wouldn't open. Well, hell. After two more tries, I decided I'd better get my coat and come back—try to figure out what was wrong.

I trod back to the jail and grabbed the doorknob, then smashed my nose on the heavy door when it didn't open under my hand and I absent-mindedly tried to walk through it anyway. Ouch! I jiggled the doorknob with one hand while I rubbed my nose with the other, and the stupid tumblers refused to disengage. Shit. I'd left the key to that door inside.

The car lights timed out and darkness descended. The sharp needles of snow had changed into lazy flakes, but it was still colder than blue blazes out here. I jiggled the doorknob harder, then gave up and knocked on the door.

"Granny! Granny!" I called. "The door locked behind me!"

No answer. I strained to hear footsteps approach, but that historically accurate door was at least a couple inches of thick wood. I pounded harder. "Granny!"

I waited a few seconds, but no dice. Oh, no. She'd probably already removed her hearing aid. A gust of wind picked up some loose flakes of snow and scattered them over me. *Brrrrrr.* I wrapped my arms around myself—which didn't warm me one bit—and tried to decide what to do,

I turned around and aimed the back of my boot at the door. *Thud.*
Thud. Thud.

"Trucker!" I yelled. "Trucker, go get Granny!"

Thud! A deluge of snow dropped off the roof, right on my head. I
batted at it, but gobs slid past my collar.

How long did it take for hypothermia to set in? I had no idea. All my
books were set in the south, and my research didn't cover that area of
expertise. Whatever. From the way my body shook, I figured it wouldn't
be long. I glanced up at more snow waiting to attack, then turned and
backed away a bit so I could kick the door with my booted toes.

Ouch! That hurt. Still, the rest of the snow that poured off the roof
missed me.

"Trucker!" I shouted. "Open the door!"

Well, crap, the dog couldn't do that. But couldn't he at least bark and
notify Granny that I was trapped out here?

Finally! Trucker yapped on the other side of the door. "Get Granny!" I
shouted. "I'm freezing out there!"

Not that Trucker could understand freezing, but he could compre-
hend from my tone of my voice that something was wrong.

His barks died away, hopefully because the dog was scatting across
the room to fetch Granny. It better be soon. I couldn't feel my fingers. I
shoved my hands beneath my armpits to try to ward off frostbite and
battered the stubborn door again with the back of my foot.

Trucker returned, but only to bark at the door some more. I quit
beating it and wrenched one hand free of my armpit, reaching for the
doorknob and hoping to feel the welcome wiggle of Granny opening it
from her side. Nothing.

Damn, it was cold. I used both hands and jerked on that doorknob
for all I was worth. Battered it some more with my shoulder and feet, but
only succeeded in hurting my body. I'd probably be covered with bruises
tomorrow...if I wasn't frozen to death. Twila would have to pick out a
long-sleeved caftan for my burial robe. And who would take care of my
cats and dog?

Sobbing, I slid down the door to the cold snow.

CHAPTER 8

"You should have called."

Tears of pain and self-pity misted my eyes, blurring Gambler's face. "I've b-b-een ca-calling!" I stuttered through frozen lips. I stumbled to my feet and continued, "H-help. The d-d-door's l-locked."

He waved a hand, and tumblers clicked. When the door opened, I fell inside. Luckily, I landed on the welcome mat, which at least padded my tailbone from a crushing blow. Trucker jumped out of the way, then returned to slurp my face and whine in concern.

Icy wind blew into the room, washing away the heat, and I groaned and forced myself up. The door closed on its own...I thought. Yet Gambler now stood inside with me, so he'd done it. He levitated my coat, and even held it courteously so I could slide into it. It didn't help much, since melting snow soaked my blouse and hair.

"You shouldn't go out in this weather without a coat," Gambler cautioned.

"I d-didn't...I mean, I thought I'd only be a minute. The car keys won't work. Do you know if these stupid things have batteries?"

"What things?" he asked at the same moment I realized I didn't have the keys.

"S-shit!" I sputtered. "I dropped the keys in the snow somewhere when I went out to the car to get our blankets."

Gambler sighed in a tone I deplored in a man, since it echoed the one Jack used when he *little-womaned* me. However, I bit my tongue—another pain to add to the pile. Right now, I needed Gambler.

"I'll see if I can find them," he said as he dissolved.

"Thank you!" I called after him. Trucker trotting behind me, I hurried across the room in search of Granny.

The cell block door was propped open, the oak chair from the desk under the doorknob. Granny must have feared the door would close and lock her in. Two barely eight-foot square cells were inside a room half the size of the main one. Old-timey iron-barred doors with skeleton key locks crossed the front of the cells, and each one contained a set of bunk beds.

The cell door on the left was pushed open, the one on the right closed. On the lower left bunk, Granny curled beneath her coat, snoring, her sock-clad feet sticking out beneath the hem of her white flannel gown. Her boots set on the floor beside her open suitcase, her clothing folded neatly on the suitcase lid. Plastic false teeth holder, hair pins—and hearing aid—were laid out tidily next to her clothing.

The bunks at least had sheets, each one a puke-green. No pillows, though. Warmer now, I shrugged out of my coat and laid it over Granny's feet. I'd let her sleep and replace the coats with the blankets—if I ever managed to get them out of the rental. If not, I guessed I'd be sleeping without covers.

In the rear of the tiny room was a shower stall, a commode and sink beside it. Our bathroom. A few towels lay on a shelf over the commode, and I retrieved one to rub over my hair. I had one arm out of my sweater before it dawned on me that I didn't want to be half-naked in front of Gambler. I'd just have to suffer the wet.

By the time I walked out of the cell block, the stack of blankets lay on the small table, the keys on the countertop. Granny had ignored me and cleaned up, since I didn't see our cups or paper plates, and the cracker box sat beside the keys, the opening neatly secured.

"Gambler?" I said.

He didn't bother to appear, only thrust into my mind, *I have no idea whether your keys have a battery or not. If they don't work in the morning, I'll come back and open your car for you.*

"Where will you be?" I asked.

Near. Just call.

"Someone did this to me," I growled. "Do you have any idea who?"

No. But it wasn't me. I'm going now.

"Wait!" I insisted. "I have more questions."

He didn't answer, and I didn't sense his presence. He'd withdrawn.

Crap. His words agitated me more than soothed my fears. I paced the small room. Having a ghost *near* wasn't a whole lot of protection, given I had no idea how many powers Gambler possessed. Or even if he carried a gun hidden somewhere in his immaculate attire. Or even if the gun would shoot after over a hundred years of dis-use. Or even if ghost bullets would do any good, should someone attack us.

Damn, we *should* have shipped Granny's shotgun!

Could Karen's murderer still be hanging around? Nearly tripping in my haste, I barreled over to the door and checked to see if Gambler had re-locked it. He had, but I unlatched the deadbolt and re-latched it anyway. Then I propped one of the table chairs beneath the doorknob and knelt beside Trucker, who had continued to follow me around.

"Trucker," I said. "On guard, O.K?"

He slurped my face, hopefully in acknowledgement of the order.

Nope. As soon as I rose, he padded over and laid down beside Miss Molly and closed his eyes. A moment later, his snores matched Granny's.

Surely, though, my dog wouldn't conk off into sleep if we were in danger. And he'd be on guard even in his dreams. A light sleeper, I'd seen Trucker bolt to wakefulness in an instant. I envied the animals' and Granny's sleep. Exhausted as I was, I knew I would only toss and turn. Gosh darn my writer's mind. I brushed away the thought of all the gunfighters and outlaws who'd stayed at the hotel. The multitude who'd died there.

Brushed away the vision of Karen hanging from a noose.

Brushed away thoughts of Wyatt Earp and the gunfight at the OK Corral.

What on earth could I do to fill the hours before dawn? Oh, at least I could make Granny more comfortable.

After I replaced my coat with blankets, without Granny even stirring, I stared longingly at the shower stall. No way in hell would I take advantage of it, though. There wasn't even a shower curtain to pull closed. Even if there were, visions of *Psycho* would keep me from enjoying it.

Instead, I returned to where I'd left my overnight bag inside the front door and carried it back to open it on the bunk opposite Granny's. Five minutes later, teeth brushed and clad in my own flannel gown and thick robe, kitty slippers on my feet, I wandered over to the fireplace beside the sheriff's desk.

Maybe watching fire flames flicker would sooth me into sleepiness. Sometimes that worked at home. I opened the damper and laid a log in the grate, then lit it with a long handled matchstick from a basket on the mantle.

Trucker's eyes popped open and his head swung towards the fire. He rose gracefully to his feet and nudged Miss Molly. At home, they loved to lie in front of the fire. I retrieved a blanket and laid it down a few feet back from the hearth, then secured the fire screen. My pets settled on the softer padding as I tried to decide what to do next.

The hell with it. I dropped another blanket beside my pets, rolled the last one up for a pillow, and laid down beside them. The fire log burned steadily, bright orange flames flickering and smoke lazily drifting upwards through the open damper.

I smiled to myself as I recalled the night I'd forgotten to check my fireplace damper back in Six Gun. The computer had been giving me problems, and I'd been putting off buying a new one, hoping it would last through another tight deadline. I backed-up, then ran a defrag program to try to free up a tiny bit more space on the overextended hard drive. While that worked its magic, I lit a fire log and hurried outside to re-fill the log carrier with real wood.

I got sidetracked watching a cute squirrel chatter and tease one of my cats and returned to a house full of smoke! Luckily for my pets, I'd left the patio door open, and cats and one dog lined the flower pots on one side of the concrete. They could have also escaped through two different doggie-kitty doors in my house, but they probably preferred to fill me with guilt as they turned their accusing eyes on me when I hurried past.

I lost another hour of writing time as I choked my way across the room, opened the damper, and than gathered fans to clear out the gray smoke. Whether from the pets' reproachful glares or my own determination not to let that happen again, it was a lesson learned.

Lesson learned is lesson earned.

I sat up with a jerk. "*Grandmere* Alicia?" I asked. "Are you here?"

No one answered. For a moment I'd hoped maybe my several-times-great-grandmother had accompanied me on this trip. I could use her counsel about now. However, my thought wasn't a communication from my long-past relative, only a remembrance from the depths of my mind.

The jail was a solid, adobe building, so despite the wind outside, there weren't any creaks or groans. The only two windows were foot-wide slits on each side of the entrance door, perhaps to protect deputies who used to man the jail at night from bullets, in case vigilantes stormed the structure when a particularly nasty outlaw had been captured. I'd watched enough old cowboy movies to visualize the crowd outside shouting for the deputy to turn over the prisoner for the hanging tree. The stout door would withstand a battering ram for a long while. Of course, the tall-dark-and-handsome hero marshal would appear and stand firm in front of the crowd, reasoning even with their drunken minds.

No hero protected us, though. I didn't consider Sheriff Carson hero material. With a murderer on the loose, why hadn't he thought that maybe two women alone might need a guard? Sure, he admitted he worked with a limited staff. Sure, Granny and I had intended to stay in the hotel alone anyway. Sure, we had a watchdog. Yet we hadn't planned on arriving just minutes after a murder!

The difference between men and women is that women aren't troubled by logic.

Shoot, I knew where that thought came from: Not a communicating ghost, rather Jack-memories. We'd seen a comedian once in N'awlins who based his entire routine around that premise. Jack had thoroughly enjoyed the show, while I gritted my teeth in exasperation.

Who could have killed Karen? Who would want her dead? I had never met the woman, so I knew absolutely nothing about her, thus had no way to even begin to ponder on who could commit such a dastardly deed.

Who had been around the hotel? The sheriff would dust for prints, but in a public building, I supposed it would depend on when the house-keeping staff had last cleaned and polished. Outside, snow would have obliterated any footsteps.

More importantly, who could have had access to the hotel? Danny, of course. The real estate woman would have a key.

Was Karen killed first, then mutilated? Did that matter? Well, maybe, since it might tie into motivation, at least as far as who the perp was and why he'd acted like he did. Or she.

After completing his scene-of-crime investigation, the first thing the sheriff would do was back-track Karen's previous hours, try to find out who'd seen her last. Then he'd widen the investigation into her friends, family and associates, searching for motive, means and opportunity. Alibis would be important. Not that Granny or I would need one, but we were at the restaurant for nearly an hour before we drove on over to the hotel.

He'd take our statements, though, to be thorough.

Sheriff Carson wouldn't consider a ghost might have information. He'd concentrate only on live subjects.

I gave up the quest for sleep and the fight against my writer mind. Rising, I walked over to the shelves to search for a can of coffee.

* * *

"There you are." Joleen propped her hands on her hips and glared at her brother. "Where've you been, True?"

"Around," True answered.

"How am I supposed to help you if you don't cooperate? I went to a lot of trouble to get someone here who can give us a hand."

"You have no idea if they can or can't," True corrected. "Besides, the boss lady ghost hunter hasn't shown up yet."

"Her plane was grounded. You'd know this, if you'd been at the hotel when I asked you to."

True walked away, towards the graveyard gate. Given their state of being, Joleen couldn't track his path, since he didn't leave footsteps in the snow. She knew where he'd be, though. Not at their mother's grave. True made sure that grave was cared for, to the point of scaring the bejeesus out of the elderly maintenance man if he so much as left a weed untrimmed around the headstone. Yet he spent most of his time at Marina's grave, hoping against hope she would visit at least once.

At first, True had refused to even come near the cemetery, wouldn't even acknowledge that the woman he loved so utterly without restraint had passed from life. The last year or so, though, the graveyard had become True's second home, although he wouldn't explain his change of attitude. Had become his haunt, Joleen corrected herself, since she and her brother understood their circumstances. They were ghosts, tied to a realm at least she wished they could leave.

Joleen caught up to her brother at the gate. "You're not helping yourself," she said. "How can we cross over if we don't tell Alice and Twila what we want?"

True halted, his back to her so she couldn't read his face. His shoulders were taut, fists clenched by his sides. She floated a step back, not that True would ever harm a woman. He kept his explosive temper under control in death, as he had in life. The few times he had erupted in the living realm, someone had died. Here in this half-afterlife, she'd only seen him explode once, the day some other passing-through ghost had pinched her bottom in the saloon and then told her she wasn't worth paying for anyway. Not that she had made extra money on her back as some of the other girls had when she was alive. She'd sold drinks, not herself.

She never wanted to see True in the throes of that type of anger again.

"This was all your idea, Joleen," True whispered. "Getting those two women here so we could cross through the so-called light. You didn't ask me whether or not I agreed with you."

Joleen gasped and stomped around in front of him. "You never said anything about *disagreeing* with my plans! I thought this was what you wanted!"

"You were gone—headed back to that Six Gun town—before I could tell you how I felt."

"So tell me now," Joleen demanded. But before he could answer, she blathered on, "I spent years trying to get you to agree to leave with me. All we have to do is ask Twila and Alice to help us overcome the mistake we made when we didn't continue on once we died. They've helped others time after time."

"Yeah," True said with a snort of disgust. "So they say."

"What do you mean? You know it's true."

"No, I don't," True denied. "And neither do you. It's all based on *faith*. They *supposedly* open some door into some other world...other realm...other state of existence. *Supposedly*, it's where our souls should have gone as soon as we died. *Supposedly*, we'll be with our loved ones, in a blissful state of being. *Supposedly*, Joleen. No one knows for sure."

"I'd rather not exist at all than stay like this," Joleen fumed.

"That's your choice. But think of this. *Suppose* it is true. *Suppose* there's also retribution. I have no doubt that you'll be fine...if this other place exists. You didn't kill anyone when you were alive. Yet *if* this place of bliss exists, who's to say that hell doesn't also exist? Who's to say that I won't be trading this existence for one much worse?"

Taken aback, Joleen shook her head. "But...but—"

"I'd rather be here, in this existence," True went on before Joleen could marshal her thoughts, "where I at least have my memories. *If* this other realm exists...should I agree to give it a try, I have no assurance I'd end up with Marina."

"So you're just going to hang around here and hope Marina comes back and tells you that you can be with her if you cross over?" Joleen asked in astonishment. "Hang around experiencing your death in that hallway over and over again?"

"Death doesn't hurt," True murmured. "It's the pain and separation afterwards."

"But what if she never shows up? How long will you wait?"

"I've got nothing but time."

"You had time when you lived," Joleen said. "How much time did you spend waiting for Marina to make up her mind whether or not to leave her husband?"

She wished the words back immediately, but too late. She only caught a glimpse of the thundercloud on her brother's face before he was gone.

"I'm sorry!" she pleaded. "True, come back. We can work this out."

Even as she called to him, she understood it would do no good. Darn her wayward tongue. She knew better than to disparage the woman her brother had placed on a pedestal broaching sainthood. It might be weeks...even months...before True would speak to her again.

And she hadn't had a chance to tell him the other reason they should be anxious to cooperate with Twila and Alice. That threat might burn down the fuse on his temper until it exploded in a thunderclap bad for all of them. She also had no idea if the dead could retaliate or protect themselves from living hoodlums.

So how would she explain to Alice that she might have to wait weeks to talk to True? That lady wouldn't hang around until a ghost condescended to cooperate with her. She didn't believe in allowing ghosts free rein. Alice believed in discipline. Joleen had read The Ghost Agreement tacked up on her cabin wall.

Maybe Twila ....

No, the senior partner in that ghost hunting relationship had helped Alice draw up that agreement. Howard had been adamant during his explanation.

Lacy snowflakes drifted down once more. Overhead, clouds added to the dark night, although here and there a bright star managed to shine through. The full moon was only a fuzzy hint behind another bank of heavy clouds billowing over the mountaintops, carrying a new layer of snow.

Joleen shivered, but not because she was cold. And not because she stood on the edge of the graveyard near her own plot. She hadn't cared for cemeteries in life, yet she'd come to understand...perhaps hope...they held some answers.

She drifted over to her mother's stone. She shouldn't have chastised True, since she fervently wished someone would come back for a few minutes, also. She sorely needed her mother to talk to her, give her hope she was doing the right thing. Safely advise her daughter, as she had in life. The gravestone only sat there, though, a darker gray shadow against the snow; a lifeless piece of marble, even the lettering eroded until someone who didn't have it memorized would have a hard time reading it.

Pulled against her will, Joleen glanced to her right. Behind the rusty, neglected fence, another gravestone hadn't worn away over time. Secrets lay beneath that one. Or perhaps the one four stones away. Harvey hadn't allowed Marina to be buried in his family plot, saving the dual gravesite for him and his second wife. The cemetery hadn't expanded yet when Marina died, so her husband didn't have much choice about his wife's resting place. Only four graves separated the two lovers in death; however, in actuality, much more than that small space divided them in the afterlife.

Joleen frowned. Something had been bothering her about True's story as to why he didn't cross over. Her brother had never been afraid of retribution when he lived. The two men he killed, other than the ones during his enlistment in the Confederate Army, were not murders but instead defense slaying. One man had ambushed True to try to steal his horse, the stallion he planned to use for his breeding program some day. The other man had been preparing to rape an Indian woman. True had been too far away to beat the man senseless and rescue the woman. He'd taken what many would think an impossible shot to keep the woman from suffering a horrible indignity and pain.

So why did he insist he wouldn't cross to where he would have a hope of seeing Marina due to fear there might truly be a hell? Or that there might possibly not be an afterlife?

Those stories didn't sound like the brother she had loved and cherished for so many years. He had to be, if not lying, at least evading the truth. What was he hiding?

CHAPTER 9

D rat it, where was it? Jittery due to half a pot of coffee, I carried my suitcase out of the cell block and laid it on the small table to dig through it more thoroughly. Finally, I tossed the contents on the floor and shook the suitcase upside down, just to make sure I hadn't unloaded one case into another. There wasn't really room, but I also felt in the zippered suitcase sides.

My protections were missing. I'd memorized that list Twila gave me, even written it down and checked off each and every single item to make sure not to forget anything.

Sea salt. Olive oil blessed with chants. White candles treated with both special oils and words of blessing. The belladonna-laced lotion Cat Dancer had supplied. Incense, both sage and jasmine. More importantly, the quince seed soap, bracelets and necklaces. I'd forgo everything else if I could just locate the quince seed stuff.

Nothing. Not even a lone quince seed that might have survived from a broken necklace or bracelet.

The protections were all missing! Someone had taken them. It couldn't have been one of the ghosts we'd encountered. Ghosts couldn't touch items meant to control them.

My suitcase had been in the rental ever since Granny and I left the airport. The small satchel with the protections had been....

No, now I remembered. A mile or so after we'd gotten on the road, we'd exited to a filling station with a small grassy area to allow Trucker a potty break. Then I'd dug in the suitcase, searching for the credit card I had brought along to use. Granny and I bought snacks and drinks there to sustain us on the drive to Red Dollar.

Evidently, I forgotten to replace the satchel of protections in the suitcase. Now it was probably lying in the hatchback...unavailable, unless the key worked now.

Well, even in close proximity, the protections would do some good. There was always the white light. Mentally, I pulled down a thick layer and surrounded the adobe building and the car in its shield.

Yet...if the satchel wasn't in the car...if I'd lost it somewhere...maybe it fell out way back at the filling station?

Damn, damn, damn. Twila would give me hell if she arrived and found I'd misplaced those important safeguards. We didn't always carry them, of course. Well, not all of them. Were we visiting a benign haunted place, we pretty much depended on the White Light. When we were forewarned about uncooperative or unpleasant entities, however, more powerful devices were called for.

I *had* to at least go out to the car and see if the satchel was indeed there.

Sure, and get locked out again! No way.

I could wake Granny and stake her on guard at the door. Granny had only had an hour or so of sleep, though. I really shouldn't disturb my elderly companion. Besides, a determined entity might bar the door anyway. Maybe hurt Granny in the process.

"Why ain't you sleepin'?" Granny asked from the cell block doorway. "An' why's all your stuff on the floor? Somethin' been in here agin?"

"Oh!" I gathered the clothing and jammed it back into the suitcase before I turned to face Granny. "I...well...." No sense trying to cover up. Granny was at risk here, also. "I can't find my satchel of protections that Twila told me to bring."

Rubbing sleep from her eyes, Granny toddled forward. "We can't's be without that. Where'd you have it last?"

"At the filling station where we bought snacks. At least, that's the last time I recall actually seeing it."

"You look in the car when you were out there earlier?"

"I guess not. I ended up with something more important on my mind."

I sighed and explained what had happened and how I'd finally gotten back inside the jail. After I finished, both our gazes centered on the heavy oaken door.

Granny shook her head. "No h'ep for it. You gots to go out there agin."

Granny's tone indicated no need for discussion. Well aware of the consequences, she didn't want to run the risk of being protection-less either, if some entity realized we were at risk.

"I've pulled down a strong layer of White Light," I said. "I can add more, if necessary."

"I got's my asafetida, too. But it might's not be e'nuf. What iffen you get all discombobulated a'fore you kin do that, iffen we needs it? You's already nervous from drinkin' coffee this time a'night." She looked at my jumbled clothing in the suitcase. "What iffen we's attacked by somethin' strong? What iffen there's a gang of 'em? There could be a bunch of 'em hangin' 'round, bein's there's a long list of passed-on's over in the hotel."

I nervously edged over to one of the slit-windows and peered out. New snow drifted through the illumination from the security light, lacy and white rather than the stinging sleet-like pebbles of earlier. The beauty should have taken my breath away. Instead, I stared at the stark, leafless branches on a nearby tree, coated with snow inches thick and bowing beneath the weight of such splendor. I couldn't see the roof over-head, but assumed new layers gathered there to await an ambush on an unwary or careless person who tarried too long beneath the eaves.

Trudging back to the counter, I picked up my cell phone, then carried it over to the window. Even though I held it into the opening, *no signal* wouldn't disappear.

"I'm going to get dressed before I venture out there," I told Granny.

"Me, too," she agreed with a nod. "Jist in case." She walked into the cell block, but returned a moment later with a piece of red clothing in her hand. "Here," she said as she handed it to me. "I brought's two pair. This'un should fit you. It belonged to my husband."

I held up the one-piece set of long underwear. It felt thick and warm in my hands, and I even giggled at the square flap in the rear, secured by bright gold buttons on each side.

"Thanks, Granny."

A few minutes later, we were ready, both bundled up as warm as possible: boots, gloves, wool pants and sweaters. Long underwear resided beneath our clothing, our coats were on and wool neck scarves tied in place. Granny wore a fluted red ski cap I hadn't seen before, one with a dangling ball of white yarn. Maybe it was part of the Santa Claus suit she wore when we visited the children's ward at Christmas time.

I was sweating already beneath the clothing, but that wouldn't last long. I didn't intend to close that door behind me.

I woke Trucker, who'd snoozed through our preparations, and instructed him to come with me. At the door, I opened it and secured a chair beneath the doorknob. Cold rushed in, and the central heating unit ignited with a comforting purr.

"Good idea," Granny said with a nod at the chair.

"Now," I told her before I went outside. "If things should happen to get out of control, you make sure you're safe before you worry about me."

"Got's ya," Granny agreed. "Oh, wait's a minute."

She hurried over to the countertop and opened one of the drawers. When she returned, she handed me a heavy flashlight. "Found's this when I was lookin' around. It works. I checked."

"Great. Now, I'm just going to look in the car to make sure the satchel's there. I mean, in case the keys still won't work. If they do, I'll get the satchel."

"Iffen it's there."

"Yeah, iffen it's there."

We both stared at the car, now covered with a new layer of snow on windows the wipers and defrosters had cleared on the drive over.

"How far's them there keys work from?" Granny asked.

"Let's see."

I removed one of my gloves and secured it in my coat pocket. Then I retrieved the key ring from the other pocket, aimed it at the car and flicked the *unlock* button twice. The car lights gleamed reassuringly and even from here, I heard the *clunk* of disengaging locks.

"Well, whoop de do," Granny chortled. She'd heard it, too. She obviously had her hearing aid back in place.

Excitedly, I took off down the trodden path to the car, Trucker obediently padding after me. Too excitedly, a small voice warned me. I halted halfway and looked back at Granny. Her small figure stood in the doorway, and I noticed Miss Molly beside her boot.

"Go on's!" she called. "Get it while the gettin's good!"

I strode on to the car, a tad less hurried, though. Too good to be true usually was. However, the hatchback easily opened and I shone the flashlight in. Yes, the satchel! I lunged in and grabbed it, then scooted back out. Victory! Clasping it to my stomach, I unzipped it before I closed the hatchback, then walked around to try the driver's door. It opened with no problem.

"Damn spooks," I muttered, then realized my mistake when Trucker growled. Discipline was one matter—an important one—but deliberately antagonizing a nasty entity was only asking for trouble. I stared over the top of the car...and there it was ....

The smelly man from the café stood between my dog and me and Granny. He threw back his head and laughed, then said, "What you gonna do now? I ain't movin'. You can stay out here the rest of the night. Pretty soon, even those clothes won't keep the cold off."

I didn't even have to open the satchel, though. Nor did Trucker have to interfere. One of Miss Molly's cat squalls split the air, and despite the flurry of snow that landed on her back when she stepped out the door onto the path, she continued her stalk. Still beside the hatchback, Trucker sat down to watch the show, tongue lolling.

Mr. Smelly swiveled in the path and took a step backwards. Then his stance firmed.

"I ain't afraid of no blasted little kitty cat!" He shook his fist at Miss Molly. "You ain't big enough to bother me!"

Ears back and mouth open in a hiss, sharp teeth exposed, Miss Molly continued towards him. With every step, she flicked each foot to toss off the snow, but she didn't stop.

I hadn't noticed the gun holster on Smelly's hip. Now I did, and so did Trucker. We became aware of it because Smelly drew the pistol and cocked it with a crisp *click.*

"Get back, cat," he ordered. "Or you're a dead pussy."

Trucker lunged...just as I threw the first thing my hand clutched— the bottle of blessed olive oil. At the same instant, Granny drew back with a move worthy of a five star pitcher and lobbed her asafetida bag at Smelly.

Dog, cat, olive oil and asafetida all converged amidst Smelly's YOWL. The intended victim—Smelly—was victimized. Not even a whisper of mist remained when he disappeared. I swear, had they known the gesture, Miss Molly and Trucker would have high-fived. Instead, they woofed and meowed for a moment, then touched noses. That was as good of a victory action as any. Granny and I celebrated with a glance and nod of satisfaction.

Trucker dug in the snow and came up with the bottle of olive oil in his mouth. Miss Molly—bless her tiny self, since I knew exactly how vile the asafetida smelled—grasped the edge of Granny's handkerchief in her teeth. The animals split again, Trucker returning the olive oil to me, Miss Molly mincing toward Granny. Miss Molly dropped the handkerchief in Granny's outstretched hand, then sneezed.

"G'zunkite," Granny said. "And thankee kindly, Miss Molly. Let's get them there cold footsies out of that there snow." She picked the cat up and cuddled her.

I replaced the olive oil in the satchel, but left it unzipped. I also took the necessary time to slide in and start the car. The engine turned over and settled into a reassuring rumble. I let it run for a few moments while

I got back out and checked to make sure Granny and the open door were still available.

Small figure wrapped in the warmth of coat and ski cap, Granny was gazing at the hotel. And I didn't care one bit for the look on her face or her tenseness.

"What is it?" I called.

She shook her head. "Nothin' we's gonna like, I's afraid."

I shut off the engine and removed the keys. After I slammed the door, I headed back for the jail, refusing to sneak a peek at the hotel. First I wanted to get that satchel secured inside.

Trucker padded inside ahead of me, and I urged Granny back in, then closed the oak door. I started to take off my coat and scarf, but Granny shook her head.

"We's might as well stay dressed. I 'spect we oughtta go see what's goin' on over there."

"We're not going anywhere," I said sternly. "We're going to get some sleep. If anything's happening over at the hotel, it can wait until morning. Or the sheriff can handle it."

Granny cocked her head, her bright blue eyes examining me, her toothless mouth pursed in thought. Then she nodded and carried Miss Molly over to set her down in front of the fireplace. "Good kitty," she said as she stroked the cat once, then walked toward the cell block.

I gritted my teeth so hard I nearly ground a layer of enamel off. But I was *not* going to say a word. I'd already fought two good fights against these rambunctious entities this evening. No sense pushing my luck. Even with the satchel in hand, it sometimes took a lot out of me to control spirited ghosts. I needed my rest...and so did Granny.

"All right!" I burst out as I stomped across the room and entered the cell block. Granny sat on her bunk, still wearing her coat and ski hat. The smirk on her face said she'd expected me. "What the hell did you see over there?"

"Ain't sure," she replied. "But seein's how that there's the only phone workin', and iffen there *is* a fire over there, not jist some spooks playin' 'round...."

CHAPTER 10

The trickle of smoke smell drifted to us this time when I opened the jailhouse door. From this distance, we could barely make out the roof of the old hotel. My gaze immediately locked onto it. From what I'd gleaned of the building layout while we were there earlier, the tiny flicker of flames and trail of black appeared to be rising from a broken window in True's room, the one where Karen's body had hung.

Granny was right. Fire. The hotel was on fire! And the only workable phone was at the hotel.

Trucker woofed and raced to the SUV. Within fifteen seconds, we were slipping and sliding down the slick roadways, Granny belted in on the passenger side with Miss Molly in her arms, her walking stick propped between her and the car door. Trucker cringed on the backseat each time the tires lost hold.

"You might's want to slow down just a tad," Granny finally said, her right hand grasped tightly on that little bar over the passenger side that I called the *oh-shit* bar. "We's ain't gonna be able to report the fire iffen we's in a ditch."

I let up on the gas and drew in a deep breath, pushed it out slowly to try to calm myself. Headlights on high-beam, we crept on to the hotel,

89

Trucker relented and sat up, his nose against my ear, his little *woof* what I hoped was a hint of confidence in my driving. As soon as I had the hotel in sight, I realized I'd been expecting all the cop cars and authorities to still be there. But *nada*. They'd all left.

Hell, it should have taken them a lot longer to go through that huge crime scene. Shouldn't it? Maybe they'd decided to finish up in the morning.

I pulled up...well, slid up...in front of the hotel and left the engine running.

"Stay in here, all of you," I said as I opened the driver's door. "No sense in all of us freezing to death."

They obeyed me as I raced up the sidewalk...O.K., I again slipped and slid on that damned white mixture of snow and ice that appeared so pretty in the moonlight but proved so treacherous to navigate. The fact several law enforcement and investigative types had trodden this path down to a dangerous layer of now-frozen slush didn't help matters.

Of course, the stupid front door was locked! I should have realized that. There was even yellow crime tape across it.

I didn't hesitate. I plunged into the knee deep drifts off the path and waded through them to the side door. At least the ground wasn't slippery beneath my boots now.

Until I encountered a damn hole in the turf and half-twisted my ankle, flying ass end over teakettle, as Granny would say, into a heap of boots, blue jeans and jacket, my muffler held tight under my butt and strangling me.

"You's O.K.?" Granny called in a worried voice.

I scrambled up and wrested the muffler free before my elderly friend took it upon herself to toddle out through the drifts and rescue me. "I'm fine!" I yelled back. "Stay there! I'm going in through the side door!"

I made it to the door without further incident and jerked one glove off. Thankfully, a security light shown out there, giving enough light to illuminate the keypad.

Now all I had to do was remember what sequence Danny had used to unlock the door.

My first try failed. I took another one of those indrawn breaths and whooshed it out slowly, easing the tension and turbulence in my mind. The second try ended with a reassuring clunk of entry.

I could smell smoke in here, also. Still, it was faint. Maybe the fire hadn't gotten too out of hand.

First, I rushed to the check-in desk and fumbled the gate open. I grabbed the phone and heard a reassuring dial tone. But when I pushed 9-1-1, only one of those infuriating *beep-beep-beeps* of a mis-directed call sounded.

Oh. I needed to dial the 9 for an outside line. Who the heck had set up that stupid system, delaying an emergency call?

"9-1-1. What's your emergency?"

"I'm at the Red Dollar Hotel—"

"Ma'am, that's a crime scene. You shouldn't be there."

"I know that, darn it! But—"

"If you're aware of it, what are you doing there?"

"If you'll shut up—"

"Ma'am, I don't have to tolerate your disrespect!"

"Damn it, I'm trying to tell you—"

"Ma'am, I'm going to hang up. When you are sober and more respectful, call back."

"It's on fire!" I screamed. "The hotel's on fire!"

"Well, why didn't you say so immediately?" the blasted woman said this time, her voice filled with exasperation.

For an instant, I debated telling her exactly what I thought of her attitude, but that would prolong the time the fire had to do its damage. So I shut up...about her, anyway.

"The fire's on the upper level," I went on. "It doesn't look like it's got too good of a start, but we need help."

"We?" she said. "How many are in the hotel messing up the crime scene?"

I gritted my teeth. She still felt a need to put me in my place.

"I'm the only one in here," I growled. "It's the only place with a working phone. Are you going to send help?"

91

"Of course," she spat back. "The fire trucks are on the way, with the rescue personnel. I dispatched them as soon as you finally told me what you were calling about! But the roads are bad."

"I know that. I just drove over here!"

"Ma'am, you need to get out of the hotel."

"I'm going!"

I allowed myself to at least slam down the phone in her ear, hoping the blast of noise dented her ear drum. Then I took another one of those calming breaths...breaths that weren't doing much soothing tonight. And turned around....

...and bumped straight into Granny. Her walking stick knocked off a container of pencils and pens as it crashed to the floor.

I grabbed my elderly friend to steady her before my jolt sent her tumbling after her stick. That's all we needed, Granny hurt. Or heaven forbid, with a broken hip.

"I'm so sorry," I said as I gripped her tightly. "How did you get in here?"

She held up a heavy bobby pin. "Works on these old timey locks."

"The smoke's getting worse. We need to get out of here." I glanced over her shoulder. "Where are Trucker and Miss Molly?"

"Bad as they didn't like it, I left 'em in the car."

"Then come on." I bent down to retrieve the stick and hand it to her, then took her arm, despite the risk she would bat me away. Granny's pride was too strong to admit she needed an assist once in a while. "Let's get out of here."

We didn't even make it to the door. Just outside the check-in desk gate, a fire extinguisher swooped through the air and hovered in front of my face.

"Oh, no," I said, staring around to see who the culprit ghost was. "I'm not fighting a fire. We'll wait for the fire trucks!"

I dodged the extinguisher and half-carried Granny to the front door. I barely got it open and shoved her through before something wrenched the door from my hold and slammed it. I manipulated the lock and jerked at the handle. The door remained securely bolted over my escape route.

"Alice!" Granny called from the other side.

"Go get in the car and keep it running so y'all don't freeze!" I ordered. "This door's stuck! I'll come out the side!"

But when I turned to retrace my path through the hotel to the side door, the fire extinguisher hit me in the stomach.

"Ooooph!" I grabbed the extinguisher and threw it across the lobby as I glared around and continued my stomp toward the side door.

The fire extinguisher beat me to the door. This time, Gambler materialized with it in his hand.

"We're trying the best we can," he said. "But it's hard to carry water in our state. The fire's not that bad yet. I think this thing might work, but we don't know how to operate it."

I pointed at the handle. "You just pull that little clip thing out and squirt."

"We still need your help," he said stubbornly. "We need more hands."

I sighed and bowed my head. "Get the hell out of my way," I ordered in a quiet voice. "I'm not going to die from smoke inhalation or burns just to save a bunch of already dead people!"

"No, no," he insisted. "We're trying to save the room. We can't die again. We know that. Please."

I lifted my eyes and stared into his worried face. "What's so important about the room? The cops have already gathered their evidence."

"It's True's room," Gambler explained in a tone indicating that should suffice to show the importance.

"And?" I demanded.

He frowned, then nodded in understanding. "True's why we had to get you and your aunt here. And if he gets pissed and hauls off somewhere, it will all be in vain and devastate Joleen."

"Someone's life has already been lost here in vain," I said. "Get out of my way."

He didn't really have to move, of course. I could have walked straight through him and escaped. If the stupid door would open. And I could counteract that, too, if necessary. I'd just have to ground myself and override Gambler's abilities with my superior ones.

"I saved your life earlier tonight," he reminded me.

"If I forgot to say it before, thank you," I said. "Now move."

"Please," he whispered in entreaty. "Just give it one try." He held the extinguisher out to me.

We played Mexican standoff with our eyes for another five seconds or so. I recalled how miserable I'd been locked outside the jailhouse door. How cold. How certain I was going to freeze to death. Die. Join those darn entities we chased all over kingdom come and enjoyed so much. Most of the time.

How I'd wondered if I'd be able to communicate with Twila from over there. We'd discussed that a few times....

I grabbed the extinguisher and tromped over to the saloon sink, where the bartender washed dirty glasses.

"Where...what...?" Gambler sputtered.

"I'm not going up there without something to cover my face from the smoke," I said as I turned on the spigot and held a bar towel under the stream of cold—yikes!—icy water. I laid the extinguisher down long enough to wring out the cloth, then picked it up and headed for the stairwell off the lobby, Gambler leading the way.

"Who's Joleen?" I asked as we hurried to the stairwell.

"She's the woman you keep calling Lady in Red."

"Oh."

The further up the stairs we went, the stronger the smoke smell grew. Even the stuffed puma on the landing seemed to blink in irritation. At the top of the stairs, I stared down the hallway. The smoke wasn't as thick as I had imagined it would be. Still, I held the towel up to my nose as I slowly walked toward the next to the last door on the right hand side.

The door and transom were open, so I assumed True was out roaming, maybe even watching all the disruption from his own dimension. Cloth secure on my nose, I stepped into the room.

Over in the corner stood Lady in Red/Joleen. She had just dumped a pitcher of water on the flames struggling to expand up the wall. The fire didn't seem much larger than what I'd seen through the window a while ago, probably due to the ghosts fighting it.

I caught the odor of lighter fluid. Someone had deliberately set the room on fire. Despite the window someone had opened a few inches, which allowed us to spot the smoke, the smell lingered with the smoke scent. It was also as cold as blue blazes in here.

Lady in Red rushed past me with the pitcher, probably heading for the hallway bathroom.

A different pitcher flew into the room, Smelly carrying it. He rushed over and flung the water on the fire.

I lifted the fire extinguisher, then realized I needed both hands to manipulate it.

"Hurry, darn it," Gambler demanded.

I flung the wet towel over my shoulder, grasped the extinguisher in both hands and pulled out the clip. First I pointed the darn thing at Gambler.

"Go get more water to help," I ordered. "Or I'll blast you back into your own dimension before I take care of the fire!"

Gambler disappeared and I hurried over to the flickering flames. The foam gushed out as soon as I depressed the lever. Until then, I'd had a small niggle of worry in the back of my mind that the extinguisher might be expired, need refilling. But within a few seconds, the flames were as dead as the supernatural firefighters.

Just to be sure, I sprayed again, until all the foam was gone. Then I dropped the extinguisher.

Gambler materialized with his pitcher, and for good measure, tossed it on the sodden carpet. He wiggled one hand at the window, and it slid closed.

"Thank you," he told me.

"Someone set this fire," I said. "I can smell the accelerant."

"Ak-aksel-huh?"

"Things an arsonist uses," I explained. "Things that will make a fire burn faster and destroy whatever the arsonist wants destroyed. This one used lighter fluid. Did you see anyone?"

He shook his head negatively as it dawned on me the fire-starter might still be lingering, to see if his handiwork did as intended. Rather than continue my discussion with Gambler, I said, "Come see me at the jail later."

"The jail again?" He cringed, but I glared at him.

"The damn jail's not operating right now! Didn't you realize that when you got that door open for me?"

"Yeah. I guess so. It's just not one of my favorite...uh...."

"Haunts?" I supplied. Then I hurried out of the room, back down the hall, and down the stairwell. In the lobby, I could hear the sirens approaching.

The front door opened easily this time, and I trod down the path and around the SUV to slip into the driver's seat just as the fire engine pulled in.

The driver stuck his head out the window and shouted, "You need to move your damn car!"

I'd had it with rude people tonight. I opened my door, stood outside and shouted back, "The goddamn fire is out! I put it out! And I'm moving my damn car, but because I want to. Not because you—"

Abruptly, I sighed and got back into the car. I slammed the door closed, dropped the gearshift into Drive, and put a tad too much pressure on the gas feed. I managed not to sideswipe the fire truck, though it was close. I wouldn't have wanted my fingers in between the two vehicles.

Granny remained quiet for a few seconds, unusual for her. "We's'll probably need to give 'em our statement on this, too," she finally said.

"Let them find us first," I muttered.

CHAPTER 11

Back at the jail, I settled my pets in while Granny snuggled down in her bunk bed inside the cell. Then I started to undress. I still wore my coat, and I laid my cheek on my left shoulder as I pulled my right arm free. And got a face-full of soggy cold!

Oh, yeah, the bar towel I'd grabbed to cover my nose when I went upstairs to fight the fire with Gambler. It still lay on my shoulder, now thawed to wet disgust. I tried to grab it with my right arm, which of course ended up with me twisted in an awkward position, hand snagged halfway free because my garnet birthstone ring caught in the coat lining. The more I tried to extricate myself, the worse I got entangled. If possible, I didn't want to rip the lining beyond the hole I'd already managed, and yet even when I tried to shove my hand back into the sleeve, the snag didn't give.

I started to call Granny to come help me, but she'd probably already removed her hearing aid. Besides, I was too tired to listen to her cackles at my position. First I grabbed the stupid towel in my teeth, yanked it free and spit it on the floor. Then I took a calming breath—one that worked this time—and twisted enough to free my left arm. Carefully, I grasped my ring through the coat material and worked it off my finger

97

Leaving it hanging in the lining, I pulled the coat off. I'd worry about freeing the ring tomorrow.

I finally crawled into the bunk across from Granny's wearing my comfy gray flannel PJ's. Exhausted with all the flying, driving, body discovery, and irritating stress of dealing with rude and insensitive people, I knew I would sink into sleep immediately despite the coffee I'd consumed.

I did, too...for about five minutes. I could tell how long it had been by checking my wristwatch, which I'd forgotten to remove.

What the hell woke me?

Beep!

Oh, crap, my least favorite interruption—the stupid cell phone beep indicating a missed call or text or voice mail. Well, it could wait until morning! I turned over and pulled the blanket up far enough to cover my ear....

Which left my darn feet exposed! Even though I still wore my socks, the chill in the cell bit into my toes. I can't abide cold feet. So I curled my legs so my feet drew up under the blanket.

Then my legs cramped in the awkward position. Deciding I could ignore the....

Beep!

...I shifted enough to re-cover my feet and laid an arm over my head to block my ear. There. Peace and quiet. Except....

I didn't like being buried like that. With my ears unblocked, I felt that, no matter how deep I slept, at least my subconscious was on alert if anything happened I should hear. After all, we were in a strange place. After all, I was responsible for Granny, Trucker and Miss Molly. After all, the paranormal was prowling big-time here. After all....

Beep!

...the stupid cell phone should be on its last legs battery-bar-wise. Surely it would finish dying in another beep or two.

Tense and expectant, I waited for the next beep. None came. Great. Now I could get back to sleep. But...what if it was a call I needed to get? No one phoned this time of night without it being important. And how the heck did anything even ring in? We hadn't had reception earlier in the evening. Sometimes, though, text messages could penetrate when phone calls couldn't.

I'd only given in to the text message craze recently and found I rather liked that form of communication. Truth be told, Jack had taught me all the basics, on one of his now-and-then drop-bys to have an early morning cup of coffee.

Jack and I both agreed our divorce was for the best. We just could not live together. He got on my nerves, I got on his. He didn't understand my writing and need for privacy for hours on end, sometimes deep into the night, if the Muse was working well. When I did have time to spend with him, I didn't understand his occasional dark moods due to any especially horrendous or heartrending case he happened to be lead detective on. Well, I did understand to a point. However, all my efforts to cheer him and have an enjoyable time together fell short at times...as did my temper when our moods stayed so polar-opposite for long periods.

We did much better as friends. Not *friends with benefits*...yet, anyway, although I had to admit the thought crossed my mind. Our sex life had definitely not been one of the marriage problems. Still, Jack had never made a move in that direction, and I sure didn't want to get slapped down if I did.

Oh, hell. I threw the covers back and stomped out into the main part of the jail. Now where the heck did I leave the stupid cell phone? Normally, I made sure I replaced each necessary gadget in my life in its specified location. The cell phone was something I usually paid attention to at home, since my editor was prone to forget which number was my landline and call the cell. I now bought purses with a slot for it, and even carried it in my pants or muumuu pocket if I were expecting a call or text.

Trucker snuffled and groaned, irritated at the disturbance to his slumber. He didn't bother to get up, only shifted to his back and flailed his legs until he folded onto his other side. With a preliminary snort, he started snoring.

"Hey, dog," I said to be perverse, since I felt perverse, "you seen the cell phone?"

He didn't answer, and Miss Molly slit her blue eyes at me in a disdainful gesture telling me exactly what she thought of my insanity. She didn't vocalize anything, though, just snapped her lids shut once more.

About then, I realized my feet were cold again. I'd neglected to jam them into the pair of kitty slippers I had remembered to place beside the bunk. I gave up the hunt and strode back to the bunk, sat down and started to put on the slippers. Sighed and decided the danged phone could wait until morning.

Laid down...and gave that up to stalk out again even before I pulled the blanket up. This time I remembered the slippers at least. A few minutes later, I found the phone right there in the little pocket on the side of my purse where it belonged. I'd forgotten I'd changed purses before I left for New Mexico, and this old purse had a pocket for cigarettes and phone both, bought back before I grew some sense and quit smoking. I sighed silently in disgust at myself. Sheesh, I'd checked the cigarette pouch instead of the one for the phone.

I pulled the cell out...but of course the darned battery was dead! I spent a few more precious sleepless minutes finding the charger shoved down in the side of my briefcase. I got it plugged in, waited ten seconds or so for the darn thing to realize it had juice again, and turned it on.

Text message. I pushed *read* and found a message from Jack.

U all right? Heard the news. U involved again?

Without thinking, I started to type a scathing reply, then remembered to check the time of the message. Oh, he'd sent this prior to his phone call, or right before, maybe. I'd talked to him since then.

Surprised at the yearning tug I felt to send him a text back anyway—and not a nasty one—I sighed and laid the phone down to finish its charge. Then trundled back to the bunk to try to get some sleep. I don't do sleeplessness well at all, so I fervently hoped I would get my wish.

I didn't, of course. I'd barely drifted into the lovely state where the next step would be peaceful oblivion when a whisper drew me back to full consciousness.

I'm here.

Darn, I'd forgotten I'd asked Gambler to meet me here. And when did I start recognizing the different voices on the ghosts populating this historic old town? Or perhaps it was that sixth sense Twila and I shared, somehow knowing who had "paged" me telepathically. I turned over to face the wall and pulled the pillow over my head again.

You're the one who asked me to meet you. Remember?

Crap. "Later," I said quietly, just in case Granny was sleeping with her hearing aid in place. "Come back later. I'm still human. I need some sleep."

"I's'll talk to ya." Granny evidently received the gambler ghost's communication.

"Uh..." I began, hoping my reference to her physical disability didn't stir up one of her crotchety spells, "did you keep your ear piece in tonight?" At least I didn't use that proper name a lot of old...older folks despised.

"Figgered I best keep an ear out, case you needed me," she said, not at all irritated. She went on, "But I heered him without my ears, likes you do. And I's ain't past the stage where I don't enjoy the company of a good-lookin' man in the middle of the night." Her bed clothes rustled as she got up. "We kin go out in the other room, so's we don't bother Alice."

All right.

By the time Granny fumbled around to find her slippers and slid her feet into them, I was half-awake again. She tried to be discreet, but when she groaned under her breath in response to her arthritic aches and pain, then rose and grabbed her walking stick to thump-slide out of the room, I was totally awake. Still, I slowed my breathing and tried to at least slip into the meditative state to get a measure of rest, which might lead back to sleep.

You might want to hear what he has to say.

"Damn it!" I didn't try to keep my voice down this time as I jerked up in bed and stared over at Granny's bunk. Lady in Red sat there in all her saloon girl finery, breasts spilling out of the red gown that ended mid-leg, a white feather waving as though in a gentle breeze decorating her lavishly styled blond locks.

I gave up and threw back my blanket to sit on the side of the bed and blindly search for my own slippers as I stared at her. She stared back, and it didn't take a psychic to understand she didn't approve of the dark gray flannel PJ's.

Aren't you a bit young to be wearing something like that? she projected.

Huh. Had she given me a compliment? Or made a derogatory remark?
Compliment, she assured me.

Uh oh. I needed to put up some mind barriers. She was advanced enough to be able to read my thoughts when I didn't mean for her to.

"It's cold here," I found myself explaining. "We don't get continuing cold like this in Texas, at least, not where I live."

Oh. Well, Gil isn't in any state to be stirred up. Although he hasn't lost his ability to flirt.

"Gil? Oh, Gambler?"

Uh huh.

I sighed and decided I might as well make some more coffee just as the delicious smell of fresh-brewed drifted in and tickled my nose. That made it a bit easier to stand and slide on my housecoat. Sort of.

Yawning, I wandered out into the main jail, Lady in Red drifting along behind me. Granny sat at the table, but Gambler Gil stood by the coffeepot. He must have made the coffee. Again, I reinforced my mind barriers, a skill I practiced often and had honed to where it only took a split second. The paranormal residents of this town had obviously worked hard to develop their abilities. Twila and I would have to be on guard to stay in charge of them.

I nodded at Granny, but she only had eyes for Gil. I shook my head tolerantly. At her age, Granny had the right to ogle all she wanted. By the time I joined her at the table, Gil was manipulating the coffeepot to fill two cups. He waved a finger and they moved over to the table, one sliding into place in front of each of us.

I noticed the longing look on Gil's face as I reached to pull the dried creamer toward me. He caught my gaze and shrugged.

Used to live on the stuff, he told me. Didn't drink booze, only to be sociable now and then. It was hard to get coffee out here, but we managed.

"Drinking problem?" I asked as I stirred.

No, he denied. It clouded the mind and lost me too much money at poker or craps.

After a few stirs, I took a tentative sip. Hot, but tolerable. A couple more swallows and a hint of caffeine buzz lifted my eyelids. Granny obviously decided to keep herself in Gil's mind and, batting her eyelids in the myriad wrinkles on her face, she cleared her throat to get his attention.

"An' what do we owe the pleasure of your handsome company here in the middle of the night to?" she asked.

Gil shrugged. Alice asked me to come. I'm not sure what she wanted.

Probably to find out why we were so insistent she get here. Lady in Red sashayed over and tucked her arm in Gil's, giving Granny a look that said in no uncertain terms the gambling man already had a girlfriend. Gil smiled down at her, but also surreptitiously winked at Granny. Lady in Red was right. He did still remember how to flirt.

"We didn't come here in response to a bunch of ghost manipulations," I told the two of them in a stern voice. "We came because Danny talked Twila into it. I told you back in Six Gun—" I shot Lady in Red a glower "— that I wasn't interested in taking on another ghost's problems. I've already got a houseful, and I haven't had time lately to open the door into The Light and talk some of them into crossing."

Lady in Red sent me back a look just as stubborn as mine to her. *Well, we aren't going to cross without True.*

"Who's True to you?" I asked.

My brother, she responded. His murder keeps happening over and over, and I'm sure if you and your aunt could find out who killed him, that would stop the...."

"It's called a residual haunting," I explained. "We don't know for sure a revelation like that will make a residual cease. It might, though."

Well, some dastardly coward snuck up behind True in the hall one night as he was going back to his room. Shot him in the back of the head! That's what happens at least once a night. I'm pretty sure it was Bob

Dalton. True had won all Bob's money in a poker game that night. Bob swore True cheated, but I know my brother. He doesn't cheat.

"Didn't cheat," I automatically corrected her.

Doesn't, she replied defiantly. And I promised Mama I'd take care of True. I didn't do a very good job of that in life, but I'm not going to leave True behind here to suffer his death again and again and again.

"Y'know," Granny interrupted, either tired of being ignored or ready to retaliate for Lady in Red's proprietary possession of Gil, "we's should separate 'em and ask 'em questions."

"About what?" I asked before I caught her drift. "Huh uh. Oh, no, my friend. It's bad enough we ended up in the middle of Karen's death. I'm not about to get involved in a two-hundred-year-old murder."

One hundred and forty-two, Lady in Red corrected.

I shoved my chair back. "I don't care how long True's been dead." Uh oh, I shouldn't even have used the name of the other ghost. That formed him in my mind and made him too real to me. "I'm going back to bed."

"You's won't sleep with that coffee in you."

"I darn sure will." I glanced at my wristwatch. "We left Six Gun before dawn. We've been up for nearly twenty-four hours. Nothing is going to keep me awake."

You still haven't said why you asked me here, Gil reminded me.

I waved a negligent hand. "Never mind. I thought we might help out the law enforcement folks by seeing if y'all had noticed anything suspicious about Karen's death. Maybe who had murdered her. It has to be murder, because I sure can't see her cutting off her own hands."

Stupidly, I'd slowly sat back down in the chair as I spoke. My darned inquisitive mind was already going to where I'd been warned away—into the current investigation.

CHAPTER 12

I jumped to my feet so abruptly, the chair flew backward.

"Huh uh. No way! I am *not* getting involved in either one of these deaths."

"Yeah, but we's the only ones 'round here who can see our friends here," Granny said with a nod at Gil and Lady in Red. "Only one's who kin ask them if they saw anythin' and mebbe he'p find out who killed Karen."

"We already have a job here, Granny. Jack will be pissed at me if he finds out I'm again involved in a murder investigation. Especially if it also includes ghosts!"

Granny frowned. "My, my. I thought's you an' him was dee-vorced. Why's you worryin' 'bout what he will think?"

"We a-are. D-d-dee-whatever." I sputtered to a halt. Granny had a point. Why on earth was I taking Jack's preferences into consideration, given we'd signed those dee-...divorce papers over two years ago? So what if he dropped by once a week to chat? So what if now and then we went to a movie we both wanted to see? So what if the last time we'd done that, we sat in his truck and talked while I waited for a break in the pouring rain to make a run for the house? A talk that lasted until dawn broke before either of us noticed the rain had ceased and the sun was rising.

We'd both moved on with our lives. Right? Not that I was dating anyone else. Well, not seriously, anyway. I'd seen that grocery store manager for a while, the one who always brought Trucker a t-bone and Miss Molly a box of her favorite Kitty Kisses. I hadn't known of anyone Jack picked up...uh...dated. But he was over in Angel Fire with a *friend*. Angel Fire, a notorious ski resort for couples, married or co-habiting.

Still, he took time out to call me....

I found myself sighing an awfully lot recently. I did it again, retrieved the chair from the wall, and re-seated myself at the table. Jack and I were dee-vorced and he had his own separate life now, one that included looking for another woman...wife...co-habitor, whatever.

"All right, give," I said in the direction of the ghostly couple who appeared as solid as the living two of us.

I told you. True is unhappy—

Joleen made a promise and—

The two of them spoke at once, both broke off at the same time, then stared politely at each other.

You first, love, Gambler Gil said.

Joleen? Oh, right. The woman's name. I liked Lady better.

No, no, dear, she responded. Go ahead.

"See's?" Granny broke in. "I told's ya we need to separate 'em." She rose and crooked a crooked finger at Gil. "Let's you an' me go back to my bedroom." With a cackle under her breath, she limped toward the bunks, confident he would follow.

Lady/Joleen gave her own ghostly impression of a sigh, a gesture recognizable even though she had no breath. She unclasped Gil's arm and waved a hand after Granny.

Jealous, love? Gil whispered in a teasing manner.

Just go on, she replied as she glided into Granny's vacated chair.

From the corner of my eye, I noticed Granny pause. When I glanced at her, a smirk deepened the myriad of wrinkles on her face. She disappeared into the bunk room, and Gil de-materialized.

Arms crossed, Lady leaned on the tabletop, breasts spilling out of her low-cut bodice to the point her nipples were in danger of exposure. She said, *You have to help us. I had no idea True stayed behind as a ghost when he died. Not until I died myself fifteen years later. I was going through the tunnel, and I stupidly looked back. True was standing there, watching me. I'd missed him so much! I just wanted to hug him one more time, but when I did, the tunnel closed.*

"It's very easy to re-open the door into The Light," I assured her. "I can do it like that." I snapped my fingers, and she grabbed at my hand. Hers, of course, passed through mine, but left a cold chill.

Don't! she pleaded. *Not yet, anyway. Not without my brother.*

I ignored persistent ghosts—most of the time, anyway. Sir Gary and Patrick flashed through my mind. However, I had walked away from others.

Please—

The reasons ghosts stayed behind had always fascinated me. So many lost souls wandered this earth, mystified at times by their state of being, not even knowing they were dead. Other times, they had no doubt they'd left their bodies behind, but for various reasons were adamant about not travelling through The Light to whatever lay beyond. Perhaps they didn't want anything to do with someone who had dealt them a raw hand in life. Other times, like my Head Ghost Howard, there wasn't anyone on the other side they were anxious to reunite with. They actually enjoyed their current state of existence and would cross if and when the urge took over.

Neither Twila nor I could force a ghost to cross, even when we assured them there was peace and forgiveness, not punishment, waiting for them. For one thing, neither Twila nor I had died yet, so we couldn't be one hundred percent sure what we said to the ghosts was accurate. Our Spirit Guides had assured us over and over this was the truth, but as humans, we would carry a tiny tad of doubt until it was verified. And when verification happened...well, we would be over there ourselves. Even if she or I tried to communicate with whichever one of us remained behind, we would probably doubt the accuracy of the telepathic message.

I kept the fact of not being able to force a ghost into The Light to myself. It always paid to hold back a bit of threat in case we needed to discipline one of our paranormal acquaintances.

"Let me recount what I already know." I rose and poured myself a new cup of coffee. I couldn't stop myself from glancing in the direction of the bunks when I heard a muted cackle of glee from Granny. Surely she wouldn't...nah.

I sat back down and continued, "True is your brother, Gil is your boyfriend. True was gambling one night...here in the hotel, I assume."

She answered with a yes nod.

"True won a lot of money—"

And land.

"—and land from someone. After the game broke up, he headed back to his room. Someone stole up on him and shot him dead. Robbed him and escaped."

That's about it.

"O.K. Here are some questions: First, maybe it wasn't about the money. What land did he win?"

That's not it at all. But she frowned. Well, True was a cowboy at heart. He planned to buy some property and raise cattle. Horses, too, since he really loved them and had an idea for breeding something special, using a stud he loved. I didn't get a chance to talk to him after the game, but I'm sure he was already planning his breeding program as he headed back to his room. Whoever stole the money, though, wasn't interested in the land. The murderer discarded the deed up in an old line shack he hid in before he hightailed it out of here.

"And you know this how?"

The man who lost the deed in the poker game found it. By accident, he said. He also owned this hotel, and he was part of the posse formed to go after True's murderer. Volunteers, since we didn't have any law enforcement here in New Mexico during those days. It was a haven for outlaws. There's an old register around the hotel somewhere with names like Jesse James and members of the Dalton gang listed in it. Later, Wild Bill Hickok and Buffalo Bill even stayed here. Other famous people, too. After I died, I didn't have much else to do except watch the guests come and go.

"Until you came to Six Gun. I assume you somehow found out about Twila and me through our association with Danny."

Actually, that was part of it. But I saw you on one of those morning shows once. A guest was watching the show over in the new section they built years ago. The one where they have TV's in the rooms. The only one we have in the hotel is in the lobby. None in the rooms.

That's one thing Twila and I didn't miss, TV's in the haunted rooms where we stayed. They were only a distraction from our sought-after entertainment: appearances and disappearances of apparitions and the antics they displayed for us.

I'd been on several morning shows, a necessary part of book tours I totally detested. Not only was I not a morning person, I also enjoyed my privacy. Not that I was a movie star or anything, but sometimes I resorted to disguises when I shopped in a town where I was doing a book signing. I was one of the authors, also, who enjoyed the new bent towards digital book tours, and even tolerated those danged computer cameras. At least most of those interactions with readers took place in the evenings, when I had time away from writing to fix my hair and makeup. Anyway, I didn't bother to ask Joleen which show she had seen.

"There are lots of suspects," I mused. "It could be—"

It had to be Bob Dalton! Joleen insisted. He hated True and was the one who lost the most money. Probably money he and his gang got in a stagecoach or bank hold-up. And he disappeared right afterwards.

"You're possibly wrong," I refuted. "Emotions run high in a poker game. People do things they wouldn't do when they're in a rational state. So second: who all was in that game? Were you there?"

I saw my briefcase leaning against the wall beside us. I didn't notice that Joleen hadn't answered until I had a tablet of paper in front of me, a pen in my hand. When I looked across the table, an irritated scowl on my face, she was gone.

"Get your butt back here!" I ordered. "Or go find yourself another ghost hunter to help you out."

Nothing. She didn't even thrust a thought into my mind. The hell with it. Leaving the paper and pen on the table, I stood and headed for the bunk room.

A few feet from the door, I paused, noticing the silence. Was Gambler Gil still there? I didn't hear Granny talking to him. Surely they wouldn't...surely *she* wouldn't...but she sure had been flirting with him. Lady hadn't appeared threatened or jealous, though. And Granny was too old to do the deed with a ghost. Wasn't she?

Shaking my head at my imaginary foolishness, I walked in the doorway. And found myself with my head down, examining my feet rather than looking at the bunk across from mine. Surely I didn't think Granny and Gil were....

I had to force myself to turn toward the other bunk...but not before I first sat down on my own mattress. If shock weakened my legs again, something would already be beneath my butt to catch me.

Whew. Granny lay peacefully on her back, blanket tucked under her chin. She wasn't even snoring. She did, though, have a silly smile on her face.

We could wait until morning to discuss what we'd both found out. A glance at my wristwatch told me I could catch quite a few winks before then. Removing the watch, I placed it in a side pocket of my suitcase. I laid down on the bunk, snuggled my blanket over me, and managed to catch an entire hour's sleep.

* * *

The eyes woke me this time. He sat there patiently, tongue out in a quiet pant. No way on earth would my wonderful Trucker wake me up unless I made him wait until he had to try to cross his legs to keep from peeing on the floor.

I reached out and patted his head. "Trucker, there's no one else in the world I'd crawl out of this bed for right now except you and Miss Molly."

"Meow." My cat sat on her haunches beside her huge friend, overpowered by his larger body.

With another one of those sighs, which I tried to hide so I wouldn't upset my pets because they had intruded on my sleep, I crawled out of bed. Across from me, Granny snored peacefully, that tiny smile still curving her non-collagen-injected lips. Even the little sleep I'd gotten had improved my temperament, and I found myself hoping she was enjoying a pleasant dream of either a live or other-dimensional man.

Granny and her husband had had a long marriage together, and she never lost a chance to let me know she thought Jack and I should have tried harder to work out our differences. At times, I agreed with her. At other times...well, I was still working on that.

I shrugged into my heavy clothing and trudged to the door on the front of that jail. With an anticipatory shudder at the cold on the other side, I slowly opened it and stepped back to allow Trucker to precede me and his feline buddy.

The dog plowed a path through the snow, Miss Molly daintily following. After making sure the damn lock wouldn't engage behind me, I edged outside and pulled it nearly closed. All right, I wasn't exactly positive it wouldn't lock, so I kept a hold on the door. I couldn't be sure Gambler Gil would arrive to save me again, either. He and Joleen had left without giving me any idea of how to contact them or if they would return soon. Well, at least Joleen had. I wasn't sure what Gambler Gil had said to Granny to put that smile on her face.

What a gorgeous night. I glanced at my wrist to check the time, then remembered I'd taken my watch off. Still, it had to be getting onward toward daylight. Then I recalled glancing at the microwave clock as I walked to the door. Granny must have set it, because the bright red digital numbers read 3:15. Given the short days of winter, there were still more hours of darkness ahead.

Overhead, brilliant white stars sparkled against an obsidian background. No new flakes fell and no wind dipped the icy temperatures to a minus wind chill. In fact, from the corner of my eye, I saw an icicle drip a drop into the snow. I'd heard of a Chinook warning hitting soon after a heavy snowstorm and hoped perhaps one was filtering in to this end of New Mexico. That would make it a lot more tolerable for us Texas folks.

In the meantime, I decided to fill my senses with the scenery, storing images to draw on later if I needed a lot of snow in my writing. Brilliant white drifts softened sharp edges on everything from buildings to signs. Snow had already blanketed our earlier footsteps; Trucker's deep paw prints were the only thing to deface the smooth layers now. Miss Molly's tiny prints disappeared in his. New inches covered the SUV, but the thought of having to brush it all off the windows before I could drive didn't bother me. Not much, anyway. Besides, I figured I wouldn't be driving anywhere until that Chinook completed its work, if the slightly warmer temperature did indicate the presence of a creeping melting trend.

The quiet stillness overwhelmed a bit at first, but when I listened closely, a few sounds declared themselves: more drips from the icicles; faint puffs of air from Trucker's mouth; the shuffles of his body as it plowed through the drifts looking for a specific spot to lift his leg. My pet was particular about that. Miss Molly had given up following him and waited patiently for the dog to return. She would probably also wait until she went back inside to do her business in her portable litter box.

Far off, an owl hooted. I don't like owls. Seems they always portend some sort of trouble. This one sounded distant enough that the misfortune wasn't ready to drop on my shoulders, but rather on someone else's.

Darn, Trucker was stomping around awfully loudly....

The dog's furious barks split the night like lightning bolts. A brief urge to retreat flashed, but Miss Molly leapt into my arms. I grabbed her close and nearly lost my hold on the door behind me. Luckily for my sanity, I gripped it tighter as I stared across the snow at the damned elk.

I wasn't sure if it was the same one or not. Probably not, since the other one was dozens of miles away. But who knew how far and fast an elk could travel? I sure didn't.

"Come here, Trucker!" I yelled. "Get away from that thing before it sticks its horns in you and guts you!"

Trucker ignored me. His white fangs flashed in the night as he roared his anger at the intruder to his domain, an intruder similar to the one that antagonized him earlier in the evening. Instead of retreating, he advanced on the monster, which outweighed him at least ten times.

I turned and shoved Miss Molly into the jail, then left the door agape as I plunged toward the dog.

"Trucker!" I ordered. "Get your fanny back here!"

He deigned to glance at me, but refused to obey. He wasn't about to let some monster animal attack me, the person he loved the most in the world.

The elk lifted its head and glared down its long nose at the dog. They were probably fifteen feet apart, but Trucker kept narrowing the distance. The elk snorted, a stream of white steam emerging from its nostrils. Then it lowered its head.

I managed to grab Trucker's collar. Not that it did any good. Did you ever try to drag a hundred-fifty-pound dog when he didn't want to budge?

I jerked. Trucker jerked back, baying his continued defiance at the elk.

The elk shook its antlers—antlers tipped with horribly sharp points. It snorted again.

I tried to pull Trucker, but he dug in his paws and refused to move.

"Please, boy," I whispered.

That got his attention. He didn't like the fearful whiny pout I put into my voice. He stared up at me, his barks dwindling to growls, then stopping. When I tugged his collar this time, he obeyed. But not without one last woof of warning to the elk.

At the door, I made the mistake of looking behind me. And stared straight into the elk's muzzle. The monster animal had followed us, hoof beats silenced by the noise Trucker and I made!

I screamed, a deathly shriek that burst full bore out of my chest and shattered the night air.

The elk jumped back, hind legs caving under it until it sat on its haunches. If elks had any sort of emotions, this one looked surprised. I took advantage of its shock and ducked inside after Trucker. Slammed the door behind me, then turned and jammed the deadbolt in place.

I reached over to lift the curtain beside the door and see what the elk was up to now. Trucker beat me to it. Front paws on the windowsill, he shoved his head under the curtain and looked out the window. I stepped over behind him and pushed the checkered material back.

The elk was on its feet now, but it still stood there...frowning at us? Naw, I was trying to put human emotions into an animal.

Not that Trucker and Miss Molly didn't have their share of feelings. But an elk? A wild animal?

The elk turned and trudged off through the snow, casting a glance back at the jail a couple times. Finally, it disappeared into the night around another building.

"Woof!" Trucker's bark carried a satisfied ring as he dropped to the floor and padded to his rug in front of the fireplace.

I, on the other hand, shrugged out of my coat and hung it on the hook beside the door. Something hard brushed my arm, and I remembered the ring caught in the lining. It could wait until another time for retrieval.

The coffee was cold now. At least I'd remembered to turn the pot off. I bit my lip as I tried to decide whether to make fresh or try for more sleep. Wide awake now after the fright from the elk, I knew catching more Z's would be a hopeless cause. Maybe food would help.

Of course, all we had were the snacks from the hotel, and I wasn't in the mood for more cheese and crackers. Then I remembered the candy bars I'd picked up at the convenience store. I dug in a bag on the floor and retrieved a Milky Way, tore off the wrapper and devoured a huge chunk. Initial appetite satisfied, I sat down and nibbled on nougat, then caramel, then nougat again. Yum. It was my favorite way to eat that candy.

"You get me one?" Granny asked as she toddled over and sat down in the other chair.

"Yep." I reached in the sack and handed her a Milky Way. She gummed hers in bites filled with nougat, chocolate and caramel together all at once.

"What was all that hollerin' out there?" she asked between chews.

"You must be sleeping with your hearing aid in," I said instead of answering the question.

"Sometimes," she said with a nod. "'Specially if I wanna hear sweet nothin's whispered by a good-looking' man."

I blocked that vision and said, "Remember that elk that attacked our car earlier?"

"Uh huh."

"Either his brother or father or some relative is wandering around here." I quickly explained what had happened, watching Granny's eyes twinkle with humor as I talked.

She swallowed the last piece of candy bar. "Might be's someone's pet. Lookin' for a handout, since it's feed's all covered up."

I shrugged, not that interested in whether or not the animal, which had scared the crap out of me, ate or not.

Beep.

Shit!

CHAPTER 13

One of these days I was going to learn to use that menu thing on the phone and change the text message waiting tone! I grabbed the cell phone before it could irritate me again.

1 new message

I punched the *read* button.

Go home!

"Who is it?" Granny asked. "Jack?"

"No," I said in a puzzled voice. "Someone's telling me to go home."

"Lemme see."

I gave her the phone and she punched some buttons.

"What are you doing?"

"Tryin' to see who this here stupid person is," she said in a distracted voice. Then she frowned, the same puzzled expression on her face as was probably on mine. "Musta been a ghost. Ain't takin' my reply message."

Never doubting her conclusion, I heaved an irritated huff. "As if we don't have enough trouble around here! Now we've got a ghost that's developed enough ability to manipulate an electronic device! Remember how *Great-grandmere* Alicia would type things into my computer?"

"Yep," Granny agreed. "But this ain't a helpful message like she'd give to you. More like it's a warnin'."

I glared around the room. "I don't take well to warnings or threats," I warned back at whatever ghost had the audacity to try that with me. "And soon as Aunt Twila gets here, this ghost that's trying to bully us will have double trouble on its hands!"

"Yep," Granny agreed again, her own eyes gleaming with icy menace. "An' mebbe triple."

"Triple," I agreed.

Well, hell, the voice said audibly. I wasn't threatening y'all. I don't treat women like that. I meant that for your own good. Already been one lady killed here. I don't want to see that happen to either of you, especially as pretty as you both are.

"O.K., Gambler Gil," I said. "Come on out. Your flirty ways won't get around the fact that you're trying to order us around. We're not some delicate western flower. Women these days don't take orders from men."

"Yeah," Granny said, but I noticed she preened a bit over his calling her pretty. "We don't's kowtow to no men these days. 'Course, I never did that all durin' my marriage. Why, I never had no tolerance for those there women that had to ask permission to run to the store and grab a gallon of milk. Or ask their menfolk how long they's would be allowed to go shoppin', how much they was allowed to spend. Why, I got so diddly darn ticked at my friend Gert one time. We's had planned to have us a girl's night out for my birthday. My husband knew better than to forbid me. He just said he'd take me to dinner the next night to celebrate. But Gert's man decided she needed to stay home and fix snacks and fetch beer for him an' his poker buddies, who was comin' by that night."

Granny could ramble on and on when she got going, but I was rather interested in this story, so I asked, "And what happened then?"

Granny cackled. "Seems like somebody cracked open every one of the caps on those there longneck bottles on the two cases of beer Gert's man had on ice. Every one of them there beers was flat! Them men was so pissed off, they decided to go on down to the bar and play pool instead. Soon's they left, Gert called me to come pick her up."

"Good for Gert," I said. "But too bad she had to waste all that beer."

"Oh, that weren't Gert," Granny said with a wink. "She didn't have the spunk. Me, I had a key to her house, and she'd forgot 'tater chips. So she borrowed my car and ran to the store."

"Didn't her husband suspect anything?"

"Naw. He thought it was the guy at the liquor store who'd done it. He'd griped about the price goin' up ten cents a case when he bought the beer."

I laughed with her, and we actually heard a third laugh. Which reminded me another person...uh...once-person was listening in.

"Are you going to show yourself, Gil?" I asked. "If not, it's not polite to eavesdrop."

I'm not Gil. And I really do think you ladies should leave. But if you won't heed me, then I'll politely take my leave.

The atmosphere in the room lightened, and I understood the ghost had been true to his word.

"Wonder who it was, iffen it weren't that there handsome Gambler Gil?" Granny mused.

"No idea. He kept himself hidden, except for his voice. Well, should we try to get some more sleep?"

"I ain't really sleepy no more. And we's supposed to be talkin' to the ghosts, tryin' to get them to behave themselves, so's they can sell that hotel," she reminded me.

"With Karen dead, I don't even know if they'll still want us here," I said. "This was Twila's deal, anyway. She's the one who set everything up through Danny." I walked over and opened the door to check the weather again. "Look, Granny. One of those Chinook's must have hit. The temperature is climbing and the snow's melting. If this keeps up, we should be able to travel by daylight. Not that I'm taking orders from a ghost to leave, but I don't see any sense in staying here. We can head out, and soon as I find cell phone reception, call Twila. Tell her what's going on and that we're heading on back to Texas. We won't be allowed access to the hotel anyway, now that it's a crime scene. And I really don't want to sit around here, trapped inside a jail."

"Me neither," she agreed. "Mebbe we could stay over in Albuquerque instead for a day or so. Do some tourist stuff. Hit one of them casinos and have a little fun."

"Sounds good to me. Let's pack up our stuff again."

Since we didn't have that much un-packed, we had our things loaded into the car by the time the sun rose. It was a beautiful sunrise, the eastern sky at first a pale rose, then a diversity of reds, violets and even gold. In the pollution-free atmosphere, the sun peered over the brim of the earth ever so slowly, the dazzling yellow orb clear and vivid. Despite our desire to leave, Granny and I couldn't bear to miss a second of this breathtaking show. We stood there silently for long moments, and when I heard a snuffle, I glanced down to see Trucker and Miss Molly sitting beside us.

But my pets weren't watching the sunrise. Heads cocked to one side, they stared at something else. I hoped it wasn't that stupid elk. I traced the direction of their gazes, but didn't see anything to merit their rapt attention. Besides, if it were the elk, Trucker would have disrupted the peace with his ferocity.

CHAPTER 14

The faint sound of an engine reached us first. A few seconds later, we could see the snowmobile making its way toward us. In the warming temperatures, the driver had forgone a helmet and even a hat. Soon we recognized Danny's face.

"Woulda thought he'd be nursin' a hangover this mornin'," Granny mused.

Me, also, but I didn't answer her. I wasn't sure whether Twila considered Danny a friend or just an acquaintance who happened to have a fascinating ghost hunt she could get involved in. I made a mental note to ask my aunt about that as soon as I saw her. Until then, I'd treat Danny as cordially as I could manage, given I hadn't been very impressed with him when we found Karen. He'd buried himself in that bottle pretty quickly.

Danny pulled the snowmobile to a stop several feet from us and dismounted the huge machine. Black and yellow, the engine rumble was rather pleasant, even though it disturbed the quiet. Danny turned it off, but left the key dangling in the ignition. Trucker growled softly, and I laid a hand on his head, assuming he didn't recognize Danny in his heavy clothing.

"Ladies," Danny said, removing his gloves as he approached. "I figured you'd be resting in this morning."

"Huh," Granny began, perhaps getting ready to tell him about all of our ghostly visitors during the night. She evidently thought better of it, because she glanced at me with a hint of warning on her elderly face. "We was headin' back to Albuquerque."

"What?" Danny asked me in a worried tone. "But you're here to help sell the hotel. Get those ghosts under control so buyers won't be scared off with all the trouble they might cause."

"That deal was between you and Twila," I reminded him. "We haven't been able to talk to her and see if she wants us to stay with Karen gone. Besides, I've been around enough crime scenes to know we won't be allowed access to the hotel for days, maybe weeks. And I've got Christmas shopping to do."

"Oh, don't worry about access." Danny waved a hand as though to push away the problem. "I've already talked to the medical examiner. He's ruling Karen's death undetermined until all the evidence the techs gathered is processed. And the sheriff said they've done all they can until the lab results come in, so he's releasing the hotel. He also said the techs really didn't find a thing in that room except dust and Karen's blood."

"W-w-what?" I sputtered. ""What sort of medical examiner do you have here? That woman was murdered! No way could she have cut off her own hands!"

And what about that pentagram on the door? I kept that inside, though, because...well, hell, even then I knew we would hang around if possible. My darn curious mind was as interested in the crime here as it was the ghosts, already examining things I'd noticed. And I still caught myself being reluctant to discuss things with Danny.

"That's right," Granny confirmed. "I didn't see that there body, but Alice told me what it looked like."

Danny shrugged. "All I know is what Eddie told me."

"Eddie?" I repeated, then recalled the sheriff who had introduced himself to me in the hotel. The one I was supposed to give a statement to before I "left town." Uh oh.

"We was supposed to talk to him a'fore we left, wasn't we, Alice?" Granny said in confirmation to my unspoken reminder to myself.

"Don't worry too much about that," Danny said. "Eddie knows you ladies don't need to be driving these roads. He said he'd call you on the hotel phone and talk to you."

Danny seemed awfully close to the sheriff. Again, Granny voiced my meanderings.

"You seems to know that there sheriff pretty well," she said.

"We all know each other out here," Danny said with another one of those nonchalant passes of his hand. "It can be lonely territory, especially in bad weather. Now, I guess if you were planning to head out to Albuquerque—which I must tell you is a bad idea, since even with this warming trend, it will be hours before that highway is safe for folks unfamiliar with snow driving—I assume you're packed up again. You want me to drive your car over to the hotel for you? We'll get you settled in one of those nice rooms there. I'm sorry you had to rough it in, of all things, a jail cell."

I gazed around me at the drifts, the town streets still covered in several inches of the pretty but potentially deadly snow. I'd already put one dent in the rental, which would thankfully be covered by insurance. Since I'd used my own personal insurance, I imagined my rates would reflect the new claim. I'd had several *claims* the past year or so, all due to the darned messes I got myself in during a ghost/murder investigation.

I handed Danny my keys. "But what about your snowmobile?"

"Would you like to drive it over to the hotel?" he asked with a snappy wink.

I stared at the huge monstrosity. Would I? Damn right! I smiled eagerly and nodded.

"Uh..." Granny spoke up. "...think's I'll ride in the vehicle. An' I kin take the animals with me." She bent down and picked up Miss Molly.

Trucker had different ideas. As Danny and I started over to the snowmobile for him to give me an operating lesson, Trucker padded right by my side. In fact, he kept his large body between Danny and me. At the machine, I had to gently shove him aside so Danny could show me how to run it.

"There's nothing to it," he began. "Even a woman...uh...anyone can drive one of these new machines."

I straddled the smooth leather seat, and Danny reached over and turned the key. The machine rumbled pleasantly between my thighs.

"This is the brake," he said, pointing at the lever below the left handle. "It's an automatic transmission, so all you need to do to go forward is turn that handle where your right hand goes."

I nodded. "Rather like a motorcycle."

"Well, not really, but if you can ride a bike—"

"Not me, Jack. My hus...ex. I'm closer to the ground on this, though, in case I dump it."

"You shouldn't have to worry about that. It rides on a tread. Ready?"

"No," I said adamantly. "Isn't there a helmet?"

"Oh. Yeah, here." He removed a helmet I hadn't noticed snapped around the pole holding a flag, which stuck in the air near the rear of the bike. As I settled it on my head, he went on, "In case you're wondering, the flag's so other riders can see you, if you're travelling in deep drifts. They'll have their own machines running, so probably wouldn't hear yours."

"There aren't any high drifts in this snow."

"No. Just be careful at the corners."

Trucker jumped on behind me, and I knew it would be fruitless to try to remove my pet.

"I don't supposed you have a helmet for Trucker?" I asked, only half in jest. The snowmobile seemed safe enough, but I'd heard stories about people dumping them. It would probably be my own foolishness if I got hurt, my fault if I injured my beloved Trucker.

"No," Danny said with a half-laugh, which I somehow found a hint of smirk in. But I brushed the concern aside in my eagerness to try out this new mode of transportation.

A moment later, I pleasantly buzzed along a few yards behind the SUV. I'd fastened the helmet securely, not so fascinated with learning something new I wanted to forego safety precautions. Trucker snuggled against my back, head over my shoulder to help me keep an eye on the roadway, tongue hanging out the side of his mouth. I'd have to remember to give my pets water when we got settled again. I'd seen them both sniffing and nibbling at the snow, but I'd read somewhere that wasn't a good source of moisture for the body.

* * *

Joleen stared out the upper-story hotel window as the SUV and snowmobile pulled up in front. She'd wondered if she had antagonized Alice when she disappeared from the table. True had given her no alternative, though. He'd appeared behind Alice and glared at her until she de-materialized and followed him.

"Those ladies need to leave here!" he said when they were back in his room at the hotel. He'd pointed at the blood spatters left by Karen's hanging body. "Look what can happen to them. Darn it, Sis. You might be older than me, but I've had a lot more experience with bad guys than you have."

"Then let's leave ourselves, True," she pleaded with him again. But as before, he set those stubborn lips and refused to answer. He only wandered over to the Jack Daniels bottle and stood tracing the outline, back to her. She'd given up and wandered out of the room, then spent the next few hours in the saloon.

Below her now, Alice and that beautiful dog climbed off the snowmobile and the bothersome Danny emerged from the vehicle Alice called an SUV, a square, bulky thing reminding Joleen of an old stage coach box. Danny rounded the truck and helped the elderly Granny out. She carried the gorgeous cat Alice had brought with her, which terrified LeRoy. Danny helped her up the steps to the front door. He opened it with his key, then assisted Granny inside. Alice still stood by the machine, and Joleen realized she was staring straight at her.

Rather than retreat from Alice's gaze, she stood her ground for a few minutes as Danny returned to the truck and started carrying suitcases up the steps. On his return trip, Joleen left the window and went down the hall to the other place that drew her in the hotel, Marina's room.

"Oh, my friend," she mused as she went through the door without bothering to open it. "Why didn't you stay behind, too? Maybe between the two of us, we could have talked True into crossing over. But even knowing he'll probably see you when he does won't get him moving."

The room wasn't anything special, and didn't even need a window air conditioner. One set of owners over the years had even put carpet on the bathroom floor, to try to help counteract the cold often permeating the air in here. Most of the owners who did accept the paranormal believed Marina herself haunted here. They didn't know she had gratefully gone into The Light when she died, hoping to find True. Joleen impersonated her friend once in a while, as much to keep her memory alive as anything else.

Joleen noticed a rose out of sync in the bouquet on the dresser on the far side of the room. She started over to correct that, but halted and stared at the floor, then around the room.

"Marina?" she whispered. But as usual, she received no answer.

She'd developed her abilities a lot over the long years she'd existed in this state, and she bent to pick up the tiny, fluffy white feather on the floor. On her palm, the brilliance glowed as though lighted from within. It had to be a feather left by Marina. Marina had loved the white doves she tamed for pets.

Her friend hadn't penned the doves up. She had one of the workers her husband, Harvey, kept around build a coop, kept food and water out, and missed them when they left in the fall. They always returned in the spring, though. The first year after she and Marina met, her friend had given her a beautiful scarf she knitted, with some of the white feathers woven in. The scarf had disappeared after Marina's death, and Joleen always suspected her friend's husband had destroyed it, as he had tried to do with all remembrances of his first wife.

She clasped the feather firmly and carried it with her to True's room. He didn't bother to turn when she entered, although she knew he could sense her presence. Silently, she laid the feather on the dresser beside the whiskey bottle and left. True would know where she got the feather. It wasn't the first one she'd found and passed on to him.

In the hallway, she paused and looked back. True still had his back to her, but the feather had disappeared—hopefully, into True's hand.

Downstairs, she watched Alice and Granny settle into a room with a twin bed against each wall. A fireplace stood in between the two outside windows, kindling and a few smaller pieces of wood laid over a pressed fire log. Larger logs filled the carrier beside the hearth. Most of the rooms had fireplaces, and over the years, those commercial fire logs became prevalent for convenience.

"If it wasn't such a climb," Danny said, "you could have one of the suites upstairs. But there's no elevator, and I don't think Granny should have to go up and down those stairs. But you'll have to use the bathroom across the hall with this room."

"It's all right," Alice told him. "We probably won't be here that long. As soon as Twila gets here, we'll get this ghost thing over with and leave."

"Good," Danny replied with a nod. "Twila can use the room next door. There's even a connecting door between the two rooms." As Alice and Granny opened their suitcases on the beds, he went on, "We stocked the kitchen for you, since that restaurant we ate at last night is only open for evening meals. I'm sorry I didn't think to get you some of the fresh food last night to take to the jail with you."

Sure he didn't, Joleen mused. He'd had too much to drink to think of that.

"I've even asked one of the summer girls to come in and do the dishes and clean up for you," Danny told them. "You won't have to bother about that."

"Reckon I been doin' dishes for 'most eighty years," Granny said. "An' cookin' and cleanin', too."

"I wouldn't think of it," Danny said. "You ladies are here as our guests."

"We're here to work for you," Alice corrected him. "And I don't recall whether or not Twila said we were getting paid."

"Your aunt refused to take anything except the promise of expense reimbursement and a week of free rooms now and next summer," Danny said.

Alice nodded, an expression on her face as though Danny had passed a test. Joleen had been there when she and Twila talked during the phone conversation about the request to come to the hotel. She and Twila never accepted any sort of payment for their investigations. But they did love to travel and stay in interesting historical places, so when Twila told Alice about Danny's offer of free accommodations later, Alice had eagerly agreed.

It was going to take them a while to settle in and be ready to talk to her and Gil again, so Joleen left before Alice or Granny could detect her presence and floated back toward Marina's room.

* * *

As I had when she left the second-floor window, I watched Lady float away, not revealing her presence to Danny. I still didn't understand why I kept testing the man, but I did. He'd been quite the affable pilot during our balloon rides. And I didn't believe Twila would have agreed to help him if she were suspicious of his motives. Still, we'd both been fooled by underhanded people before. Instincts as to a person's inner morality wasn't our strongest psychic power.

The roar burst overhead without warning. All three of us cringed our heads into our shoulders and stared up. Of course, we couldn't see anything. The ceiling was overhead. Trucker barked ferociously and disappeared out the door, Miss Molly hot on his huge heels. Granny and I went after them.

Well, Granny toddled far behind me, using her walking stick to try to up her pace. Knowing my friend, she was anxious rather than fearful of the noise, as I was. I didn't bother to see if Danny joined us. I assumed he would.

I caught my pets at the door, prancing in impatience. They couldn't open it themselves. I didn't, either. I pushed aside the window curtain

127

to try to see what was going on. I had to shift a couple times before I pressed my face against the cold pane and gazed toward where the noise appeared to be centered. If the loud roar hadn't been enough, the snow whipping up in a high flurry indicated where things were happening.

A helicopter landed on the street, rotors whirring so rapidly they made an illusionary complete circle in the air above the body of the copter. The snow the blades kicked up enveloped everything, hiding the occupants. After a moment, the pilot must have turned down the power, because the blades slowed until they circled lazily, and the snow settled down.

The pilot-side door opened, and a man climbed down. First, he removed a huge suitcase, then two smaller satchels and set them in the snow. Then he held up a hand to assist his passenger out.

She was trussed up for the cold, boots, snow pants and a ski jacket. Only a set of earmuffs protected her head, though, and I'd know that shiny red hair anywhere.

"Twila!" Granny and I both squealed in unison. I hadn't realized Granny had joined me at the window, and I squeezed her shoulders in delight.

"She's finally here," I said, releasing Granny and heading for the door.

"Me'n Miss Molly'll wait here," Granny said.

"Good idea," I said as I opened the door and Trucker and I tore out.

My dog made it fine. I'd forgotten how slippery the snow-covered sidewalks could be. But I did myself proud. I caught myself on the first slide before I ended up on my tailbone. More carefully, I made my way down the steps and up the street to where the copter had landed.

Twila immediately held up a forestalling hand, and I knew what she was going to say before she said it. I was right.

"Now, Alice, I'm not considering this ride something to cross off our bucket list. We'll still do a helicopter tour together one day."

I tossed her a phony scowl, stifling my grin. We had a long bucket list, things to do before we entered The Light ourselves. An unspoken pact to do them together existed, but once in a while, circumstances interfered. A tiny bit of competition also festered between us.

Though only four years older than me, my aunt did serve as a guiding hand, especially in the ghost business. As to life experiences, I once in a while beat her to the punch. Seems she had the most fun experience this time, however. A faint twinkle of one-up's-manship glowed in her pretty brown eyes.

I allowed myself a tiny smirk. Nodding behind me, I said, "Well, I drove a snowmobile first, so I'll keep that one on our list, too, for us to do together some day."

Then, forgetting about any rivalry, I grabbed her in a death-grip hug. "I'm darned glad you're finally here."

"Me, too," she agreed, returning the tight embrace. "It's always too long in between our times together, and phone calls don't always suffice. I'm not sure what we've gotten ourselves into this time, but we'll see it through together."

I pulled back and studied her face. If she was worried about this investigation, I wasn't sure I wanted to stay.

"Maybe we should hitch a ride back in the 'copter," I said. "Granny and I were just talking about leaving here and spending a day or so in Albuquerque."

"No," she said with a somewhat sad shake of her head. "I have a feeling whatever happens here is part of our destiny. When someone asks for our help, we shouldn't ignore the gifts the Universe gave us."

I gritted my teeth. There would be no arguing with her when she set her mind to something.

"Well, at least tell me how on earth you managed to catch a ride in a helicopter to get here."

"Danny," she said, then went on without further explanation, "Let's get up to the hotel so you can show me my room."

I made a mental note to dig into her lack of information later as she grabbed the large suitcase and pulled out the handle to roll it behind her. That left me in charge of the two smaller satchels, one of which I recognized as containing a multitude of consecrated and blessed protection materials. My similar bag now rested back at the hotel. Still, sometimes Twila brought things she had sensed might help in a certain investigation, or even new things she had learned about through some of her paranormal contacts. I picked up the protection satchel first, then started to get the other one. Trucker beat me to it, and took off after Twila, bag dangling in his strong jaws.

I glanced at the pilot, but he was already climbing into the 'copter.

"Soon as you get out of the way, I'll take off," he said. "Don't want to blow you away."

Taking his caution to heed, I trudged after my aunt and pet.

CHAPTER 15

After Twila greeted Danny and left her suitcase and satchels in the room she would use, she said, "I saw a room with a card table on a television show about this hotel. Isn't it close?"

"Next one down the hall," Danny said. He walked out of the room, and we followed.

Danny opened the door on the card room and people and animals trooped in. A round game table sat in the middle of the space, a window on the wall behind it. Four chairs surrounded the table, one for each of us to sit. Which we did when Twila motioned.

"Now," she said, eyes on Danny. "Refresh us on what sort of problems the ghosts here are causing."

"Still the same ones I told you about on the phone," Danny said.

"Tolerate my forgetfulness," she said, although I knew her mind was just as sharp as Granny's. "Tell me aloud. I want the ghosts here to know what behavior we won't put up with. What we're here to discipline them for. Over the years, I've found it best to let the accused know what accusations are leveled against them."

Danny cringed and glanced around the room. "Are they here now?"

"Some," Twila informed him.

Appearing on the verge of flight, Danny was probably aware that if he gave in to his desire, we'd pack up our belongings and head out, also. We didn't believe in being evasive with ghosts. They needed direct confrontation and castigation for any and all illicit actions, a lot of those the same ones not acceptable in their living lives.

"Well," Danny finally said around a release of breath, "they cause the internet site where we have the sales information to crash."

"That appears to be quite the stretch of paranormal abilities for a ghost," I put in.

Twila shrugged. "Since I have no idea how all this byte and wireless stuff works, I'll bow to your judgment on that, Alice. What else, Danny?"

"We can't keep a For Sale sign up out front. It's either yanked out of the ground and tossed down on its face or sometimes even missing. And whenever Maddie, the real estate agent, brings a prospective buyer through for a tour, doors slam, and she hears chains rattle. Moans and all those...ghostly noises."

"I just thought of something," I said. "With Karen dead, won't the hotel be involved in probate? Until that's settled—"

"Karen gave me a Power of Attorney," Danny said. "She doesn't live in New Mexico, and she didn't want to be bothered with all the closing paperwork. Or the appraisals, all that stuff. Maddie's in her sixties, so she was more than happy to let me handle some of that for her. I checked with an attorney friend of mine before I came over here this morning. I read him the document, and he said given the language in it, the POA's still valid for us to go ahead with the sale."

"You don't live here in Red Dollar, either," Twila said. "Isn't Roswell your home?"

"I've got a summer cabin in the area," Danny replied, but didn't bother to give us any direct information as to its location. "And you can see I have a snowmobile to get around in bad weather, so I'm in good shape to stay here and help."

"Where does...did Karen live?" I asked.

"Arizona," Danny answered.

The crash that split the air sounded as though every dish in the kitchen had smashed to smithereens. I gasped, and met Twila's eyes before I moved an inch, although Danny and Granny were already on their feet, heading toward the door.

"Wait," Twila ordered the other two without taking her gaze from mine. Then she stood. "Alice and I will go check. You both stay here."

"Trucker, guard!" I added, so my Rottweiler would remain with them, on the lookout for danger.

"But you might need me...." Confronted with Twila's don't-be-stupid gaze, Danny shut up.

The two of us rushed down the hallway and turned left through the saloon, toward the kitchen. The noise had ceased, but the moment we opened the door, we both screamed and dropped to the floor like old timey gunfighters killed with one bullet. The two knives whooshed over our heads and buried themselves somewhere behind us with a *twang!*

"Are you all right?" Danny yelled, evidently having heard our screams.

"Stay there!" Twila yelled back.

We both scrambled up and took shelter against the wall, one on each side of the doorway.

"Now what?" I asked in an angry rather than frightened voice. "Who the hell is that and what are we going to do to him?"

"Her," Twila said. "I think it's the woman who was killed here."

"Karen? Shit. She's got to be royally pissed and bent on revenge."

A flurry of pots and pans flew out the door, landing with crashes and thuds on the floor and pool table behind us. An inane thought popped into my mind.

"How the hell's she throwing things without any hands?"

"Now, now, Alice, you're going a bit overboard with the cursing," Twila chastised.

"Sorry. But how is she? She can't have been dead long enough to develop pitching power."

"We don't know for sure how quickly ghosts can develop," she reminded me, "We're always learning new things."

She eased her head around the door jamb.

133

A heavy cast-iron skillet zoomed out, far above Twila's head, but the angry fire that suited her red hair flashed in her brown eyes as she jerked back. Her gaze searched the room behind us, and paused on the huge mural painted across the back wall. I examined it a bit closer for the first time. In it, Lady in Red flirted with two cowboys at a card table. The one she leaned the nearest to was Gambler Gil. The knives that had whizzed past us were buried in the chest of a bartender, wiping a beer glass with a stained towel.

Not finding what she wanted, Twila ordered, "Wait here. I'll be right back." She rushed past the door fast enough for the teapot to miss her, then paused a few steps away from me. "And don't try to handle anything yourself."

Ha! I wasn't about to confront this antagonistic ghost on my own! As she raced off, though, I found I didn't have a choice.

A ball of red burst out the door. It landed on top of the pool table and flared into a human: a naked mid-forties woman, whose blue eyes centered on me and glared daggers of hatred. She raised one handless arm and pointed.

"You can see me! Can't you?" she demanded.

"Uh...no...uh...well...yes, but...."

"Don't lie to me!" she screamed, although I was fairly certain the words only sounded in my mind. There was a hollow effect to them, indicating telepathic communication. "I've been lied to far too many times in the past few months!"

I stood my ground and waited for Twila to return. In the meantime, maybe....

"Who lied to you?" I questioned.

She frowned, a tiny bit of her fury deflating with her slumping shoulders. "I don't know. Darn it, it's all so confusing."

"I can talk to you...help you figure things out," I soothed in a soft voice.

"Sure," she sneered. "Just like...like...."

Her frown deepened. "I can't remember who," she wailed.

Then she disappeared in the blink of an eye as Twila rushed up.

"Shoot," my aunt said. "She's going to be a troublesome one. We can't even keep her around to reason with her."

I was glad she used *we*. A measure of guilt at not handling Karen better intruded on my senses. No doubt that was who the ghost was. The handless arms proved her identity, even if I hadn't recognized her from her body in True's room.

"It was Karen," I informed her. "The woman we found hung."

Yeah, and there's still a mess in my room.

"And that's True," I told Twila, knowing she had heard the communication. "He's Lady in Red—Joleen's brother. We've made contact also with a ghost we call Gambler Gil, although his name is just Gil. He's Joleen's boyfriend, and Granny's latest male attraction. See that mural back there?"

She examined the painting and nodded.

"The one in the red dress is Lady. Joleen. She's got her hand on Gil. I don't know who the guy that ended up with the knives in his chest is."

She didn't appear interested in the painted players in our drama.

"There's more," I said, "but you keep looking back toward where Danny and Granny are waiting. Maybe we should finish our discussion with Danny before I tell you everything else."

"Probably," she agreed. "Unless this True wants to talk further."

Silence met our ears and psychic minds. But now was as good a time as any to start making True understand I was tired of his attempted manipulations.

"True's already ticked me off," I told Twila, sensing that, though the ghost wouldn't talk, he hovered nearby. "He's about as uncooperative a ghost as I've ever encountered. He's so obnoxious, I don't understand why his sister refuses to cross through The Light and stays around here to be with him. Gil's probably only doing it because he cares about Joleen. So far, though, all I've seen as far as True goes is a moody, selfish moron who's too involved in his own misery to care about anyone else."

"We can banish his butt with no trouble," Twila said, joining in on my quest to start the discipline it would take to handle the problematic True. "At first, I'd consider just doing a partial banishment. Leaving him wander around cut off from the hotel until he decides to cooperate. But if he causes too much trouble or intrudes on our attempts to calm this place down, we can make the exile permanent. Then he can meander around unfamiliar territory until he finds another set of more compassionate ghost hunters to help him out."

"Yep," I said.

We both waited for a response from the recalcitrant ghost, but the only recognition we got was a brilliant burst of white that formed into a large orb, zoomed through the back wall, and disappeared.

"There's more to that one than we've learned yet," Twila mused. "I'm sensing a star-crossed lover complication."

"We can't let that make us sympathetic to him," I reminded her, a rule she had taught me herself.

"Right. We just need to take everything into consideration to control this one. It will make us stronger than him when we eventually do confront him."

"Oh." I should have known she had a reason for her conclusion.

Before we left, we grabbed an armful of the pans and skillets scattered behind us and walked in to inspect the kitchen. We laid the pots and pans on the counter, then stared around. There wasn't a sign of any broken dishes. In our experience, that was realistic in a location infested with paranormal activity. Many times there were sounds of violence or breaking glassware or dishes, even moving furniture. Yet upon examination, nothing would be out of place or broken. We had no idea how the ghosts or other entities were able to manifest such noises without actually causing the destruction or furniture dislocation, and neither did any of the other investigators we chatted with. So we only shrugged.

My stomach growled, reminding me we hadn't eaten breakfast yet, so I opened the refrigerator door and found it well-stocked. The freezer portion held several white-paper-wrapped meats, identified in black marker as steaks, pork chops, chicken patties, etc. Further examination of the cabinets revealed just about anything we could want to prepare our own meals.

"I'll fix us something to eat in a bit," I told Twila.

To quell my stomach for now, I grabbed a package of white-powdered-sugar donuts before we headed back to the card room.

Danny and Granny waited with my pets. Granny sat at the table, dealing out a hand of solitaire from some cards I'd noticed lying on a shelf. Danny stood at the window, and he turned at our footsteps, apprehension on his face.

"What was going on? And how much damage was there?" he asked.

"Nothing like it sounded," Twila told him. "We'll handle it. And right now, we need a little time to get more settled in and talk among ourselves. Leave us a key for the front door, and we'll see you later."

Appearing quite willing to take orders from a woman—or perhaps just to escape the haunted hotel—Danny dug in his pocket and gave Twila a key already connected to a keychain containing an inlaid photo of the hotel.

"When do you want to talk to me again?" he asked, already heading for the doorway.

"We'll let you know," she said, then quietly gazed after him until we heard the front door shut. "Let's go to my room. I want to set out some protections."

Granny, my pets and I followed her. I opened the door between our rooms and Granny sat at a small lady's desk in Twila's room with her cards and started a new game. As Twila dug in her satchel and started removing items, I set my pets up: water and food bowls, Miss Molly's portable litter box. I carried a collapsible pitcher with me to the bathroom across the hall and returned to fill the water dishes to the brim. Both pets immediately walked over to quench their thirst.

In her room, Twila had some candles burning and a few things lining the top of the fireplace mantle. I didn't bother to examine her preparations. Whatever she put out would be meant to protect us. She carried some more things into mine and Granny's room and set them around.

"How did Danny afford that helicopter ride for you?" I asked without preamble.

"That's been bothering me, also." She sat down on the bed Granny was using. "I called him when my red eye landed in Albuquerque. I didn't even have to leave the airport and find a room to wait until the mountain passes cleared. He sent the pilot to meet me and take me over to the helicopter. Then we flew here."

"There's more to this than just ghost busting," I declared.

"Yes, but we do have some ghosts here that need our help. You know how we work. The dead are more important to us than any of the livings' illicit activities."

"Yeah, like the time we almost got blown up by a bomb in that old hotel in Mineral Springs!" I reminded her.

"There was that," she agreed. "So I guess we better keep an eye and ear out in both worlds."

Granny toddled in and sat beside Twila. "When's we gonna get to talk to that there handsome Gambler again?"

Twila laughed and hugged her. "It's so good to see you. And we'll try to round up our ghosts after Alice cooks breakfast."

Granny glanced at me with a frown. "Mebbe I ought's to help her out. Spire of what she says, she ain't that she a bad cook, when she puts her mind to it. She just gits distracted now an' then."

"Now, Granny," I said. "Just because I forgot to set the timer and hurried back to my computer when a manuscript problem solution came to me."

"She's didn't even notice the smoke pouring out the winder." Granny shook her head. "But I's did. An' I didn't embarrass her by callin' the Fire Department."

"No, you didn't." I sighed. "You just called me, and I got the fire out myself. But you did mention it to Jack the next time he came around."

She grinned and stood. "My belly thinks my throat's cut. We's gonna do some cookin' or not?"

I'd forgotten about the donuts, and I opened the bag and offered it to Twila first. She took a few, as did Granny. Carrying the sack with us, I munched on the walk to the kitchen. Granny and I both ate about a half-dozen of the small pastries, enough to take the edge off our hunger.

* * *

An hour later, we sat around one of the smaller cafe tables, tummies full and minds refueled by starch and sugar to work on the ghostly problems. Twila had sat in a chair facing the mural this time, and she glanced at it a couple times, but didn't discuss it.

"Go ahead and tell me what's been going on since you got here, Alice," Twila said. "Then we'll decide what our next step is."

I started with seeing Jack in Albuquerque, although that didn't have a thing to do with our presence here. Still, that veered into the first elk, led into my tale, and ended up with the second elk and our current situation. Since I'm a writer, I always tell a good tale. A written one, anyway. Granny piped up now and then to interject anything I verbally left out.

She finished up for me, "An' Alice didn't burn my eggs."

Twila shuddered. With an egg allergy, she didn't even like the mention of those orange orbs surrounded by white, no matter how appealing they looked on a plate. She even closed her eyes when she had to crack one for some of the marvelous baking she did.

"So now what?" I asked.

She stood. "Now we track down True and see just what his problem is."

I grimaced. That room up there was already beginning to smell from the dried blood.

"And, she went on, "I've not forgotten about Karen. I feel sorry for her, even if she did try to knock me on the head with an iron skillet. But first, let's go greet our new guest."

"Huh?" I said, then shook my head. If she said someone was coming, then someone was coming. Pets and people all trooped through the saloon and into the lobby to the front door, where just then someone knocked loudly.

"Not psychic," Twila said with a laugh. "I heard the vehicle pull up out front."

"So who is it?" I asked, playfully prodding her to open her senses and try to predict who was at the door.

"We'll see in a minute."

Since she didn't respond to my teasing attempt to prove her abilities,

I didn't know whether or not she hadn't *seen* or didn't know. Probably didn't know. Even as strong as she was, sometimes she—and I—had blocks. My conclusion came because when she drew back from lifting the curtain before she opened the door, a surprised expression filled her eyes, along with a look of delight.

She opened the door and stepped out to hug my ex-husband tightly. "Jack! It's great to see you!"

Trucker and Miss Molly echoed her delight with a woof and meow, while Granny and I waited our turn, my own delay rather unenthusiastic.

Jack returned Twila's embrace, but over her red hair, his gaze centered on me. He wore his ski jacket and the hiking boots he'd had on in the airport baggage area. As soon as Twila released him, he wrapped an arm around me and Granny, who had both stepped out behind Twila.

"Are you two all right, *Chère?*" he asked after he released us but kept one arm around my waist, staring down at me from his over six foot height.

"We're fine." Reluctantly, I pulled away. He might be worried now, but I didn't need psychic sense to tell me how he would express his irritation, perhaps even anger, when he found out we weren't going to leave the hotel just because we'd happened upon a murder. "You must have had a dangerous drive through that canyon I saw on the map between here and Angel Fire."

"I borrowed a four-wheel-drive from a friend in law enforcement out there in Angel Fire. She said it was an extra one they shouldn't need for a few days."

He went on to say something about the storm's path going south, Red Dollar being on the edge so there wasn't that much snow west in Angel Fire, a fact that disappointed some of the skiers. Most of that bounced off me, since I kept hearing *she* linked with the law enforcement official.

"Didn't your friend you were skiing with get mad when you left to come over here?" I interrupted his explanation.

"Naw," he replied. "Since the snow wasn't that great, we weren't missing much." He glanced around. "Too bad they don't have a ski resort here. But then, I left my equipment back in the room."

Damn. He still didn't say whether or not his ski friend was he or she.

We're dee—divorced, I reminded myself for perhaps the thousandth time since we signed those damned papers in New Orleans.

Twila linked arms with Jack. "Let's get inside and shut the door before we lose all our heat. Or get locked out."

Jack bent to pat both Trucker and Miss Molly before he swept Granny into his other arm as he passed her, leaving me to follow behind.

"No wind blowing," he said. "No reason for the door to slam shut."

"I know the combination for the side door in case something like that would happen," I put in, giving Twila a warning nudge not to say anything about prankster ghosts who might decide to play a trick on us.

Unfortunately, I neglected to nudge Granny.

"Alice already got locked outta the jail," she said. "Good thing that there Gambler Gil ghost came by."

Jack halted so abruptly both Twila and Granny lost their grips on him. He turned and stared at me, thankfully with an expression of anxiety rather than anger on his face. His words belied his calm expression, though. "Jail? Ghosts?"

"We couldn't stay in the hotel after we got here, since it was a crime scene," I justified. Wrong response, because *crime scene* only reminded him of the murder he most definitely wouldn't want us involved in. Just because once I'd been accused of one murder. Just because he'd rescued me from landing in a jail cell once. Just because—"Let's go get some coffee. I think we drank it all, but it won't take but a minute to make more."

I strode away from the sigh of disapproval he couldn't stifle, or maybe didn't want to hide. In the kitchen, I busied myself with a new pot of coffee while the others sat at the table we'd been using.

"Want somethin' to eat, Jack?" I heard Granny ask. "Alice made us a purty good breakfast. Even got some cinnamon rolls, tho' they's them ones out of a can."

"I'll have a roll," Jack said. "I grabbed a bite in Angel Fire with Caroline when I picked up the truck."

"Good ol' fashioned name, Caroline," Granny replied, probably fishing for information, given her propensity for curiosity.

Jack laughed. "Her grandmother's name. Believe me, she's way too young to suit a name like that, but she rather enjoys it. They're a historical family in the area, so it's important to them to keep their history alive."

He sure knows a lot about her, I mentally groused, wondering if Granny indeed was trawling for her own information or trying to pull something out of Jack to rouse my jealousy. Granny made no bones about the fact she thought Jack and I should never have gotten divorced.

"She ski?" Twila asked, evidently going for her own pole and worm to dangle for details of Jack's love life.

"No, but her brother does," he said. "He and I were supposed to hit the slopes again this morning."

I'd been too interested in Jack's love life details myself to pay attention to what I was doing. "Ouch!" I jerked my hand away from the hot coffee spilling over the cup, hoping no one had heard my screech of pain.

No such luck, though. Heavy footsteps entered the kitchen as I ran some cold water on the burn.

"What happened, *Chère?*" Of course Jack had been the one to respond, probably with both Twila and Granny's blessing. Come to think of it, probably Trucker and Miss Molly's, also.

"Nothing, nothing." I waved him away. "Just spilled a little coffee."

"Let me see." He was right behind me, close enough to feel the warmth from his body. A warmth I'd always treasured on cold nights....

He pulled my hand from under the stream of water to examine it. I stilled as he grabbed a paper towel and tenderly dried the burn.

"I saw a live aloe vera plant in the entranceway," he said. "Probably part of the decorations they used, thinking it might look like a cactus. I'll get some of it to ease the pain."

He hugged me briefly before he turned away and walked past Granny and Twila, who stood in the kitchen doorway. They didn't smirk until he passed them, then directed their mischievous gazes at me for only a second before heading over to the coffeepot.

"We's'll get the coffee," Granny said. "You let's Jack take care a'you."

Without even bothering to see if I agreed, they filled three more cups and returned to the table as Jack came back with a split aloe leaf.

"Here, *Chère*. Let me see your hand again."

He grasped my hand and tenderly rubbed some of the aloe juice on the burn. The pain receded immediately, as it always did with aloe. When he was done, he started to lift my hand. I thought he was going to kiss it to make it well, but he abruptly halted the gesture and released me to step away.

"Better?" he asked.

"Lots." I chanced a look up at him, my curious brain taking in his face. It appeared benign...except for the tight jaw, as though keeping himself in check for some reason.

Perhaps at the close contact between us?

I sighed, wishing I was right but unable to ascertain whether or not I'd reached the right conclusion. He nodded and left the kitchen, grabbing one of the cinnamon rolls from the tray I had left on the counter as he went.

Heaving another one of those darned sighs that seemed to be becoming part of my personality these days, I stood there another moment. One of our major marriage differences had been my interest in the paranormal and Jack's total disbelief. Even after confronted with undeniable evidence, he refused to accept that area of my interests in life...and death. Maybe we could talk him into heading back to Angel Fire and leaving us alone before we had to deal with any of the problematic entities here.

Twila screeched in anger, then yelled, "I'll make you sorry you didn't go through that tunnel, you creep!" at the same moment Jack shouted, "You sorry s-o-b! Get the hell back here!" and Granny cackled, "Go get 'em, Trucker!" as the dog's furious barks joined Miss Molly's meow-shrieks of fury.

CHAPTER 16

Since all living occupants in the dining area were spoken and accounted for, whatever was causing the disturbance had to be paranormal. Rather than rush into the fray, I decided to let the others handle it. Even though I had a cup of coffee waiting for me, I poured another, dashed in a liberal dose of flavored liquid creamer, and thought yearningly of the full bar close by. I'd be willing to bet there was another bottle of Crown Royal out there, which would taste great in this coffee— as well as lower my stress level. However, that would mean walking out to see what all the ghostly commotion was about.

I grabbed a cinnamon roll and leaned against the countertop to munch.

* * *

Fighting the urge to chase after LeRoy, Joleen remained frozen in her place in the mural painted on the rear wall, although she noticed the new woman's eyes scan over her, leaving no doubt she was aware of her presence. Twila, she'd heard Alice call the woman when she arrived, the

144

person they all had been waiting for. The one who carried a lot of power inside herself and in the satchels she brought along.

Joleen admired this Twila. She'd felt the energy in those bags when she stood at the card room doorway as she tried to eavesdrop. Once again, Twila had immediately noticed her presence, so she quickly left. She wasn't quite ready to deal with either of the new folks, even the handsome man Alice seemed captivated with. Not without Gil to support her.

She didn't have a choice, though. That handsome black-haired, brown-eyed man they called Jack stomped after LeRoy, who had levitated a glass of ice water on the table and dumped it over Twila's head. Twila grabbed a bunch of napkins to wipe her face, then crooked a finger at Joleen in a demanding gesture.

Joleen shook her head, but Twila's glare made her think better of defiance. She emerged from the picture while the woman called, "You might want to get back here, Jack! That's a ghost you're chasing after!"

Something crashed in the saloon. It sounded like someone threw a glass against the wall.

Jack shouted, "You bastard!"

Twila pointed at the vacant chair, her unspoken gesture an order to Joleen to sit her transparent butt down. Then she crossed the room to the hallway to the saloon and stood there shaking her head of red hair.

"Waste of good booze," she said. "But I'd advise you to come on back here, Jack. The next time that one pours whiskey on you, it'll probably be lots more than a shot glass full."

A second later, Jack returned to where they sat around the table. He reeked of whiskey, a grim expression of disgust on his face. He didn't look so handsome now. Instead, he reminded Joleen of a gunfighter she wouldn't like to meet in a dark alley.

Twila shoved the napkin dispenser at him. "There's a sink in the kitchen."

He mopped his face with a handful of napkins rather than head toward the kitchen. "Before I clean up, I want to know what y'all are into here, Twila."

"Not that it's any of your business, Jack." She lowered her brows in a clear warning expression to each and every one of them, directing a particularly strong glance at Joleen. "But I got called here to handle some ghost problems. My plane was delayed, so Alice and Granny arrived before me."

"And walked into a murder." Jack shook his head without waiting for her to respond. "*Ma Chère* needs a keeper sometimes."

"Far as I know—" Twila shot him a grin "— the job's open."

He glanced toward the kitchen, but didn't move.

"Where'd Trucker go?" Twila asked.

"I's grabbed Miss Molly," Granny said, showing them the cat on her lap. "Last I seen of Trucker, he was after that there ghost."

"LeRoy," Joleen said. "He's..." She grimaced. "...a far, far distant cousin of mine."

"Thanks for speaking audibly," Twila said, her tone and expression making Joleen feel better this time. "Jack doesn't hear ghosts."

"Huh?" Jack said. "What am I supposed to be hearin'? Who are you talkin' to?"

Twila sighed, as did Granny, and they shared a look of tolerance.

"How's come Jack seen an' heard ol' LeRoy but cain't tell the lady's here?" Granny asked Twila.

"She's not fully formed enough for his senses to pick up." Twila pointed at the mural on the wall. "See that painting over there, Jack?"

"Yeah," he agreed.

"See that woman in the red dress?"

"There's nothing wrong with my eyesight, Twila. Yes, I see her, too."

Twila nodded at the chair beside where Granny sat with Miss Molly. "Well, she's in that chair. She's one of the ghosts here at the hotel."

He glared at the chair. "One of the problems?"

Joleen cringed, but Twila's comment eased her discomfort. "I don't believe so, although I'm keeping an open mind for now."

"A psychic mind," Jack said.

He got the glare this time, and had the grace to do the cringing.

"I'm going to be talking to her about what's been going on around here," Twila went on. "Since you didn't hear her a moment ago, I can repeat things for you, or you can just sit out."

"About the murder?" he asked.

"Not necessarily. Only if it spills over into what I was called here to take care of."

Jack pulled one of the chairs out from an adjacent table, turned it around and straddled it to place his arms across the chair back. He nodded to Twila to continue, although her expression clearly informed him she didn't need his permission.

"Materialize better," Twila ordered. "I've changed my mind. It's too much bother to repeat everything you say."

Joleen obeyed, and could tell the instant Jack saw her. His face paled, and he sat up in the chair, nearly scooting off the seat before he remembered the chair was turned backward. She smiled flirtatiously at him, receiving not even a hint of response to her charms in return. He recovered quickly, although he didn't relax. Instead, he kept his shoulders stiff, as though prepared for her to lunge at him.

A quick glance at Twila let her know her act would probably meet with tolerance. Instead, she only whispered, "Boo," and Jack's jaw clenched in reaction. But he didn't jump.

* * *

Things had quieted down out in the restaurant dining area, but I still didn't feel like dealing with that. Lack of sleep was catching up to me, although I should have felt guilty. Granny wasn't showing the same effects, and she was quite a few years older. I didn't want to think about how my years at times made me feel like I was closing in on her.

If I could escape the kitchen, I could sneak back to the room. I saw an unobtrusive door on another wall, walked over and opened it. The next room was the formal dining room. Breathing a sigh of relief and tamping down the guilt complex at leaving Twila to handle things, I slinked out the door and closed it silently behind me.

I crept like one of the wraiths Twila and I chased and made it through the lobby to our rooms without discovery. For a few seconds, I debated whether or not to close the door and change into my PJ's, then put out the do-not-disturb sign I found on the dresser. The desire to be clean won. Carrying PJ's, robe and a towel, as well as my toiletry kit, I hurried to the bathroom Danny had told us to use.

The decorations reflected an old-timey elegance, muted yellow cabbage roses that could have been ugly on the wallpaper on the left and right walls. Instead, a mellow background color of faint green worked well. A pedestal sink centered beneath a mirror with an intricately carved wooden frame. The housekeepers must have had to dust that with a toothbrush, but it was spotless. I hung the PJ's and robe on a hook and set my kit on a spindly-legged walnut table in the corner. A plain white outer curtain kept water from spraying across the room. Drawing it and the plastic liner back exposed an old claw foot tub. It set high enough off the floor to tempt a person to use the stool on the yellow bath mat, but I figured I could manage to crawl in without that assistance. I'm not the most stable person on ladders or stools, and I didn't want to twist an ankle or suffer a bruise.

I locked the door and turned on the shower. While the water warmed, I stripped and laid out shampoo, liquid bath soap, loofta, and after-bath lotions. Last came the bottle of body mist Jack had given me for Christmas last year: southern jasmine, my favorite scent. I bit my lips in indecision, then shrugged and put it with the other necessities instead of shoving it back in the kit. If Jack noticed me wearing it, so be it.

In the shower, I luxuriated in scrubbing myself clean for several minutes. I even shampooed and rinsed my hair. I was sitting on the side of the tub, the water still cascading down as I scrubbed at a bit of callused buildup on my heel when the door burst open.

I jumped to my feet and they both slid on the bathtub mat, which was supposed to keep crap like that from happening. My head hit the tiled wall as I fell, then the porcelain rim of the tub.

Blackness descended.

. . .

Cold water in my face woke me. For a moment, I couldn't remember where, even who I was. I inched up to prop myself against the slope of the tub. Inadvertently, the back of my head slid on the wall behind me.

"Ouch!" I tentatively touched the knot protruding from my skull, just above my neck. It felt at least as big as an extra-large egg.

A man whistled, and my gaze centered on the head peering through the shower curtain.

Not bad for an older broad, the ghost said. He looked young, but damn sure not cute. Something caused him to miss handsome by several inches. Maybe his shifty eyes. Maybe his over-large nose and the fact he apparently died after he hadn't shaved for a few days. His beard wasn't a sexy shadow type, either. Instead, the shabby patches of bristle left bare spots on his chin.

He erupted in a snotty, phlegm-filled laugh and ducked back to where I couldn't see him.

Fighting nausea and pain, I scrambled to my feet and twisted off the water knobs. Wrapping the shower curtain around me at first, although the damn ghost could probably see straight through it, I started to step out of the tub.

My damn foot slipped again, but I caught myself on the side of the tub before I fell this time. Still, my knee hit the hard-as-stone porcelain with a thud, and I bit my tongue.

"Damn! Shit! Hell!" I yelled, but that didn't help the pain one iota. I tasted for blood, but thankfully my teeth hadn't penetrated the tongue.

I realized I probably should try to telepathically contact Twila and let her know I was in trouble. But Jack was there, and I was naked. I'd added a few pounds since the divorce, mostly on binges of ice cream and chocolate.

Gritting my teeth, I managed to keep my balance and climb out onto the bath mat. I dropped the curtain and yanked a towel off the rack to wrap around me.

The door still stood open, and I cupped the pain in my head as I peered into the hallway, looking for that blasted ghost. Now that I had a moment to think, although the process had to filter through pain, I realized the snoopy voyeur ghost must be the bothersome LeRoy who Joleen had mentioned—the nasty prankster who showed up at the jail and probably locked me out in the cold.

With shaky hands, I re-gathered my toiletries to carry back to the room to use, rather than try to fight all my hurts in that small space. Out of sight, out of mind, my robe and PJ's remained on the hook behind the door.

I'd taken two steps into the hallway when LeRoy flew past me, Trucker hot on his heels. For some reason, my dog wasn't yapping or growling. I jumped back, but as unsteady as I was, I didn't make it out of the way in time. Trucker's shoulder hit me, and I crashed first into the wall, then to the floor. Trucker skidded to a halt and reversed direction to return to me.

No way would the others not hear that pair of tremendous thuds. Crap, what was I doing? I should be worrying about what further damage I'd done to my already over-abused body. I started to take inventory before everyone arrived, the dog standing over me, whining in distress.

"It's not your fault, Trucker," I assured him. "Here. Maybe you can help me get up before they find me here on the floor."

I laid a hand on his broad back, then removed it to wipe at what I thought might be blood running down my cheek. I didn't see any red, and when I instinctively touched my finger to my tongue, I tasted saltiness.

Tears? Was I crying?

A sob answered me. My own sob.

Foregoing the dog, I scrambled to my knees and tried to stand. The others weren't quiet as they rushed down the hallway.

Jack's arms captured me first. Without even a hint of effort, he swept me up and cradled me, my head on a shoulder I recognized from using it numerous times. I didn't look up to see where Granny and Twila were, but their footsteps halted, then turned and faded. I also heard Trucker's toenails clicking as he followed them, leaving me alone with Jack.

"What happened, *Chère*?" he asked, voice laced with concern.

"I-I-I...." I shook my head, the sobs escalating.

"Did one of these damn ghosts do this to you?" he growled.

"Uh...no...yes...." I quit trying to talk and buried my face in his neck, wetting it with my tears.

Jack moved, and a few seconds later, laid me down on a bed. I assumed we were in the room Granny and I were using, but I wasn't sure. He didn't release me. Rather, he laid down beside me and cuddled me into his arms, letting me wail while he whispered *it'll-be-all-right,* Chère.

At long last my misery abated. However, instead of taking inventory of my injuries, I wrapped my arms even tighter around Jack and went to sleep.

CHAPTER 17

Again, I felt like I'd just closed my eyes when I woke up, this time to someone playing with my eyelids. I resisted the attempt to open them, then caught the scent of man in my bed. Not just any man: Jack. My eyes flew open.

"Huh? Wha-what are you doing?"

"Shhhh. Just need to make sure you don't have a concussion, love," he said. "There's a hell of a knot on the back of your head. What happened?"

I lay still for a moment, events of the past half-hour intruding into the pleasure I couldn't deny as the man I had once loved with my entire heart and soul held me so tenderly. Then I remembered how he'd found me: naked except for a towel, wailing and sobbing in pain and....

The other reason I had dissolved into a tear fountain probably had to do with lack of sleep and anger at my clumsiness. Sometimes it seemed like every step I took ended up in an injury. Hell, once I'd even been shot!

Reluctantly, I tried to push out of his arms, but Jack refused to relinquish his hold.

"I need to check you over and then get you to a doctor, *Chère*. Your eyes look all right, not dilated like you've got a concussion. But I don't like the size of that knot on your head." He lifted up far enough to stare down at my legs, then ran a hand over one of my knees. "Or the look of that bruise. You might have cracked a knee cap."

The feel of his hand on my leg was way too much. In a minute, I'd be going where we both decided not to after we resumed our post-divorce friendship: to that "friends with benefits" place.

I struggled more insistently. He frowned and sat up. I clasped the towel tightly as I scooted to the bottom of the bed and slid my feet to the floor. Not tightly enough, evidently, since one breast threatened to peek over the top of the terrycloth.

I yanked the towel in place, then slid a glance at Jack—chocolate eyes smoky with desire, which had definitely *not* been a problem in our marriage....

He glanced away quickly, and I examined the room just as fast, looking for my robe...which I now clearly recalled hanging in the hall bath. So I tugged the bedspread off and wrapped it around me, then wobbled to my feet to pull the damp towel out from under it.

"I'm all right now, Jack," I said. "Can you go get Twila? Please?"

"No!" he growled, standing abruptly and grabbing me by the shoulders. He firmly but gently pushed me down on the bed and stood over me. "I want to know what happened in there. And I want to know why you were cryin' like that. Did one of those blasted *ghosts* you chase after do somethin'?"

I vacillated between anger at his continued denigration of my paranormal investigating and pleasure at his concern. Unfortunately for Jack, and perhaps for me, too, anger won.

I stood to face him, trying for nose-to-nose even though my five-foot-five fell over six inches short. "I didn't get any sleep last night except maybe fifteen minutes! And yes, it was partly due to some ghosts. And I fell in the tub...due to a damn ghost. I fell in the hall partly due to a damn ghost! I was crying because I'd just about had it with a lot of things about this entire place and the pain probably sent me over the edge! But I agreed to come here to help Twila out. Yes, with some damn ghosts! I mean to do that. Because following through on my commitments means a lot to me! And I'm sick and tired of your attitude about my ghost hunting! Again! For about the fiftieth time! Now get the hell out of here and go get Twila for me!"

I held the bedspread up with one hand and shoved at his chest with the other to squeeze past him. "Forget it. I'll go myself!"

His arm captured me around the waist before I could take that second step. His other arm swept under my knees and lifted me back onto the bed. He released me and I only caught a brief glimpse of his set mouth and eyes stormy with anger now rather than what I'd nearly welcomed, before as he strode off.

"I'll go get Twila."

As soon as he left the room, I slid out of bed. Wavering with dizziness and sore muscles, I staggered across the hall, the bedspread trailing behind me. In the bathroom, I shut the door, then took down my robe. After I shrugged into it, I tossed the PJ's over my shoulder, opened the door, picked up the bedspread and dragged it behind me back to the room.

I found the pervert ghost there. Gritting my teeth, I pretended not to see his leer and tossed the bedspread on the bed before I sat and pulled my own satchel of protection elements from beneath the bed. I set it beside me, opened it, and slid the zipper clasp back on a plastic bag of consecrated sea salt.

Then I acknowledged LeRoy.

"You depraved piece of protoplasm!" I tossed a fat handful of salt on him. He howled in pain.

"Get out of my room! Get out of my life! If I ever catch you spying on me again, I'll make you wish you were more than dead!"

Brushing at his clothing, even though the salt had gone straight through his non-corporal body, LeRoy fled, still bawling his distress. He didn't even bother to de-materialize. He raced out, the echo of his voice tracing his path down the hallway, past the bath.

"Good job," Twila said as she came in, followed by Granny, Miss Molly, and Trucker. "Let me look at where you got hurt."

My cat jumped onto the bed and placed her front paws on my chest to stare into my eyes. I stroked her in reassurance that her mama was all right, then laid her on my lap so Twila could examine me. She inspected the knot on my head, then gestured for Granny to hand her an ice pack I hadn't noticed her carrying. Twila placed it against the knot, murmured, "Hold it there," and knelt to look at my knee. I flinched when she touched it, but bit my lower lip and endured as she ran a finger over the kneecap.

"I think it's just a bruise," she said. Since she had years of nursing experience, I felt good about her diagnosis. "Let me check your eyes. Did you lose consciousness?"

I cooperated as she cupped my chin and stared into my eyes. "For a second or two only. I think. Probably it was more a blackout due to all the stars in my mind from the pain. Do you know, you really do see stars when you hit your head?"

"I've heard that," she murmured. She stroked my cheek before she dropped her hand. "I'd agree you should see a doctor, but I don't know how we'd get there now."

"What do you mean?" I frowned. "Granny and I were getting ready to leave. The roads are clearing."

She sighed. "Not now. Right on the heels of that Chinook, as Granny called it, came a sleet storm. The temperature's dropped about thirty degrees in the last half hour. The helicopter pilot told me there was a Blue Norther blowing in, but the reports said it wasn't supposed to hit until tonight. So much for accurate weather forecasts."

"Yep," Granny agreed. "We's looked outside and they's already ice all over everythin'. Roads, cars, on top of the snow. An'...."

She clamped her mouth shut as she glanced at Twila, her expression indicating she thought she'd blabbed too much.

Twila exhaled before she said, "The phone's out. I think the ice built up and broke the line to the hotel. I can see a black wire on top of the snow, hanging from a pole out by the street."

Not that concerned, I said, "Well, we've got a job to do here. And plenty of food. I saw a couple cases of bottled water in the kitchen. We'll be all right until this lets up."

"I agree," Twila said. "But Jack can't leave, either, even though he wants to. So I'm..." She glanced at Granny. "...we're hoping you and he can work out your differences and get along for a while."

I huffed out a breath. "I'll get along with him as long as he keeps his mouth shut about our ghost hunting."

"Is that what the fight was about this time?"

I paused, not wanting to lie to her. Was that all of it? No, not really. It was also the two of us—maybe more me than Jack—fighting desire. I decided evasion was the better tact for now, at least until I figured things out for myself. As close as I was to Twila, there would probably be a point where I wanted to sit down and talk to her about Jack, but first I wanted to get it straight in my own mind. At least, as much as I could.

"What about the murder?" I asked instead of answering her.

She took the conversation shift like a good sport, probably realizing I would come to her when I was ready. "Granny said you and she were supposed to give statements, but with the phones out, that can't happen. Where's your cell?"

Ice pack still clasped to my head—the throb had eased to a dull roar —I gently shoved Miss Molly to the mattress, stood and limped over to the dresser. When I checked the phone, *no service* stared back from the screen. I shook my head.

"You saw that damn ghost running down the hall, right?" I laid the phone back on the dresser. "The one who caused all my aches and pains? He was even spying on me in the shower!"

She clenched her teeth and included both Granny and me in her next comment. "He's just a trashy piece of bumbling no-good. But he's a ghost, so don't underestimate him. He's got an aura around him that shows he's a muddled mess, so he could go either way in his pranks."

"An aura?" I couldn't stop myself from asking. "Ghosts have auras?"

"I know," she replied. "I've seldom seen one myself, but they do exist. Anyway...." She took my arm and led me back to the bed. "I want you to rest for a while. Get some sleep."

She pulled back the covers, and I slid in. After she smoothed the sheet and blanket around me, she picked up the bedspread and laid it over me, too.

"Lie right here for a few seconds." She hurried into her room and returned with a pretty bas-relief jar in her hand. When she unscrewed the top, a pleasant lavender scent filtered out. She exposed my knee and gently smoothed salve on it. I flinched at her touch at first, but immediately, the pain disappeared.

"Nice," I said. "Thanks."

"It's something I got up in Amish country," she said. "Not one of my own recipes."

"It's wonderful," I said.

"I'll leave it on the mantle. You can use it whenever the pain comes back." She recapped the salve and said to Granny, "You, too. Get some rest,"

"I ain't that tired." But she trudged over to the other bed and allowed Twila to settle her in.

"I'll take over for a while," Twila said as she pulled down the blind on the window and turned out the light. "You two rest so you can help me when I need it. This is far from over around here."

I checked the red glowing numerals on the digital clock on the dresser and hoped the next time I looked at it, at least eight hours would have passed.

* * *

Nope. Only an hour. But it was a good solid hour of deep sleep, one of those down-under rests you hated to emerge from. You could tell your body needed more, and you were luxuriating in the floating sensation of healing rest. You tried everything from ignoring the wakefulness to pulling a pillow over your head, striving to recapture the relaxation and slide back down the ramp into slumber.

The darn gut instinct sensation wouldn't quit, though. Something wasn't right.

I turned my head and slit my eyes to look over at the other bed.

Granny lay there peacefully, not even snoring. I couldn't help watching her closely for a few seconds. After all, I'd brought her here. After all, she was old. After all, she could die peacefully in her sleep. By the time her chest rose slightly and coasted back down, I was wide awake.

Taking care not to wake Granny, I eased out of bed and took stock of my body. Pain, of course, but I decided to forego the salve in case I overused it and it lost effectiveness. The headache was back, but I'd forgotten to ask Twila if it was safe to take anything for it. One step indicated the knee ache would plague me for a while longer, but maybe exercise would help. I hadn't noticed the soreness in my right ribs before, and when I opened my robe and looked, I found the bruise. Nothing broken, though, or it would be far worse than what I now felt.

I quietly limped to my suitcase lying on the luggage rack and removed some clothing. The mattress on my bed was solid and didn't squeak, so I sat back down and dressed in clean underclothes, jeans and a soft flannel sweatshirt with deer standing around a snow-covered pine tree in the woods. Rhinestones outlined the tree and would sparkle in the light. It was one of those semi-gaudy pieces of bling I loved to wear.

Feet encased in warm socks and brown suede flat-heeled boots, I wandered out into the hallway to look for Twila and see if my inner sensation meant she was having some sort of problem with our paranormal inhabitants. Every once in a while, we found we needed our combined powers to handle a sticky or malevolent situation. And besides, I needed to ask her what I could take for my headache, which movement was aggravating.

I didn't find her on the bottom floor, though I didn't search every guest room. She had no reason to be in one of those. I stared at the steps to the upper floor for a moment, dreading the ache the climb would increase in my knee. Heaving a sigh, I started up.

Forced to pause and let the knee recover, I stopped on the first landing. I even patted Ol' Tom on the haunch, then soldiered onward. At the huge painting of the conquistadors, I halted again, but not from pain.

"Huh." The extra explorer stood in that empty spot. He was a shadowy figure of white mist, but I saw him clearly. Wishing I had my camera with me, I nodded at him and went on. He didn't acknowledge my gesture of greeting.

Now which way? I tried to contact Twila with my mind, but the body aches kept me from drawing deep enough to reach that place in my library of senses.

"Ennie, meenie, miney, moe." My waving finger led me to the right, rather than the left, towards True's room. Before I walked off, though, I glanced down the hallway. The transom was open. I'd already figured out that meant the problematic ghost was out roaming. I didn't necessarily care to visit the death site again, but I still wondered why I wasn't being led there.

Knee rested and able, if not exactly willing, to navigate, I walked down the other hall. This time I decided perhaps I should look into the rooms I passed. However, the first door I tried was locked.

Studying the keyhole beneath the doorknob, I pulled out my own door key. I'd automatically jammed it in my jeans pocket before I left the room Granny and I shared, something I did in reaction to the time I got locked out on the balcony of a hotel room in Sedona, Arizona. I'd spent a half-hour in the blazing afternoon sun before I managed to get the attention of a groundskeeper. Unfortunately for me, he wasn't the one who came to my rescue.

"You're not supposed to lock the door behind you when you go out on the balcony," the snot-nosed teen said when he unlocked the sliding glass door.

"No shit?" I'd responded.

Now, I tried the skeleton key from my pocket. As I thought, it fit the lock. And the next one, and the next. All the rooms on the right side of the hallway were empty of living guests, and I was too cranky and cantankerous to check and see if any of the paranormals were about.

I left each and every door behind me open, then started up the other side of the hallway. Near mid-hall, I found a door cracked a couple inches and pushed.

Inside, I found Twila and Jack. Heads bent, they were examining something on the wall in front of them so intently, they didn't hear the faint squeak of the door hinges.

"Maybe we can draw it, Jack," Twila said. "See if Alice can do a search on that computer she carries with her."

"I totally doubt we have internet access with the phones out," Jack replied.

"Isn't what she has called wireless?"

Jack chuckled. "Not that wireless. Me, I don't know how it works, either, but I'm pretty sure you have to have a signal to tie into."

"You do," I said as I walked over to see what had their attention.

They stepped apart so I could view the drawing. I frowned and shook my head. "That thing looks like someone just threw blobs of paint on the wall and then drew circles in it."

"It's not paint, *Chère*," Jack said. "It's blood. I can tell by the smell."

Still working on my emotions, I tried not to acknowledge him. But, hell, that drew my eyes to his. My mouth gaped and I backed away. "Who's?"

A stupid question, of course, but he answered it the only way he could. "No way to tell until we can get a sample to the lab."

"The main thing is," Twila added, and I thankfully edged closer to her, away from Jack, "those circles didn't draw themselves. I think they're important."

"To True's or Karen's death?" I asked.

"Who's True?" Jack asked, but we both ignored him.

"Well, Karen is the only one the blood could have come from," Twila pointed out.

"Not necessarily," I refuted. "It could be blood from someone else. Or animal blood." I gasped and stared around. "Where's Trucker and Miss Molly?"

She patted my arm. "They're both asleep in my room. I frankly didn't want to have to worry about them while I looked around, so I closed my door."

"Did you move Miss Molly's litter box into your room?" I asked with a quirked eyebrow.

Her face fell. "No."

We both hurried toward the door.

"What about this?" Jack called.

"Draw us a picture," Twila said over her shoulder. "You can fax it to the sheriff when we get phone service back."

"Or take a picture with your cell phone," I added. "Even without service, the camera still works."

Twila raced ahead of me, since my knee wasn't cooperating yet. I heard her clamber on down the stairwell and made the mistake of glancing toward the other hallway before I followed her.

I froze.

CHAPTER 18

At first I thought the man walking away from me was Gambler Gil, but I noticed he was shorter, maybe five-eight, a wiry hundred-fifty pounds. He wore black pants and boots, a checkered vest, a black coat jacket slung over his shoulder. With his back to me, I couldn't see his face, but his hair was as black as Jack's and had the same healthy sheen. The pistol slung low on his right thigh and well-cared-for gun belt around his waist would have told me I was looking at a ghost from the Wild West era of the hotel, had my senses not already confirmed it.

"Uh...Twila?" I whispered. She'd already bounded down the steps to fetch Miss Molly's litter box, before we ended up with cat-urine-soaked carpets.

A foot or so behind the ghost, a room door opened silently. Another apparition slipped into the hallway. A sound the figures in the other dimension could hear but I missed must have warned the first ghost. He started to turn.

But the second man already had his pistol out, pointed straight at the first man's head.

Boom!

The first man fell...and so did I. Someone tackled me from behind, and we both crashed to the floor. In a corner of my hearing, I recognized booted footsteps racing towards us.

Boom! Boom!

"What the f—?" Jack's voice.

I tried to rise, but Jack cupped me to his chest and sheltered me with his body. The footsteps clattered past us and on down the adjacent hallway. Jack released me and jumped to his feet. I opened my eyes in time to see him on the verge of chasing after the ghost, aiming his Glock again.

"Don't!" I screamed. "It's a ghost! You can't kill it by shooting it!"

He dropped his pistol, resignation on his face, and...yeah, a blossom of red embarrassment. He finished muttering the interrupted *fuck* from a second ago.

A couple things flashed through my mind: First, I'd just watched True murdered in the distant past, but since Jack tried to protect me from a non-existent danger, I hadn't been able to see the killer's face. Had I managed that, Twila and I would possibly have been able to reason with the rest of the ghostly crew around here and get then to agree to cross into The Light. Joleen wanted the residual haunting to cease. Punishment for the killer wouldn't be possible, but we could publish our results on the internet and maybe satisfy the need for justice. The result would hopefully diffuse yet another residual haunting and leave the hotel in peace for a sale.

Second, Jack was still seeing ghosts. He'd acknowledged that ability in himself a few times before, reluctantly and highly annoyed at having it. He'd seen Sir Gary in Jefferson, Texas, as well as watched the ghost and Bucky, reunited with his missing head, cross over. He couldn't deny also seeing Patrick, who loved to wander around in all his naked glory at the old hotel in Mineral Springs.

In this instance, he had obviously watched the murder go down in full glory, clear enough in his mind to mistake it for an actual event. Intensely enough to pull his own pistol and try to protect me when the killer raced toward us.

"Uh oh." I gritted my teeth at the knee and rib pain my fall had renewed and sat up to stare down the hallway and assess the bullet damage. Traces of gun smoke still lingered in the air. I didn't see True's body lying there, though. And the faint glimmer of a pool of blood faded as I watched.

Sure enough, at the far end of the hallway, past where the events had played out again after so many years, a large hole marred the wide window frame. Luckily, the bullets had missed the panes, but cold air already cascaded in through the ruined wood.

A glance at Jack's face told me this was not the time to tease him about seeing the gunfight or shooting at a ghost. At some point, I did want to question him as to whether he might give me a description of the man who killed True, but not right now.

"Can you help me up?" I asked, keeping my tone of voice as non-provocative as I could. Inside, I gleefully admitted to satisfaction at Jack witnessing the same thing I did. No way could he deny that!

When he hesitated, I went on, "We need to stuff something in the holes you blew in the wood down there. How did you get your pistol on the plane?"

At least he shoved that pistol back into a holster in the small of his back before he held out a hand to me. I reached for him, but instead, he changed his mind and placed his hands under my armpits to lift me to my feet.

"Wow," I murmured. "You must have been working out. I haven't lost any weight, and you're sure hauling me around easily."

The teasing jibe didn't lighten his mood. Releasing his hold on me so quickly I nearly hit the floor again, he glared down the hall, then over his shoulder.

I shrugged and quit evading the confrontation.

"Yes, it was a scene from the past. They were ghosts. I'm pretty sure it was a re-enactment of True's murder. One of the things Twila and I are going to have to solve to do our job here."

"True," he said.

When he didn't go on, I continued, "True won the hotel and a lot of other property from the original owner here. He was killed on his way back to his room that same night. What we just saw. There's more to the story, but right now, could you possibly tell me if you could identify the killer?"

"The killer," Jack muttered. "The ghost who killed another ghost."

"Yeah, that's about it." I stifled the guffaw of laughter threatening to erupt and spoil any chance I had of pulling the information I needed out of Jack.

He zeroed his gaze on me. "You were never in any danger. They couldn't have hurt you or shot you. It happened a hundred years ago."

"A little longer than that," I said. "But can you help Twila and me out?"

He shook his head and walked away, continuing on down the staircase.

"Crap," I muttered instead of the *fuck* that would have mirrored my feelings better. I limped down the hallway to try to find something to stuff in the bullet holes. I'd worry about how to explain those to Danny later.

* * *

I found Jack on a stool at the saloon bar. His poison of choice had always been Jack Daniels, and it hadn't changed. A bottle sat on the polished surface beside him, a half-empty double jigger between his finger and thumb. As I watched, he downed the whiskey and poured another double shot.

The bottle was only about two-thirds full, and I hoped that meant Jack wasn't its first customer. Surely he couldn't have killed all that booze while I stuffed toilet paper in the bullet holes. I'd used an entire roll, and covered the repair with adhesive tape I found in the upstairs bathroom medicine cabinet. I wasn't that handy with do-it-yourself stuff, but I could make do when necessary.

I'd also kept an eye out for LeRoy, but the sea salt had evidently arrested his voyeuristic trait sufficiently.

I started to go to Jack, but noticed a slight stiffening in his shoulders at my approach. Deciding to retreat for the moment, I reversed direction to the lobby. There, I found Joleen.

What happened upstairs?

"I saw part of the incident when True got killed," I answered aloud, but quietly so I wouldn't draw Jack's attention away from his booze. If he found me chatting with a ghost, and was able to see Joleen, he might take the entire bottle somewhere and settle in for a more private drinking session.

Who did it? she asked excitedly.

I shook my head. "I didn't see that part."

No sense in explaining it all to her. I needed to find Twila instead of trying to reason with an apparition who had already proven perverse.

Why not? she insisted.

"Go away." I waved her off and limped toward our rooms.

She, of course, perversely followed me.

But—

I whirled on her so fast, she nearly walked through me. I did feel a shiver of paranormal coldness on the palm I held out to warn her off.

"Did you hear me?" I yelled, forgetting to keep my voice down.

Immediately, footsteps hurried towards me from the direction of the saloon. By the time Jack could see me, though, Joleen had de-material-ized. From the corner of my eye, since I decided not to acknowledge him, I saw Jack shake his head and turn back to the bar. I continued on to my room.

Both doors were closed. I opened the one on mine and Granny's. Neither Twila nor Granny were there, but the connecting doorway was ajar so Trucker and Miss Molly had access to both areas. More importantly, Miss Molly could get to her litter box.

I looked into Twila's room. No one. Where could they be?

I did see the jar of salve in Twila's room, so I limped over to get it. Before I sat down on her bed, I unzipped my jeans and pulled them down to expose my knee. A few seconds later, welcome relief lifted the pain. I even rubbed some on my rib ache. Maybe now I could get some more much-needed rest.

Half a minute later, I kicked off my boots beside my own bed and laid down. Miss Molly jumped up beside me, and Trucker stretched out on the floor where I could touch him if I reached over the side of the bed. I did, and one hand on him, the other stroking my cat, I closed my eyes.

Even though I tried to meditate, which sometimes helped me slip into slumber, I couldn't sleep. So I decided to lie there and think.

Tap-tap-tap.

I frowned, but didn't open my eyes. The noise had to be sleet hitting the window. It came from that direction, and I'd noticed it falling upstairs when I looked out as I plugged the bullet holes with toilet paper.

Tap-tap-tap.

Shoot. I opened my eyes and stared at the window. Through a slit where the blind didn't completely hide the window, I could see tiny beads of sleet bouncing on the glass. The distraction, once identified, ruined any attempt at sleep. My thoughts whirled.

Shifting Miss Molly with me, I turned on my side. Trucker must have missed my touch, because he rose, walked to the foot of the bed and lunged up onto the mattress. I didn't protest when he stretched out behind me, even though he barely left enough room for me and the cat. We'd lain like that more than once, although my king-size bed at home in Six Gun was better suited space-wise.

Six Gun. Gun. Six-shooter. Old West.

Those thoughts rolled over each other in my mind. How many firearms were around us here? True carried a pistol, and so did his killer. No doubt Gambler Gil had a hidden gun or two on his person. No card shark worth his salt would deny that a game could erupt into danger when paired with booze.

LeRoy probably had a pistol, perhaps even a gun belt and holster. I hadn't paid that much attention to him. From now on, though, I probably should take note of the weaponry involved in this paranormal investigation.

Did that frilly skirt Joleen wore have pockets? Probably. And she would carry a lady's derringer, at the least.

Jack's pistol was real-time. He'd never answered me about how he happened to have it with him, but I had recognized it as the one he carried on the job. I'd even gone to the range with him one day and fired it until I felt proficient with the semi-automatic. Being law enforcement, he would have permission to carry it on the plane.

I wondered if Danny carried a gun. Probably, since he had a cabin in the area. To men, that usually meant hunting. They used rifles to kill the animals, but I'd never known a man who owned a rifle and didn't keep a pistol around, also.

Twenty-six men had died here in this hotel, most of them from the Wild West era. I'd lost count of all the guns, but there was enough weaponry around here to reenact the gunfight at the OK Corral, had the ghosts and living inhabitants the desire.

Oh, and one woman had died. Karen. She was in a fine fettle over her death, according to the interaction Twila and I had with her in the kitchen. Her weaponry there had been knives and pots and pans. I didn't know that much about the woman, since she was Danny's friend. However, I imagined New Mexico, like a lot of other states, had enacted a concealed carry law. A woman who worked late in a hotel or carried funds to a bank might avail herself of that law.

I had, as soon as I moved to Texas. Not that I hadn't *carried* anyway when on a lonely trip, and even sometimes when Twila and I travelled. I grew up a tomboy, guns and fishing poles childhood toys.

I already knew I wasn't going back to sleep. For one thing, the niggling worry over not finding Twila and Granny anywhere wouldn't die. Oops, wrong word to use in this situation. Jack might have seen them on his way to the saloon. I should brave our redundant argument and go ask. Plus I hadn't checked the second floor. Maybe they'd gone up there.

Giving Miss Molly one last stroke, I tossed back the covers and scooted between the two animals to the foot of the bed. My cat re-snuggled, this time beside her huge constant companion.

CHAPTER 19

Had her hair not been ghost hair, Joleen would have snatched herself bald. Irritation boiled into fury, directed at everyone here in the hotel, living...or dead like her. Directed specifically at the new ghost prowling around, who had stayed just out of reach of contact. How dare Karen get murdered and spoil all Joleen's carefully laid plans to finally reason with True and persuade him to cross into The Light with her and Gil. Joleen's anger at Karen cemented when Alice yelled at her. Part of Alice's ire had to do with LeRoy, of course, but Karen's presence complicated matters.

She would take care of LeRoy second. First, she needed to deal with Karen.

No brand new ghost had ever inhabited the hotel during all Joleen's years of being one herself. The few glimpses she did catch of Karen indicated the woman who owned the hotel...used to, since Joleen didn't believe ghosts could possess property...embraced a wrath rivaling Joleen's right now. Joleen couldn't even blame her own pissed-off state on a monthly, since she hadn't been pestered by that bothersome female trait in her current state of being.

She had to get rid of the interfering Karen. Until she attacked Twila

169

and Alice, Joleen had been willing to ignore the most recent ghost. Now, though, she'd seen the woman hovering one too many times. And bushwhacking Alice and Twila couldn't be tolerated. Despite Alice's prickly attitude, she and Twila had a job to do here for Joleen and True. There was a cop on the premises. If Karen wanted something, she could contact Jack!

Joleen stomped through the lobby into the hallway, wishing her footsteps could sound out her fired-up temper. Once in a while noises did penetrate from her dimension into the one humans occupied, but she'd never understood how and couldn't control that. She glanced at Jack, still sitting on the saloon barstool. He'd pushed the whiskey bottle aside, evidently satisfied with the amount of liquor he'd consumed.

As she passed the guest rooms the women were using, Alice rose from her bed. Not wanting another confrontation from the currently unfriendly woman, Joleen hurried on down the hallway, sticking her head in each room as she passed. Once nice thing of her existence— which she otherwise had come to intensely dislike—was being able to float through obstacles. At the end of the hall, instead of having to return to the stairwell, she levitated onto the second floor.

Appearing outside her friend Marina's room, Joleen looked in the open door. Yes, there were Twila and Granny. They weren't talking. Instead. Granny stretched out on the high double bed—Twila had probably had to help her up there, even given the padded step stool dating from Marina's occupancy. Twila rocked in the chair in front of the window as she stared through the ice-covered glass pane. Joleen doubted Twila could see much. Even then, the objects would be distorted.

She started to ask Twila why they were here instead of their own rooms, then noticed the white feather on the windowsill. Twila must have found it, and maybe she was trying to contact Marina. Joleen questioned whether her friend would show herself. Marina hadn't responded to any of Joleen's pleas over the years.

She didn't think her presence reflected in the ice, so when Twila turned to look at her, the psychic probably sensed Joleen. For a second,

Joleen waited for Twila to yell at her, but the woman's face remained serene and non-intimidating.

Uncertain yet around the senior ghost hunter, Joleen hurried to True's door. The transom was open, True out somewhere, but Joleen floated on in. She hoped someone would send a cleaning crew in here soon. Even in her state, she could smell the odors of blood and bowel content.

Karen could probably smell it, too. Her nose was wrinkled in distaste when she jerked around to face Joleen.

"Who the hell are you?" Karen demanded.

This was the closest Joleen had been to Karen since the woman died. She'd seen her around the hotel numerous times in life, of course, both alone and escorting potential buyers with or without Maddie, the real estate lady. Her body wasn't bad for her age, which Joleen put at early forties. A bit of a droop to her breasts, and a slight paunch to her stomach, some nearly invisible wrinkles on her face. In her apparitional state, her blue eyes and tongue didn't protrude as a result of her hanging death, but her face hadn't yet lost the dark discoloration.

The other woman shoved back a dangling lock of once-silky black hair with a forearm missing a hand, blue eyes spitting rage. Joleen couldn't really blame her. It was bad enough being a ghost, but at least Joleen had all her human parts.

The old adage, *You catch more flies with honey than vinegar,* went through Joleen's mind. She did her best to restrain her anger.

"Look," she said, "I've been around long enough to maybe help you out." She lowered her gaze to Karen's breasts, then quickly pulled it back up to the other woman's face. "At least help you get cleaned up. Find something to cover yourself with."

"What I want to *find,*" Karen spat, "is my hands!"

"I understand. But don't you want to put on some clothes?"

"I really don't give a damn. If anyone who can actually see me doesn't want to look, they can shut their stupid eyes!"

"That's your choice."

Karen's eyes lost some of the anger sparks. She sniffed, but not from

171

impending tears. "I suppose a shower wouldn't hurt. I loved reading about the Wild West when I...was alive."

So Karen did realize she'd died. Joleen nodded, and Karen kept talking. "What a hell of a way to die. You lose control of your damn bowels."

Joleen didn't remember Karen's language being so foul the times she'd seen her in the hotel. However, she'd been on display as the owner, so perhaps she'd monitored her speech.

Karen held up her arms. "But I need my hands to turn on the damn shower spigots!"

"I could do that for you," Joleen offered. "There's a shower in the next room."

She floated over to True's closet and manipulated one of his longer white shirts off a hanger. It had yellowed with age, but remained a touchable, soft cotton. She'd lost count of the times a change of hotel owner had resulted in that room being cleaned out. And lost track of the damages they suffered until they left the room alone and allowed True to return both his ghostly presence and personal items to it. The first couple times, she and he both had to use their developing abilities to move the Jack Daniels bottle, but then True handled everything himself.

"We'll take this shirt with us for you to wear afterwards."

"But won't the water just flow right through me? I read about ghosts, too, when I was alive. I was fascinated by stuff like that. I don't recall anything about them being able to shower."

"Probably none of the ghost hunters ever thought about that," Joleen answered. "But I've taken plenty of showers in my condition. You have to concentrate on your body. Like when you appear in front of someone."

Karen nodded. "I did read stories of ghost hunters finding shower curtains and bathtubs wet when they didn't think there was anyone around. Let's go."

Karen started for the door, but Joleen said, "This way."

She went through the wall first, and a second later, Karen joined her in the bathroom, a satisfied look at passing through the wall on her face. Joleen turned on the faucets. With a sigh of anticipation, Karen stepped through the curtain, into the tub.

At first the water did slice through Karen with no effect. But the woman closed her eyes, and within a few seconds, solidified enough for the water to wash over her body. She circled to focus the stream on her back, where most of the blood and other mess had dried.

Through a gap, Joleen watched, in case Karen needed her assistance. The other woman stood under the water for a while, letting it sluice away the blood and grime. She turned a few more times, and pink and gray water flowed down the drain.

"Wish I could wash my hair," Karen murmured.

"Want me to help?" Joleen asked. "I've got hands."

Karen stared at Joleen in indecision.

"Oh, don't worry about that," Joleen said. "I'm only into men."

Besides, Joleen continued in her thoughts, who would be turned on by that mutilated body? Poor woman.

Joleen squirted the shampoo the hotel left for guests onto Karen's hair and massaged it clean. As Karen rinsed, Joleen poured some bath gel on one of those modern net-things and washed off any remaining traces of dirt and blood. When they were done, she helped Karen dry as well as she could and into True's shirt.

"Let's go in another room and talk," she urged.

"What about?" Karen said as Joleen fastened the last button.

She answered as she stifled her distaste and rolled back the sleeves to expose Karen's maimed stumps. "I think you should ask Alice to help you cross on through The Light. You'll be happier over there."

"Forget it," Karen said. "I'm not going without my hands."

"You'll have new hands over there," Joleen reasoned.

"You don't get it. Whoever has my hands is probably the one who killed me. And I want his ass exposed and punished! I won't rest until then. And I'm not crossing over until then!"

"Didn't you see who hung you up there?"

"I was drugged. And whatever they gave me also destroyed my short-term memory. I'm hoping it will come back."

Too bad, Joleen mused. Had Karen known her killer, she and Joleen could go to Jack. Now that the cop had admitted seeing ghosts, he might be made to listen to crime evidence, even brought to him by an apparition.

"Look, you're complicating matters here," Joleen said. "I've got a plan I've been working on for years. I'm sick and tired of being a ghost, but I can't leave True. So I need Alice and Twila to concentrate on helping him and me and Gil out."

"Maybe I need some help, too."

Irritation jeopardized Joleen's attempt to remain reasonable, but she gave a good try at smothering it. "Then at least agree to leave my psychic ghost hunters alone and see if you can get Jack to help you. The women came here for me."

"I've already seen enough to know that cop doesn't want anything to do with any of us." Karen's voice rose in exasperation. "I'll admit, I made a mistake attacking those two. I was throwing a fit about everything. They just happened to get in the way. I'll apologize."

"No!" Joleen spat. "How many times do I have to tell you. They're here for me! And True and Gil. You take care of your own damn business. Don't stick your nose in mine!"

"I will take care of my own damn business!" Karen stuck her face up to Joleen's. "And I'll stick my nose anywhere I have to in order to do that."

Temper escaping its bounds, Joleen slapped Karen. The other ghost's head snapped back.

Immediately, Karen retaliated, evidently forgetting she didn't have hands. But her stump caught Joleen's nose in a wrenching blow. Joleen instinctively grabbed her face, then stared at her palm, surprised even after so long as a ghost not to see blood. She glared at Karen.

"Is this how you want it?"

"Your choice, bitch," Karen spat.

Joleen sneered as she slipped a glance at Karen's handless arms. It shouldn't be hard to show this stupid interferer who was boss around here. Who had been dead the longest and had developed the strongest abilities. Shoot, after all, Joleen had even managed the trip to Six Gun to talk to Alice.

Joleen lunged, reaching for Karen, She met a kneecap. A second later, she picked herself up off the floor and stared at Karen with a bit more caution as she rubbed her aching tailbone.

"Just so you know," Karen said in warning, "I took self-defense classes in addition to getting my gun license. I had to handle things alone here sometimes, and people tend to get drunk on vacations. I wanted all the protection I could get."

Joleen sneered at her. "Next time you need a shower, get it yourself."

She flounced around as though leaving. But keeping Karen in the corner of her vision, she saw when the other ghost relaxed her attack stance. She needed to knock some sense into this broad.

Having watched another fight between two men ghosts during her tenure here, Joleen knew they could wallop each other as ghosts the same as in a human cat fight. Quick as a flash, she hit Karen in the stomach with her shoulder. With an "oomph" of pain, Karen crashed into the tub and fell over the side.

Not letting Karen recover, Joleen grabbed her by the hair and shirt and jerked her out of the tub. With a roar of anger, Joleen tossed her through the bathroom door and went after her.

In the hallway, Joleen slung herself on top of Karen before the other woman could even try to rise. The two of them tumbled down the hall, first one on top, then the other. Over and over and over.

At first I thought Miss Molly had taken off on her own and run into something she was facing off with. The screeching rebounded in the hall, bouncing off ceilings and walls in a cacophony of nerve-wracking noise. But Trucker and Miss Molly, who had both followed me on my exploration to look for Twila and Granny, were still right beside me. They, too, stared down the way we'd just come, toward the other connecting hall.

"Let go, you bitch!"

"Fuck you!" a second female voice screamed.

"Omigod!" I yelled to my animals as I limped on fast as I could toward the noise. "Someone's attacking Twila or Granny!" I paused long enough to wave Trucker on. "Sic 'em, Trucker! Go on!"

He obeyed and disappeared down the hallway with a roar that joined the rest of the noise ricocheting off my eardrums. Miss Molly, though, stayed with me.

I suffered the pain of rushing to the assistance of my dear friends and managed a trot. But at the Y in the hall, I ground to an abrupt halt beside my dog.

Not Twila and Granny. Joleen and Karen circled each other. Joleen's hands were fisted in a pugilistic stance. Karen, with no hands, held up her forearms defensively. The hotel owner had found a shirt somewhere to cover at least part of her nakedness.

"Had enough?" Joleen yelled.

Karen answered with a karate move as skilled as any I'd seen in a movie. Unfortunately for her, Joleen seemed ready for it. She reared back, caught Karen's foot before it connected with her head, and twisted the other ghost into the air. She let loose, and Karen dropped to the floor with a *kerthunk*.

She didn't stay there, though. Joleen gloated a second too long. Karen swept her legs into Joleen's knees, and the saloon girl crashed to the floor beside her. Karen jumped on top, one forearm pinning across Joleen's throat, a knee digging into her stomach.

"Give!" Karen shrieked.

Instead, Joleen bit Karen's arm.

Karen screeched and pulled back, crossing her other arm over the injury. Joleen bucked and Karen flew off. Joleen didn't bother to get up. She kicked Karen in the side hard enough to send the other woman sliding down the hallway on her back.

Then Joleen rose. She must have caught sight of her human and animal audience, because she glanced at me. My own gaze drifted behind her, where Granny and Twila stood in the hallway.

"I've been looking for y'all—"

"Uh oh." Granny pointed just as Karen shoved her feet beneath a spindly legged table against a wall. Legs strong, she heaved it at Joleen.

The rim hit Joleen's head, the legs tangling in her arms as she batted at it. Abruptly, Joleen froze, wavered for a moment, then slowly fell to the floor and lay without moving.

As Twila and Granny edged past the two opponents to where I watched the show, Karen got to her feet and stomped over to Joleen. She held her forearms out, and it looked as though she wanted to brush her hands together in a that's-finished gesture. For a brief instant, she stared at the end of her forearms sorrowfully, then propped her handless forearms on her hips.

"You'll get the same thing if you ever bother me again, you sleazy saloon tramp!"

Joleen's pointed-toe red shoe caught Karen right between the legs. The other ghost howled in agony and cupped her armless forearms to the pain. She backed away a step before Joleen surged to her feet and tackled her.

"We's gonna do anythin'?" Granny asked.

"Not me," Twila said.

"Me, neither," I agreed. "For one thing, I don't know what we could hold onto to separate them. For another, we might get cold-cocked ourselves."

The two female ghosts screeched and cursed each other as they rolled over and over, first away from us, then towards us. Karen's shirt didn't help much. We caught glimpses of her gray-streaked black bush. She needed a dye job to match her hair.

The rolls brought them back to the table, and Joleen grabbed it by one leg before Karen could.

Joleen pushed Karen away far enough to swing the table down on the other woman's head. The table leg broke, and I expected Karen to fall unconscious. Instead, the ghost roared in rage and slapped a forearm hard enough across Joleen's cheek to knock the other woman completely off her.

Joleen scrambled to her feet along with Karen. She crouched defensively, but Karen stayed upright. She used her karate skills again.

Her first kick sent Joleen crawling into the wall. Joleen screamed and pushed off...right into another kick from Karen. This one tumbled the blonde to the floor, and Karen caught her in the ribs with the next one, shoving her a few feet down the hall.

Joleen spun on her back. She tangled both her legs around Karen's and thrust, sweeping Karen down with her on the floor. The women joined again for another set of tumbles over and over and over.

"This could go on a while," Twila said. "Should we leave them to it?"

"Shouldn't we try to stop them before they get hurt worse than they are?" I asked. "Maybe toss some sea salt or something on them?"

"How bad can they get hurt?" Twila reasoned. "They're already dead."

"Oh," I said.

We turned toward the stairwell...and there stood Jack. He drew his gaze away from the women, now tumbling back towards us, and glanced at us. Shaking his head, he headed down the stairwell.

We followed. Continuing to fight pain, I dropped back and allowed the others to precede me, including my pets. I took one last look at the combatants. Joleen was on top, her fist drawn back to punch out Karen's lights...if a ghost still had lights. But Karen shoved a handless forearm into Joleen's stomach. Before her blow landed, Joleen tumbled off Karen.

Although my headache had dulled, my knee was killing me again. Oops, I shouldn't think of that word in connection with my own body in this house of the dead. I leaned on the railing as I stepped down the first stair.

"Owwww," I moaned under my breath. I ended up having to put both feet on each stair step before I could navigate the next one. It was taking me forever to hobble downward, but I gritted my teeth and persisted, determined to have Twila fetch me some salve and also pain medication at the first opportunity.

The cold warned me briefly. I had just enough time to grab a tight hold on the bannister when the two bodies whooshed through me. It could have been the surprise. But there were stories of ghosts pushing people, so maybe the force of their bodies loosened my grip. Whatever.

The ghosts crashed to a halt on the first landing. Both of them recoiled off the wall, then lay without moving. Right on top of me!

I screamed. There was no quashing it.

Brushing at myself as though a million spiders had crawled out of the wall and covered me, I pushed myself back with my good leg. Shit, I used the throbbing one, too.

I screamed a second time and managed to get to my feet. I bounded down the steps as though I had two good legs and hit the deck a'running.

Right into Twila's arms. I nearly knocked both of us to the floor, but Jack was right behind her. He grabbed hold and steadied us.

"What is it?" Twila demanded.

I buried my head on her shoulder and refused to answer. I couldn't speak. I tried. Keeping my head down, I pointed back at the stairs, and babbled something idiotic. To me, it sounded like: "Gobble-ikky-ooosshee-gabaldeeee!"

Twila tried to hand me off to Jack, but I dug my hands in and held her in a death grip, refusing to let go.

"They...ghosts...J-J-Joleen. K-K-K...cold. So damn cold," I managed to gulp against her shoulder.

"Shhhhh," she soothed. "It's over now. They're...." She couldn't quite contain her snicker. "They're dead now, Alice."

That straightened me up, probably just as she intended. I jerked back and glared at her. "Of course they're dead. They're damn ghosts!"

Then I bit my own lip. It didn't work. A giggle emerged. Then a couple more. This time when we held each other, Twila and I howled in half-hysterical laughter. Well, mine was half-hysterical. Hers was probably total glee and relief I'd come back to myself. Neither of us did panic very well. We either stifled it or got the hell out of Dodge.

Jack stomped away. I heard his boot steps even on the carpeted hallway. Twila and I drew back from each other, mopping at our streaming eyes with the backs of our hands. Then we both looked over at the stairs.

Granny stood there, looking up at the first landing. Where the two ghosts still lay unconscious...If ghosts could be unconscious. Which must have been possible, since these two looked completely knocked out.

"Huh," Granny said. Then looked at us and shook her head.

Twila and I howled again. I stumbled away from her to the lobby, where I fell into one of the soft lounge chairs. Right behind me, Twila dove into the one beside me.

It took us a good two to three minutes to control ourselves. Every thirty seconds of so, we'd think we had it handled, then make the mistake of looking at each other or Granny, who had settled herself on the couch across the coffee table. Granny would catch our gazes and cackle just a bit, and off we'd go again.

CHAPTER 20

"They's both disappeared just a'fore I left," Granny said when Twila and I finally each grabbed a sweater hem and dried our dripping eyes and cheeks. "Guess they's went on back to wherever."

"Darn, I hope so," I said. "I've had enough of ghosts for a while."

"Never thought I'd admit it," Twila put in, "but I'm hoping they leave us alone for a while, too. I'm ready to sit down to a nice lunch with maybe have a couple beers!"

"Hey, I saw some frozen pinà coladas and margaritas in the 'fridge freezer," I said.

"Maybe one of each, along with the beer," she said with a nod.

Before we rose, I asked, "What were you two doing in that end of the hall? I was looking everywhere for you."

Leaving the murder room for last, I went on in my mind. And that's the direction they appeared from.

"There's a room down there that I feel has something to do with that evasive ghost," Twila explained.

Granny caught my shudder and broke in, "Naw, not the one where that there ghost lives...uh...usta live. It's one catty-corner."

"Any luck figuring him out?" I asked my aunt, relieved we didn't have to discuss the murder room, with all that blood.

"Not a bit." She sighed and got up from her chair.

Even though it was a little early for lunch—breakfast hadn't been that long ago—we all headed toward the kitchen. However, before we were even out of the lobby, we heard a snowmobile engine outside. The noise ceased abruptly, fairly close to the door.

"I'll get it," I said, but Jack came out of the saloon and headed for the door.

"I'll see who it is first," he said.

Actually, I realized I'd rather Jack took charge for now, drained as I was from dealing with those blasted ghosts and my half-hysterical breakdown. Even though I tried to block it out of my mind, that icy feeling of those two ghost bodies plowing through me made me shiver harder than recalling the bloody room.

Granny and Twila continued on toward the kitchen, but I lingered.

Jack unlocked the door and stepped in front of the opening so I couldn't see who was there. "Yes?" he said.

"Uh...I'm looking for Twila and Alice." Danny's voice.

I walked over behind Jack. "We know him. It's Danny."

Jack stepped back and opened. As Danny walked in, he held out his hand. "Jack Roucheau, Homicide."

I wasn't sure whether Jack automatically included his job title or it was a warning to Danny. It did cause the man to hesitate a split-second before he accepted Jack's handshake. Or maybe Danny just needed to pull off his glove.

"Danny Smith." He caught sight of me and I decided Jack's job title maybe had indeed given him something to hesitate about. Relief eased his face muscles, and he dropped Jack's hand to walk over to me.

"Homicide?" he asked in a whisper.

I shrugged in answer, and he raised his voice to say, "I figured I should stop by and see how things were going, Alice. So how goes it?"

Inwardly, I felt like telling Danny what he could do with his haunted hotel, but this was Twila's game. Instead of the irritated huff of breath I wanted to blow out, I calmed my aggravation and said, "Twila's in the kitchen with Granny. Have you had lunch yet?"

He pulled back a sleeve and looked at his watch. His frown said he agreed it was a little early, but he seemed to change his mind about that.

"It would be nice to have a bite with some lovely ladies," he said. "Just let me divest myself of this heavy snowmobile garb."

I started to walk away, then noticed Jack not following.

"You're invited, too, Jack," I said.

He drew his attention away from watching Danny, who had gone back over to the door to unzip his heavy suit of protective gear. He glanced at the other man once more, but I couldn't read that stone face he could drop into when he grew suspicious of something. And I wasn't about to question Jack in front of Danny, since it appeared Danny was the focus of suspicion.

I limped toward the kitchen, reminding myself to get those darned pain pills. Jack did follow me, but he headed for a coffee pot someone— probably Granny, who enjoyed her coffee—had set up in the café area.

"Danny's here," I told Twila and Granny. "I invited him to have lunch with us."

"Ugh," Twila said. "I was hoping we could have a nice meal without talking about the stupid ghosts here. Now I'll have to go over it all with him."

"Probably," I said. "I didn't tell him anything. He's sort of your client."

"Yeah," she said with a twinge of disgust. "This may have been a mistake. He got me here by offering us that free stay after we cleaned the place up. I think I'd rather just pay for a stay on our own."

"Well, we's cain't do nothin' with all this here ice coverin' them roads," Granny said. "But we's kin eat well. I'm thinkin' of makin' a pot of gumbo for supper. I found some shrimp an' sausage an' a chicken. More'n I could expect, to find crawfish, but the rest will do."

"Yum," Twila said. "I love your gumbo, Granny."

Granny grinned at the praise, deepening the road map of wrinkles on her face. "I'll get started soon's we eats lunch."

Since those two had things under control meal-wise, I made the mistake of wandering out to the coffee pot. At home, I would have had a huge morning latte, but here I had to content myself with a cup of half coffee, half flavored creamer. Knowing my preference, Granny had left a bottle of the crème brule flavor out for me.

I turned around and barely rescued my cup before it spilled its contents down the front of Danny's plaid flannel shirt.

"Oops, sorry," he said, backing away far enough for me to see he'd removed his boots and now walked around in his socks. "I was just wondering why a homicide cop was here. I mean, he wasn't part of our deal."

"Not my deal," I denied. "Twila's. But Jack is my ex-husband. He's...well, he happened to be in the area."

"Oh," Danny said. He stared around the room, an expression on his face I couldn't read. I did sense he wasn't happy with Jack's presence, but what could he do? Should he try to throw Jack out onto those icy roads, he would have three of us to contend with.

Yes, I admitted, I still worried about Jack. After all, he would always be one of my dearest friends.

Even though I fought to keep the rest of that comment—*with benefits*—buried, that little tingle between my legs indicated my lack of success.

"So where'd he go?" Danny asked.

"No idea," I replied, walking away from him to take a seat at a nearby table. I only wanted to sip my coffee in peace, but it was my own fault he kept intruding, since I'd invited him.

He sat down across from me. "How's it going with the ghosts?"

"You should be asking Twila that," I said with a yawn the caffeine couldn't quell. "She'll tell you about Joleen and Karen."

He froze. "Karen?"

"She's a..." I yawned again. "...ghost now, too. You've currently got a houseful."

I'll admit to a certain amount of satisfaction at the look of horror on his face. For some reason, I didn't care for the man. He hadn't bothered me that much when he'd been our balloon pilot back in Ohio, but now I noticed his plastic demeanor. Some men were any easy like right from the first. Others seemed to have to put on an effort to be amenable, like politicians. Danny was the type of man who firmed my decision to write Donald Duck in every spot on the election ballot!

Twila and Granny came out of the kitchen, large plates filled with greens, strawberries and grilled chicken in their hands. Twila set one plate in front of me, the other in front of Danny.

Danny scooted back his chair. "It looks lovely, Twila, but you know what? I just remembered I've got another appointment. I'll go through the kitchen and check your supplies, then let myself out."

He whispered off on his stocking feet, without a glance of goodbye at either me or Granny. Twila frowned after him for a second, then shrugged her shoulders and motioned for Granny to sit.

"What sent him off in such a hurry?" Twila asked, obviously mistrusting his appointment excuse, as I did.

"All I did was mention that Joleen and Karen were around here as ghosts," I said. "He didn't seem to care about Joleen, but he blanched as white as...a ghost, when I said Karen's name."

"I'll go get the other salad for Jack," she said, "and the iced tea. You two go ahead and start eating."

I dug in, and forgetting my manners, said with my mouth full, "Strawberries. Where'd they come from up here this time of year?"

Granny said, "Prob'ly from down South Texas."

As Jack walked in to join us, Twila came back with a pitcher of tea and some plastic cups somehow clasped in one hand, a plate of salad in the other. Jack hurried over to take the pitcher and cups from her.

"Thanks, Jack."

She started to set the pitcher on our table, then scowled. "Shoot, looks like I spilled salt into the tea when I dropped that salt box out of the cupboard. I'll go make a fresh pitcher."

"How do you know that?" I asked.

"See?" She pointed with her other hand at the pitcher handle. "There's white stuff in the crevice here. And I didn't put sugar in it yet."

Jack took the pitcher from her. "You sit down and eat your salad. I'll make some more tea."

He left us, and I toyed with a strawberry as I glanced at the doorway where he had disappeared. Then I shoved my chair back.

"I'll see if Jack needs any help finding the tea."

In the kitchen, I watched Jack brush the white granules off the pitcher handle into a plastic sandwich bag, then seal it up and stick it in his jeans pocket.

"What's going on?" I asked while he washed his hands at the sink.

He didn't appear to be surprised at my presence. Yet he only said, "Y'all got some instant tea or do I need to boil some more bags?"

I opened a cupboard door and handed him a box of teabags. We both noticed the spilled salt that Twila had mentioned, a few grains she'd missed when she wiped it up. I started to brush them into my hand, but Jack dropped the box of teabags and pushed my hands away. He wet a paper towel and cleaned up the spill, tossed the towel in the trash, and sealed the salt shaker into another plastic bag.

A large box of salt sat on the next shelf, and I glanced at it the same time he did. He pulled it down and opened it, sniffing for a second, then closing it back up to replace it.

"It's probably all right."

Jack rinsed out the tea kettle Twila had left on the stove, even using soap in it to clean it completely. I didn't bother to tell him Southern women didn't clean their tea kettles. He knew that.

After he had the water heating on the stove, I grabbed his arm.

"What the hell was that white stuff? Obviously, you didn't think it was salt."

"It might be," he denied. "But I wasn't about to taste it and see."

"You think one of the ghosts around here might be trying to poison us to make us leave?"

"Don't have to be a ghost."

Danny's journey through the kitchen to supposedly check supplies flashed in my mind. "Danny? Why would he want to hurt us? He wants us to clean up this hotel."

"People's plans change sometimes, *Chère*."

"Not his. At least, not about the hotel. He even has one of those power of attorney things from Karen. So he can still sell this place, even with her dead."

"Interesting," Jack said. "Uh...isn't this Danny the guy you and Twila met in Ohio?"

"Our balloon pilot. Yeah."

"Jess told me about him. Said you and Twila were all thrilled 'bout ridin' with him all over the skies up there."

Jess was Twila's husband, and Jack and he were best of friends, even across the distance separating them. Twila and I, also, didn't let living far apart bother our closeness, but most men had a different type of friendship. They didn't usually talk relationships, just sports and guy stuff. Jack and Jess nurtured another closeness, though. They discussed male-female stuff, rather like Twila and I did sometimes, although not as in depth.

"Gee, Jack, you sound jealous," I said, unable to resist adding the smirk in my voice. "But for what it's worth, the only contact I had with Danny was when the balloon basket shifted and threw both me and Twila into him once. But, remember? As Granny says, we's dee-vorced. Neither of us has the right to question who the other happens to date."

Me and my big mouth. My tone of voice trailed off into woebegone and stifled any attempt at derision. A sharp stab from a green-eyed monster of my own buried it.

"That dee-vorce wasn't my idea, Alice," he reminded me, chocolate gaze pulling me into its center.

"You didn't fight it," I said. "You didn't even show up at the final hearing."

"My lawyer said I didn't have to put myself through that," he said quietly. "I thought it was what you wanted, and I wanted you to be happy, *Chère*. But I didn't have to sit there and watch it end."

"You sound like you think we should try again."

He glanced away from me, then sighed. "I don't know."

My stomach plummeted. Had I wanted him to say something else? I'd have to think on that later.

"Well," I said to cover up my disappointment, "things haven't changed in either of our lives. I still need hours and hours alone to write. And I'm still chasing after ghosts, something you despise."

He gazed back down on me, that damn stone face in place. "I don't necessarily despise it. Just don't understand it. And I still get snowed under when I have a particularly brutal case. Ain't the best person to have to live with durin' those times, but it's the only way I can work. It's not as bad now that I'm in Longview, smaller town. Not as many sickenin' cases as there are in N'awlins."

"Seems petty when we take it out and look at it honestly, huh?"

"Yeah," Jack agreed.

I dropped my eyes and picked up a spoon from the counter. Running my fingers back and forth on it, mostly to have something to do while I spoke, I said, "I've been thinking of not submitting my next option book. Maybe going indie and getting out of the New York rat race. My agent's talking about an audit, since we think there's been a couple fishy royalty statements."

"What would that do to your schedule?" he asked.

"I wouldn't be under deadline all the time. And if it went well—"

The teakettle whistle blared into the kitchen, and we both jumped for the stove at the same instant. Jack wrapped an arm around me, already knowing, I'm sure, that clumsy me might twist an ankle in my haste if he didn't save me. He'd rescued me a lot during our years together. Even afterwards....

He kept a tight grip as he grabbed a potholder and lifted the teakettle off the stove. Then he released me and said, "I'll make the tea, *Chère*. You go on and eat your salad."

I toddled towards the door, legs woozy. Not from pain, though. From close contact with that Cajun who had stolen my heart a few years ago.

And...I sighed. Probably still had at least a piece of it. Maybe more.

At the door, I paused and turned around. "Jack...."

He shook his head. "Let's talk after all this is over, *Chère*."

"When we have time to concentrate," I finished for him, and he nodded.

"All right." I wandered on into the dining area, and nearly walked right past our table before Twila reached out and tugged on my sweater.

"Uh...where you going?" she asked when I looked down at her in question.

"Oh. I was...uh...just going to finish my salad."

I sat down in the chair, but didn't eat another bite. Instead, I drank my glass of the tea Jack brought out while the rest of them ate. Jack had taken the chair beside me, and once in a while, his knee brushed my leg.

CHAPTER 21

Twila pushed back her chair and crossed her arms. Since she hardly ever did that, believing, as I do, it interferes with our psychic reception when we investigate a haunted location, I knew she was also checking her temper. You didn't want to be on the receiving end of one of those blasts. Her jaw set, and her words emerged in a crisp manner that demanded attention.

"What the hell was that white stuff you were so interested on the iced tea pitcher, Jack?"

She hardly ever swore, either, so this was serious business. I chased away any musings about maybe getting Jack his own room and—

"Pay attention, Alice," she ordered.

I did.

"It just didn't look like salt to me, Twila," Jack responded after a few seconds. "Salt's grainy. This looked more powdery."

"So someone's trying to poison us?" she asked.

He spread his hands in an at-a-loss gesture. "We all saw Danny go through the kitchen. But he wasn't in there very long."

"He made a poor excuse," she said. "He'd already stocked this place with enough supplies to last us several days before we even arrived."

To show her I was indeed paying heed, I repeated what I'd said to Jack in the kitchen. "Why would Danny want to get rid of us before we're finished here?"

"An' I sure ain't ready to go through that there light yet," Granny said. "Why'n't he just say he figgered he'd wait a while a'fore he tackled them ghosts, Karen bein' gone?"

"Karen?" Jack asked.

"Uh...if we go there, Jack," I interrupted, "we have to explain about the ghosts. Karen's the woman we found dead when we arrived."

"She's a ghost now?" he asked as though truly interested.

"Uh huh," I replied.

"I know a little bit about how y'all work, *Chère*. Could be whoever killed her knows she's a ghost now. Might be afraid she'll tell you who did it."

I couldn't decide if Jack was interested due to the paranormal aspect or his crime investigation brain. No doubt, the latter.

"I imagine every one of us has already thought about that," Twila said. "And as far as we know, the only other person who knows Karen's stayed around as a ghost is Danny. Alice told him."

"Then logic says he has to be the one wantin' rid of y'all now," Jack reasoned in that male reasoning.

I wasn't so sure, and when I glanced at Twila and Granny, they both shook their heads in a tiny negative sway. Without words, I agreed with them. It was *too* logical.

But it could be true. If our lives were in danger, we couldn't overlook anything.

Trucker and Miss Molly wandered in. At first I thought my dog needed to go out, but he plopped his huge head on the table right beside my plate.

"Trucker!" I chastised. "That's a no-no."

Before he lifted his head, he cast me a soulful look, then another one at my plate.

"Oh, crap," I said, scooting back my chair. "I need to go feed my animals."

Jack rose. "I'll go with you."

Twila shook her head. "You haven't eaten your salad, Jack. I'll go. Alice and I will be fine."

"He prob'ly don't like rabbit food," Granny said. "I's'll make you a hamburg, Jack. How 'bout that?"

"Sounds great, Granny. And you're right. Rabbit food isn't one of my favorite dishes."

"Let's go get some real man food, then." Granny led off and he followed her as though on a tether, not even bothering to look at us.

I laughed. "He does love Granny's cooking. Maybe if I'd been a better cook, we'd still be married."

"There's always tomorrow," Twila reminded me. But her evasive manner indicated the subject wasn't her top priority right now. She crooked a finger at me, picked up my iced tea, and walked away.

Animals following, we didn't stop until we got to our rooms. We left the doors open, and I made my pets wait a few more seconds as I started to ask Twila for something for pain. I didn't even have to speak, though. She was already in her room, and she came back and handed me a couple tiny round white pills and my tea.

"What are these?" I asked. "They don't look like aspirin."

"I got them from my doctor a while back," she explained. "They're for arthritis pain. I brought them with me, knowing we were going to have bad weather. I don't like taking stuff like that, but this getting older isn't for sissies. Don't worry, they're non-narcotic. He says they're the last stop before narcotics, though. And they work great."

I swallowed the pills with a sip of tea, then fed both Trucker and Miss Molly. As usual, my cat wasn't satisfied totally with her own food. She had to taste Trucker's first. I never understood why. She knew he always got the same brand. He stood back until she had a nibble, flicked her tongue in distaste, and sauntered over to her own bowl, tail held high like her Egyptian forbearers. Then finally Trucker settled in to gobble his meal.

Twila sat down on Granny's bed and gestured for me to do the same on mine. "If we weren't iced in," she said, "we'd be on our way back to the airport. This isn't worth it."

"No, but it's probably what the Universe has in mind for us," I reminded her.

"The hell with the Universe. It's not the be-all, end-all. We have free will and can change things."

She hesitated as though unsure she wanted to say whatever she had on her mind, then blurted, "Did you see that big black safe in the saloon?"

"Yes, but what's that got to do with anything?"

"I think we need to see what's in it."

"Oh, Twila, it's probably totally empty," I said with a hand wave. "No owners are going to keep any money in a safe these days. I doubt they ever have much cash at all around, other than tips when they're open for meals. Most of those go on a credit card, too."

She contemplated for a while, so I teased, "And we don't steal money."

"I'm not talking about money," she said in a serious tone. "I think there's something else in that safe. Something we're going to need at some point."

She bit her lip, and I prodded, "What?"

"Guns."

"Guns? Like in bang-bang, Clint Eastwood and 'Make my day'?"

"How could I know, though?" she asked with an annoyed-at-herself expression. "We haven't looked in it yet."

I defended her, "It's what you're sensing, isn't it?"

"Yes, but...."

"How many times have you cautioned me not to dismiss a message I get just because I think I might be imagining what I heard. If you think we need to get in that safe, we need to get in that safe. Let's go try to open it."

"Actually," she mused, "it's got a protection spell on it. You remember that blood sketch Jack and I found?"

I nodded. "There was a pentagram drawn in blood in True's room.

193

Where we found Karen. Probably some black witches or maybe even Satanists at work here."

"I don't think they're Satanists," she said. "I think we would have definitely sensed those. Satanist evil is plain nasty. But black witches can work in the...well, in the dark. They're hard to discern."

"You discerned the protection spell."

"It was meant to be discovered," she said. "No one other than a thief would normally try to get in that safe, and he'd never be able to open it. If someone who could sense the magic tried...."

"Gil opened the jail door for me."

"A ghost would never get through the spell."

I blurted, "Jack knows how to pick locks."

"I figured he did, although I don't know how much *picking* would be involved with a safe. More like figuring out the combination. Think you can talk him into it?"

"Me?" I laid a hand on my chest. "Why don't you talk to him?"

"Maybe Granny could," she said.

"Yeah," I agreed. "Jack's not real amenable to either one of us right now. He's dealing with being able to see *those damn ghosts y'all chase after* again."

"Let's wait until Granny fills his belly first."

"Definitely. Jack's always easier to deal with after he eats."

Trucker lifted his head and growled at the doorway. Twila and I both froze. Then we cautiously turned our heads.

How long had he...she?...been standing there? Since Trucker had only growled a second ago, I didn't think long enough to overhear more than us discussing Jack's appetite.

At first, I took her for a man. But she pulled off her knit cap and a tangle of snow-white hair tumbled over her shoulders. She smiled, her teeth even brighter than her hair.

"Hi," she said. "I'm Maddie English. You know, the real estate lady?"

"Oh," I said. "Danny mentioned you."

I introduced the two of us, and she nodded. "I'm so sorry I didn't get here sooner. Especially after...." Her voice trailed off and she wiped at her eyes. "Especially after I heard about Karen. But that's really why I couldn't come. I was so devastated. It took me a while to gather my wits enough to make it over here."

"We didn't hear you drive up," I said.

"I live just around the corner," she explained. "I walked." She stuck out one foot to show us her suede boots with the waffled soles for traction. "And I have a key, of course, since the hotel is one of my listings."

Trucker laid into his bowl of food again, and she said, "What beautiful animals. Will they allow me to pet them?"

"After they eat," I cautioned. "Even the cat can scare you with one of her bitchy meows if she's not done eating."

"I see," Maddie said with a laugh. "Well, I need to discuss something rather distasteful." She batted at her eyes again, but missed a tear that escaped down her cheek. "I...oh, this is hard. Karen is...was such a dear friend. But life does go on."

"Would you like to sit down?" I asked.

"That might be nice."

She walked over and sat beside me. I patted her a couple times in comfort, then Twila said softly, "What is the distasteful matter?"

"Well." She heaved a huge sigh. "Well, Danny said he wants the hotel to stay on the market. In fact, we've got a couple representatives from one of the Native American tribes in the area scheduled for a tour tomorrow. If the weather breaks up enough. And the reports say it should."

"Good," Twila murmured under her breath. I agreed, since I knew both of us were glad the roads wouldn't keep us imprisoned after today.

Maddie caught her comment. "I understand. You must be upset at being penned in here."

"We'd planned to stay a few days," Twila said. "But I was hoping we could get away once in a while."

"You're very welcome to come over to my house for a visit," Maddie said. "In fact, why don't you both come for dinner this evening? It's only a block from here. And I noticed you had a four-wheel drive. You wouldn't even have to get out in the cold for long. Just to your SUV, and a block to my house."

195

"There are two more here," I explained. "A...friend of ours, Jack Roucheau. And another friend, Granny Chisholm. Granny's elderly, so we definitely would want to drive with her."

"Jack and I might walk," Twila said.

"Now, Twila, my driving isn't that bad on ice!" I fumed.

"No, no, no," she denied. "I'd just welcome the fresh air. Unless you want Jack to drive your vehicle."

"You know," I said, "I'd like to take a walk, too. Jack and Granny can ride together. Oh." I looked at Maddie. "Unless your invitation didn't include our friends."

"The more the merrier," she said. "I'll plan on four guests. Maybe five, if Danny wants to come."

"But what about the matter you came here for?" Twila asked.

Her face fell. "I have to get the room where they found Karen cleaned up," she said. "Danny told me the sheriff had said it was O.K. But with the roads so bad, I don't know how I'm going to get any cleaning people here."

"You should reschedule the tour," I said.

"I should." She nodded. "There's a wonderful cleaning service over in Angel Fire that does great clean-up. Even...blood. They do infrequent jobs for the cops. They can't get here today, of course. And Danny's so adamant that he doesn't want to upset the apple cart, as they say, with these potential buyers."

It dawned on me what she was about to say when she studied Twila and me with a contemplative gaze.

"No!" I said, rising and moving over to sit beside Twila in a united front. "We can't help you. I don't do cleaning well, for one thing. And I don't do blood at all."

"I agree," Twila said. "You'll have to find someone else."

"Or do it myself," Maddie said in a mournful voice. "It won't bother you girls if I'm in and out for a while, will it?"

I conceded to Twila to answer her, since this haunt was her baby.

"Of course not," she said. "But are you sure you still want us for dinner, if you're going to be busy...uh...cleaning."

"Yes, yes, yes," Maddie said. "It will be a nice break for me to have people over. And I love to cook."

"Granny was making gumbo for dinner," I recalled aloud.

"Oh, that would be wonderful," Maddie said with a clap of her hands. "I'd thought about broiling some red snapper fillets I got on a trip to the coast this past summer. They would be scrumptious with gumbo, and I can fix jalapeño cornbread."

"You better go check with Granny," Twila said, and we both rose and started out of the room. "She's a bit touchy about the meals she plans."

After a few steps, I realized my pain had vanished. I vowed to get the name of those miracle pills from Twila, since I didn't care for the thought of something addictive as I aged, either.

Maddie followed us and it turned out our worries were unfounded. After we introduced them, she and Granny put their heads together about dinner and shooed us out of the kitchen.

"What do you want to bet she talks Granny into helping her clean that room?" I asked.

"If she does, which I agree she probably will, make sure Granny bills her for it."

"Good idea."

"Now, let's find Jack and see about that safe."

"But we were going to let Granny ask him."

She raised her eyebrows at me in one of her don't-be-stupid looks. "She's busy cooking. You want to interrupt her?"

"No, but...." I started to turn back to the kitchen. "Maddie probably has the combination."

Twila grabbed for me and barely caught my sweater. I jerked to a halt, staring at her in surprise.

"You know what they say on crime shows," she said. "Don't trust anyone. She's new to our acquaintance. Let's do this ourselves."

"All right," I agreed, puzzled but willing to bow to her doubts. "As long as you're the one who asks Jack."

CHAPTER 22

"Y"ou want me to what, *Chère*?"

Twila had forced me to blurt out the request to Jack by the simple measure of just standing there, looking at me, until I could take Jack's frown of annoyance at our lack of words no longer. She knew me and my blabber too well sometimes.

"Open the safe in the saloon," I repeated.

"Why?"

Figuring I'd get back at Twila, I gestured at her to speak. Darn, she was stubborn. She stared past Jack at a buffalo head hung on the wall.

I sighed. "It has to do with the ghosts. So do you really want to know?"

"Yes." He matched Twila's silence.

I could be as stubborn as my aunt. After all, we shared half a gene pool. I gestured at her again, then casually strolled over and started examining the historical items encased under glass on the check-in desk counter.

"Even though I'm psychic, Jack," she said, "I don't know everything. It's a feeling I have. One of those intuitive things."

"Like a gut instinct?" he asked.

"No, that comes from a different chakra spot," she replied. "You see—"

Oh, good lord. We'd be here all day if she gave Jack a lesson on the different sixth sense variations. Despite the thought she was playing me again to get me to blab our plans, I interrupted, "She thinks there's some guns in the safe."

Jack fixed us both with a steely stare. "And why do you two need guns?"

I gestured at Twila.

"Like I said, it's an intuitive feeling. Like cops sometimes get."

That got Jack. He couldn't deny all good cops knew better than to ignore their intuition.

"But if you don't want to help us," I added, "we'll see what we can do on our own."

"So you're going to do it, whether I help or not."

"Yes," Twila said, the two of us now in sync. "And you do owe me one. Remember when you came to visit us last time?"

Jack's face reddened. He glanced at me so quickly, a person who didn't know him wouldn't have caught it, then immediately back to Twila. I'd already heard all about his and Jess's escapade one night on the motorcycle. The few drinks too many as they rode and reminisced about their younger days. The bike wheel stuck between railroad ties at a crossing. The cop who caught them trying to light a fire in an abandoned church to keep warm until morning, when someone would be awake and they could borrow a phone to call Twila.

But I held my tongue.

"I'll see what I can do," he told Twila, and stomped toward the saloon. We all had to stand back before we got there, however, because Maddie and Granny paraded past. Maddie carried a bucket filled with cleaning supplies, and Granny had found some aprons and rubber gloves in the kitchen. She grinned and flicked the gloves at us as she passed.

Twila held Granny back a moment and whispered in her ear, "Make sure you get paid."

"Gonna," Granny replied with a wink.

We continued on into the saloon.

"At least we'll have privacy to do this, with them busy upstairs," I said.

"Doin' what?" Jack asked, but he was already fiddling with the safe dial.

"Just some cleaning," I answered vaguely. It probably wouldn't have hurt to tell him they were cleaning up blood, but he was pretty protective of Granny. He might not like the idea of her doing that. I didn't much, either, but I knew better than to argue with that feisty elder.

Within ten seconds, I heard a *click* and Jack twisted the round steel handle on the safe and pulled it open.

"There," he said. "It's so old, it was easy to open."

Twila and I shoved at him in an attempt to see inside the safe, but Jack pushed us back. His warning expression immobilized both of us, even though we were anxious to see if Twila's intuition proved correct. Jack started to reach into the safe.

BAM!

The safe door nearly took of Jack's nose as it slammed shut, and he shook his hand as though burned.

"What the fu-hell?" he sputtered.

"Are you all right?" I anxiously pulled his hand to me. It didn't look injured, so maybe the spell had more mind power than physical damage potential. I stared at his nose, which looked fine, also.

Indignation on his face, Jack jerked his hand free and reached for the safe door again. But Twila firmly stayed his arm. "Explain to him," she ordered. "I'll be right back."

She hurried off, and I stiffened my shoulders. This was our bailiwick, and Jack would just have to listen, whether he believed or not.

"It's a black magic protection spell," I explained. "Twila's probably gone to get some things to use to break it."

Jack contemplated me for a few seconds. "Well, I sure didn't slam the door and nearly take off my own damn nose. And you two have more experience in this sort of thing than I do. So just tell me what you need me to do."

I swallowed my shock at his cooperative attitude. I couldn't help the thought that maybe this wasn't Jack. Maybe some entity at the hotel had possessed him. But possession was another thing both Twila and I were good at discerning. I opened my senses and felt nothing but Jack there with me. Except....

I whirled around to shake a finger at Joleen. "Stay there!" Gil stood behind her, and I added, "You, too. We don't need your interference."

Gil held up his palms and backed off a few steps. "Yes, ma'am."

Recalling the cat fight a short while ago, I studied Joleen: the bit of disarray in her normally well-maintained hairdo, a faint hint of bruise on her rouged right cheek. For the most part, she didn't appear too bad off for having been in such violent combat. Until she grimaced and walked with difficulty as she moved a few feet to stand back with Gil. Too bad she couldn't take a couple of Twila's pills, but I doubted a ghost would benefit from human pain meds.

Joleen's feet were bare, shoes dangling from one hand. At my glance, she responded aloud, "I'm recovering a lot faster than when I was alive. But it still hurts. And heels aren't made for walking in when you're in pain."

"What's the other guy...woman look like?" Jack asked, humor in his voice.

Surprised at Jack seeing and speaking to a ghost, let alone kidding around with one, I stole a fleeting look at him, then back to Joleen. She actually blushed, and Gil slipped an ownership arm around her waist, perhaps jealous of a living man's attention to his girl.

"About the same as me," Joleen told Jack. "Except she's still searching for her hands."

Twila hurried back with purple velvet bags dangling by yellow cords from her right wrist. I'd probably given her those bags from my empty Crown Royal bottles. We carried our protection materials like that, both for the color and softness. Purple is a spiritual color, the softness protects our bottles of various liquids from rattling against each other and breaking. Twila preferred a different type of alcohol, her tastes changing now and then, but hardly ever Crown. I kept us both supplied.

She didn't bother to give Joleen and Gil any attention, but I knew without doubt she acknowledged their presence to herself. So did they, because their expressions grew even more wary, and they moved further away.

Or it could have been the ghosts feared the vibrations from what she carried. We were used to the power emitted by our protection materials, but it could disturb the unversed.

Twila set the bags on the bar. First, she took out a white votive candle and a light blue one, along with two glass candle holders.

"What all's in her bags?" Jack asked, as though truly interested. "And why does it work?"

I answered his second question first, as Twila removed three small packets tied in purple ribbons and a plastic bag of salt from another bag. "We don't exactly know why our stuff works, but I'm sure the friends who supplied us do. Everything has been consecrated and blessed against malevolence. As to what they are, the white candle always symbolizes good. The blue one has powdered five-finger grass and sandalwood mixed in with the beeswax. They're for protection against evil, as is the salt."

Twila slowed her hands, partially, I thought, to allow me to continue enlightening Jack as to the coming ritual. Also, she would be grounding herself, sinking deep roots beneath her to secure herself spiritually as she touched each item.

She clarified what was in the purple ribbon packets herself as she approached the two of us, giving me a chance to concentrate on grounding and preparing myself.

"These contain consecrated and blessed protection herbs, Jack." She pinned one over his heart, then did the same for herself and me. "We'll keep these on until this is over with."

"What about us?" Joleen asked.

Twila frowned, returned to the bar and drew two more protection packets from the purple bag. She tossed them up and down in her palm. On the fourth toss, without even looking, she sent them flying through the air toward the ghosts. Gil caught them.

I couldn't help myself, and I guess Jack couldn't, either. We both gaped at the ghosts, wondering where the heck they were going to pin those packets on their other-dimensional clothing. They surprised us. Gil stuck a packet down Joleen's bodice and placed his in the pocket on his vest closest to his heart...or what had once been a beating heart.

Twila slipped a peek at the two ghosts and giggled softly. I snickered, but quickly controlled myself, digging back into the necessary solemn mindset for what would come.

Twila opened a bag to pull out a wire-bound journal I'd seen before. It held white magic spells we'd collected from various friends over the years. Our own *Book of Shadows*, probably the most important thing we carried into our investigations.

"Here." Twila handed me the *Book*. "Find what we need."

I leafed through the neatly-handwritten pages while she opened the last bag, but I paid attention to what she was doing so I could continue to enlighten Jack. When she pulled the items out to place them on the bar, though, dread stilled my searching fingers. Twila laid out two small chicken bone wings, a piece of black thread, a bottle of Power Oil, along with packets of *Gris-Gris* Faible and Circle of Protection Incenses.

Omigod. Major heavy-duty tools.

"That looks like some stuff y'all got from Uncle Clarence's lady in N'awlins," Jack murmured.

He referred to Cat Dancer, my dearly departed Uncle Clarence's lover from New Orleans. She was a formidable practitioner, and we continued to study under her guidance whenever we could find the time to visit.

"Exactly," I whispered back as I waited to see what Twila would do about a necessity we didn't have with us.

My aunt didn't hesitate. She went into the lobby and returned with a hurricane lamp. She set it on the bar and removed the chimney, then unscrewed the cap holding the wispy white wick.

As she smelled the lamp contents, I cleared my throat of the apprehensiveness clogging it. This was no time for my courage to forsake me.

"She's seeing if that's true kerosene in the lamp or that fruity lamp oil some people use," I told Jack quietly as I inwardly strengthened my mental preparations for the coming confrontation. Cat had made us practice strengthening techniques over and over, until a lot them were second nature.

I nodded. "Evidently, it's kerosene because the vial she's opening contains Protection Oil. And Cat always told us to use it in kerosene."

Twila didn't pour the oil in, though. Instead, she looked over at me and held out her hand. I'd already found what we needed, since I'd studied that *Book* as much as she had over the years, trading back and forth when we visited each other. I had my finger stuck in the appropriate page, and I opened the *Book* and handed it to her. Then I stood shoulder to shoulder with her for a while, as we both silently read the incantation written there.

Finished, we stared at each other for a long moment. I'd been too involved up until now to reflect on what we were doing as much as I should have. Probably just as well, since we had no choice. Still, neither of us was all that experienced in messing around in this realm.

As though she had read my mind, Twila murmured, "First time for everything."

I gulped, and we faced each other. We held hands as we combined our forces to fortify ourselves even more by binding our gifts. We didn't forget to concede the danger of what we were about to do.

The moment I acknowledged that thought, I sensed the sizzle of a completely different type of energy around us. I picked up on our ancestor, *Great-grandmere* Alicia, a strong, capable woman, and even sensed Cat with us. Still alive, Cat could nonetheless psychically cross great distances when we needed her. Attuned to each other, we gratefully accepted the unseen support our silent pleas had garnered.

Satisfied we knew what we were doing—as much as possible, given we weren't sure what we were going to encounter on the other end of our ritual, what would be working against us—we dropped hands and hugged each other tightly. I left her with the *Book* and backed away to stand by Jack again. It wouldn't take both of us to do what else was necessary. In fact, two people would only muddy the mental waters.

Crooning under her breath, since the spells would weaken if shared with the others listening, Twila poured the entire bottle of oil into the kerosene. After she reassembled the lamp, she pulled some matches from her jeans pocket and lit it.

Leaving it to burn on the bar, she removed a silver chain from around her neck and stretched it out beside the lamp, making sure the chain lay on top of the black thread. She picked up the fragile chicken bones and formed a cross on the thread, then tied it all together. The cross dangled from the chain when she replaced it around her neck.

"That looks like *gris-gris* to me," Jack whispered.

"Yes," I said. "The marrow in the bones will absorb evil."

"Not much marrow in them tiny things," he said.

"Enough. The other stuff is incense. One's called Circle of Protection, the other *Gris-Gris* Faible. I have to help now."

I went over to the bar as Twila placed the two small votives in the glass holders and lit them. She set them on the floor close to the safe door, but left the lamp on the bar. She lit several stems of Circle of Protection Incense and handed them to me. I picked up the bag of salt, which she'd already opened for me, and carried it with me. Murmuring my own protection incantation, I walked as much of a circle as possible around us, starting from one side of the safe, ending at the other. I scattered salt as I went, and made sure the circle enclosed even the ghosts.

"What about Granny and that other woman?" Jack whispered as I passed him on my way back to the bar.

"If they happen to return, Granny knows enough to steer clear of our ritual," I answered. "But they're going to be a while." I grimaced again at the thought of all the blood in True's room.

Twila had four sticks of the *Gris-Gris* Faible Incense burning and lying across some upside down shot glasses. She'd laid out more glasses for me, and I placed my still burning sticks there, left the salt bag gaped open in case we needed more of it, and set it on the bar.

We both turned to stare at the safe. Our hands fell loosely at our sides, but not for long. We each cupped one hand palm up to accept whatever help the Universe would give us and clasped our other hands together.

"Please," Twila said. "Everyone stay quiet. Jack, go over with Joleen and Gil."

"I—"

"Now!" Twila barked. "Don't argue with me. There are enough complexities in the air around here to deal with. We don't need any more mixed energy."

The spell would be aware of what we were doing, also, but we weren't about to tell Jack that. Whoever put it in place didn't even have to be here. She...or he...was without doubt skilled in the mores of magic, or wouldn't have weaved the spell in the first place. There would be consequences, dire ones, for anyone who tried to bypass it. Anyone watching needed to be away from the danger. We would have preferred Jack and the ghosts to entirely leave the hotel, but Jack would never go for that.

As soon as Jack obeyed my aunt, we each took a deep breath and reached our joined hands out toward the round handle used to open the safe.

Before we touched the steel, the wind roared into an inferno around us, carrying the ear-splitting sound of breaking glass. The noise nearly deafened us. Crystal behind the bar exploded, and shards of deadly glass daggers whooshed through the air.

CHAPTER 23

Twila and I never moved, except to turn slightly to see the responses of Jack and the ghosts. Both men had their guns out before they realized the glass hadn't penetrated our circle of protection. In fact, our incense still smoldered on the intact shot glasses, while the lethal shards shattered and fell to the floor with clinks and thumps of defeat.

We both sniffed the air at the same moment, checking for the smell of alcohol. The spell-caster must have been a booze lover, too, since the bottles were still on the shelves. No odor gagged us, and it would have penetrated even our protection barrier. Only the empty glassware had been flung in attempt to harm or kill.

We returned our attention to the safe, our fingers only an inch away. We didn't withdraw when the flames shot out around the door. We could feel heat—cold heat, though. Too cold to burn. It would have, had we not done the incantations.

"*Chère*," Jack whispered in a panicked voice.

"Shut up, love," I hissed back.

Knowing the spell wasn't done with us—or more frankly, the spell's caster—neither of us moved to grasp the safe door. The flames died, and for a long moment, nothing else transpired. I could sense Jack and the ghosts in the background, wondering why we didn't open the damn thing. Still, we waited.

Suddenly, the lamp flame brightened until it filled the entire chimney. The incense embers flared, and dark gray smoke gathered above the sticks. Beneath our feet, the floor trembled.

"Stand tight," Twila said. To the others, not me. She and I had been ready for this, and the only move we made was to hold tighter to each other's hand.

The floor wobbled into waves undulating as though on a beach. Knowing it was only an illusion, we kept our balance easily. I didn't hear Jack fall, so I assumed he was fine, as were the ghosts. The wave-like motion wouldn't bother the paranormals in their state.

The surf effects continued as the first chair shattered against the barrier. It flew in from the formal dining room doorway on our left, straight at us. Another chair followed, and crashed and splintered, falling on top of the first one. Six more chairs dashed at us, and the undulations frantically rocked at our balance. By the time they died, a pile of chair kindling scattered outside our circle.

"Guess Maddie will have some more clean-up to do," Twila said with a wry chuckle, never taking her eyes from the safe.

"Think it's done?" I asked.

"Maybe."

Fingers within reach of the round handle, we remained motionless for another minute. Finally, we ventured to touch the steel.

A barrage of silverware from the dining room hit our barrier. It crashed and fell...except for one heavy silver butter knife. The tip of it penetrated the protection bubble.

For an instant, the bubble held. The knife hung there wobbling. But the force behind it sent it flying at us.

Twila and I were ready. We both ducked, and the knife zoomed harmlessly over our heads, landing on the floor inside the circle. As she stood back up, Twila swooped the blue candle into her hand and carried it with her. She jammed the flame against the area the knife had torn open—invisible to others, but not to the two of us. With a hiss of hot wax, the tear sealed. When she pulled the candle back, a tinge of light blue hovered there.

Twila returned to my side, clasped my hand once more, and waited. No more glass shattered. No more chairs flew. The floor stayed smooth, and no silverware took flight. In fact, the entire atmosphere lightened.

Our lamp flame settled down to glow at its normal inch-high height. The smoke around the incense sticks lightened from dark gray to white.

But we heard the sound of something crawling behind us. I turned.

That damn knife wiggled frantically toward me. It lifted off the floor an inch, plopped back, then rose two inches, doing its darndest to fly at me. I grabbed the salt bag from the bar and scooped out a good-sized tablespoon. When I poured it on the knife, a scream of anger and frustration exploded around us.

From the corner of my eye, I saw Jack and Gil waving their pistols in the air, searching for something to protect us from.

"It's virtual," I said quietly. "The spell-caster left it behind in a last attempt to scare anyone off who tried to get in the safe."

"Or kill them," Twila reminded me.

"Yeah. Black magic."

"Last?" Jack asked, quietly but with a tenseness in his voice.

"Yes," Twila assured him.

She and I both grabbed the safe handle, twirled it to the left, and swung the door open.

The tinge of light blue where Twila had repaired the bubble fell to the floor. We had totally destroyed the black magic spell. Our incantations no longer felt the need to protect us.

Jack started to move forward, but I held out a hand to warn him back. Before we examined the safe's content, I re-walked my circle, using a mental broom and sweeping motions to open it, since I didn't have a true broom with me. Though we weren't initiated Wiccans, Twila and I both had our own; however, they resided in our homes, to help cleanse them now and then when necessary. I left the salt lie, and anyone with knowledge of magic would know what it meant. We didn't care. If another battle came to pass, at least our opponents would understand they weren't dealing with amateurs in the various other realms.

I nodded at Jack, and he stuck his pistol in the holster behind his back and joined us at the safe. Open, the door exposed an area four feet across, and the space extended at least four feet back into the wall.

Twila and I stepped back and allowed Jack the pleasure of pulling out the firearms, which confirmed her instinct. He lifted out two rifles first, both old Winchester lever-action carbines from the late 1800's. I'd done some research once for a book, so I recognized them.

Jack gave Twila the satisfaction of meeting her gaze and nodding a validation, then propped the rifles against the wall. He reached back in the safe and removed several pistols, every one a six-shot revolver. Those he placed on the bar, and before he walked away, I stopped him.

"Look," I said. "Those are all loaded."

"Damn sure are," he muttered.

He picked up one pistol and dumped the bullets into his hand. Then he looked around for something to put them in. Since every glass around us was shattered, he started to stick them in his pocket, but shook his head.

"I can't carry all these on me. Can one of you go get a bowl from the kitchen?"

"Let me help," Gil said. He turned and wiggled his fingers. A second later, a red plastic bowl floated into the saloon and landed gently on the bar. Jack just shook his head and dumped the bullets in, then picked up another revolver.

Evidently tired of waiting, Twila brought two more pistols over to us. I went back to the safe with her, and by the time we were done, ten rifles and fifteen pistols were propped against the wall or lying on the bar, all weaponry from the Wild West age of the late 1800's. All spotless and in what appeared to be excellent working order.

"We need to unload these rifles, too." I glanced at the bar and saw Jack and Gil closely studying the pistols. Joleen laughed at them and floated over to us.

"Men and their toys," she said. "I heard that on television once."

Twila and I chuckled in agreement. Then Twila said, "I'd really like to leave these things loaded. Isn't there a safety thingie on them?"

"They're lever action," I told her. Recalling my tomboy days, I picked up a rifle and held it barrel pointed away from all of us. I also recalled a few of the Ten Commandments of Gun Safety I had studied until they, too, were one of my second-nature instincts: Never point a gun at anyone unless you mean to use it. Always treat a gun as though it were loaded. If you do aim a gun at someone with the intent to use it, kill them. Dead people can't testify against you in court.

After my mental review of safety rules, I demonstrated the action on the rifle. "To load a bullet, you pull this lever down, then back in place. Thus, lever-action. It moves the bullet into the chamber. After that, you can gently squeeze the trigger and shoot. But there might already be a bullet in there, so you have to be careful. However, a chambered bullet would eject when you pulled down the lever."

Twila and Joleen both studied the rifle's mechanism for a few seconds.

"How do you know they're loaded?" the ghost asked.

I carefully jacked the lever open and showed them the exposed shell. When I replaced the lever, the hammer on the rifle was pulled back. Gently, I grasped the hammer with my thumb, eased on the trigger, and laid it back in place.

"Not that you really need to know," I said, "but that hammer hits a firing pin, that hits the shell. There's gunpowder in it, and a spark ignites that. Boom, the shell blasts out the barrel. The spent bullet stays in the chamber until you eject it."

I went on to warn: "Remember another important fact. Once you pull the trigger, you can't recall the bullet."

One after the other, I examined the guns, with Joleen watching my every move. Twila reached for the last rifle and did the examination herself before she propped it with the others. I decided not to test Joleen's abilities, and didn't offer her a rifle to inspect.

"Then they're all already on safety," the ghost said before I could.

The sound of bullets rattling drew my attention back to the bar, where Jack...and, yes, Gil, too...were reloading the pistols.

"Good idea to keep them loaded, Twila," Jack said. "We'll leave the hammers on an empty chamber, though. Remember that, if you need to use them." He halted in the middle of shoving a bullet into a chamber of the pistol in his hand, then pushed it on in and said with a groan, "What the hell am I talkin' about? We don't need a bunch of pistol-packin' women and ghosts shootin' at each other around here."

Neither Twila nor I laughed at what he...perhaps...meant as a joke.

Twila answered his jibe with, "Tell us the safe combination, Jack."

He tossed her an incredulous look. "Are you sure? When did you learn to use a gun?"

"Jess taught me," she said. "What's the combination?"

Just then, we heard Granny and Maddie walk into the lobby, chattering with each other in the same vivacious fashion as they had since first meeting. The clean-up must not have tired them out as much as I'd anticipated. But they both halted at the saloon door. For some reason, I looked at where I'd last seen Joleen and Gil, but they had both vanished.

"What on earth happened in here?" Maddie asked. "Look at this mess."

"Sorry," Twila said. "We'll clean it up."

"How did you get that safe open?" Maddie asked.

"We were just fooling around," Twila said with a vague wave of her hand. "Doing our job here, checking things out."

Granny wandered over and stuck her head inside the safe door. When she stood back up, something hung in her hand.

"Lookee!" She held up a gun belt and holster. "An' they's more in here."

Granny took it upon herself to remove the rest of the gun belts, six in all. She passed them around as she took them out, all except the last one. That, the smallest one, which looked as though it might have been made for an older child, she placed around her tiny waist. Snugging it tight, she pranced over to the bar and picked up one of the pistols to shove in the holster. None of us had the guts to stop her, but Jack cringed.

I knew Granny a lot better than Jack. She also understood firearm basics and safety. She didn't play with the gun by pulling it out and aiming it around. Instead, she scowled, propped her hand on the gun butt, and toddled around the saloon.

"You's best not mess with me, you bastids," she said with a growl. "I's the sheriff in this here town."

Her antics broke the last vestiges of tension in the room. We all laughed, then got to work cleaning up the mess and replacing the firearms in the safe. As we finished, Jack tucked a piece of paper in my hand, and another in Twila's. We both stuck what I presumed was the safe combination in our jeans pockets.

* * *

"Look, sweetheart," Gil said, as the two of them stood at the foot of the bed in the last room on the second floor. "We can't. You know what they said when they found out you'd took off and talked to Alice. If we mess with them, they'll send us out to wander around lost somewhere."

"If they can get rid of us themselves, why did Danny have to ask Twila here?"

"I don't know," Gil admitted. "And we don't know for sure if Danny's a coven member. Or even who all of them are."

"You saw what Alice and Twila did. I think they're stronger than them. They can protect us."

"It took those two time to prepare," Gil reminded her. "What if they retaliate the minute we start talking? It would be too late for them to save us. We'd be gone and probably never get back here to help your brother."

"You don't give a darn about helping True," Joleen accused.

Gil rolled his eyes. "If you make me admit it, I don't. But I do love you. And I'll do anything to make you happy, even if it means putting up with your kid brother. Who, might I remind you, made quite a few women unhappy in his life."

"None of them were right for him," she defended. "But he loved Marina."

"Yeah, he did. But she was married to another man. That's adultery."

"Her husband hit her!" She walked over to Gil and looped her arms around his neck. "He wasn't a wonderful man like you." Gratified, she felt Gil pull her close. Even in their state of being, they could feel each other's bodies.

"I love you," Joleen said. "Forever."

"Well," Gil said in a wry tone. "I'm glad we're in this forever business together." He dropped a kiss on her lips. "And you've always been my forever love."

She drew his head back down and showed her love this time with another kiss. Gil backed her towards the bed.

"But we should decided about—"

"Later," Gil murmured, cupping her hips to draw their bodies together and capturing her lips again.

The blood curdling scream brought all of us to our feet from where we sat around one of the restaurant tables. My water glass of Crown and Seven crashed at my feet, spattering my jeans with alcohol and soda. Without any bar glasses to use, we'd cleaned up the saloon, then grabbed our booze of choice and carried it into the restaurant area, where Granny had set up a new make-shift bar, complete with ice and mixers, along with glasses from the kitchen. None of us would have more than one drink, but we all needed that.

Jack lunged away from the table first, his pistol already in his hand.

Damn, I mused as Twila and I followed him more slowly, *that gun's in his hand a lot lately.*

Twila and I both halted at the kitchen door. I was recalling what happened the last time we'd found trouble in that room—the attack by the handless ghost. We separated, and each one peeked around a different side of the door jamb.

In the far corner of the room, Maddie stood behind poor little Granny, holding the elderly woman against her far larger body like a shield. She gasped and looked on the verge of hyperventilating. Granny inattentively patted the arms Maddie clasped tightly around her waist with one hand and pointed across the room with the other. The back of Jack's shirt bulged from his replaced pistol, and he gazed at the open freezer door on top of the refrigerator, then back at Granny.

Jack pointed his own finger: at Granny, then the freezer.

Granny nodded.

"What's in there?" Jack asked.

Granny opened her mouth, but only a gabble of half-formed words emerged. "Goo-ugh-ha-ha-ugh-na-na-na...."

"Good grief," Twila whispered. "If what's in there has Granny stupefied, it must be bad."

"Should we...?" But I answered myself. "No way in hell. Let the man do it this time."

"I agree."

Jack didn't. He grimaced in distaste and didn't make a move towards the open freezer door. Glancing over, he saw us standing there.

"You ladies leave something in there to scare folks off?"

"Not us," Twila denied at the same moment I said, "Nope."

With a thud, Maddie collapsed on the floor. Lucky for Granny, her faint loosened her muscles and her arms dropped from Granny's waist. Without thought, I raced across the room, Twila right behind me. We both ignored Maddie and helped Granny over to sit on a chair beside the small kitchen table.

Twila plunked a bottle of Jim Beam I hadn't noticed her carrying down, then apparently realized she needed a glass to give Granny a fortifying shot of alcohol.

Glasses which were in a cupboard over near the freezer door. Twila stared at me, an order in her eyes.

"Uh...I better check on Maddie."

"Alice!" she demanded. But I scurried around her and Granny to bend over Maddie, who was already moaning and regaining consciousness.

"Here," Jack said, as he set a juice glass on the table. He didn't wait for Twila, though. He poured it nearly full and handed it to Granny.

She slugged it down without pause...until it hit her stomach. Then she gasped and held her chest. Before we had cause for alarm, she said, "Whooeee. Thankee, Jack."

He stared over at the freezer door instead of answering her.

"What's in there?" Twila asked Granny.

"Uh...." She clacked her false teeth together, something her pride hardly ever allowed her to sink to. Then she shook her head without answering.

Jack sighed and walked over to the freezer. Maddie groaned again and distracted me. I helped her sit up, and when I looked back at Jack, he still stood staring into the open compartment, condensation from cold hitting warm air feathering in a cloud around his head.

"I's...." Granny poured her own drink this time, although she managed to get as much on the table as in the glass, what with her trembling hand. She drank another swallow. "I's was digging down deep to try's to see if mebbe I missed some crawdads to use in my gumbo."

"And?" Twila prodded.

Granny only shook her head and drank more Jim.

Twila and I both stared at Maddie, but she swung her head back and forth a lot more violently than Granny had. She scrambled to her feet, and before anyone could stop her, rushed out the back kitchen doorway.

"Wonder iffen that means she ain't gonna want us to come for dinner?" Granny mused.

I giggled at first, but it died quickly. All three of us turned to stare at Jack.

"Come on, Jack. Show us," Twila said—unfortunately for our sensibilities.

He picked up a dish towel from the counter and reached into the freezer. Granny stood abruptly and followed Maddie's path in as quick a toddle as I'd seen her manage in years.

Jack turned around.

A hand hacked off at the wrist dangled in Jack's grasp. He held the index finger, which was frozen into a splay with the rest of the digits.

My stomach lurched.

I heard Twila gag.

But the sink where we needed to puke was over there close to Jack.

We both slapped our palms over our mouths and went after Granny and Maddie.

"Well, you wanted to see," Jack called, then let go of a wicked cackle.

Comeuppance wasn't long in coming to Jack. In fact, we didn't even get five steps from the kitchen before something forced us to forget our churning stomachs.

A piercing howl of both victory and rage split the air.

"Hey!" Jack shouted. "Get the hell out of here!" Then, "Alice! Help!"

Twila and I skidded to a stop. The last thing on earth I wanted to do was go back in there. But how could I ignore a plea from Jack? He'd never asked a woman to come to his aid since diapers.

CHAPTER 24

Another shriek split the air. I instinctively rushed forward, but halted after two steps and cast Twila a silent plea.

"He's your man," she said.

"Alice!" Jack yelled. Then added, "Twila! Damn it!"

"He wants you, too," I said unnecessarily. "And he opened the safe for us."

"Crap," she muttered.

We both rushed to the door, which opened inward into the dining room. I pulled it back, expediently jamming it against the wall by stepping in front of it.

Twila and I gaped. Karen stalked Jack, who backed away from her. The hand still swung in Jack's hold, but he used his other hand to jerk the small table away from the wall, sliding it between him and Karen. I didn't have the heart to remind him that wouldn't stop a ghost.

"Give it to me!" Karen screamed, both her handless arms extended.

"It's evidence," Jack yelled back at her.

Oh, god. Only Jack would point out something that absurd to a ghost! Twila and I held our stomachs and collapsed forward in uproarious laughter.

Karen lunged straight through the table. Quick as a cat, Jack jumped away, heading for escape through the other doorway.

Karen beat him to it. Her body, enough of a body to thwart Jack, anyway, blocked the opening. She held her arms up and shook them.

"They're mine!" she screamed.

Jack retreated. Giggling and choking, Twila and I wedged our backs against the wall and slid down to sit on the floor.

Catching a motion in my side vision, I turned my head to see Trucker and Miss Molly prance in. They sat down on the other side of the doorway. Neither of them laughed, but Trucker's tongue hung out in a pant. Miss Molly only lifted her head in her normal haughty gesture and circled her tail around her rump.

I managed to control myself long enough to say, "You should let her have her hand, Jack."

He turned his glare on me...and that was all it took. Karen swooped over and stuck her right arm onto the cut-off wrist. The *slurp* rocked my stomach, but my interest overcame the nausea. When Karen jerked back, the hand came with her.

Jack didn't bother to argue. He slowly withdrew and stood with Trucker and Miss Molly on their side of the door.

Unfortunately for Karen, she'd stuck her wrong arm out. Her left hand now protruded from her right arm.

"Damn it!" she barked.

Wondering what she would do stilled every other bit of sound in the room. We watched in fascination as Karen grabbed her left arm with her left hand and pulled. Nothing happened.

Karen groaned and heaved harder, the strain clear on her contorted face.

The left hand stayed on the right arm.

Karen gave up...we thought. Instead, she loosened her hold, then stuck her left handless arm to the juncture of the wrist on her other arm.

Slurp.

The hand jumped to the correct arm. Karen flexed it for a few seconds, then zeroed her glaring eyes on Jack. "Where's the other one?"

Jack clamped his lips, but I blurted, "In the freezer on top of the 'fridge."

Jack didn't even bother to slide me a chastising glower.

Karen swiveled and stuck her handless arm into the freezer compartment. When she withdrew it, her right hand was attached. She grinned in victory...and vanished.

Jack slid down to sit beside my dog and cat.

We broke our one-drink-during-an-investigation rule. Neither Twila nor I would walk through that kitchen, though. I shuddered at how close I'd been to those hands earlier while I cooked. Even knowing I might have to get into the 'fridge if we ended up being here long enough to need future meals couldn't force me to overcome my distaste right now. Twila, neither, it seemed, since after Karen vanished, she only stayed in the kitchen long enough to grab the bottle of Jim Beam.

Perhaps to overcome his humiliation at a piece of protoplasm from another dimension horrifying him, Jack stalked over and slammed the freezer door shut. He continued on out of the room.

Followed by Trucker and Miss Molly, Twila and I circled around through the dining room, then the saloon, into the café to fix new drinks at Granny's bar. Jack already had one in his hand. Luckily for me, since my glass had shattered on the floor, Granny had put out extra. I also fixed Granny one, although I wasn't sure if I should, given the amount of alcohol already in her tiny frame. She could handle quite a bit, though, as I'd found out during our late-night *tête-à-têtes* in Six Gun. And she could lambaste with the best of them, if I left her out when she wanted another drink.

I didn't have to worry. Granny lay sprawled in one of the lobby chairs, gray hair splayed from her normal neat bun around her head propped on the chair arm. Her snores shivered against her lips, false teeth in her lap.

In order not to disturb her, we headed for the far corner, under a large elk head with glassy brown eyes. I handed Twila the drink I'd prepared for Granny, Jim always being my aunt's top booze choice. We sat on a loveseat, Jack on a couch across from us. My pets crawled up beside Jack, one on each side. Jack laid a hand on Trucker's head, then swigged his Jack and Coke.

After he swallowed, Jack said, "Now what?"

I didn't take any pleasure in Jack bowing to us being in charge. I sipped my drink and raised my eyebrows at Twila. She shrugged and lifted her own glass to her lips.

The three of us drank for several moments in silence, all evidently totally without a clue as to our next move.

Jack finally gently shoved Trucker's head off his lap and rose to walk over to the window. He drew back the curtain and said, "Still iced over out there."

"Warming trend's not supposed to hit until tomorrow," I told him.

"When you don't know what else to say," Twila murmured, "talk about the weather."

I swallowed more Crown and Seven, glad I'd mixed a double.

"Well," I said into the new silence. "We should try to find out what happened to Maddie. Maybe the phones are working. Surely they've got utility repairmen out."

Jack strode over to the desk and lifted the phone receiver. He shook his head and replaced it. His ski jacket hung on a hook inside the door, and he pulled his cell phone from a pocket. That, too, garnered a negative head shake.

Twila stood, leaving the drink I'd prepared for Granny untouched and placing her own half-finished glass beside it. "Didn't you say the truck you borrowed had chains, Jack? Back home, we drive on ice that way when we have to. I, for one, am about half-claustrophobic."

"In this huge place?" Jack said, then went on before we could censure him, "Never mind. I know what you mean." He glanced at Granny and the pets. "But the truck won't hold all of us."

"And we're not about to leave Granny or the animals alone here," Twila assured him.

"Granny made sure our SUV came with chains," I said. "They're supposed to be in a side pocket in the hatchback."

Jack wiped a hand inside the door window to clear the frost. But at least an inch of ice had frozen on the outside of the glass, blocking the view. He turned the knob, and the door opened easily.

"Wasn't this locked?" he asked me with a frown.

"Definitely," I said. "Maybe Maddie went out that way and forgot to lock it behind her."

He glanced outside, then shut the door and twisted the dead blot into place. "I'll get my gear on and put the chains on your tires. You ladies make sure the rest of our crew is ready."

Rather glad to see Jack back in his take-charge mode, I didn't argue. We headed for our rooms to get our coats, boots and other warmer gear, as well as Granny's. If we needed to, we could dress her and even have Jack carry her out to the SUV.

Jack followed and reminded me to give him my car keys. He finished with the chains before we were all ready to go and waited at the front door. I'd even found the heavy sweaters I'd brought along for Trucker and Miss Molly, and made them wear those in case we got stuck somewhere and had to walk back.

Trucker didn't mind his red one with the dancing white snowmen amidst the green pine trees, but Miss Molly snarled at me. Too bad, she found out I was the boss about this. She looked just too cute in her merry red and green Christmas knit with reindeer leaping into the air pulling a sled-load of gold-paper-wrapped presents. I left the Santa hat dangling, though, rather than risk dire injury if I tried to cram it over her ears. I also decided not to push the ON button for the flashing lights outlining the deer and which would also pulse on Rudolph's nose. She won those two.

We didn't have to dress Granny. She woke as chipper as though after a full night's sleep. I'd never seen her with a hangover, although she'd nursed me through one or two. She donned her own warm winter wear as I explained we were going out to reconnoiter the status of the utility repair work and try to find Maddie's house.

When she joined him at the door, Jack handed her the walking stick she carried sometimes. "I's'll still hold onto you, too, Jack," she said.

"My pleasure, Granny," he responded. "I left the vehicle running, so it's already warm for us."

"Good thinkin'," she said with a nod of appreciation.

We were ready to be on our way. I locked the door behind us. Jack reached past me and checked the security of it.

"If we find it unlocked when we get back," he cautioned, "I'll go in first."

"That's fine with us," Twila said.

I didn't protest when Jack helped Granny settle in the back seat and walked around to the SUV's driver side. He wasn't listed on my rental policy, but since I already had one nick to explain, I decided he would be the better one to navigate us around in this mess. Twila would also be capable, but she didn't oppose Jack's intention, either.

I'd already lifted the hatchback. Trucker leaped in himself, and I settled Miss Molly beside him. My cat tossed me a disgruntled look. You'd never think cats could communicate. Maybe others didn't, but every one of mine sure did, with Miss Molly at the top of the interface ladder.

Twila got in the passenger seat behind Jack, leaving me to ride front shotgun. A moment later, Jack shifted into four-wheel drive and slowly drove down the street, chains clanking.

"We should probably check on Maddie first," I said. "She told us she only lived a block away. But I don't know which way."

Despite the security of the chains gripping through the ice, he carefully turned at the corner. "We'll drive around the hotel and see if we can find her footprints."

Problem was, several sets of imprints marred the top of the snow, which was now covered by ice, so they punched through the slick surface. Without getting out of the vehicle, we couldn't tell if they were men or women's boots, or maybe animal tracks. Some led up to the hotel windows, then back away. Others trailed along the sidewalks and disappeared in tracks from snowmobiles. I'd only heard the one machine

Danny drove, but we could have missed the sounds of others as we slept or our attention became distracted otherwise. There had to have been others, because we noticed several trails. Not all of them kept to the road, either. Some led across yards.

We actually didn't have any trouble finding Maddie's house. Jack pulled up in front of the ice-covered real estate sign in her yard.

"Doesn't look like she's home," he said. "I don't see any lights on. And no one's walked up that sidewalk for a while."

"Maybe she comes and goes through the back," I said.

He glanced at me, then out the side window, towards the hotel behind us. "Would be the long way around to the hotel," he said logically.

Still, he dropped the SUV into gear and drove on around the corner. Only another line of houses occupied that half of the block, and we couldn't see the back of Maddie's house.

"We'll check here again before we go back to the hotel," Jack said, maneuvering onward.

After several more blocks, we came to an area of town where numerous stores lined what appeared to be the main street. No lights showed in any of those buildings, other than several signs, which twinkled on and off to identify the names of stores. But at the end of the street, we found a welcome sight: a pair of utility company trucks.

The lettering on the doors indicated they were from a telephone repair company. Evidently, this town hadn't had the funds yet to bury their utility lines, and the company hadn't bothered to buy a truck with one of those cherry-picker things to ride their repairmen up in the air. One man clung to the pole, a set of climbing cleats on his boots and a safety belt holding him in place. He studied something in his hand intently.

Jack pulled over and shifted into Park. He opened the driver's door, but left the vehicle running to keep us warm.

While Jack talked to the repairmen, I checked on Twila and Granny. Granny's eyes sparkled back at me, but Twila leaned against the window, taking one of what she called her Power Naps. She could slip into sleep for five minutes and wake as alert as though after a full eight hours. I questioned her once about why her naps were so short, even when we weren't doing much and she could have slept longer.

"Don't want to miss anything," she'd said with one of her quirky grins.

Even as I watched, she woke and looked around at the animals in the back, then at Granny and me.

"Jack's seeing if we might get phone service soon," I said. "And there's nothing else at all open."

"Ain't nobody in any of them there homes 'round here, neither," Granny said. "What's these folks do? Go to South Texas for the winters?"

Since we had no idea, Twila and I didn't attempt to answer. I'd also noticed the lack of population. It hadn't seemed that deserted when we arrived the night before. The restaurant where Danny took us to eat had several customers. Come to think of it, though, there were also plenty of empty tables.

Jack got back behind the wheel and said, "They think we might have service sometime in the next hour. If one of the rebuilt parts they have with them will work. Otherwise, they'll have to go back to their home office over in Angel Fire and get another one."

"Murphy's Law," Twila mused. "They'll probably have to go to Angel Fire."

"Should we head back?" Jack asked.

"Oh, please, no," I said. "Can't we just drive around a little longer?"

"My thoughts, too, *Chère*," he said. "But what about the rest of y'all?"

"I's vote to drive some more," Granny said, and Twila nodded in agreement.

My pets didn't voice a vote, although I jokingly lifted myself from my seat to see them lying in the back. "They both say, 'Onward Ho.'"

We laughed, and Jack agreeably drove on down the street and around the corner. He glanced in the rearview mirror and slammed on the brakes. Even with the chains, we slid sideways, barely missing a parked car.

Disturbed, Trucker lunged to his feet and looked out the rear window.

And erupted into a frenzy of deep-throated barks so loud we covered our ears. Miss Molly leapt to the window and propped her feet on it. Her shrill meows joined her buddy's fury. The four of us swiveled to see what the problem was, but I guess Jack had already seen the elk.

The darn animal stomped up to the utility truck nearest the telephone pole. It batted those long, sharp horns at the driver's door, and we could hear the screeching scrapes even through our closed windows. The driver already had the window on the rise, his shoulder shaking as he cranked the handle. He made it, but unfortunately caught the tip of one elk horn.

The huge elk jerked away, and the window shattered. Made of safety glass, it crumbled into harmless pieces. The driver didn't bother to hang around and see if the elk stuck its head in the truck. He scrambled out the passenger door and raced to the second truck. The elk spied him, and gave chase.

The men in the other truck already had the door open for their fellow worker to scramble in, and they slammed it shut only an inch from the elk's nose. The antlers hit hard, and the animal bounced back. It stood there shaking its head as though stunned.

"What the hell is wrong with that animal?" Jack asked.

"Horny," Granny said. "This is the time a year they's mates. Must not be able to find him a girlfriend."

The elk threw its head back and...bugled, I guessed they called that. His upper lip drew back, exposing a set of teeth meant only to eat grass and vegetation. I wouldn't have wanted to be on the receiving end of a bite from them, though.

The elk attacked the telephone pole next. The poor repairman hugged his arms around it and held on. The horn jabs didn't really shake the large pole, yet the man had to be terrified to see that animal waiting for him to climb down. Plus, it was damn cold out. Even through heavy clothing, he might develop hypothermia, if he remained motionless up there for too long. As bothersome as that majestic elk had been, I would have hated to see him put down to save a human.

The elk evidently decided he was going to wait around right there for one of the men to give him another opportunity for a game of chase and catch. He backed away from the pole, but wandered a circle around it, then one of the trucks, then back to the pole.

Jack opened his door. "Maybe if I shoot in the air, it'll scare that stupid animal off."

"Stay here by the door, Jack," I warned.

Trucker lunged into the backseat, his fury unabated. Jack didn't have time to close the driver's door and thwart my dog's escape. Trucker continued into the front, barreled into Jack, and Jack ended up on his ass on the ground. Trucker ignored his sprawled body and took off around the truck. I grabbed for Miss Molly, but only succeeded in snatching her sweater. She tugged, and I tried to gather a stronger handful of wool.

Miss Molly laid her ears against her skull and rolled onto her back, waving paws with exposed claws in the air as she growled her anger. I instinctively let go. With a *meow-ser* of victory, she scrambled to her feet to face Jack, blocking the door again.

"Miss Mol—" he began.

I missed her again when she lunged straight at Jack's chest, then over his shoulder.

"Ouch!" he yelled as she sprang away. He'd unzipped his jacket, and Miss Molly's claws found no barrier to grabbing a hold to propel her leap. Having been on the receiving end of my cat's claws myself a time or two, although both were accidental injuries, I winced in sympathy.

Jack drew his pistol. He held the barrel pointed into the air, but then his mouth gawped in astonishment. The windows had started to fog up, so I pushed the button on the keychain dangling in the ignition to roll down the hatchback glass and see what had stunned him.

Granny, Twila and I stared through the opening. Trucker sat on his haunches in front of that elk, his barks and growls silenced. Miss Molly padded the last couple feet over the packed snow and ice in the street and cuddled close to her dog pal. The elk held his head and antlers up in that haughty gesture elks use, staring into the distance. Then it slowly lowered its head and touched noses with Trucker. Even Miss Molly accepted a tender thrust from the huge animal.

"Aw, they're making friends," Twila said. "How cute."

I wasn't sure the repairman on the pole thought it charming. He stared down at the elk, now joined by a huge dog that had a reputation for viciousness and a cat with a supposedly similar nature.

I started to get out of the car. "I better get my dog before he scares that repairman to death."

"Alice!" Twila barked. "Get back in here right now."

"But—"

"Did you not see that animal attack those men?" she said. "Call your dog all you want from here, but don't you dare go over there."

"Oh," I said, and shut my door again.

Just then, Trucker stood and trotted off down the street.

"Trucker, get back here!" I yelled through the rear window.

He ignored me, but Miss Molly ran towards us. She didn't stop until she got to the SUV and leaped in through the open rear window. Not even then. She jumped over the seat and cuddled on Granny's lap.

"Poor cold kitty," Granny said.

Still a bit pissed at the cat, I ignored her as my gaze searched for Trucker.

Jack got back in behind the wheel and said, "Don't worry, *Chère*. We'll find him."

And find him we did, only a couple blocks away...with another elk. A cow, since it didn't have antlers. It followed Trucker obediently as he totally disregarded us where we were stopped in the street. Jack U-turned the SUV and drove after them. Every one of us knew where the dog was headed.

He was. He led the cow into sight of the bull. It bellowed a cry filled with a mixture of what I considered thanks and anticipation of release of sexual tension. It galloped at the dog and cow.

I tensed, sure the huge elk meant to toss Trucker out of the way of its mounting. But it skidded to a halt, touched noses with the dog, and

Trucker trotted off to leave the two of them in privacy for mating. The bull bugled again, then rushed at the cow.

Perhaps she didn't like his off-key song. Perhaps she wasn't ready yet. Or perhaps she wanted a bit more foreplay than just him jumping her, which is what he tried to do. She kicked out with her rear legs and caught the bull in the chest. We could hear his *oomph* of pain through the still open rear window. He drew back and stared at the cow with what I considered a mournful look. His next bugle sounded like an elk version of *Taps*.

Trucker turned and walked to the elks. For a few seconds, he stood there staring back and forth between them. His last glance centered on the bull, then he walked away. So did the cow. Tail twitching, she sauntered off.

The bull followed her, its huge antlered head sunk in suitable chastisement at its display of overabundant testosterone.

CHAPTER 25

We drove by Maddie's house again, with no luck. Back at the hotel, Jack carried his duffle bag down the hall to choose a bedroom for himself. Granny headed for the kitchen to make sure we'd have one of her delicious meals for dinner, and Trucker and Miss Molly tagged after her.

I stared around, at a loss as to what to do next. Twila decided for us both. She took my arm and led me over to the lobby couch. We sat facing each other.

"How's your head?" she asked first.

I felt the knot, which had diminished to a mere bump. "The headache's gone, but the spot's still tender. I'm sure it will be fine by tomorrow."

"Knee?"

I held my leg out and tentatively twisted it back and forth. "Lot's better, too. Still a twinge, though." Before she could ask, I continued, "My ribs aren't bothering me that much, either."

"Ribs?" She scowled at me. "You never mentioned your ribs."

"They're only bruised. I put some of your ointment on them, and last time I looked, you could barely see where I hit the tub."

230

"We'll put some more ointment on both places in a few minutes. Right now, what's going on with Jack? What did you say to him in the kitchen?"

"Jack?" I asked, utterly confused at the quick subject shift. She remained silent as I tried to figure out where she was going with this. Weren't we here to investigate ghosts, not mine and Jack's relationship?

Oh. Our relationship. Now I understood. I pulled to mind Jack's teasing banter with Joleen. The fact he actually stood right beside the two apparitions while Twila and I worked to counteract the Black Magic protecting the safe. His recent lack of denigration of my ghost hunting activities.

Come to think of it, most of his anger at what we did seemed to stem from worry I might get hurt. Twila, also, of course. Still, I was the one he'd at one time professed his undying love to.

Oops. There was that reference again to dead or dying, something that overshadowed all our activities here.

"What did you two talk about in the kitchen?" Twila prodded. "Or is it none of my business?"

"Oh, Twila, it's always your business." I reached out and took her hand in mine. "I don't know what I would have done without you the past couple years, after our...dee-vorce." I chuckled wryly. Granny's designation of mine and Jack's split now appeared to be part of my regular vocabulary.

"Yes, but...." She bit her lip.

"What? We can talk about anything, can't we?"

"Well, not *anything*," she denied with her quiet laugh. "But...well, I know part of the reason you and Jack split was because of your paranormal interests. And I'm the one who led you down that trail. Who's kept you involved."

"You feel guilty because you taught me about ghost hunting?" I shook my head in astonishment. "So you're only acting like you care to ease your guilt?"

I couldn't look at her; I stared over at the black bear head hanging on the far wall.

"Oh, for pity sakes!" Now I'd gotten her red-headed dander up. "If you ever didn't want to join me, you could have said no at any time."

"Exactly." I met her brown gaze. "And I was chasing after ghosts with you long before I met Jack. He knew it was part of my life, just like my writing."

She giggled. "You were just making a point, huh?"

"Exactly," I repeated.

We laughed together in a release of tension, then hugged each other tightly.

When I drew back, I said, "Don't you ever worry about any fault on your end over mine and Jack's problems. But I am glad you brought this up. We .. uh...we did talk a little bit in the kitchen. But we decided to wait until all this mess is over with before we sit down and get serious. Did you know Jack actually quit his job in New Orleans and took the one in that smaller Texas town because he didn't like what New Orleans had done to our marriage?"

"I sort of figured that."

"He didn't exactly say so," I clarified. "But that's where he was going."

"Did you tell him about your plans to go...what did you call it? Indie or something like that."

"Yeah, indie. A couple friends have been bugging me to start our own publishing company. I don't know as I'd want to be in on the business end of it, but I'm a pretty good editor. And I can spot talent in an author —things someone else would miss."

"And your name alone would give the company credence."

Embarrassed as always at someone thinking I was a big-shot star, I squirmed on the sofa. "Well, it's all still in the thinking-about-it phase."

"As long as you *think about* Jack, too, while you consider all that."

"Definitely," I agreed, recalling the few minutes we had alone in the bedroom, which....

...damn it, had ended up in another argument....

...which was at least as much my fault as Jack's....

A crash from the kitchen brought both of us to our feet. We raced toward the sound, and Jack immediately joined us. Had he been eavesdropping in the hallway? If so, how much had he heard? No time to chew over that. Granny was in danger.

We passed Trucker and Miss Molly running away from the kitchen. They didn't bother to change direction.

No, Granny wasn't in danger. We halted at the kitchen door. Granny stood there, hands on her nearly non-existent hips, glaring down at a crystal bowl shattered on the floor.

"Dad-blasted thing just slipped right through my tired old fingers," she griped. "Was gonna make us another of them purty salads. It woulda looked nice in that there bowl."

"Let me clean it up for you, Granny." Jack headed for the supply closet, and Twila and I carefully navigated through the glass shards.

"Don't worry about it." I patted Granny on the shoulder. "You want to take a break? You've been working pretty hard today."

Uh oh. Wrong comment. She stiffened under my hand.

"An' I's too old to work?" she said with a glare up at me from her diminutive height.

"No. Nonono," I assured her. "It's just...well, if you need any help, holler. O.K?"

Twila and I both turned to rush out of the room. A disgruntled Granny could rip our ears off with her decades worth of vocabulary. Twila paused at the stove to sniff the pot of gumbo bubbling there and made the mistake of reaching for a wooden spoon to take a taste.

"It ain't ready to eat yit!" Granny fumed.

Twila dropped the spoon and stayed right behind me as we scurried on out the door.

"Whew," she said as we halted by the coffeepot. "All we were doing was trying to help."

"Sometimes Granny takes offense at offers to help. Thinks of them as digs at her age." I shook my head. "We'll just keep an eye on her. Make sure she's not getting too tired. She won't appreciate it, but we'll feel better. She's so active all the time, I forget her age."

"Yeah."

Another crash sounded in the kitchen. This time, Twila and I stood firm. We'd wait until Granny called and said she needed our help.

She didn't call, and I busied myself making a cup of tea for each of us. Someone—probably the busy Granny again—had dumped the old coffee and filled the pot with hot water. I'd have to remember to tell her how much we appreciated her thoughtfulness. None of us cared for coffee later in the day. She'd set out some flavored tea bags, also, and I opened a raspberry-peach to dunk in my water. Twila chose a wild berry mix.

A plate of oatmeal-raison cookies lay beside the coffeepot, store-bought, as Granny would call them, but they looked fairly fresh. We each picked up a couple. Then we settled at a table to nibble cookies while we waited for the tea to cool enough to sip.

"Jack should have cleaned up that mess by now," Twila mused.

"Uh...maybe he went on out the other door to his room. He might not want to talk to us right now. I think he was listening from the hallway."

"Good," she said. "If you can't talk it out, maybe you can go at the problem sideways."

"Maybe so."

She frowned. "I'm going to try to sneak a peak and see if he left, though. If he did, we'll hang around here for a while in case Granny does need us."

She scooted her chair back at the same time Joleen appeared in the kitchen doorway.

"You better get in here," Joleen said out loud, worry creases on her face.

We didn't stop to question her. She barely had time to move out of the way before we ran right through her. In the kitchen, Gil knelt over an unconscious Jack. There was no sign of Granny.

"Omigod!" I rushed over to Jack and automatically pushed Gil out of the way. Of course, my hand went straight through him, but he took the hint and moved. I knelt and scooped Jack's head into my arm to pat his cheek.

"Jack. Jack, wake up! Jack!"

Twila handed me a wet cloth, and I wiped his face. The coldness worked to rouse him, and he stirred. He blinked several times, confusion and pain in his chocolate eyes. Finally, he appeared to realize where he was—on the floor—and pushed away from me to try to get to his feet. Twila and I helped him up and into a chair.

"Where's Granny?" I asked, as Twila handed Jack a glass of water, then walked behind his chair to look at his head. I'd already felt the knot when I held him. It was even larger than the one I suffered in the tub.

He gulped down half the water as his gaze scanned the kitchen. He slammed the glass on the table. "She didn't come out to get you two?"

"Joleen did. We haven't see Granny." Worry for my elderly best friend crowded my concern for Jack in my mind. Deep dread chased after that.

"Who hit you, Jack?" Twila asked, her tone mirroring my own anxiety.

"Hit me?" Evidently he was still a bit confused. Then he shoved both of us away and stood, kicking the chair into the wall with his foot. "Some bastard crept up on me and cold-cocked me! He must have Granny!"

Despite what must have been a throbbing head, Jack raced out of the kitchen and through the formal dining room, the quickest way to the front door. We could feel the icy draft from several feet away. Jack jerked it on open, and we stared outside.

Nothing stirred, and we couldn't tell if there were any new footsteps in the ice or not. We'd all entered this way when we returned from our utility reconnoiter trip, and left our warm outdoor wear in the entrance. Our vehicles still set on the street, and there were other tire tracks there, also. Sleet fell again.

"No!" I said with a moan. "We were right there outside the kitchen when it happened. We thought Granny had just dropped something again. We didn't want to stick our noses in and have her yell at us. But it was you falling! Someone has kidnapped her!"

"We don't know for sure, *Chère*," Jack tried to soothe.

"The hell we don't," Twila said in a grim voice. "Let's get after them!"

"I'll go—" Jack began.

"You damn sure won't," I cut him off. "You're hurt! Where are my pets?" I turned and whistled loudly, then shouted, "Trucker! Miss Molly?"

Lucky for my sensibilities, they both raced towards us from the hallway where our rooms were. They'd probably been snacking. *Thank you for that, Universe,* I mentally voiced. *Or whoever attacked Jack might have shot them. Now, please, help us find Granny.*

"Gil! Joleen! Get out here!" Twila ordered as we all three started dressing ourselves and the pets to brave the icy sleet.

The two ghosts appeared immediately. "We didn't see who did it," Gil said before we even questioned him. "We like that little old lady. If we'd seen her in danger, we'd have warned you."

"Jack was the one in danger," I muttered, then corrected myself, "but now so is Granny. Someone has her."

"We should call the sheriff," Jack said. "He can put a bulletin out."

"To watch for what?" Twila said. "We don't know what they used to take her away."

I'd caught something on Joleen's face when Jack mentioned the sheriff. Without letting them know I had them in my side vision, I saw her stare at Gil, and him shake his head slightly. Enough. I whirled on them.

"What are you two hiding?" I demanded. "You've got about two seconds to come clean, or I'll banish your stupid protoplasm asses out in the cold!"

"We can't," Gil pleaded.

"One," I said.

Twila lifted her hand to point at them.

"T—"

"All right!" Joleen said hurriedly.

"Honey," Gil warned.

She turned on him in fury. "That lady's in trouble, and we might know who has her. If you don't like me telling them what we know, go play cards with True or something."

Gil glared back at her, then abruptly stomped off toward the kitchen door.

"Turn off the gumbo on your way through!" Twila called after him.

"Now," I ordered Joleen. "Give."

Gil won't find me in the card room, a mental voice interrupted. I'm right here. Have been for a while.

"True," Joleen whispered.

We all looked over at the lobby desk. There stood the illusive True. The loner ghost faced us, but I recognized his build and clothing from seeing him *die* in the hallway. He wore black: trousers, boots, and a suit jacket like those Wyatt Earp-types in the old cowboy television shows. The only spots of color were his white and gray checkered vest and a faded pink handkerchief tucked in that pocket on the left side of his chest. On closer examination, the pink was a rose.

Jack examined the other man without fear, obviously seeing him along with us.

"Did you hear what he said?" I had to ask Jack.

His only response was an abrupt nod. I assumed he was remembering his useless attempt to kill a man already dead.

Funny. I felt irritated with True for embarrassing Jack, rather than glad Jack got a measure of comeuppance from a paranormal perp.

Twila didn't seem to be prone to tolerating True, either. She cast him a sneer and said, "So you decided to show yourself, *Mr. True.* Be aware, we can *see* you even when you don't make the effort to visualize. I've noticed you several times, loitering in the shadows like a lazy bum with nothing constructive to do."

She reached down and picked up Miss Molly. "Come on. Let's get out of here and do something constructive ourselves. Like find the bastard who took our Granny."

"Just a minute...." I began. But she and Jack and the animals tromped out the door. I caught it before it shut, and turned back to talk to Joleen. Who wasn't there. Neither was True.

I finished my thought, "...we should make the ghosts tell us what they know before we leave." Then I sighed and hurried after the rest of the crew.

Even in my agitated state, I had sense enough to lock the door.

Jamming the key in my coat pocket, I half-slid down the sidewalk. When I made it to the car with all my bones intact, Jack and Twila were still fighting over who was going to drive.

Twila had the upper hand. She stood between Jack and the steering wheel. "I don't give a damn if you're male or female, Mr. Detective. I've had years of experience driving on ice. Get in the back!"

She turned and shoved Miss Molly into the car, then got in behind the wheel. I realized Jack's intention right away. He started around the SUV to claim the front passenger seat. I beat him to it, jerked the door open, got in and locked it.

"Can't do that, Alice," Twila said as she revved the motor. "That locks all the doors. Trucker and Jack still have to get in."

I unlocked the door, and Jack yanked open the rear one on Twila's side. Trucker jumped in first, and Miss Molly immediately joined him in the backseat. Jack slammed the door shut and grabbed his seatbelt.

Twila already had her seatbelt on, and she only had to slide a glance at me to remind me to lock myself in. She turned the wipers on high, an attempt to remove some of the sleet already frozen on the windshield, cranked the indicator to defrost and opened the fan wide. She didn't wait for the window to clear. She dropped the SUV into gear, and the chains clanked as she pulled into the street.

She drove off at what I considered a completely unsafe speed. I only reached up for the *oh-shit* above my door and held on.

"You better get in here instead of riding on the roof," Twila said into the air after a block. Trucker and Miss Molly must have sensed what would happen, because they leaped into the hatchback just before Joleen materialized across from Jack. She looked us over, shrugged and manipulated the other seatbelt onto her non-body. But the first time she leaned forward to talk to us, she pulled right out of the restraint.

"Do you know where you're going?" she asked toward Twila.

"You're about to tell me," Twila ordered. "Before we go too far out of the way."

"Left," Joleen said.

Twila skidded around the corner. Just when I thought she might bump the curb, the SUV straightened, and Twila pushed on the gas. "Where's the next turn?"

"Two blocks. Go right."

Twila slowed at the corner Joleen indicated, just enough to slide around it. Well, not quite enough. We did a three-sixty, and ended up headed the way we'd been going. Twila never wavered or reacted. She hit the gas again while I gulped back my screech of fright, one I knew better than to vocalize if I wanted to avoid a verbal bashing for disparaging my aunt's driving. I'd been in Texas too long, though. Sliding around on ice wasn't part of our driving game plan. I heard Jack catch an indrawn breath, also.

As I pulled my fingernails out of the indentations in my palms, I recognized the place where the utility repair trucks had been working. The trucks and men were gone. We hadn't thought to check the phone at the hotel. My cell phone was snugged in my pocket, but eyes glued to the roadway, I couldn't bring myself to pull it out. Ahead of us was where the two elk had wandered off on their way to get to know each other better before they made a baby elk. Joleen extended her arm to point that way.

"Where are we going?" I finally asked.

"Danny's cabin," Twila said. She quickly glanced in the rearview mirror at Joleen and added, "Aren't we?"

"I still don't know for sure what part he plays in this," Joleen told her. "But it's somewhere to start."

"Who else is in the coven?" Twila demanded as she pushed on the gas feed.

"Besides Karen and Maddie? I don't know the names of the others, but I recognized that sheriff who was at the hotel after Karen got killed."

"Eddie," I said.

"I hate crooked cops," Jack growled.

"Which one threatened to banish you?" Twila asked.

"All three," Joleen said. "I think Maddie's the female leader, though that Eddie is over all of them."

"Maddie and Eddie probably cast the spell on the safe," I added. Twila nodded in agreement.

We were headed out of town now, and it looked like the road led to a steep hill in front of us. I hoped like hell we weren't going to climb that on this ice.

Where else would a hunter have his cabin?

Yep, Joleen extended her finger to indicate for Twila to keep going straight up that blasted mountain.

I'm one of those passengers who's totally terrified of riding in a careening car, whether on good roads or bad...unless I happen to be behind the wheel. Then I can hand out aggression backed by a ton's worth of vehicle like the finest road-rage-charioteer. No way did I want to be the one driving in this mess of frozen sleet, though.

Searching desperately for something to distract me, I turned around to catch Jack rubbing his eyes.

"What's wrong, Jack?" I asked, keeping a firm hold on my support bar. "I forgot all about your head. Are you O.K.?"

"Eyes a bit blurry," he muttered. "I'll be fine."

"Check his pupils, Alice," Twila said.

Anxiety riddled me as I recalled how long it took me to get over my knock on the head. I wanted to crawl over the seat and examine him closer, but there was no way. Twila slid around another curve. If I tried let go of that *oh-shit* bar to wriggle into the backseat, I'd probably slam into her on the next bend.

Through the layer of snow and ice on the road, the SUV shook when it hit a washboard-like series of bumps. I gripped the bar harder, and said, "Look at me, Jack, so I can see your eyes."

After a preliminary, pure male hesitation at being ordered around by a female, he caught my gaze, distracting me for a few long seconds. I'd always loved the way we looked at each other....

I dragged my thoughts back to worry mode and eye-balled his pupils. They looked equal-distant, but I'd probably need to get closer to be positive. A no-do right now.

"They look O.K.," I said to Twila, and Jack turned to stare out the side window.

We'd been climbing now for a couple minutes. As soon as that thought hit me, I couldn't keep from gawking out the window past Twila's shoulder. A steep drop fell away on that side of this stupid mountain. At least there was a metal guard railing preventing us from crashing over.

Maybe. I supposed it would depend on how fast we hit the blasted thing.

I couldn't see Trucker or Miss Molly in the back. Probably they were flattened on the floor, holding tight to keep from slithering back and forth in the hatchback. The wicked ride didn't seem to bother Joleen. Grim lips set, she peered ahead. I could hear the wipers sliding on glass now, rather than ice.

"Damn," I muttered as I spied a tunnel through the rocks around the next curve. I hated tunnels. At least it didn't look that long. I could see the other side. We entered on the fly, since Twila didn't slow. Before we emerged on the other side, an avalanche of snow and ice jarred loose from overhead. Twila slammed on the brakes. But unable to stop at this speed, we smashed into it.

The SUV shuddered from the impact but still didn't halt. It skewed sideways and hit the guardrail with a sickening crunch. Metal screeched on metal, and I yelped. My mind flashed a picture of us hovering on the edge of a straight down drop into oblivion.

Snow covering the hood and windshield, we sat quietly for a few seconds, the only movement Twila shutting off the wipers. Jack opened his door first.

"Don't, Jack," Twila commanded. "You can't see. So you don't know what you're going to step out there into. Let Alice check things on her side first."

I gulped and got out. Something thudded against the guardrail at the same moment a rifle blast boomed and echoed around us.

I didn't need Jack's shout of "Alice, get the hell in here!" to motivate me. I dove back in the car. Before I could slam the door, I heard a snowmobile engine roar away. Another shot erupted, right there with us. On the seat, Twila's head lay beside mine, since she'd thrown herself down, also. I peered through the gap in the bucket seats. Door open, Jack stood outside, shooting at the shooter.

He only fired the one shot. Then he cursed a few words I rarely heard him use and got back in the car. Gun still in gripped in one hand, he reached through the seat gap with his other to touch my face. "You O.K.? And Twila?"

Twila answered. My throat was clogged with the need to say *Someone shot at me again!* and the fear blocking the words.

"We're all right."

"What the fuck is going on around here?" he growled.

With a gasp, Twila sat up and leveled an index finger at him.

"Whoa, whoa," he said before she could lambaste him. "I didn't mean it was y'all's fault. I'm not sayin' you got yourselves into this mess. Even that your messin' around with ghosts did. There's somethin' a hell of a lot deeper here than someone wantin' y'all to calm down a pack of spirits so they can sell their stupid hotel."

"Ghosts," I said, as I sat up and swallowed the fear into the pit of my stomach, where it festered and burned.

"Huh?" Jack said.

"A pack of ghosts. Ghosts and spirits are two different entities."

He closed his eyes briefly, as though keeping a rein on his irritation. When he opened them, he said, "Where's that ghost who was ridin' with us?"

"I suppose, even though she's a woman, Joleen took off to see if she could identify who shot at us," Twila said with a tinge of sarcasm, obviously still ticked at Jack's hint of condescending tone. Before Jack could defend himself, she went on, "Did you manage to see who it was?"

He clenched his jaw for a second, then decided to validate himself against Twila's unspoken accusation. "I've learned over the years to accept any type of assistance against murders I can get, male or female." When Twila let the looming argument drop, he continued, "It was the same type of machine that balloon pilot rode. But I imagine there's lots of that make around here."

Our worry over Granny would have us at each other's throats before long. We needed to cooperate, not argue. I didn't voice that aloud, concerned it would escalate the tension. Instead, in an attempt to lighten the air, I said, "If it was Danny, he's a piss-poor shot."

"Thank you for that, Universe," Twila murmured.

"Yeah," Jack added. He leaned forward and threaded his fingers through my hair. He stared at me for a long moment, and I sat there entrapped in his gaze. Then, despite Twila watching, Jack pulled me toward him and kissed me. A long kiss. A thrilling kiss. One I never, ever wanted to end. I sat there helplessly, wanting desperately to wrap my arms around Jack's shoulders. But I was so weak with pleasure and desire, my muscles wouldn't cooperate.

Until he started to pull away from me. I grasped his head and recaptured his lips, lingering in the tenderness and exhilaration until Twila cleared her throat.

"We need to get out of this mess," she reminded us.

Jack sighed and sat back. "You two wait in here until I check things out."

Still, his gaze lingered on me. Mine on him. Past his shoulder, Trucker and Miss Molly's heads peered over the rear seat. I could have sworn they both had huge grins directed at mine and Jack's kiss on their faces. But I could have been mistaken, since they both ducked down as soon as I looked at them.

Jack re-opened his door. It banged against the guardrail before the space measured even six inches.

I asked, "How did you even stand up out there to shoot?"

"It was tight," he growled. He started to wedge himself out again, then gave up. "But I can't get around the vehicle this way."

He scooted across the seat as I opened my own door. I needed to do something. Truth be told, I hoped the cold outside would lower my body heat, which Jack's kiss had sent soaring despite my fear for Granny's safety.

Jack didn't protest when I joined him. He kept his pistol in his right hand and wrapped an arm around my waist to hold me still until he scanned the area. With a nod, he indicated it was safe. Probably safe, anyway.

First we looked the front of the SUV over.

"How on earth did whoever shot at us manage to make sure we'd get hit by that snow at the right minute?" I asked.

Jack pointed at the tunnel exit. "He shot into the rocks to make it fall. He couldn't have been certain that would happen, but it was worth a try. And worked. We didn't hear that first shot inside the tunnel."

The snow and ice covered the hood and windshield. There wasn't really a pull-off here, and if someone happened to drive down the mountain, our vehicle would sure as hell stop them, unless they saw us in time to swerve into the other lane. If we could get moving, we might be able to pull back onto the road.

The whine we heard indicated Twila tried re-start the stalled wipers, but she quit almost as soon as she turned on the switch. The snow was too deep to clear off that way. She couldn't tell from inside, but at least six inches of white covered the glass.

Cautiously, Jack and I high-stepped through the drifts to see exactly where we'd ended up. My fears were realized. I should have screamed louder.

"Pretty view," Jack said.

I didn't laugh.

A whir sounded as Twila rolled down her window. "Uh oh," she whispered. She had leaned out far enough to see the steep, thousand-foot drop on the other side of the guardrail.

"How's it looking as far as us getting out of this mess?" she asked quietly.

"Not good," I told her. "But do we have a choice?"

Jack said, "Alice and I are going to have to push. You know how to use four-wheel drive, Twila?"

"Jess had it in his pickup. He showed me how it worked once."

I studied Jack. He weighed in at close to one-ninety, all of it muscle.

He kept in great shape...when he wasn't injured. He was right, though. We didn't have any choice.

First we put on our gloves and cleared most of the snow from the windshield and hood. There was probably a scraper in the hatchback somewhere, but we'd already wasted enough time, and neither of us made a move to search it out. Then we walked around to the rear of the car.

"Can you roll down this back window, Twila?" Jack called.

When she complied, he said, "You two into the backseat," to the animals. He pulled out the rubber mat the car rental company had put there to protect the carpet from slush deposited by uncaring drivers of a vehicles not their own. In fact, Jack shook off a couple puddles of water from snow melted from Trucker's feet.

Jack slid the rubber mat under the rear wheel closest to us, then motioned for me to join him behind the car. When I did, he called through the open window to Twila, "Rock it first. See if you can get some traction."

"I've been stuck before, Jack," she said in an I'm-not-stupid tone. "You just push when I'm rocking forward."

She rocked the SUV back and forth a few times, with us grunting and straining on each forward thrust. Then she stomped the gas hard. The tires dug in, and the SUV hurtled forward. The mat flew from beneath the tire, but Jack slapped it away from me before it hit my face.

Thank you, Universe, and every other deity watching over us!

Twila slammed on the brakes, and I hurried forward and made it to the car without falling on my butt. Jack shook out the rubber mat first and replaced it before he got back in. As Twila rolled up the rear window and my pets jumped into the hatchback, we belted ourselves in.

Joleen appeared in the rear seat. "I couldn't tell who it was. He was covered up too well in his suit and helmet."

Twila drove on as Jack questioned her further. "Where did he go? Anywhere that might indicate who he is? Did he notice you following him?"

"He stopped a ways from here and took out a pair of binoculars,

Watched what you were doing back here for a while. I was up in a tree, so he never saw me."

"Do you ever need a coat?" Jack asked inanely. I noticed he slid a glance at her overabundant breasts in the low-cut bodice, but quickly looked back at her face.

She giggled. "Not now that I'm dead. And the man...I guess it was a man, he was built like one...waited there until he saw you were going to get out of this mess, then took off. I figured I needed to get back here and show you where to go, so I didn't follow."

"You're right, we do need you," I assured her. "You did fine."

She smiled with pleasure, then pointed between Twila and me. "There. Turn right on that road."

Chains clanking and driving a bit more cautiously now, but still, in my opinion, too fast for the road conditions, Twila swerved into the side road. There, she met a layer of undisturbed ice-covered snow and a gate a cross the road. A huge log chain with an enormous lock secured the gate to a large post. Twila slammed on the brakes in time to halt the front bumper a whole inch from impact.

"Can I ask something?" I said as Twila glared at the gate. "How do you know where the cabin is, Joleen?"

"I found you in Six Gun, didn't I? It gets boring around here, especially when there aren't many guests to watch in the winter. When I found out I could travel around, I followed Danny here a time or two. Didn't like watching him kill the deer, though, so I quit coming."

"Doesn't look like he's been here," Twila said.

"He doesn't always come up this road," Joleen explained. "There are back trails they can ride those snow machines in on."

"They?" Jack asked.

I stared at him anxiously again. His face was pale, beads of sweat on his forehead.

"I don't know who all the men are," Joleen said. "Some I've seen around town. The second time I was here, there were some women with the men. I figured they were gonna get drunk and party, so I left. I watched enough of that in my job when I was alive."

"This isn't finding Granny." Twila opened her door.

I grabbed her arm. "You need to check on Jack. I don't like the looks of him."

"I'm fine," Jack growled. He pushed his own door open and got out. Avoiding Twila's jutting driver's door, he stomped through the ice to the gate. Without pause, he pulled out his pistol and shot off the lock.

The gate dragged against the snow and ice, but Jack shoved on it until it moved back far enough for Twila to drive through. She did just that, waiting on the other side for Jack to get back in.

The cabin was only a few hundred feet down the road. We wouldn't have made it if not for the chains. They clanked and broke through, edging us steadily forward. Around a bend, a one-story log cabin appeared.

The cabin was dark. No smoke rose from the chimney. Hell, we'd picked the wrong place to find Granny.

"I'm going to go look in, just in case," I said. No one contradicted me, so I got out of the car to plod a new trail. At a sound behind me, I glanced bapriestessck. Jack stood with his arm steadied on the car rooftop, pistol following my path. Instead of the warmth I should have felt at his protective effort, worry over his wellbeing stole through me. The effort to help free the car had drained him, or he would have never let me do this alone.

Then I noticed a flash of red. Before fear suffused me, I recognized Joleen high in a treetop, scanning around in case someone tried to approach. Jack had overcome his male dislike of showing any physical vulnerability in front of the supposedly weaker sex and sent her up there. I made a note to insist we get Jack taken care of before we continued our search for Granny. Try, anyway, since his stubbornness rivaled mine. We didn't need two emergencies on our hands, though.

A small porch extended across the front. I grabbed a railing so I wouldn't break my leg on the icy steps and climbed up the two of them. The door was locked, the windows without blinds. I could see inside: absolutely no sign of life.

Just to be sure, I walked to the edge of the porch and stared out through the woods. No trail marred the whiteness. A heavy snowmobile would have left tracks. Huge trees barricaded the other side of the porch, so it was useless to look over there.

Back in the car, I refastened my seatbelt. We still had that dangerous drive back down the mountain to contend with.

CHAPTER 26

Twila waited until we were down off the mountain before she said, "Sorry about the car damage, Alice. I'll help you pay the insurance claim."

"Don't worry about it," I murmured. "Where are we going to look next?"

"Maddie's," Jack said from the backseat.

Just as I glanced back at him, Joleen dematerialized. By the time we pulled up in front of Maddie's house, she was waiting outside. As I rolled down my window, I shivered in sympathy at the incongruous picture she made, standing there in the ice and snow in her low-cut red dress. As she'd said, though, ghosts weren't bothered by the temperature. They didn't even react to the cold they inflicted on others with their very presence.

"No one's here," Joleen said.

"Did you look everywhere?" Jack asked, leaning over the back seat to see her better.

I still had a major problem with Jack's recent casualness with ghostly sightings and conversations, but I kept my mouth shut. About that, anyway. As soon as Joleen answered, "Just about, I think," I felt Jack's forehead. My hand came back wet from a film of sweat.

"We need to get you back to the hotel," Twila said before I could.

Jack ignored us and opened his car door. A second later, he strode up the walkway. He'd either inattentively or intentionally left the door open, and Trucker bounded over the seat after him. Jack jiggled the doorknob only a second before he once again used his pistol and shot into the lock. When the door still stuck, he drew back and smashed it open with a leg kick. He didn't seem that physically bad off, I mused, as he disappeared inside. But that could be macho effort on his part.

Twila and I were out of the car in a flash. Halfway up the walkway, I halted at the loud distress call from Miss Molly. She stood in the driver's seat Twila had vacated and stared back and forth from me to the icy pavement. Twila went on, and knowing she would keep an eye on Jack, I sighed and slipped and slid back to the SUV to grab the cat in my arms. I made it up the walk again without injury, and by the time I hurried through the door, no one was visible.

I listened, and even tried to tune into Twila's thoughts to locate her. Nothing worked. Joleen had informed us Maddie was a coven member, its female black priestess, so my senses were no doubt blocked. Cuddling the cat, since I didn't want to let her roam, I wandered through the living room. The next room, rather than a dining room, had been set up as Maddie's office. I didn't pay much attention to it—the layout of desk, filing cabinets, office chair and visitor seats—until I noticed the "sleep" light burning on the computer monitor.

Walking over, I shifted my cat to a one-armed hold and jiggled the mouse. At first, all I fathomed were the normal icons on the screen. Then I saw a document file among the others. When I clicked on it, a list of folders popped up. One was named *Red Dollar Hotel*, and I opened it. The documents inside appeared to be named innocuous things that would pertain to the hotel sale, and I didn't think they would give us a clue as to where to find Granny. In fact, I started getting the feeling I was wasting time, when I should have been helping the others search. Then I noticed another file inside the *Red Dollar* one. The new one just said *Junk.*

It obviously wasn't. Who would password protect a *Junk* file? Curiosity aroused, I sat down and placed Miss Molly on my lap. What would a woman like Maddie use for a password?

I couldn't believe it, but I hit it on the first try: *money.* The file opened to show only one document: *Map.*

I wasn't that good with maps, but this one wasn't hard to figure out. It showed Maddie's house and the hotel...along with the tunnel under the street connecting them.

"So you came and went with a key, huh?" I growled, tracing the screen with a finger. "And maybe that's where you've got Granny."

"Where?" Twila said, peering over my shoulder and scaring the hell out of me. I screeched and jumped to my feet, barely rescuing Miss Molly before she tore eight or ten scratches down the front of me. Jack came running with his ever-present pistol in a two-handed grip. He crouched and waved it around to encompass the room as Trucker whined behind him.

"Twila did it," I said, pointing at her with one hand and securing the cat with the other. "Shoot her for scaring me!"

A second later, we giggled, and Jack even chuckled and re-holstered his pistol. "What are you looking at?" he asked.

Twila stepped back in a show of letting me reveal my discovery. I nodded at the monitor.

"There's a tunnel under the street between this house and the hotel."

Jack studied the map. "You're right, *Chère.* Now all we have to do is find the entrance down in the basement. Twila and I were just there, but we weren't looking for anything like this."

"Where's Joleen?" I asked. "Wasn't she with you?"

"Haven't seen her in a while," Jack said.

"I'm here," Joleen said as she wavered into sight behind Jack. "I couldn't go down in that basement." She shuddered. "I can't stand those dark, smelly places. Once LeRoy locked me in the storage room at his house and told my aunt I'd walked home. They didn't find me until late that night, after my mom came looking for me."

"I hope Leroy got his butt whipped," Twila said.

"He did," Joleen replied. "But I still have nightmares."

"Do you actually sleep and dream?" Jack asked.

"Oh, for pity sakes," Twila said. "You can ask your ghost questions later. Right now, we need to find Granny."

"Yeah, before Granny tears whoever has her a new asshole," I said.

"I sort of wondered myself if whoever grabbed Granny had any idea what the hell they were in for with that feisty woman," Jack agreed.

After we crossed the kitchen, Jack blocked the basement door.

"Jack," Twila warned. "We're going down there."

"I know," he said. "I just want y'all to think about somethin'. There's a good possibility whoever took Granny did so as bait. To draw us to her."

"For what reason?" Twila asked. "This whole thing isn't making sense."

"It's not like on television," Jack said, softening his tone so he wouldn't stir Twila's anger. Or mine, as far as that went. "Criminals are stupid. They don't always think things out. I agree, it's not making sense. Y'all were asked here, and now it appears someone's either tryin' to run you off...or do something more drastic."

"Kill us," I said flatly.

"Yeah," he whispered, then continued, "or maybe not. Anyway, I want y'all to stay behind me. Let me go first. I *have* had a little training, so I know what I need to watch out for."

I laid a hand on his arm. "You've also had some first-aid training. And you're still sweaty. If you're ignoring dizziness from that knot on our head...."

"Would you, if you were hurt and Granny needed you?" he asked.

I look away. He was right.

He started to turn, but I dug my fingers in. "Promise us that if you don't feel well, you'll let us know. If for no other reason than you could endanger all of us if you passed out."

"There's an extra gun in my boot," he said, and opened the stairwell door and flicked the light switch on.

All five of us descended the stairs, three people and two animals. I still carried Miss Molly, and Trucker insinuated himself after Jack. My dog always considered himself the alpha unless Jack was around.

In the basement, we separated, checking different areas to find the secret entrance. Jack and I both headed toward the same wall first, where I thought, from reviewing the map in my mind, the connection would be. It confused me, however, when Jack waved me on and walked over to a different area.

Jack found it. We heard the *click*, then the squeak of hinges. Twila and I hurried over to the gap in the wall.

"I thought the map showed the connection in the spot where I was looking," I said.

"You didn't notice the small hallway off it," he said.

He pulled a flashlight from his jacket pocket and shone it to the right. The open area just inside the door led that way, then branched off in a ninety-degree angle to the left. Examining that design in my mind, I nodded. It would lead under the street.

"Remember, y'all stay behind me," he said as he started forward.

The sudden bright light illuminated the tunnel, making Jack's flashlight unnecessary. Overhead, a line of neon bulbs glowed. I stared at Twila, who had her hand on the switch on the tunnel wall.

She shrugged. "I didn't think Maddie would want to walk around in an unlighted tunnel."

Jack strode on, but I noticed he kept his flashlight in hand. With the overhead illumination, I couldn't tell if he had left it burning or not. We followed him and Trucker, and after a dozen feet or so, Miss Molly struggled to get loose. I set her down and kept moving.

We made a sort of parade: Jack and Trucker side-by-side, Miss Molly behind Trucker, Twila and I walking together. The tunnel was wide enough for that, and it looked well used and maintained. I had expected dampness and spiders and cobwebs. What we got was hard-packed dirt under our feet and stone-cut walls on each side. Water did dribble down here and there, and once we bypassed a puddle, unfrozen this deep in the earth even in the winter weather. Nothing impeded us, though.

What we didn't find was what I, at least, had anticipated: another door anywhere along the tunnel route. Somewhere we would locate Granny, hog-tied and muffled with a piece of duct tape. I doubted the lawbreakers would think we could find the hidden map and discover the tunnel, so why should they try to hide a room down here? Though thinking in Jack-mode—rationally—I supposed it would have been a heck of a job to also dynamite out an adjacent room in this rock.

We walked for approximately two blocks, until we came to a huge steel door, which encompassed the entire width of the tunnel. At least six feet wide, the dull metal was only marred by a round gold lock, which appeared to need a modern key. A doorknob centered below it.

"We aren't going to be able to get through there," I said.

Jack started to lift his pistol, then shook his head and murmured, "Better not use this in these confined quarters."

Twila walked over and took Jack's flashlight. The light here was dimmer, since a couple of overhead bulbs had burned out, and she shone the beam up and down the door seams. Then she started playing it over the wall on the right side of the tunnel.

Sensing what she was looking for, a trip switch for the door, I walked over and started feeling along the left wall. With nothing to do, Jack watched us for a few seconds, then pulled what I recognized as his lock-picking kit from another coat pocket and got to work.

Trucker wandered over and nudged Jack aside.

"Hey, dog." Jack tried to shove him away, but Trucker wasn't easily shove-able. I'd seen him do what he did next at home now and then—infrequently, only when he thought I was too slow letting him out the front door so he could cross the road and visit the lake.

He stood on his rear legs, placed his front ones on each side of the gold lock, and grabbed the doorknob in his mouth. He twisted his head, and the door tumblers clicked. Trucker pulled back, and the door swung open.

Trucker sat down and stared up at me, as though to say, "What do you want me to do now?"

I slapped my forehead. "We've been wandering around like fools, and we might have the answer to finding Granny right here!"

Before I could say it, Twila ordered, "Trucker, find Granny!"

Trucker cocked his head. Instead of going through the door, he raced back down the tunnel.

Undecided, I stared after the dog, then at Jack. He handed me his Glock, then reached down and pulled his backup pistol—a small revolver—out of his boot.

"You be careful," I said angrily, torn in half with worry over his head injury and the need to find my dear friend.

Twila took my free hand and squeezed it. "Let's go with Trucker," she said.

I heaved a breath and took a few steps. Even with Twila dragging at me, I halted and turned to see Jack go through the door, pistol held up in search mode. My cat dogged his steps, and I didn't try to call her to me. Maybe she knew what she was doing. I sure as hell wasn't sure we did.

We trotted back down the tunnel and came out in Maddie's basement. Trucker waited there, tongue lolling, but he immediately raced up the stairs and continued until he got to the front door. There, he clearly indicated we needed to let him outside. Twila obeyed the dog's unspoken demand, and we exited with him.

Trucker continued past the parked SUV and down the street. Twila and I looked at each other in confusion, but she headed for the vehicle and slid in, waiting until I joined her in the passenger seat before she drove off. After we travelled a couple blocks, one lonely building with a tail of smoke emerging from the stone chimney came into view ahead of Trucker.

"He's going to the jail!" I said with a gasp.

Twila stopped the vehicle. "And we could be walking straight into an ambush, just like Jack warned."

I frantically opened the window and stuck my head out. "Trucker! Come!" I shouted. "Wait!"

The dog immediately reversed direction. I got out, then let him in the backseat and climbed in the front again. "Where the hell's Joleen?" I fumed.

"She's with your boyfriend," Gil said from the backseat. We both swiveled around to see him sitting there, Trucker in an on-guard stature, but not growling.

"And you're right," Gil said after a cautious glance at the dog, even though he had to know Trucker couldn't bite him. "There's a man waiting for you in the jail. With Granny locked in a cell."

"How long have you known that?" Twila spat.

He held up a hand. "Barely a minute or so, I swear. Before she went with you, Joleen ordered me to start looking around town for that wonderful little lady. There's a lot of buildings here, and I'm not that partial to the jail. It was the last one I looked in. When I came back out, I saw you parked here."

"It's always the last one," I muttered inanely. "Or you would keep looking. Who's in there? Danny?"

"Yes, but I don't think he's real happy about it. He was muttering something about not knowing what the bastards were up to when he got involved with them. And I did show myself to Miss Granny, so she'd know rescue was on the way. I also opened her cell door while I was there, so she wouldn't be—"

"Oh, shit," I interrupted. "You opened the cell door?"

"That's what I just said."

"Get the damn gun ready, Alice!" Twila floored the gas pedal.

* * *

He's not going to make it much further.

Joleen chewed her bottom lip as Jack, wandered around the room exposed when he went through the steel door. In one hand he held his gun, the other his cell phone, snapping a picture here and there. Joleen had been here herself a couple times, once briefly—very briefly—when the coven met, once when the members were absent. She didn't like the altar and black magic accessories spread out on it, especially the bejeweled, blood-stained knife. Nor did she care for the dingy red curtains hung on the walls and the ancient hearse wagon bed the members had dragged down here. Besides the energy that lingered from the long-ago casket occupants, blood from where they'd killed Karen drenched the wagon slats.

The cat meowed stridently at Jack, and he walked over to where she waited at the stairwell up to the hotel basement. This room was actually a sub-basement, a fact not known even by any of the more recent hotel owners. She'd heard a coven member say once that a leader from years ago had altered the floor plans.

Jack followed the cat up the stairs and slid back the door. It was another hidden one, but if you knew where to look behind the huge furnace room, you could also open it from the other side. Joleen accompanied him and the cat through the furnace room into the laundry area. Jack made it all the way to the next stairwell before he collapsed. The cat sat beside him and frantically licked at his face, trying to rouse him.

* * *

Granny came out the front door just as Twila skidded into the pole I'd hit on my first drive over to the jail. She leaned on a fireplace poker in her hand and waited for us. Twila backed up and swerved far enough around the pole to miss it, then steered us more slowly up to where Granny watched our progress. I was out the passenger door and, without even a slip of foot, had her in my arms before Twila stopped the SUV. Trucker had followed me, and he raced a happy circle around us, his barks welcoming our friend back to his circle of care.

"Omigod, are you all right?" As Twila hurriedly joined us, I stepped away to pat Granny's elderly soft cheek and run my palms down her arms. Granny wore a blanket from one of the bunks around her shoulders, her snow boots on her tiny feet.

"I's fine, girls," she said, soothing me instead of me taking care of her. She lifted the poker, then stabbed it back into the ice. "But Danny ain't. Hope I didn't kill him, but don't much care if I did."

The blanket loosened, and Twila pulled it up to secure it around Granny's neck. She wrapped an arm around our friend, and said, "Let's get in the car, sweetheart. I'm so, so glad we found you."

"First we's best drag that there hoodlum into the cell he had me locked in," she said. "Just in case he ain't dead."

She turned and led the way into the jail. She'd left the door open, and I shut it behind us and Trucker. Not that we would be hidden from anyone who decided to check on whether Danny was doing his job or not. Our vehicle still waited outside, and Twila had left the engine running.

When Gil materialized beside us, Twila said, "Go watch the car. If anyone shows up, tell us so Alice can shoot them."

"Yeah," I said, lifting the gun out of the pocket I'd dropped it in when I hugged Granny.

The ghost disappeared, and Twila went over to kneel beside Danny, prone on the floor and not moving other than to barely breathe. She placed her knees to avoid a pool of fresh blood shimmering around his head and checked his pulse before she stood.

"He's got a strong heartbeat. He'll probably be all right when he comes to. Well, with a sore head. You must not have hit him too hard."

"I's tried!" Granny lifted the poker and stabbed it into the holder beside the fireplace. "He's was sittin' there mutterin' all 'bout his bad luck when I's snuck out after that there purty Gil unlocked my cell door. 'Course I peeked out first to check on him. Had his back t'me, or I never could've done it. I sneaked over and got hold a that poker without him hearin' me. Cold-cocked him hard as I could. He never knew what hit him."

"You did good, Granny," I said. "But we do need to lock him up, like you say. He could come to and cause us more trouble." I handed Granny the gun.

"You'uns take care a that," she said with a nod as she toddled over to the barred window beside the front door. "I's'll be the lookout."

Twila and I each grabbed a foot. None too gently, we pulled Danny through the door and into the open cell. We left a trail of blood the first six feet or so, then it disappeared. The floor was cold, but I wasn't about to try to lift him onto the bunk. We conceded to the temperature by laying a blanket from the bunk over him.

When we walked out of the cell, Twila banged the barred door shut hard. She manipulated it back and forth and checked the lock until she was sure it wouldn't open again.

"You know where the keys are, Alice?"

I led her into the office area and showed her the keys, hanging on a nail hammered into the wall. She removed them and stuck them in her jeans pocket.

"Ain't nobody showed up," Granny called. "We's can go ahead and make a break for it."

We did. A few seconds later, we were all ensconced in the SUV and headed back to the hotel.

CHAPTER 27

"Anyone take ker of my gumbo?" Granny asked as we entered the hotel lobby.

"I did, ma'am," Gil said. "I turned it off, so it wouldn't burn."

"Why, thankee, you great big handsome hunk." Granny slipped her hand in his arm, although I assumed she would pull right through if she weren't careful. "Let's you'n me go check on it."

"Granny," I said, and she halted. I cupped her face. "Are you sure you're all right? I'm so sorry this happened. Please don't think I'm making cracks about your age, but if you need to rest for a while, don't hesitate. You've been through a horrid trauma."

She patted my cheek. "Thankee for caring, Child. But the best therapy for me right now is to cook up somethin' y'all will smack your lips over. And—" She batted her eyes at Gil. "Do it with a good lookin' man helpin' me out."

"I'll do my best to take care of her," Gil said seriously. "I know a few tricks, and I can telepathically contact either of you within a second or two."

"As much as we hate to leave you, we do need to find Jack," Twila said.

260

Granny frowned. "Jack's in trouble?"

"We aren't sure," Twila told her. "We had to separate while we searched, so we need to look for him. It might be best if you came along."

Granny shook her head. "You's go on. We won't take no chances. If we hears anythin' funny, you'll be the next one to know."

In a quandary, Twila and I hesitated a moment longer. I said what I assumed we were both thinking. "Come with us first, Granny. We'll get you a weapon."

"Now that there sounds like a by-crackie fine idea," she said with one of her wrinkled grins.

All of us, including Gil and Trucker, hurried into the saloon. I pulled the piece of paper Jack had given me out of my jeans pocket and read off the combination as Twila dialed. We hit it on the first try, and she reached in. When she pulled her arm back, the small holster was in her hand. She gave it to Granny, and I helped her belt it around her waist as Twila retrieved a revolver.

We closed the safe, and I gave the gun to Granny so I could notice how she handled it, whether her hands were steady or not. They were. She shoved the pistol home and patted the butt—perhaps the way she would like to pat Gil's butt, if her hand wouldn't slide straight through.

"We's'll be fine now, girls. Go find Jack." Without another word, she headed for the kitchen, Gil trailing her like a faithful dog. The other faithful dog, Trucker, stared back and forth between Granny and me, undecided as to which one needed him most.

"Go with Granny, Trucker," I said to release him. He bounded off.

"Where do you think that tunnel comes out here in the hotel?" Twila asked.

I thought for a moment, examining the map in my mind, then answered, "Probably in the last room down the hall. On the opposite side from where our rooms are located."

We took off in a hurry, through the lobby and down the hallway. I glanced in our rooms as we passed, but didn't see Jack. Across the hall, another door stood open. His duffle bag sat on the floor in there, the bed un-rumpled. We went on to the last room, and Twila twisted the knob,

Locked.

"Damn it," she muttered. "Alice, the gun."

"Here." We both looked over at Joleen, who had appeared in the hall beside us before I got the gun completely out of my coat pocket. She pointed at the door and tumblers clicked. We rushed inside.

"Gil showed me how to do that," Joleen said as she floated in behind us. "And you need to get down there quick. Jack's unconscious at the foot of the stairs."

"No, I'm not." He emerged from the closet doorway. "Miss Molly licked me awake. There's a door in the back of the closet wall." The cat sauntered out between his legs.

Jack wavered. I ran over and slid an arm around his waist, drawing his other arm over my shoulders. He didn't protest as I helped him to the bed. Miss Molly gracefully leaped onto the bed and walked across the mattress to curl up on the pillow beside Jack's head. Before she dropped into a loud purr, she licked his cheek.

"Good girl," Jack said as he gave her a quick stroke. "Thanks for the help."

"You need to rest, Jack," I said in a worried voice.

He looked past me at Twila. "You got any more pain meds?"

She nodded, but gently pushed me aside. "Let me look at you first."

As she examined him, Joleen caught my eye and wiggled her fingers, evidently indicating she was leaving, because she disappeared.

"You gave Alice pain pills," Jack reproved Twila.

"She let me make sure she didn't have a concussion before I did that. You can either do the same, or I'll let you think you're taking pain meds and feed you a sleeping pill instead."

"How do I know you won't do that anyway?" he asked. "And by the way, did y'all find Granny?"

That he'd waited until now to ask that important question confirmed he was hurting. Yet pain didn't necessarily translate into a concussion.

"Granny's in the kitchen," I said. "With Gil watching over her. Now lie still and let Twila look at you."

He mostly obeyed as my aunt stared in his eyes to check his pupils, but he asked, "Where'd you find her?"

"The jail," I said inattentively. "How is he, Twila?"

"I think he's got a hard head," she said, then added with a soft chuckle and glance that took in both of us, "There seems to be an epidemic of hard-headedness around here lately. I'll be right back."

She left, and Jack's expression, as I'm sure mine did, reflected we'd caught Twila's nuance about our stubbornness over our relationship.

We're going to talk about it, I grumped in my mind. After this is over.

"Yes, we are," Jack said, and I gasped as I realized I'd spoken aloud.

Jack patted the mattress beside him and said, "Sit down and tell me how you found Granny."

I sat on the bed and explained about our trip to the jail. I dramatized Granny's actions and got a laugh out of Jack when I told him how she sneaked up on Danny and knocked him out. I noticed his wince of pain, however, and none too soon, Twila returned with a bottle of water in her hand, a wet wash cloth wrapped around it. She held out the other palm to Jack, and he picked up the two white pills.

Twila removed the wash cloth and gave him the water. After he took the pills and laid back against the pillows, she draped the wash cloth over his forehead.

"I'm not going to sleep," he denied. "We need to decide what to do next about this mess of perps. I think we should go over to the jail and see if that balloon pilot is awake to answer some questions."

His eyes drooped closed, and for a second, I thought maybe Twila had given Jack the threatened sleeping pills. But when I glanced questioningly at her, she shook her head no, and answered Jack, "Danny might be awake by now. He's another hard head."

I automatically felt the back of my head. My fingers encountered only a slightly sore small bump to remind me of my injury.

"I'd like to bust a few more heads," Jack said grimly. "If we can figure out who needs it."

Remembering how we'd left Jack, I asked, "What was on the other side of that door down there in the tunnel?"

He opened his eyes. "You don't really want to know, *Chère*. Let's just say, it's where Karen met her end."

"Oh," I breathed. "Where the black coven met?"

"Yeah," he said. "And we'll leave all that to the law enforcement, when we can get them here."

"You check your cell phone lately, Alice?" Twila asked.

"No, but I will." First I pulled out the Glock. Jack reached for it, but I avoided his grasp and handed it to Twila. Then I found the cell phone buried in the pocket recesses. When I checked the screen, the welcome picture of Trucker and Miss Molly greeted me, along with three service bars in the left corner.

"Yippee," I said. "We have a phone. But who should I call? The local law's crooked."

Jack dug his phone out and checked it. He held up a finger to silence us and pushed a couple buttons, activating the speaker while the phone still rang.

"Hey," the female voice said. "I've been wondering when you would call."

The wash cloth slipped down over Jack's eyes, hiding his expression, as he said, "Hey, Carrie."

Caroline, I translated in my mind. He knew her well enough for a nickname.

"I'm still over here in Red Dollar," Jack said. "I was wondering what the road situation between here and there is like."

"Is that all you were wondering about?" she asked, a pout in her voice.

"For right now," he said with a chuckle. "There's an important reason why."

"You know I'd give you anything, Jack," she purred in a tone not nearly as pleasant as Miss Molly could produce. In fact, my cat roused herself and stalked down the bed to re-settle by Jack's feet. When she and I stared at each other, I swear she curled her lip back off her sharp fangs in a sneer at Copy Cat Carrie.

I nodded at Miss Molly, then turned my back to hide the sneer and the fact I mouthed: *I'll just bet you would. Bitch.*

"Even if it is just road conditions for now," she purred on. "Fact is, the second front that moved through socked us in over here. And the Canyon between here and Red Dollar is closed."

"Could you reach Charlie and ask him to call me? I left his cell number back at the hotel before I got it programmed into my phone."

"If my brother's out on the slopes, he won't have his phone with him. He doesn't like being bothered when he's skiing."

"He wouldn't be skiing on ice, would he?"

"Oh, we got as much snow as we did sleet. In fact, snow on top of the sleet. So the slopes are open. Snow didn't reach the Canyon, though. The reports we've gotten back say it's a skating rink."

"Maybe you could just give me his number, then, so I could keep trying to reach him."

I was looking back at the bed now, and Jack pushed up the wash cloth and motioned with his hand to indicate needing a pencil to write something. Being a writer, you'd think I'd always have pen and paper available, but Twila was the one who opened the bedside table drawer and withdrew a small note tablet and pen while Miss Purr Voice said, "Just so you don't lose my number by mistake."

"I won't," Jack assured her. This time his expression cheered me when he rolled his eyes in irritation.

She repeated a phone number and Twila wrote it down. Jack spent another minute getting her off the phone—I'd have preferred he do it in five seconds, but I held my tongue. Then he disconnected and dialed the number from the tablet Twila held up for him to see.

"Charlie," he said when the man answered in a stern voice after the first ring. "It's Jack. And just so you know, I've got you on speaker and there are a couple citizens here with me."

The official tone of Jack's voice warned me he wasn't fooling around now.

"What's up, buddy?" Charlie replied.

"Is there any way you can get over to Red Dollar?"

"Maybe if I could hijack the local hospital helicopter. Canyon's closed."

"That's what your sister said. Any possibility you might get the copter to bring you here?"

Charlie didn't speak for a long moment, then, "What's going on?"

"I'd rather not tell you over the airwaves. If you can't make it, could you maybe convince somebody in Albuquerque to help us out here? Preferably somebody from the Feeb office."

"Nobody local, huh?"

"No."

"Let me see what I can do. You gonna be at this number?"

"Yeah, but let me give you my wife's number, too."

"Wife?" Charlie asked.

Jack didn't bother to correct him, and only repeated my number from memory.

I flushed with pleasure and tried to stifle the warm glow in my heart to no avail

Take that, Copy Cat!

I definitely needed to think about this thing between Jack and me more seriously than as a just-friends thing. Which it was only outwardly, I admitted, and sliding downhill towards benefits with the speed of a bobsled. After we got done here, of course.

"Why the FBI?" Twila asked after Jack disconnected from Charlie.

"They investigate when it has to do with possibly crooked local cops," Jack explained. "I've had my suspicions about that since I got here. Y'all just arrived yesterday and found the dead woman. There's no way the investigation into that death could be complete by now. Yet there's a crime scene upstairs that's not cordoned off."

Fearful of his reaction, I didn't mention the murder room had also already been scrubbed clean. However, Twila and I exchanged an uneasy glance as Jack went on, "There doesn't seem to be any sort of investigation going on at all, despite the fact there's no way that woman died by her own hand. There's some other stuff, but you get the idea."

I giggled, and Jack frowned at me.

"I'm sorry," I said. "It's not funny, but when you said *by her own hand,* I thought of Karen's hands...." My voice trailed off, the levity disappearing.

Not to Jack and Twila, though. They snickered, then guffawed for at least half a minute. I broke down and joined them.

Jack pulled the wash cloth from his forehead and wiped his face. He sat up on the side of the bed, and when Twila acted as though she might protest, he fought her back with a warning look.

"We need to make some plans. Also, we've left Granny in the kitchen alone. From now on, we need to either stay together or be separated for a damn good reason."

Twila rushed out of the room, no doubt headed for the kitchen. Miss Molly decided to go with her, and she leapt off the foot of the bed. Twila still had the Glock, and I wouldn't have wanted to be the person she tried to protect Granny from. I followed more slowly with Jack, to keep an eye on how he was doing. He staggered a tiny bit when he first started out of the room, but soon grabbed my hand and pulled me down the hall at a good pace.

We found Granny and Twila in the kitchen, a ghost, a dog and a cat on guard.

"How are you, Granny?" Jack asked. "I'm sure sorry that had to happen to you."

"I's'll be fine, Jack. Truth to tell, I's'll prob'ly have a couple night-mares now and then. But you's can bet that there Danny is sorrier that he got tangled up with me." She grinned at Gil, who stood with a bottle of Red-Hot levitated at just the right height for her to reach if she needed it. "My feller here is takin' ker a me."

I noticed Joleen waver into sight behind Gil and prepared myself for a possible spat of trouble between her and Granny. But the saloon girl only smiled at the two of them and shook her head. Then she headed back into her own dimension and whatever private quest she was involved in.

I guess she caught my thoughts, because *I'm looking for True,* flashed through my mind.

Be careful, I instinctively sent back to her, before it dawned on me she didn't have a whole lot to worry about in her state. Well, come to think of it, yes, she did. I recalled her battered and bruised appearance after the run-in with Karen.

"I'm going to hang around here in the kitchen," Twila assured me. "Where will you two be?"

"Just a few feet away," Jack told her. "In the saloon."

I followed along with him, and he went straight to the safe. When I realized he had forgotten the combination, I pulled it out again and read it off. Door open, he removed four carbines, three revolvers, and three holsters. Shoving the safe door shut, he twisted the steel handle to make sure it was once more secured.

I didn't bother to tell him the spell-caster and any ghost on the premises could open that safe easily if he...or she...felt so inclined.

Jack studied my lower body, and I sighed and let my eyes drift into half-slits, preparing for him to pull me to him, now that we had some privacy. But hell, he wasn't looking at me with desire. He reached over on the bar and picked up one of the holsters.

"This one should fit you, *Chère*." He slipped the holster around my waist and buckled it. I recognized that particular Jack-face—the one he wore when he was deeply involved in a case versus the on-the-way-to-the-bedroom one.

He chose a pistol from the array and put it in my holster. I felt like Annie Oakley, but it wasn't a fun Oakley feeling, as she would have had performing with Buffalo Bill. Maybe, I mused to myself, I should gear myself more toward a Calamity Jane persona.

No, she was a lost cause as far as Wild Bill Hickok was concerned. Hope for a different outcome with my law enforcement guy bloomed in me.

Even though I knew Jack had a gun in his boot, and Twila had his Glock in the kitchen, he donned one of the holsters and pistols himself. I could have drooled over the handsome picture he made, all dressed up as an old-timey gun fighter. He put Gil's good looks to shame.

Maybe I did drool a bit, or maybe it was the dreamy gaze in my eyes, because Jack said, "Sorry, *Chère*. We don't have time to waste right now."

He reconsidered and added, "Not that any time with you is a waste, love. But right now, we need to flush out some rats before they do any more damage to this great old place."

I bobbed my head in agreement as he picked up the rest of the guns. After all, we were talking about compromises in our Jack-Alice world, and I might as well start accepting him in his cop-mode now. Jack handed me one of the rifles, and like a good little soldier, I propped it on my shoulder and followed him to the kitchen.

"Trade you, Twila," he said, holding out the last holster, which now held the third revolver.

Twila agreeably handed Jack the Glock and settled her gun belt around her waist as Jack replaced his in the holster on his back. I inanely wondered if that empty leather hadn't bothered him when he lay on the bed with us taking care of him. There were more important things to worry about right now, though.

Instead of giving Twila and Granny the carbines, he leaned those two against the wall inside the kitchen door.

"In case you need them," he said with a look at the two other women.

"Thankee," Granny replied as she stirred the large pot on the stove and shook in a few drops of Red-Hot.

Jack caught Twila's eye and flicked his head to indicate she should come with us as he went back into the café. We all ended up with cups of the fresh coffee, doctored to our own preferences, and sat around a table, our preferred roosting spot.

CHAPTER 28

"Can you get Joleen in here?" Jack asked me.

"Probably." I sent out, *Joleen?*

She appeared immediately, and so did her brother. Joleen settled into the remaining chair at our table. True hovered between us and the door to the saloon.

"You gonna join us or stand there bein' rude and eavesdroppin'?" Jack asked, indicating he, too, had a clear view of the male apparition.

True disappeared, and Jack shrugged and turned to talk to Joleen. A chair slid across the floor, and Jack stiffened. He dropped his hand to the gun butt protruding from his holster. Twila and I only watched calmly. The chair squeezed between mine and Joleen's. I scooted over a few inches.

Two cowboy hats floated into the room, one the height of a man's head, the other a couple feet lower. Jack had started to relax his hold on the pistol, and I lifted my coffee cup to hide my grin when his fingers re-tightened.

True appeared in the chair beside me, one of the hats on his head. holding the other one. He flicked a finger on his free hand at his hat and said, "This one's mine. One of the bar maids nailed it up there a night after I'd had a few too many." He handed Jack the other hat. "This one looks like it might fit you. It's pretty clean, not all sweat-stained like some of the others."

To Jack's credit, he accepted the hat and plopped it on his head. I bent my arm and set my elbow on the table to prop my chin on my fist. He looked more than ever like an old Wild West hero.

Under the table, Twila nudged me with her knee. In my mind, I heard her communication: *We've got some serious issues here, Alice. Pay attention.*

This is serious, too, I shot back, and grinned at her. She chuckled silently and nodded agreement.

I did straighten in my chair and readjusted my mood to a more sober vein. None of us knew what was going to happen next. We were dealing with some nasty people, one a ghost. Karen hadn't hung around...oops, wrong word to use in connection with that departed person...hadn't *stayed* around long enough to question to our satisfaction. Karen, Maddie, Danny and the sheriff were all involved in the coven. Whether or not that had anything to do with the people conking us on the head and shooting at us, trying to run us out of Dodge, or Red Dollar, was yet to be determined.

Here we sat, all dressed up in fighting gear, and no one to shoot.

Jack meant to get to the bottom of it, though.

"As we were leavin' to go look for Granny," he said to Joleen, "you were gettin' ready to tell us something you'd been warned to keep quiet about. Given a threat to make sure you listened."

"I tried to point someone to what was going on without getting myself banished. I drew the pentagram in True's room and the other design you and Twila found. I saw them in a book one of the coven members left open down in their room."

I shuddered at the thought of sticking a finger in blood to draw with. She caught my distaste and even seemed to understand the reason.

"I had enough ability to not have to touch the blood they'd collected in a chalice," she said, that recollection giving her and everyone there a jolt of revulsion.

Jack seemed to have had enough of that inquiry direction. He included True in his glance. "You can feel free to chime in anytime."

"Chime?" True asked. "Like a bell?"

I chuckled and explained, "It's an expression. It means for you to add in anything you want to tell us. You seem to do a lot of wandering. Did someone threaten you, too?"

"I don't let them know when I'm around," True said. "Guess you'd say, I don't let them *see* me. I'd rather work on getting rid of these hoodlums my own way."

"You're the one who's been causing the problems with the hotel sale, aren't you?" Twila asked. "Destroying the sign. Crashing the web site." She frowned. "Although it's strange, at least to me, that a ghost can manipulate something on the internet."

"Easy as pie," True said with a smug look.

"All it takes is the right amount of energy, Twila," I explained. "And I'll bet he's the one who sent me a text message."

"I've had plenty of lonesome time to practice," True said without actually admitting to manipulating the cell phone.

"And he's kept us tied here with him," Joleen said. "When he'd be a lot happier over there with Marina."

True started to waver and disappear, but Twila barked, "Get your ass back here and face up to what you did! I know there's something you're living with...uh...you died with that you're not telling us!"

In direct disobedience, True faded more. She only stared at him without voicing any further menace of what would happen should he continue to thwart her order. When he was merely a faint glimmer of pixels, he sighed and materialized into his full body once again.

"How did you know?" he asked Twila quietly.

"She reads minds," Joleen said.

"No," Twila denied. "Well, sometimes, if I concentrate hard enough. It's mostly reading body language. It didn't take a mind reader to figure this out. It's got something to do with the night your hat got nailed up."

True hung his head. "I didn't drink a drop after that night."

"You dumb, stupid...man," Joleen said.

272

"Well, she wouldn't leave Harvey." True spread his hands. "We'd had that same fight again that very afternoon."

"She had a child with him," Joleen said. "And don't say you could have taken care of both of them! Harvey St. Paul had friends in high places. He would have made life miserable for all three of you, chasing you down until he found his son. He didn't give a damn about Marina, but he knew Tadd would be the only child he ever had. Before you showed up on the scene and fell in love with Marina, Harvey had the mumps. When he couldn't get Marina pregnant again, he had a talk with Doc Holiday when he dropped by once. Doc told him if a man caught mumps that time of life, he usually ended up sterile."

Jack leaned on the table. "So let me get this straight. You got drunk because the woman you loved...a married woman...wouldn't run away with you. So in your misery and tanked-up state, you went to bed with the barmaid. She kept your hat as a souvenir and nailed it up over the bar."

"And Marina saw it the next day," True whispered. "Before I recovered enough to take it down. She'd heard what that meant."

Jack leaned back in his chair and crossed his arms. "So the married woman you were sleeping with found out you, her lover, slept with another woman and got pissed. And broke up with you."

"I'm not sure what you mean by broke up," True said. "She probably would rather have broken my head. I wish she'd done that, instead of freezing me out for the rest of my life."

"Which didn't last too long after that," Joleen added.

I scooted my chair back. When everyone jerked their gazes toward me, I said, "I need some water." I kept my cool pretty well until I made it into the kitchen. There, I leaned against the wall and bit my lip—hard—to keep from screaming.

Granny was at my side as fast as she could toddle.

"Child, what's wrong?" she asked, her bright eyes peering deep into my soul.

"I...can I talk about it with you later, Granny? It's something I need to work out in my own mind first."

And it was, I inwardly mused as she nodded and went back to her gumbo. I hadn't thought to look for Gil, but now I saw him in the same protective stance beside his new girlfriend.

Girlfriends might be the problem. It had hit home with me with the impact of a meteorite straight from the Universe. I'd been drowning in high hopes for Jack and me to renew our girlfriend/boyfriend status. Possibly with an eye towards more, maybe even a together-forever happy-ever-after. Yet I'd blindly ignored the years we had been divorced...dee-vorced. I knew Jack's libido. Very well. I couldn't imagine him going without sex for long.

Miss Pouty-Purr over in Angel Fire sure had seemed to think there might be a chance for her to take Jack home with her. Or share his hotel room, when he went back to Angel Fire.

Where he would go after we were able to get out of here. He had to take the borrowed pickup back to Pouty-Purr. He still had some things in his hotel room....

With an effort I dredged up from somewhere, I shouted inside my mind: *Enough!* It had taken years of practice for me to be able to use that helpful mind control feature, which would halt black thoughts in their tracks. I also knew I had to re-focus, so I grabbed a bottle of water out of the 'fridge beside me, not even shuddering at the thought of its proximity to some unwrapped frozen meat earlier in the day. I twisted the cap off, took a long swallow that forced me to loosen my gritted teeth, and leaned on the wall again. I wasn't quite ready to look Jack in the face. Instead, I'd follow the conversation from here.

"It's like this," Twila was saying. "Things that bother us on this side —in the earth dimension while we are alive—aren't necessarily the same things that make a difference across The Veil. Yes, Marina was probably so angry she never wanted to see you again. While she was alive anyway."

"She sure as hell was."

"Whether she had a right to be or not," Jack said in a low voice.

"That's a discussion we can have another time, Mr. Detective," Twila warned, and I swallowed more water in an attempt to soothe my sour stomach.

"I didn't go into The Light at first because I was hoping there was some way I could get her to forgive me before I left," True explained.

"That would have been nice. And yes, it probably would have meant something to your growth over there."

"And," True said when Twila paused as though trying to decide how to explain our beliefs to an un-initiate, "after she also died, I was filled with so much guilt, I couldn't face her in the afterlife."

Twila took a deep breath, and I knew she was ready to give yet another ghost her you-need-to-move-on talk.

"As I started to say," my aunt said in a tone that indicated she would not take well to any interruptions, "the same things that are important to us here aren't inevitably what matters in the afterlife. Rather than carry her anger over your betrayal with her, she now can see the entire picture. Face up to her own part in the wrongness of what happened. Understand there was shared guilt and be more accepting of the fact you both need to forgive each other."

I caught Granny's gaze on me, her sympathetic expression changing to one reflecting her perception. I managed a sickly smile back.

Without peering around the doorjamb, I couldn't see what was going on in there, and the silence was getting to me. Truth be told, I wanted to see Jack's reaction to all this. Truth be told, I wasn't a damn bit ready to think of his fine body sweating and pumping over another woman.

Thankfully, Twila had evidently given True long enough to ponder her revelations and said, "You ever hear of the word faith?"

True laughed briefly. "Sure. It's something preachers use to get you to drop money in their collection plates."

Twila pushed out a disgusted sigh. "You're missing the point. You don't have to believe what I tell you. But there's a good possibility Alice and I can arrange a meeting between you and Marina to forgive each other. We can't do that, though, if you continue to glory in your self-imposed pity party and wander around here like a poor, ill-treated Lancelot."

"Who?" True asked.

"A knight who was in love with King Arthur's wife, Guinevere," Twila explained. Evidently, True must have still looked confused, because she continued, "Never mind. Part of contacting those on the other side is faith that they will come to us. And when they do, faith that they are really there, rather than just rubbing your eyes and explaining it away as an hallucination. Something you could not have possibly seen."

True was still stuck on another point. "I'm not just sunk in a pity party," he grumped. "I really am sorry for what I did."

"As you should be," Twila said without mercy. "And it's your choice whether or not to stay that way until you're one of the last souls left after Armageddon or face up to what you've done and get over it. Grow your soul. Accept your faults and misdeeds and learn from them."

"It's a lot to think about," True said.

"And always your choice whether to do that or not." A chair scooted back, Twila's I guessed, because she said, "I'm going to get some water, also."

She never made it. The explosion rocked the entire structure.

A second one followed before I could get to Granny, but the wobbling pot of gumbo on the stovetop gave me the impetus I needed to lunge the last few inches and pull her to the floor with me. I didn't stop there. I kept her sheltered in my arms, on top of me, as I frantically pushed backwards with my feet, trying to escape the coming cascade of boiling gumbo.

Which never hit us. A safe distance away, I saw it frozen in mid-air. Gil stood there, a grim expression on his face, his finger poised at the shower of roué, chicken, shrimp and spices. With a supreme effort, he manipulated the pot and its contents back onto the burner, then flicked the knob to turn off the flame. He waved his finger again to soar the lid onto the pot. All within a second or so.

I scrambled to my feet and pulled Granny up into my arms. None too gently, either. I didn't even wait until I was sure she hadn't broken anything. I lifted her and carried her to a chair and sat her down.

Then I thought to look for Trucker and Miss Molly. Miss Molly was right there, and she leaped into Granny's lap, placed her paws on her shoulder and frantically licked her wrinkled face. Trucker jammed his head beneath my right hand and stared at me with so much concern, I knelt to wrap my arms around his neck.

"I'm fine, boy," I said. "And so glad you and Miss Molly are, too. I love you, Trucker." I ruffled his ears and stood. He remained protectively by my side as I turned again to Granny.

"I'm all right, Child!" Granny insisted, though she clung tightly to the cat and stroked it with a shaky hand.

"Are you sure?" I scanned her frail but sound body.

"You's the one who landed hard, Alice. And I thankee from the bottom of my heart."

That reminded me, yes, I had landed hard. On my back. Luckily, hip padding protected my sensitive tailbone, part of the ten pounds I kept meaning to lose. Some stinging filtered up my spine, but the heavy sweater saved me from having to ask Twila for more pain meds.

"I'm O.K.," I told her.

"Then you'd best gets out there and see what happened to the others."

I took her advice. As I raced across the room, Trucker with me, I heard her say, "And thankee for savin' my gumbo, Mister Handsome."

In the dining area, I found Twila blocking the door to the saloon, one arm stretched palm out to stop Jack. "I said no, damn it!" she yelled into his face. "We wait for Alice!"

"I looked in the kitchen," he growled back at her. "She and Granny are all right."

Twila saw me in the kitchen doorway. She still held her arm out. "Here she is."

Jack said to me, "Tell your aunt this isn't something you two need to look into. There was a damned explosion out there."

"Two," I said as I walked over to join Twila. Trucker stayed where he was. He didn't much care for arguments between people in his circle of love. "And there was a reason for them. Think about it, Jack. There was also a reason the explosions happened where they did and not here, where we would have been injured. Or killed."

"Because whoever did this wasn't sure they'd manage to kill the right people," Twila added with a nod. "So they tried to destroy us another way."

"By getting rid of our protective elements," I confirmed.

"The rooms," Jack said. "Where your things are."

"Yes. Now that you know what we think is going on, find some fire extinguishers and let's go," Twila ordered.

Granny toddled out, a fire extinguisher in her frail arms and Miss Molly trailing her. Gil followed, levitating two more with him. "I seen another one in the saloon there, an' one by the front desk," she said.

Gil sailed an extinguisher through the air, and Jack caught it easily.

"I think I know where the other explosion came from," True said. "I'll go check that." He disappeared.

Twila stepped back to let Jack lead the way, and she picked up the red canister behind the bar as we passed. Twila, Granny and Joleen waited until I got the one at the front desk and ordered Trucker and Miss Molly to stay there, so we wouldn't have to worry about them. By then, Jack and Gil were already down the hallway at our room doors, where streams of dark smoke filled the air.

Jack pulled his shirt up over his nose and opened the canister. Foam exploded, and Gil joined him as they walked into Twila's room. It made sense hers would be the target of the most damage, since she had the satchel of strongest protection elements.

I couldn't help myself. Although still muddled over my feelings for Jack, I shot a telepathic plea to Gil: *Take care of Jack!*

Done! he replied. And since he'd already proven himself a worthy guardian, I believed him.

Twila and I pulled our sweaters over our noses, but Granny used her apron. Joleen, of course, didn't have to worry. Our gang of women firefighters hurried down the hallway to the room Granny and I used.

Twila and I blockaded the door to protect Granny and squirted foam. The smoke stung my eyes, and tears streamed down my cheeks, wetting the collar of my sweater. I really couldn't see what I was aiming at until a couple flame flickers penetrated the smoke, giving us a target.

Too soon, our extinguishers ran out. I reached for Granny's, but her bright eyes warned me I better not touch it. With a huge amount of trepidation, I moved back so she could use her canister. She planted her feet and squeezed the handle. Her apron slipped off her nose, and she didn't protest when I reached around her and pulled it back in place.

Twila left us, and I divided my attention between protectively hovering over Granny and watching where my aunt was going. Twila coughed a time or two but ducked through the smoke. A few seconds later, I noticed the dark clouds start moving. The color lightened, enough of a change to see Twila had opened the window at the end of the hallway. She continued to protect her nose as she hurried back up the hall to where we stood.

Smoke still seeped out of the room when Granny's extinguisher ran out. The three of us backed away and moved on down the hallway. A second later, Jack and Gil joined us.

Jack took in the path of the smoke, now gliding down toward the open window, and nodded his approval.

"We'll have to wait until things clear more," he said. "I can't tell much yet, but from what I could see, I think someone used an accelerant and torched that before they set off the explosive. The explosives wouldn't have started that much of a fire, since the building's stucco. And they wanted to get rid of what was in the room, not necessarily damage the building beyond repair."

True appeared beside us, and Jack looked at him in question. "You find the site of the other explosion?"

"The room down where those crazies met," True said with a nod as I once again stifled my amazement at Jack's easy conversation with a being he'd denied the existence of for so many years. To Twila, True said, "You talk about faith. Those nuts have it. A mis-placed faith in some nasty entities."

"Those are dangerous nasties," Twila said. "Jack's already determined that's where Karen was killed."

"I thought she would be the logical victim, given what I judged the age of the blood down there to be," Jack corrected in what I recognized as his detective persona. "I hadn't heard of anyone else getting killed around here."

"You think she mighta been one of them there sacrifices?" Granny asked.

"Maybe," Twila replied.

"How bad's the damage down there?" Jack asked True.

"They used powerful stuff. Not magic, physical explosives. It's a pile of rubble. I tried to determine if part of the basement would collapse without that room's support, but I don't know."

Jack thought for a moment, his comments indicating he'd been examining the floor plan on the map in his mind. "That other room's not directly under the basement. It's set off to the southeast. Was."

"Let's get out of here and wait for the smoke to clear," I said. "And I need to check on Trucker and Miss Molly in the lobby."

They weren't in the lobby. When I passed the stairwell where I'd tangled with those ghostly bodies, I saw them sitting on the first landing. Both stared up at Ol' Tom, and had I not known better, I'd have sworn the puma was staring back at them. I *know* an animal dead for decades couldn't have twitched its tail.

Jack, Twila and Granny must have experienced the same misconception. They halted abruptly, and when I turned to see what caught their attention, they were staring at the puma. I shook my head and went on into the lobby.

"Trucker, Miss Molly, come on," I called back. I didn't want to wait around and see if Ol' Tom included himself in the invite.

I guess we were all too wired to sit down and try to relax. Jack leaned against the lobby desk, and we three women gathered in a group in front of him, joined obediently by my pets. The three ghosts stood to our left. No one alive or dead said anything for several long moments. I instinctively examined those around me, searching for any signs of injury or blisters from the fire.

Particles of ash had settled in everyone's hair—except for the ghosts.

The upper portions of the living faces were all dark with soot. I found myself wishing I could clean up in either the hall bath or the kitchen sink, but I settled for brushing at my own hair to dust out the ash. I certainly wasn't going off by myself around here anytime in the foreseeable future. When Granny and Twila noticed what I was doing, they ran hands over their own hair. Granny also dug a handkerchief from her apron pocket and scrubbed at her face, wrinkling it into even deeper paths.

Jack finally broke the silence. "Sorry about y'all's things."

"Whoever did that obviously doesn't know all the facts about magic or protection," Twila said in an unconcerned tone. She walked over to the desk and reached behind the wall around it to pull out a box of tissues. She took out a handful, then handed me the box.

"We don't need the actual elements," Twila went on. She stopped smoothing the tissues over her dirty face and picked up a paperweight with a tarantula entrapped inside it from the desk. "I can take this and infuse it with protection. Within a few seconds. And we can call on Cat's assistance from hundreds of miles away. From what I'm learning about these neophytes, they're just dabbling. I've studied for years, and I've passed a lot on to Alice. We aren't afraid of these wannabe black witches."

"Good," Jack said. "I'll let you take care of them with my blessing, because I don't know anything about dealing with that type of lawbreaker. What I'm worried about more is whoever's trying to kill us."

"It's a joint effort," someone said from across the lobby.

I assumed every one of us saw the shoes first, those lovely, outlandish shoes.

CHAPTER 29

My gaze traveled upward. Karen was fully dressed. She wore a soft wool, navy pantsuit, a pale blue blouse under it with a ruffle around her neck to give her a hint of femininity. Of course, she hadn't presented herself at her best hanging naked from a rope, tongue protruding, face dark and blood congealing on her arm stumps. No fault of her own, I hastily mused.

But those shoes! I lost interest immediately in her neat business attire and landed my gaze back on the most awesome sight I'd seen in this old hotel: those sensational marvels on her feet, a far cry from a match to the business apparel. She noticed Twila, Granny and me gazing at them. Granny's expression, especially, bordered on worship. I slipped a quick glance at the ghost men and woman and caught them as enthralled as the rest of us.

"Like them?" Karen asked. "I used to wear them under my robe during ceremonies." She stuck out her foot and pulled up a pant leg so we could better see one of the shoes.

I had no idea how she could even stand up in those, let alone walk. When she was alive, anyway. In her present state, she could float. She didn't have to worry about falling off the eight-inch heels on those shining black leather slippers.

We stared at the shoe in even more awe after she exposed the rest of it. Gold carvings of what appeared to be elk antlers encased toe to heel and curled up her leg another six inches. On the end of the shoe sat a small white skull with a crown of diamonds. The skull grinned into the ether. Tiny red jewels sparkled on the tips of each antler, glittering in the light. All in all, it was a shoe any woman from nine to ninety would drool over.

"Kin I have them when you cross over?" Granny asked in a mesmerized voice.

"By my guest," Karen said, lowering her leg and dropping her pant leg. "If you help me give Maddie her comeuppance."

Granny sighed in disappointment. "I's don't deserve 'em. That there Maddie fooled me well and proper. All she's had to do was tell me what I was cookin' was better'n anything she ever et before, and I lapped it up like a cat an' cream." She glanced down at my cat, which now sat at her feet. "Sorry, Miss Molly, but she did. An' I did."

To Karen again, she said, "An' she still owes me fifty bucks for helpin' her clean that there room!"

"You're not the first one she's fooled," Karen said. "And these shoes cost a lot more than fifty bucks. You can sell them on E-bay when you get tired of wearing them."

"Oh, I couldn't ever sell 'em," Granny said in horror. "Pro'ly couldn't ever walk in 'em, either, not even with my stick. But I's sure would like to put 'em on a shelf and look at 'em."

"Like I said," Karen told her, "be my guest. But first I want to see Maddie behind bars. And Eddie and even Danny. Then...." She hesitated and cast Joleen a cautious look. "I...uh...would like to have Alice and Twila help me cross over."

Joleen huffed a sigh of annoyance—not that any breath passed her lips; the gesture and sound got her point across. "I told you they were here to help me!"

"Look," Twila said. "Alice can cross over one, two or dozens when she opens a door. So there's room for each and every one of you on the path through The Light."

"Thank you," Karen said. "And thank you all for what you've done to expose these murderers. I know I was part of it, but I didn't realize at first it was going to be more than just casting a few spells to better our lives." She directed her next comments at Jack. "I want you to know there's a diary with my things in Angel Fire. I wrote some more in it while I was there."

Jack frowned, and I could tell by his expression what was running through his mind. If we managed to get the murderers locked up, how would he explain an entry in a diary after the victim was already dead? Talk about a problem with chain of evidence.

"You's already learned to travel place-to-place?" Granny asked in interest.

"It was easy, since I knew it was possible from listening and learning Joleen had actually gone to find Alice. And I'm ready to face whatever retribution is waiting for me," Karen said to Twila and me. "But, as I implied, I'm not going until I see Maddie behind bars. And the others who need to be there with her."

"Give us a list," Jack said.

Karen held up a re-attached hand with manicured nails covered in gold, silver diamonds set in a shape of a cross in each one. I hadn't noticed whether her frozen hands had been manicured or not. Perhaps she had done her nails herself since we'd last seen her. She placed her thumb on each finger as she spoke, starting with her index finger: "Eddie, Danny, Maddie, and the other nine coven members." She combined the last nine on her small finger.

"Names of the rest?" I asked her.

"They're in the diary, but they aren't important. They're just towns-folk who thought it would be cool to try to use magic to better them-selves. We'd help them on a business deal or something. Maybe give them an ointment to smooth their wrinkles, make them look younger.

They weren't in on my murder. Eddie never would have gotten them to do something like that."

"So you were the thirteenth," Jack said.

"Yes," she admitted. "And Maddie's the one who told them I was getting ready to betray their plan to buy the hotel for themselves. So they wouldn't have to worry about being found out when they did their ceremonies in that hidden room." She looked at Twila and me. "They never expected you two to get rid of the ghosts, just confirm the place was haunted so they could buy it cheaper."

"I thought you owned the hotel," Twila said.

She shook her head. "Not alone. With this economy, I had to find some investors. When that didn't work out, when the ad campaign still didn't bring in enough guests, Eddie came up with the idea of buying the hotel himself. But he wanted it cheap, and the investors had to be convinced to write off their losses instead of demanding all of their money back in a sale."

"You and Maddie were showing the place to other possible buyers," Joleen said.

"We had to make it look good. But it was mostly to prove to the investors it would never sell for the market price we had on it."

"Why were you used for the scapegoat sacrifice?" Twila asked astutely.

"Maddie wanted Danny," Karen spat. "Even though he was young enough to be her son! I'd made the mistake of telling her Danny had proposed to me, and we were going to Albuquerque to look for rings within a week or so. Then I caught her down there one day when Eddie, our High Priest, didn't have anything planned. She was working a love spell. I had no idea who she meant it for until the night they killed me."

"Ah," I said when she stopped talking due to her sobs. "I wondered why Danny was so upset when we found you. He must have been under the love spell during the ceremony. Didn't even realize the woman he was engaged to was the sacrifice."

"Or, if so," Twila said, "that he was being lied to about her betrayal. But we know from Cat those spells can lose their effectiveness after a while, especially if they're cast in a relationship the Universe doesn't mean to happen. When he found her hanging in that room, the spell had broken. But he still might not have been able to recall being in on the sacrifice. Not until later."

When it looked like Karen could speak again, I said, "I don't think we have the whole story yet."

"You don't," Karen said in a tear-clogged voice. "Maddie is the one who convinced Eddie a human sacrifice would assure the dark powers would help his plan."

She paused to fight more sobs before she went on, "Her magic was piss-poor at the best. I think she doctored some recordings of calls I'd been having with supposed prospective buyers. Eddie believed her and decided to step up his powers and get some even stronger help by agreeing to give the dark side a living sacrifice. Maddie had been saying all along that was the next step, since it didn't look like we were being granted our desires as quickly as Eddie thought we should be."

She hurried on before anyone could interrupt her, as though she needed to tell us everything. "I've remembered a lot, now that the drugs they gave me in a pitcher of ice tea are out of my system."

"The pitcher," Twila murmured. "We were lucky Jack saw the residue."

"Uh...." I couldn't help interjecting. "I didn't think drugs had an effect after you died."

She shrugged. "They must. I remember now that Danny wasn't in True's room when Eddie hung me up. I still had a faint heartbeat, but I was already hovering. He was at the sacrifice, though."

"But why," Jack interrupted, "hang you where you'd be found like that? They'd already gotten away with killin' you in a room nobody knew about. Pretty much gotten completely away with murder. All they had to do was come up with some story about why you disappeared. Even if their story didn't make sense, there wasn't any evidence to link them to you vanishing."

"That's your cop mind thinking, Jack," I said quietly. "This is black art. They wanted the body found. Exposure of their horrible act would supposedly make the spell more powerful."

"Oh," he whispered with a look that told me the murderers better worry about what happened when they were *exposed* to Homicide Detective Jack Roucheau.

"This Eddie...the sheriff, right?" Jack asked.

"Yes," Karen said.

"Eddie probably started the fire," I mused. "In case he left any evidence behind."

"When we're lookin' for motive in my line of business, we say 'follow the money,'" Jack continued. "Eddie probably had more reason than just wanting this hotel for privacy for his rituals."

A thoughtful expression crossed Karen's face. "He gambled a lot. Maybe that escalated the need for a human sacrifice."

"But he wasn't an investor, was he?" I asked.

"No, but...shit," Karen spewed. "I'd already changed my will and life insurance. I don't have any other family, and Danny was my beneficiary. Before, I'd left everything to the United Way."

"Danny Boy said he talked you into one of them there pieces of paper that let him sign your name," Granny said.

"A Power of Attorney," I said.

"There's lots more to it legally than just that," Jack said. "And Danny probably would have met with an accident himself after Eddie had a deed to the hotel. Or been the next *sacrifice.*"

"Good," Karen said, but her voice shook.

"We can talk about all this later." Jack went on. "Time's passin', and you can bet they know by now we're all still alive." He grinned at the ghosts. "Most of us."

"Still, I think you've figured it out. Or we have," Karen added, not ready to let her anger abate now that she had an audience to listen to her ordeal. "I know for sure Danny listened to Maddie. Even as drugged as I was when I was in that wagon bed they laid me in, I could see her holding Danny's hand. I heard her whisper to him that now I'd get paid back for betraying all of them, but she'd make sure to help him over the hurt."

"It was a horrible way to die," Joleen said. "I'm sorry I didn't understand."

"It didn't hurt," Karen denied. "You should know that. Death doesn't hurt. It's the regrets that bother you."

"You're right," Joleen agreed.

Jack's cell phone rang, startling all of us into jumping and grabbing the pistol butts protruding from our holsters. Jack relaxed first and pulled the phone out of his shirt pocket.

"Yeah?"

I hoped for a second he would put the caller on speaker—then hoped he wouldn't. I wasn't in the mood to listen to Miss Pouty-Purr right then.

The call only lasted a few seconds, during which Jack listened in silence. "I understand," Jack said finally, and disconnected.

As he returned the phone to his pocket, he told us, "Charlie says he's still working on getting someone from Albuquerque up here. They've had a terror threat at a government office, so that's their first priority. He actually did try to get the hospital to let him use the helicopter, but no-go. The ice and snow is causing a lot of fools too dumb to stay home to crash their cars. That's the hospital's priority."

"We can understand that," Twila said. She'd missed a spot of soot on her cheek, and I found a clean spot on my wad of tissues and wiped it off. When she saw I wasn't going to do the same for Jack, whose face was still black above his nose, tanned and clean below it, she grabbed more tissues and wiped him clean. He waited until she finished before he spoke again.

"Well." Jack settled his hat more firmly on his head. "I'm getting tired of just reacting to the attacks on us. I'm gonna take the fight to the enemy."

"Not without us," I said.

"Now, *Chère*...."

"She's right," Twila said, and Granny hefted her gun belt to shift it on her hips in agreement. "There are twelve of them. This isn't some old time movie where the lone sheriff takes on the band of outlaws and wins. The sheriff's one of the bad guys. You're gonna have to take whatever posse you can dig up to stand behind you. And that's us."

"Besides, we don't know where to find them," I said.

"*I'll* start with the jail," Jack told us, emphasizing he still thought he was going alone. "Y'all will—"

The light shimmered and thunder crashed around us. It happened so fast, we didn't even have time to duck and try to protect ourselves.

CHAPTER 30

A twangy tune from a player piano shattered the frozen stillness, which had immobilized all of us in crouches, pistols halfway out of our holsters. *Buffalo Gal* ended with *dance by the light of the moooooon!* and *I Wish I Was in Dixie* launched next. Glasses tinkled. Voices laughed and conversed in raised tones to be heard over the music. A female voice shrieked giggles indicating she wasn't in danger...at least of being physically hurt. The clack of pool balls combined with the other noise.

We turned as one to stare at the saloon, but there wasn't a person in sight, only the echo of their bygone presences. Yet no doubt the building around us was now rooted in the past, as we were. The formal dining room had disappeared. Instead, wooden tables and chairs, cards and poker chips spread out on a few tabletops, filled the area. As we watched, a deck hovered in the air, and cards pealed off to complete hands in front of each pulled-up chair. Except there were no players. Visible, anyway, though the hands lifted into the air as though held.

A bottle of whiskey in the middle of a disfigured tabletop rose, tipped, and filled four scattered shot glasses. When the whiskey clunked down, the glasses lifted, floated through the air and clinked in a toast. Then they raised mouth height and tilted until the liquid disappeared.

Each glass descended to the table, and the whiskey bottle levitated again.

A haze hung over the room, the distinctive odor of cigarette and pipe smoke identifying the source. A set of batwing doors swung back and forth on the front of the building, audible footsteps indicating invisible people entered and exited. The bar now ran across the far wall, and a glass of beer slid down the shining surface, foam spilling a path behind it. The glass halted abruptly three-quarters of the way down and lifted into the air. It tilted, and the beer vanished into the mouth of whoever held the glass.

We now stood on plank flooring in the lobby, the carpet gone, the room only a quarter the size it had been. The check-in desk still sat there, but with no sign of the waist-high wall, let alone a phone or computer. An open ledger with as many X's for sign-in's as scrawled names lay beneath a pegboard with skeleton keys and hand-lettered room tags numbering to ten. A rickety staircase led to the upper level, rather than rooms down hallways on this floor.

"*Chère?*" Jack whispered, a mixture of panic and apprehension in his voice.

Even though my feelings for him continued their circle of confusion in my mind, I slipped my hand in his and squeezed.

"Hmmmm," Twila said as she placed her fist on her left hip and kept her right hand on the gun butt. "Maybe we didn't give these spell-casters enough credit. I think we've gone back in time to when the ghosts we've been dealing with were actually alive."

"What?" I said with a gasp at the same moment Jack growled, "No way in hell."

"I think she's right," Karen said, the expression on her face as astonished as the one I felt on mine.

When I looked over at her, I couldn't quell my gasp of astonishment. Maybe no one except Twila and I could tell, since these ghosts were fully capable of appearing to be as firm-bodied as we were, but now Karen was herself, as she had been when alive. And so were Gil, True and even Joleen.

"Yes, we're real now," Gil confirmed as he shoved back his frock coat to expose his own gun and holster.

"Eddie and his crew didn't do this," Karen denied. "It's way beyond their capabilities."

"It's the power of all of us combined with that of the Universe," Twila said, her own awe clear in her tone and on her face. "I've never had anything like this happen before. And...." She frowned like she did sometimes when she got a message, then nodded. "It's definitely from the Universe. How it's meant to be."

I walked away from the others to the batwing doors, feeling as though dozens of eyes watched me. I pushed open one door, as firm in my hand as though real...which it was. Outside, snow drifts lingered on the sides of the dirt street. Wagon wheel ruts and horseshoe imprints had cleared the rest away. A wooden walkway ran in front of the four buildings across from the saloon: a general store, a hardware and feed store, a café, and a different jail, barred windows on the front indicating its use.

I looked down. A similar walkway stretched on our side of the street, a railing planted beyond it for hitching horses. I couldn't see what buildings flanked the saloon without walking out there to look, which I wasn't about to do alone. I did confirm the wooden slates continued both to the left and right of where I stood. I now noticed railings in front of the other buildings, and sounds of horses blowing and stomping their feet signaled they were in use. Still, our band was the only visible occupants of this time period.

Then I did feel someone beside me and turned to say to Jack, "Are you seeing what I'm seeing?"

He nodded, his face strained and white under his tan. As hard as he was trying to bluff it out and live up to the big, brave male detective persona, the tell-tale signs showed through.

"I guess so. If what I'm seeing means Twila's right. That we've somehow traveled through time, back to when Joleen and the others were alive."

"Yes," I confirmed.

"Why?"

I shrugged. "Maybe to right some old wrongs? Maybe...I have no idea."

"Can we get back?" Jack whispered.

"I hope like hell we can," Twila said from behind us. "But you can bet, we'll have to do whatever we're meant to do here first."

"And what is that?" Karen asked, as she peered over Twila's shoulder. "I hope I don't ruin my shoes out there."

"*Out there* is where we need to go," Twila said without a hint of uncertainty.

Karen sighed. "At least give me a gun. Mine is back at the new addition to the hotel. Over a hundred-and-fifty years from now."

Twila and I exchanged glances. Did we really trust her? I stared down at those wondrous shoes and recalled Karen gifting them to Granny on her departure. When Twila noticed my expression, she said, "Go get her a weapon, Jack."

Jack went to where the safe had been...back in the future. Now the stairwell rose over that area, and there was no sign of a safe.

"Maybe the safe was a more modern add-on," he said.

Twila walked around the staircase, then leaned back to beckon us. On the other side, we found the wall with the safe. She was already turning the dial.

"Shoot," she said when she twisted the handle to open the door. "It must have a different combination."

"Let me." Jack flexed his fingers, then bent to place his ear close to the steel door. The strain on his face had tapered off now that he had something constructive to do. He twisted counterclockwise, then right, left again. No luck.

He spun the dial all the way around, then started the same procedure over again, this time clockwise. A satisfactory click sounded after the third rotation, and he opened the door. Jack reached in and pulled out another holster first, then a pistol.

He handed them to Karen and said, "I wasn't sure we'd find the same things here as before."

"Universe gives us what we need," was all Twila said.

"Have you noticed all we have are the six-shooters, none of the carbines?" I asked her quietly.

"What we need," she repeated.

Jack heaved a breath and laid a hand on the wall beside the safe. He bowed his head and shook it. Instinctively, I moved over to wrap an arm around his waist and pat his shoulder.

"What is it?" I asked.

He faced me. "This." He waved a hand to encompass everything as he walked away from the wall and into the lobby. "And that. And that, and that, and that." His gestures indicated the stairwell, the lobby desk, the saloon and the batwing doors. "I mean..." He studied Twila and me as he went on, "...over the years, you two have told me about some experiences I doubted like hell you could have had. Not that I called y'all liars, but I'll admit, I thought you'd embellished things to make a good story. But this—" His eyes widened. "Oh, shit. And that!"

Trucker and Miss Molly were climbing down the stairwell. I hadn't seen them go upstairs. Perhaps they had slipped by as we stared out into those late 1800's streets. Their parade included a third member this time: Ol' Tom sauntered behind Miss Molly. His huge paws plopped down the steps, tail waving back and forth. Those formerly glass eyes shone with life, and his sides rose and fell with breath.

None of us reached for our pistols as the three animals each navigated the last step and sat in a semi-circle, staring at us, Miss Molly in the middle between the other two huge animals.

"He's here to he'p us out, that there puma," Granny said. "Don't none's of you bother him." She toddled over and actually stroked Ol' Tom on the head, and his loud purr rumbled. "We's sorry you got shot, but you's kin enjoy goin' huntin' one last time, old boy."

From out of the nether, even though there was no sign of a grandfather clock, the bongs sounded: *BONG. BONG. BONG. BONG. BONG. BONG. BONG. BONG. BONG. BONG. BONG. BONG.*

"Don't tell me," Jack said. "Let me guess. It's high noon."

"Not necessarily," Twila answered. "Given it was late afternoon when we left our time, it could be a symbol."

The batwing doors flew back and thudded against the walls on either side. Someone had rushed in, but we didn't see him. That didn't stop us from hearing him.

"Mad Ed's callin' 'em out!" a voice deepened by booze and cigarettes shouted. "Take cover!"

Chairs scraped back from tables. Boots stomped, and the new female screams signified fear. A whiskey bottle wobbled, and an invisible hand caught it before it fell. Whoever held it jerked it into the other shadowy dimension with the rest of the unseen observers.

Unseen, and now unheard. Not another sound disturbed the air, until....

A barrage of shots split the sky outside but not that far away. Probably just about as far as the jail down the street, I reasoned.

"Well, podner," Granny growled to Jack. "You's posse's ready to roll."

Jack swallowed and stared around. At Granny. Then me, Twila. Next he looked at Gil, standing by Joleen, who pulled a small derringer out of her bodice. Jack shook his head and walked back over to the safe. He took out another pistol and holster and gave them to Gil.

"Show her how to wear them," he said with a nod at Joleen.

Next in line for Jack's perusal were True and Karen. They obviously passed his muster, and he studied the animals.

"Hey!" someone shouted, loud enough they probably used a bull horn. Sheriffs had access to bullhorns, so I decided it must be Eddie. "You yellow bellies gonna come out and meet your makers?"

Jack rolled his eyes. "He must have watched one too many old movies."

"His weapon shoots real bullets, not rubber blanks," I reminded him.

"Look," he said. "We're not about to go out there and have an OK Corral shootout! We men will sneak out the back and go down the alley. See how many of them we can pick off before they realize what we're up to."

"They already got the alley covered," a new voice said. Well, one I recognized, and so did Joleen, who glared at her cousin, LeRoy.

"What the heck are you doing here, LeRoy?" she asked, pulling her pistol from where it now hung in the holster on her hip. "I ought to shoot you now, like I should have years ago!"

"Aw, no, please." LeRoy cowered and backed up a step. "I know I did wrong, Cuz. I wanna chance to...whatcha call it? Redeem. Yeah, I wanna chance to redeem myself a'fore I go over there with y'all."

"How do you know we're going?" Joleen snarled.

"I been listening," he said.

"Eavesdropping and spying." I joined Joleen's glare.

Just then, Ol' Tom yawned, and LeRoy saw the animals. He yipped in startlement and bounded across the now-smaller lobby to huddle behind Joleen's skirts.

"I mean it," he said. "I'm sorry, sorry, sorry I done what I done. Don't let them cats take me apart. Please!"

"Oh, for pity sakes." Joleen shoved her gun back in her holster and turned around. She grabbed LeRoy by the ear and jerked him to his feet. Pausing in surprise, she said, "Why, Leroy. You took a bath. And shaved."

He nodded vigorously. "I did, I did. I seen how you was able to help that there woman clean herself up—" He glanced at Karen, and before he could finish, Joleen scowled again.

"You spied on us in the bathroom!"

"Just to see how you did it," LeRoy pleaded. "I wasn't sure how to use them new-fangled spigot things. And I knew you wouldn't talk to me when I came to ask you to forgive me, iffen I kept smellin' like I did."

"Let him come," Jack broke in. "He's an extra gun. Where did you see them watchin' the alley, LeRoy?"

"Everywhere you'd be able to sneak between a building and get a shot at them," LeRoy said. "If you started pickin' them off one by one, the others would be on you like coyotes on fresh meat. And there's a bunch of them out there. Some are wearin' them black robes, like when they did all that there loud chantin' downstairs."

"Where they murdered me," Karen muttered.

"I didn't see that happen," LeRoy assured her. "Don't know as I coulda done anything to help you, but I was wanderin' around the grave-yard, seein' if I could find my grave."

"It's about four plots down from mine," the new, softly-feminine voice said.

True recognized the voice immediately. "Marina," he breathed, and started to walk over to the check-in desk, where a pretty blonde in a long pink gown with rosettes of pink roses around the neckline and cuffs stood.

Marina shook her head to indicate for True to halt. He did, and she said, "We'll have time to talk after this is over with. Don't you see? It's the culmination of some unfinished business from back in our time."

Joleen walked over to Marina, and her approach was accepted. "Hello, my best friend." She kissed Marina on the cheek, and the smaller woman hugged her back. "Let me see if I can figure this out."

She looked at Karen. "You're the betrayed woman, like Marina was. True, you're yourself. Those men out there, at least, Eddie and Danny, are the crooks who murdered you to steal back the hotel you won from Harvey. Eddie, who was Harvey, probably shot you and handed off the deed to Danny, who was one of the Dalton gang. Danny hightailed it out to that old line shack so Harvey could just happen to run across the shack while the posse was chasing the murderer and find it. Then Danny collected his payment from Harvey and disappeared."

"Yes," Marina said. "That's exactly how it happened."

"Hey, you cowardly bastards!" Eddie/Harvey shouted from down the street. "We're coming in after you!"

"Look," Jack began.

True ignored him. Face set in grim lines, he walked toward the batwings. Gil, Joleen, Karen, and even LeRoy fell in behind him. Karen didn't even wobble on her beautiful shoes. True cast one loving glance at Marina as he passed the check-in desk.

"Stay safe," she whispered. He dipped his head, then pushed the doors back.

I evaded Jack's hand and hurried after the others, Twila and Granny beside me. By the time we shoved out the door, Jack was with us, although he gave us all three an angry glower. Last in line, Trucker, Miss Molly and Ol' Tom scuttled beneath the swinging batwings.

True had stepped down into the street, Joleen and Gil on one side, LeRoy and Karen on the other. We joined them and gazed toward the jail to see what waited for us.

Two men in western garb stood down there, pistols already in their hands. We drew ours, too. This wasn't going to be one of those old timey fastest draw contests.

Behind Eddie and Danny stood several black-robed figures, hoods back to expose both male and female faces, pistols in their hands. As we watched, four more men in robes emerged from the shadows between the buildings on our side of the street until there were twelve people arranged against us.

I counted our "posse." True, Gil, Joleen, Karen, Twila, Granny, Jack, LeRoy, me. Nine. I looked over and saw Marina standing behind the batwings, watching us. Even without her, though, I figured our three animals would make up for the two opposition members that outnumbered us.

I recognized the bugle when it sounded. So did Trucker. He bounded over to greet Elk and Mrs. Elk strolling down the street. They touched noses, and the three of them came over to be part of our posse.

Ha. Now we had fourteen, two more than the others.

Jack stepped forward and said something in True's ear too low for us to hear. True took Joleen's arm in one hand, and Jack reached for Karen's shoulder. They moved the two women behind them, and the four of them, Jack, Gil, True and LeRoy, took up their stance in front of us. I knew it would be useless to protest, so we five women ranged ourselves behind them, the five animals after us.

Jack took the first step, and the other three men followed suit.

As we walked forward, the black-robed figures fell back away from the other two men.

"Hey," one black-robe yelled. "You said we wouldn't have to fight. Only throw them out of town!"

"Get back here and shoot!" Eddie screamed, lifting his pistol.

True's pistol barked first. Eddie's gun flew out of his hand, and Danny crouched to aim his. Jack's bullet hit Danny high on the shoulder, and he sprawled backward in the dirt, screaming in pain. His gun was still clasped in his hand.

We women and LeRoy and Gil spread out and started shooting at the black robes, who dropped their weapons and stood there as though confused. We had to stop shooting when the animals raced past us on the left. The elk were the farthest away, Trucker and Miss Molly beside them, and Ol' Tom in the lead, tail whipping and snarls piercing the gun smoke. They headed for the black-robes, who caught sight of them, dropped their weapons, and ran like hell.

Before they could get out of range, Karen carefully aimed over the head of the puma and snapped off two shots. She hit one, who fell and got back up with the help of the person closest. The second yelped and grabbed an arm, but didn't slacken pace. I identified that one as Maddie.

Eddie swooped Danny's pistol out of his hand. Instead of facing Jack and True, he dove behind Danny's prone body and pulled the other man in front of him as a barrier. Anyone shooting him would have to go through Danny first. Eddie started shooting.

Jack knelt, although True kept going. Eddie concentrated on True, and I knew at least one bullet hit home, because blood blossomed on the back of True's jacket. Behind us, Marina screamed.

Jack steadied his pistol with his other hand and shot. Eddie howled in pain and rolled backward. He didn't get up.

Beside me, Granny lifted her pistol to blow at the barrel, like gunfighters do on TV. She slapped it back in her holster as Marina flew past to get to True, still on his feet. Marina grabbed him, and he pulled her close. Obviously uncaring of the blood stain it would leave on her dress, Marina hugged True tightly and lifted her face for his kiss.

Intent on the two star-crossed lovers, I hadn't noticed Karen follow Marina. She stood over Danny, and I gulped back my dread that she would lift her pistol and finish off her once-fiancé. However, she only scuffed the toe of one glorious shoe in the dirt and kicked dirt in Danny's face, then walked back toward us.

"We's best go after the animals," Granny said.

"Uh ...." I looked over at Twila. "What about the people who were shot?"

"Hell," Granny answered. "Let 'em rot."

I laughed. I couldn't help it. "We can't do that."

Jack was already leading Gil and Leroy down the street. The rest of us followed, but only to watch as they discussed who would take which part of which body and drag the men over to the jail before they allowed anyone to treat their wounds.

"It's SOP," Jack said, now in full charge. "First you secure the perp, then worry whether he's gonna live or die. Especially a perp who's been trying to kill you."

I didn't hesitate. I clapped my agreement of his actions, as did all of us females.

"Nice to once in a while step back and let the men take over, huh?" Twila said with a wink at me. "Makes us feel sort of pretty and feminine."

"Yeah," I agreed with a giggle.

We didn't have to worry about the animals. They came back, herding Maddie in front of them. I had no idea how they knew which person to cut out of the black-robes and bring back to jail, but there she was. She held a hand over her bloody left shoulder and looked up from fearfully keeping Ol' Tom at a distance to catch sight of Karen, strolling determinedly toward her.

Maddie screamed, "I should have killed your friends on the mountain, instead of hoping they'd slide down the cliff and make it look like an accident!"

Karen spit in her face. Twila, Granny, Joleen and I clapped again, then joined Karen and helped her surround Maddie to herd her to the jail. We didn't even need to pull our pistols again. Outnumbered, Maddie plodded along in a tear-soaked huddle of misery, not stopping until Granny had to step around her and open the door on the jail.

As Maddie walked past, Granny nonchalantly stuck out her foot. Maddie tripped, gasped and took a header into the room, crashing to the stone floor. She laid there and yowled.

"Oopsie," Granny said.

We didn't bother to hide our smiles of satisfaction at Granny's retaliation for the way Maddie befriended and deceived her.

Jack, Gil and LeRoy were behind us. Jack dragged the unconscious Eddie by the heels, the crooked sheriff's head bumping up the wooden steps. LeRoy and Gil carried Danny. I went over to where I'd seen the cell keys hanging on the wall back in our time. Twila jingled them, and I recalled she'd stuck them in her pocket when we locked up Danny back there. Maybe Eddie had another set, or maybe the Universe sprung Danny to time-travel him back here.

This was the same jail, I realized as Twila went on in to unlock the cells. At some point it had been moved from here to the other site.

A few moments later, we had our crooks incarcerated.

The whiskey fumes hit me first, and the others smelled them, too. They sniffed the air and backed against the cell bars. The ghost who sauntered in this time wasn't exactly firm-bodied, but he looked like he knew what needed done. I recognized him from historical pictures of Doc Holliday.

"I'll take care of the wounded," he said, lifting the black bag in his hand to show us he had the medical necessities. "'Course I might have to dig out a bullet or two."

"Keep him away from me!" Maddie screeched, scooting against the wall in the corner of her cell bunk.

The other two men were only now starting to rouse, and Doc dismissed them with a glance. "I'll get to them. They'd want me to take care of the woman first. Code of the West, y'know, tho' I ain't gonna call her a lady."

He passed right through the cell bars, bag and all, and Maddie fell off the bunk in a faint.

"Twila?" I asked in a half-whisper.

"Leave Doc Holiday to it," she said with a shrug. "My medicine was all destroyed in the explosion."

CHAPTER 31

Animals eyes scrutinized us from the doorway when we all gathered in the front portion of the jail. Trucker and Miss Molly peered around on the left, Ol' Tom the right. Above them, one on each side, Mr. and Mrs. Elk gazed in.

"Whew," Granny said. "It's crowded in here."

A scream from a cell indicated Maddie was awake again. Perhaps Doc waved a bottle of those nasty old-fashioned smelling salts under her nose to bring her back and realize who was taking care of her.

"Let's go outside." Like the Pied Piper, I led the others out. The animals fell in, and we paraded to the middle of the street. I halted until Twila joined Trucker, Miss Molly and me where we stood apart from the others. The elk and puma waited on the side of the street.

"We don't need our satchels to cross over anyone who wants to go," I told the crowd.

Granny immediately grabbed Jack's arm and tugged him with her to stand behind us. "I ain't ready to go yit," she whispered as she passed us.

"We know, Granny." Twila chuckled. "But some of the others are." She stepped back with Granny and Jack. "And this is one of Alice's strong points, so it's her show now."

"I hope our gifts still work back here in this time period," I mused. "It took us years to refine them...uh...back in...the future?"

Twila shrugged. "Your guess is as good as mine. I think we need to finish this task first, though. Before we try to figure out how to—and if— we can go home."

"You mean we might not?" Jack growled, apprehension in his voice. "I've got a job back there."

"You could probably find work here now that they're in need of a new sheriff," Twila teased. Then she went on in a more serious tone, "This has never happened to us before, Jack. So no, neither Alice nor I know how to get home. Or to be honest, *if* we can. We'll have to have patience and see what the Universe has in store."

"And patience is one of the lessons I'm still learning," I grumbled. I straightened my shoulders. "What about Marina and True?" I asked no one in particular.

"Here we are." Arms around each other, the two of them walked around from behind us, joining the others. I faced Joleen and Gil, Karen, True and Marina, and even LeRoy. Only LeRoy cringed when Ol' Tom wandered over from between the two elk and sat down with the rest of the used-to-be ghosts. The others only looked at the puma and re-centered their gazes on me.

The male elk bugled and strolled over to us, its mate following. I stiffened as I watched those sharp-tipped antlers close the distance, but before he reached me, Trucker and Miss Molly trotted out to meet him. The four animals touched noses similar to the way people shook hands all around. The two elk sauntered down the street, and my animals returned to sit with us.

I said to the men, women and animal placing their trust in me, "This isn't mandatory. You still have your free will." I paused. "Even you, Ol' Tom. I'm going to create a pathway and open a door into The Light. Twila and I have both been assured by our Spirit Guides this is where everyone needs to be once their souls leave their bodies."

I frowned and studied them. They all looked like their souls were completely intact. But I sensed the little whisper in my mind from one of my Guides and knew this was what needed done.

"We're also sure you'll find happiness through The Light. And loved ones and families. It's much better than wandering around lost over here."

I didn't wait to see if any of them had second thoughts. I turned to my left, to the east, and held up my right hand. "This is the way into The Light," I said. I moved my finger upward as if tracing a path in the sky, which was a brilliant blue overhead, with meandering bunches of white, fluffy clouds. I ended my path at one of the largest and most beautiful clouds, shaped like a huge round ball. Turning my hand sideways, I moved it back and forth. The cloud parted as though a door had opened in it, which it had. A glimmer of white light emerged, brightened and formed a pathway from the ground through the doorway.

I dropped my hand and turned my head toward the former ghosts.

Ol' Tom went first, and surprising me, Karen laid a hand on the puma's neck and walked beside him. She waited, though, as Ol' Tom leapt past the people and onto the path. Waving his tail in victory, he bounded upward. At the door, he paused and looked back over his shoulder. I took the growl he gave me as a thank you.

"See you at the Rainbow Bridge," I called with a wave.

Ol' Tom showed his fangs, but in a grin, then disappeared. Trucker whined quietly, then yipped his own soft goodbye. Miss Molly meowed.

I looked at Karen. "Are you having second thoughts?"

"Not a one. I just didn't want to steal the cougar's spotlight." She stepped out of her gorgeous shoes and winked. Not at me, at Granny. I picked up the shoes and turned to give them to my elderly neighbor and friend, who clasped them to her chest.

"Thankee," she said to Karen.

"Thank you," Karen replied. "All of you. I'm not sure what I'll be facing over there." I think we all heard LeRoy mutter, "Me, neither, but I'm gonna go," from where he stood. Karen went on, "I hope some of the hell I went through here will count, even though I did bring part of it on myself."

"We wish you a good afterlife," I said, and Jack, Twila and Granny all murmured, "Amen."

Using the backs of her hands—the hands she refused to leave behind—Karen brushed at the tears brimming her eyes, Stiffening her shoulders, she turned and stoically plodded up the path and straight through the doorway.

True and Marina came next. True said, "Thank you seems weak, but it's all we can think of."

"Thank you," Marina said. Together, they, too, strolled without hesitation up the path, through the door.

Joleen and Gil walked over to me first. Joleen hugged me tightly, but Gil stepped past to grab Granny and kiss her cheek. She sniffed back a sob and patted him on his shoulder. Then she looked at Joleen. "You take ker of my feller."

"I will, Granny." Joleen hugged my elderly neighbor tightly. Then she and Gil embraced Twila and shook hands with Jack. Joleen also pulled Jack's head down and kissed his cheek.

I thought Gil had forgotten me, but he hadn't. He swept me into his arms and twirled me around before he set me down. "Thank you," he said.

That left LeRoy, and he stood over there alone, a sorrowful look on his face.

"Oh, damn it, LeRoy," Gil said. "Come on."

Joleen held out her hand and Leroy rushed over to kiss it frantically. At first, Joleen pulled back with a grimace. Then she chuckled, kept LeRoy's hand in hers and placed her left hand in Gil's right. The three of them ran up the path, laughing all the way.

"Thanks, y'all," LeRoy called back just before they disappeared.

I sobbed and wiped the tears trickling down my cheeks. This part of it always made me cry. I was so happy for the souls returning home, yet extremely glad it wasn't my time to go with them. Given all the souls I had helped cross over, I imagined I'd have a huge crowd besides my family waiting for me when I finally got there. However, as Granny would say, *Thankee very much, but I'll wait a while.*

Jack stepped up behind me and wrapped his arms around me, pulling me against his chest. "You all right, *Chère*?"

"I am now." I let myself enjoy his closeness. Later, we had to settle things. But like crossing over myself, I wanted to delay that.

Jack held me tightly, but knowing him as well as I did, I could tell something distracted him. I pulled away to study his face. He didn't even seem to notice I'd moved. He stared at the pathway for a second, then around the town.

"The door will stay open for a while, Jack. In case any others want to take this opportunity to go."

"That's not what I'm thinkin' about," he admitted. "I was wonderin' why we're still here. In this time. Haven't we done what we...or you and Twila...were supposed to do? Shouldn't we be seein' that shimmer and hearin' the thunder? Realizin' all of a sudden we're back in our own time?"

"I hoped we would," Twila said. "Obviously, not yet."

"Let's go see iffen my gumbo's still on the stove," Granny said as she walked away. Twila caught up to her and held her hand, which Granny didn't fight. I pushed out of Jack's arms and started to follow. When Jack remained in place, I took his hand and dragged him with me. Miss Molly meowed, and Jack bent down and swept her into his free arm. Trucker padded along at my side.

We didn't see another soul on the way back to the saloon/hotel. Alive or dead. I suppose we would have, if we'd checked the jail first. I had no doubt our prisoners were secured well. Twila had passed me the keys, and they resided in my back pocket. I could feel their outline against my hip in those jeans that would fit so much better if I'd ever lose a pound or two. Maybe a bit more.

None of us had worn any coats, but the weather hadn't seemed to bother us before. It did now. The cold seeped into me, and Twila dropped Granny's arm and pulled her close to share their body heat. They scurried up the walkway steps in front of the batwing doors, Granny not protesting when Twila steadied and helped her. Jack caught me close and did the same, his strong arm around me, body heat filtering even through his heavy sweater.

In the saloon, Granny and Twila stared around in confusion.

"What's wrong?" I asked.

"We's was wondering which way the kitchen got off to," Granny said. "They's used to feed folks in them bars back then, didn't they?"

We prowled the saloon for a few minutes, but couldn't find any sign of a kitchen. Then Jack snapped his fingers.

"Come on." He led us back out the batwings and we shivered as we followed him across the street to the building with the *Café* sign over the door. Jack stood back and let us enter first.

I could hardly believe it. I should have, given the strangeness of the past few hours. A long trencher table stood in the middle of the floor, behind it a wooden counter with stools. On the back wall, a wood stove emitted welcome heat. On it sat the big pot Granny had been stirring in the hotel kitchen.

When Granny walked over to pick up a potholder to lift the pot lid, I noticed the toes of the shoes sticking out of her deep apron pockets.

"Ummmm," she said. "It's my gumbo an' it's hot." She laid the lid on the counter and took down some bowls from a nearby shelf. A few moments later, we all sat at the trencher table eating her delicious mixture of shrimp, chicken, sausage and spices.

None of us spoke a word while we ate. Granny had found a fresh loaf of bread on the counter, and we'd passed it around and each torn off a chunk, including a large one for Trucker and smaller one for Miss Molly. I wasn't sure our lack of conversation came totally from our enjoyment of one of our favorite Granny dishes. My mind continued to worry the point of what else we could do to get out of this time period.

Twila voiced our fears first. "I hope we're not stuck here. I need to get back to Jess and our grandkids."

"We might's have to have a trial here, even we cain't get them back to face their music," Granny said.

"That would be a mess," Jack said. "For one thing, they have to be tried where the crime took place. For another, I'm not sure how much credence a judge in this time would give to the pictures I took with my cell phone down in that murder room."

"You took pictures?" I asked. "You were sick with pain, and you still put being a cop first?"

He shrugged. "It's the way I am, *Chère*."

"Yes," I admitted. "And it's a good way to be in order for us to have a safe place to live in. Plus, with the room destroyed in that explosion, there went a lot of the other evidence."

"That won't stop the Feebs," Jack explained. "They've got plenty of money to dig that place out of the ruins, with there bein' evidence there. They can also dig into the crooked sheriff's financials, anything else they need to do to build a case."

"You think that'll be 'nuf to send 'em up?" Granny asked. "That there Eddie needs to pay for killin' Karen, an' Maddie was in it up to her eyeballs."

"They'll probably figure Danny's the weak link and offer him a deal," Jack said. "Have him testify against the other two."

"They have a lot to answer for back there," Twila said harshly.

"If we get back," I tactlessly said, then hurriedly went on, "I mean, *when*. And I'm sure the Universe will make sure those three down in the jail come, too, so they can be punished."

Jack pushed his bowl away and leaned back in his chair. "Is there any way at all to...I don't know...talk to your Guides or whoever you consult about stuff like this?"

"I've told you a couple times, Jack," I said, "this is new to us, too. And I've been imploring my Guides to give me advice on what to do ever since we got here! I'm sure Twila has, too."

"And?" Jack asked.

"All I'm hearing is *patience*." I caught myself before I sneered at my Guide's counsel. That would have been the wrong thing to do, given we still desperately needed reassurance and assistance.

"All I hear is *it will work out*," Twila said. "I'm trying really hard to have faith in that. Still, I can't help worrying about my family in Ohio."

Granny glanced over at the stove. "I's don't guess they have a 'frigerator or even an ice box here, where I can keep my gumbo. It's pro'ly gonna spoil. Hope they's got some more food fixin's 'round, so's we kin keep eatin' iffen we're stuck here a while."

Jack jumped to his feet and kicked his chair across the café. "How the hell long can this go on?" he shouted.

"As long as it does," Twila said.

His face fell, and he had sense enough to pull over the chair beside him before he wilted into it.

"Well." Twila stood and carried her bowl over to the countertop. "We better wash our dishes, then go back to the hotel and see if any of the rooms are fit to sleep in."

She'd already filled a teakettle to heat on the stove, and she poured a tin pan full of water and looked around for some soap.

"Here." Granny walked over and picked up a plain white rectangular bar on the counter, then handed Twila a sharp knife. "You got's to shave off some a this here lye soap to wash 'em with." As Twila complied, she sighed and said, "Iffen we's stuck here, mebbe some of my know-how 'bout old-time ways will he'p us." She turned and crooked at finger at Jack. "Come over here an' put this gumbo outside where it's cool. That'll leastways give it a chance to keep for another meal or two."

We all helped clean, then waited for each other at the doorway. Halfway across the street on the way to the hotel, I turned around despite the chill air. Behind the café, the sun was setting in a blaze of stunning colors: orange, yellow, violet, even a faint hint of pink. We'd been here nearly a day now, more than a day since we'd arrived in Albuquerque.

The others had halted to enjoy the sunset with me, but I didn't stay long. Something worried me.

"How am I going to feed Trucker and Miss Molly?" I asked a moment later as Jack and I walked side-by-side through those batwing doors. "That bread's not going to fill their tummies very long. They won't eat spicy gumbo, and their food's back in the future."

Twila overheard me and said, "Faith." She pointed to the bar, where pouches and cans of the exact food I fed my animals were laid out beside two sets of bowls with my animals' names glowing in gold paint. A pitcher and a larger bowl was placed beside the cat food, and when I checked, I found cold, clear water. The cat food even had the modern lids with the pull tabs to open them. A moment later, Trucker and Miss Molly settled down to eat their meals.

"Will you ladies at least let me check the rooms upstairs first, to make sure there's nothing waiting to harm you?" Jack asked.

"Since you asked, I believe we will," Twila replied. "But Alice is going with you."

"I am...? Uh...yes, I am." I walked over to the stairwell and waited.

Jack sighed and pushed me aside to go first. My knee didn't exhibit a bit of pain as I climbed, and I realized that, despite her acceptance of assistance, Granny was walking around without her usual limp. I shook my head in awe, but found myself hoping the absence of pain would last when we returned home.

If we did.

Patience.

"Yes, I know," I said in a resigned tone.

"What?" Jack asked as he halted at the top of the stairwell to examine our surroundings.

"Nothing, just some advice from beyond," I murmured.

He didn't bother to ask me to explain. He pulled his pistol and motioned for me to stay behind him as we walked down the hallway, checking the five rooms on one side. On our return path, we inspected the others. Seven rooms were bare of even sheets on the beds. Yet surprisingly, we eventually found identical rooms to the ones we had used earlier: one with the two twin beds Granny and I had chosen to sleep in, a room with a double bed for Twila connected to it. The fireplace grates were clean except for piles of paper and kindling, the racks beside them overflowing with firewood.

Amazingly, our PJ's and robes were laid out casually on each bed, overnight cases with essentials like medicine and deodorant on the floor, smoke-stained but available. Our warm coats hung on a rack at the foot of my bed, including Jack's down ski jacket.

When we checked the last room down the hall, Jack's duffle bag sat on a neatly made-up double bed.

"I'll be damned," he murmured.

"No, blessed," I corrected.

I re-traced my steps to my room and slipped into my coat. Then I gathered Twila's and Granny's to carry downstairs. It was still chilly on the lower floor, since we hadn't found another source of heat there. When we got ready for bed that night, we'd be able to build a fire in the fireplaces. For now, I decided not to leave the flames unguarded.

As Jack slipped into his ski jacket, the weight of the other two coats in my arms pressed against something hard in my sleeve. I remembered the ring caught in the lining—had it only been last night? I laid the other coats on the bed and shrugged out of mine.

"What's wrong?" Jack asked.

"Oh, my ring came off in my coat lining last night," I said inattentively as I reached down inside the sleeve. I managed to free the ring and pull it out. I opened my hand before I remembered which ring had been hidden there.

Before I could re-clench my hand, Jack reached around me and picked up the ring. "You're still wearin' it, huh? At times, anyway, I guess. I haven't seen you with it on in a while."

"I usually wear it when I travel, especially on business," I admitted. "It's like having a part of my other life with me, something personal."

He held the ring in his thumb and forefinger, twirling it back and forth to pick up the scant light. Memories flooded me. The large garnet, my January birthstone, was surrounded by small diamonds, the stone for Jack's birth month, April. He'd given it to me for my birthday the first January we'd been married.

I sat on the bed, and a moment later, he moved around beside me. I thought he might put his arms around me, but instead, he leaned forward with his elbows on his knees, the ring held in his right palm so he could continue to look at it.

"That was a nice night we had, your birthday that month. You remember what I said when I gave you the ring?"

"Yes," I whispered. "You said you'd always be there to take care of me. Surround me with your love."

He glanced up at me. "We let things get in a mess, didn't we?"

"It was both of us," I agreed.

He straightened and reached for my right hand, where I'd always worn that ring. Then he looked into my eyes.

"I'd like to give it a better try, *Chère*. You think we might do that?"

As much as I yearned to fling my arms around him and shout yes, yes, yes, I didn't. We were both a couple years older now, a couple years more experienced with heartbreak and bad decisions. I studied his strong, masculine face, his deep chocolate eyes filled with love, need, and even desire. As I'm sure mine were. Yet I had to say it.

"We shouldn't make any quick decisions. We threw caution to the wind before and jumped into marriage. I don't think I could stand it if it didn't work out between us again."

He glanced at the ring, then back at me. "As far as I'm concerned, we should stop at the first minister we can find as soon as we get home. I've never stopped lovin' you. I want you for my wife again, *Chère*. I want to grow old with you. I want you to marry me. Again."

"I love you, Jack. I always have, and I know I always will."

I leaned toward him, yet couldn't bring myself to close the gap between us completely. We'd led different lives the past two years. We'd become good friends, but despite how we seemed to have worked on a few of our differences the past twenty-four hours, we still had a ways to go regarding other important aspects in each of our lives.

And...there were probably relationships we'd had during those years that we hadn't told each other about. I hadn't gotten serious about anyone. Had he? Could I handle it if I found out about more Miss Pouty-Purrs?

He sighed. "If a try to living together is all you can give me right now, *Chère*, I'll take that."

"Living in sin?" I teased, but I cupped his cheek in my left hand, and placed my right hand out for the ring. "Yes, I'd love to live in sin with you. We didn't try that before."

Jack smiled and slipped the ring on my finger. I melted into his kiss, and wrapped him as close as he held me. I never, ever wanted the kiss to end, and could only bring myself to pull back when something nagged at my vision.

Jack groaned in disappointment when I pointed at the middle of the room, but he followed the direction of my finger.

"Oh, shit," he said as we stared at the beginning shimmer of light. He grabbed me and pulled me to my feet with him. "We need to get Twila and Granny and the animals up here. Fast!"

"We're here," Twila said from the doorway. "Something drew us."

She stood there with Granny by her side, Trucker and Miss Molly at their feet. I could have sworn they were all four smiling at us.

"Guess that their last piece is in place," Granny said. Jack grinned back at her and squeezed my hand.

The shimmer brightened and expanded. Twila and Granny rushed forward with the animals. We nudged Trucker and Miss Molly into the middle of our circle and joined hands all around.

Then I noticed one shoe had fallen out of Granny's apron pocket.

"Oh, no!" she cried.

Trucker dashed out of the circle, nearly knocking me down, but Jack held me steady. The dog grabbed the shoe and bounded back to be with Miss Molly.

"Hang on," Twila murmured as the shimmer enclosed us.

"Don't worry," Jack said, his gaze on me. "I'm not letting go."

Thunder boomed.

Afterword

Dead Man Hand has been years in the writing. Due to some personal life interventions, it languished on my computer for a long while after I wrote *Dead Man Talking* and *Dead Man Haunt*. But I never forgot the book, nor did my Muse. Alice, Twila, Jack, Trucker and Miss Molly have lived many hours, weeks, months and years with me, and they are, indeed, part of my family by now.

When the world of e-books opened to authors, my desire to have my own books available for my readers, old and new, gave me the incentive to start publishing again. I also found the joy in my writing once more, and finished two books that had been tugging at me for years: *Winter Prey* and *Dead Man Hand*. In addition, I gave in to the urgings from friends and began rewriting and publishing some of the dozens of ghost hunting diaries I'd kept over my years as a paranormal investigator. I now have six of those out there, *Ghost Hunting Diary Volume I* through *VI*. Though true stories, they fit right in with my fictionalized crew of ghost hunters in the *Dead Man* books.

Dead Man Hand, as with the other books in this series, grew into a preliminary plot in my creative author mind during a trip Aunt Belle Brown and I took to an old, historical building in Cimarron, New Mexico:

the St. James Hotel. At the time, the hotel was owned by the wonderful Mary Ann Carpenter, and she gave us free access, even trusting us with the combination to that important side door so we could come and go as we pleased. We were the only guests during that stay...live ones, anyway. You can read about that fascinating two-night-three-day-stay in "St. James Jeepers Creepers," the first story in *Ghost Hunting Diary Volume IV*.

Dead Man Hand is fiction, as is the Red Dollar Hotel in Red Dollar, New Mexico. The story began, though, as I listened to some of the fascinating history of the St. James, as well as rumor and lore passed down through time. Always keep in mind that I took this story and made it a T. M. Simmons story, not a true tale like "St. James Jeepers Creepers." Alice, Twila, Granny, Jack, Trucker and Miss Molly are...whoops! You'll have to read on in this book to find out what happens to them!

I totally enjoy interacting with my readers, so I've also included my email addresses, as well as Facebook information. Thank you very much for buying my book. I wish you happy reading, lives full of love...and a scare now and then!

Boo!
T. M.

DEAD MAN OHIO
A DEAD MAN MYSTERY, BOOK 4

The Grassman said something, and Jack replied. To us, Jack said, "He wants to know our names. It would be a good idea if each of us said our own, to show him we're willing to get along with them."

I lifted my gaze up to the one beside us, way up, and met his eyes staring down at me. I gulped again, touched a hand to my chest, and said, "A-alice. I'm Alice."

"Twila," Twila said beside me, imitating my gesture of hand on chest.

"Jack," Jack said with a nod.

Granny didn't hesitate. She pulled free of Jack's hold and marched right over to the Grassman. She only came up to his muscular thigh, and holding her elderly hand out to shake with him, she said, "Granny. And who you be?"

I swear the mouth beneath that green fur tilted up as the Grassman gazed down at Granny. He tenderly took her hand and said, "Bob."

Jack's laughter rumbled in his chest, and despite my lingering fear, I had to bite back a giggle myself. Who would have guessed this thing would have such a everyday name? Further introductions, though, confirmed that they were all called common names as Bob turned to point at each of his companions.

The female he told us was Kate, and the other three were each Tom, John, and George. We all followed his gaze when he looked around the clearing for the little one. When we saw him, I realized why it had gotten so quiet. He was curled up on the ground beside Trucker, Miss Molly and Harley, worn out from his game of tag.

"Rascal," Bob Grassman told us.

Granny repeated all the names, ending with, "Rascal, huh? He's a cutie pie."

Well, I wouldn't have gone that far, but Granny glanced at Jack and said, "Can you tell him that for me?"

Jack nodded and repeated a few words. This time, Kate walked over and squatted down by Granny. She said something, and Jack told us, "She said, 'Thank you for saying that about my little boy.'"

Granny reached out and patted Kate on the shoulder. "You be welcome."

It didn't appear Jack had to translate that, since Kate carefully stroked a finger over Granny's gray hair.

Then Kate walked over and picked up Rascal. She led the way, and the rest of us fell in behind her. I could tell Bob was still on guard, however, because he took up the rear position, behind everyone else

* * *

Available in Paperback and eBook from Your Favorite Bookstore or Online Retailer

About the Author

T. M. Simmons lives in a haunted house on the edge of the East Texas Piney Woods, which she and her husband share with a variety of pets and paranormal residents. In between writing cozy mysteries and other stories, she delights in scaring herself silly during otherworldly encounters and visits haunted building and graveyards during both dark and full moons. Her husband goes along sometimes to protect her from the bumps in the night, although he's been know to spy a ghost and retreat rather than confront. She also pursues paranormal entities with her own real-life Twila, Aunt Belle Brown, and they are Lead Investigators of the Supernatural Researchers of Texas paranormal investigative team. SRT's motto is, "Leave Peace Behind," and the team seeks to leave peace for the people who are dealing with troubled hauntings, as well as for the ghosts. Simmons is extremely willing to discuss her experiences with anyone she can corner.

Sign up here for the T. M. Simmons newsletter and receive a copy of *Thrall Bound, a Short Story;* only available to newsletter subscribers.

https://ghostie3.wixsite.com/index1

www.iseeghosts.com

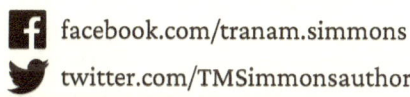

facebook.com/tranam.simmons
twitter.com/TMSimmonsauthor

www.ingramcontent.com/pod-product-compliance
Lightning Source LLC
Chambersburg PA
CBHW030639020726
47493CB00006B/1793